"No, Papa,"
Annie screamed.

Maybe the whip was meant for me; I never found out, it hit Annie across the face.

"Damn you," I screeched at Annie's father. "Give me that whip."

I was small and wiry, but I charged at Mr. Gillentine like a wet cat, spitting, clawing and breathing hellfire. Together we fell over backwards and Mr. Gillentine hit his head on some rotten slats.

Annie put her hand over her mouth, eyes wide and frightened.

"Papa! Something's wrong with Papa . . ."

ROYAL CHARLIE

ROBERT STEELMAN

CHARTER BOOKS, NEW YORK

ROYAL CHARLIE

A Charter Book/published by arrangement with
the author

PRINTING HISTORY
Charter edition/April 1983

ISBN: 0-441-73609-2

Charter Books are published by Charter Communications, Inc.
200 Madison Avenue, New York, N.Y. 10016.
PRINTED IN THE UNITED STATES OF AMERICA

Chapter 1

I never knew my father, but I was certain he had royal blood in his veins. Sometimes I thought it had to be more than a figure of speech, that about royal blood. After all, if a king is more than a man, isn't it likely his blood is different from a man's? Thicker, perhaps, filled with floating specks of courage and greatness, or maybe even faintly blue, as they say?

That fateful day when Annie Gillentine and I crouched in the shade of the green hop vines, her voice trembled.

"Charlie! No! Please—no!"

Squatting on my shanks, knife poised above my wrist, I looked down at the fine-honed blade of my penknife, the one my father had left with me in the basket that day in the place they called Sweeney's Shambles.

"I've got to see," I said. "Maybe it's turned just a little blue by now." A drop of sweat ran down my nose. I flicked it loose with a toss of my head. "I'll never rest easy till I know."

"You—you *boy!*" Annie's lips were pressed tight together in a caricature of her mother. "Always trying to scare some-one!"

"It isn't that at all!" Distressed by her ignorance, I wanted to explain how it was, but there was no time. From the next

1

hill I heard Mr. Casper Gillentine call. He would be leaning on his hoe, his bald head pink in the sun, scanning the vine-covered slopes.

"Look out," I said. "I'll go the lot!"

It was something I had heard a gambler say in the back room of the Garden House in Utica; it meant go right ahead and not think of the consequences. How I had come to be in the Garden House is another story. Anyway, I pressed down on the point of my penknife. At the last moment I had to turn my eyes away, but I pressed hard and the point stung my wrist like a bee. At the same time I heard Annie's sharp, hissing-in of breath.

"There!" I brought my eyes round. A puddle of blood lay in the palm of my hand and trickled down my fingers.

"Annie!" Mr. Gillentine sounded vexed, which he often was. "Annie, where are you? Drat it—and where's the boy?"

Taking her kerchief from an apron pocket, Annie wrapped it around my wrist, sniffling a little. "You've hurt yourself! Oh, Charlie!"

"It doesn't look any different," I said. "It's red and thick, that's all." When I shook my hand, the droplets spattered the green hop leaves.

"Annie! Will you answer me? And where is that shiftless boy? Charlie! Charlie Campion!"

Mr. Gillentine was a religious man, but I think he would have liked to swear some. Annie didn't get up yet—just knelt there beside me—but she called out: "All right, papa! I'm coming." She pulled the handkerchief tight and fastened it with a knot. "You goose! Of course it doesn't look any different. What did you expect? Oh, Charlie, you're so silly sometimes. Did you want it to be colored purple?"

I shook my head. "There must be some way to tell. And don't talk to me like a little baby. I've got king's blood, I tell you! The blood of Irish kings, and they're the best kind. Very noble and poetic—musical too—and have enchanted swords and talk Gaelic to everybody."

What is it about a moment that stays in a man's mind all his days, though at the time he may think nothing of it at all? There was hot sun coming down through the vines in patches like gold, patches that danced and moved, and the spatters of blood were like rubies flung across the emerald leaves. Annie's hair was pulled back in a knot and fastened with a ribbon, and the golden flakes of light lay thick on the dark hair, minted flakes that shimmered and danced. In our glen it was cool and quiet, far away from Gillentine's farm and Utica and the world. Her eyes were blue and moist, like the petals of a flower wet with dew, and under her shift she swelled out at the chest in an exciting way. Seeing me look at her she got red in the face, and it was nice the way the dark flush stained her cheeks. She pretended to find something wrong with her hair, and fussed at the ribbon for a while; then, seeing I was still staring, she pulled the shift tight down over her brown knees.

"Drat you, Charlie Campion!" she cried out. "If you've got Irish blood, it's only proper! You're a born troublemaker, and the Irish are a troublesome people, Papa says. Listen to him call! Oh, he's mad!"

I caught her hand in mine. "I only cause trouble when I'm crossed, remember that! We're a proud race, that's all. Look, you go that way and I'll go this! He'd better not see us together."

She gave me a long look that was hard to understand, even for a poet, and then flitted away through the vines. A minute later I heard her call from a hundred yards up the slope.

"Here I am, Papa!"

"And where have you been, Lady?"

He only called her that when he was mad. Oh, he was a good enough Presbyterian, I'd heard, but he never trusted anyone. Maybe that was why he was so rich, though very sparing in his habits; stingy, I guess you could say, which is certainly not the habit of kings. A lot of beer is drunk in this world, and they must have hops to brew it. Twenty acres of hop vines in the good New York soil, and hard work sawing vine-props and hoeing weeds had made a lot of rich men around Utica. I didn't care much about hop vines; they weren't mine. All that was mine was the hard work, and Annie's and Grover's, and Abraham's and Follett's and the rest of the Gillentine children's. Right there was where Mr. Gillentine had an open hand. Thirteen children, there were in all.

"I was hot," Annie explained. "I was just taking the shade, Papa."

"Didn't you hear me call?"

Annie was smart enough, but Mr. Gillentine scared her, the way he did a lot of people. Sometimes when you're scared you don't think too fast, even I, Charlie Campion, who have in most instances a very quick mind.

"I—I maybe I took forty winks, Papa."

"Where's that boy?"

"Charlie?"

"Now don't be clever, Lady. Yes, of course. Charlie."

"I haven't seen him, Papa."

"The Lord," Mr. Gillentine warned, "loveth his creatures to speak true, and not do the Devil's business."

"Honestly, I haven't! He was hoeing up yonder." I could imagine her, slender and frightened, caught in fealty to me, flinging an outstretched arm towards the slope. "Up there is where I saw him last, Papa. Maybe he got thirsty and went to the house for a drink from the well."

A king has obligations, even a fifteen-year-old one in patched breeches with a battered maybe-gold penknife his only estate. I hated old Mr. Gillentine; though I was wiry and quick, I was small enough so he could beat me real handily and often did. This time I'd catch it, but I didn't want him to touch Annie.

"Here I am!" I called.

Mr. Gillentine peered down the hill. "So you are."

It seemed like a thousand steps it took me. Hop vines pulled at my bare ankles and the sun was hot and my stabbed wrist throbbed. Once a little snake rustled the dust and slid across my bare foot before I could draw back.

"So you are," he said again. The long dank hair hung down his crisscrossed red neck, and he leaned on his hoe. Not taking his eyes off me, he called over his shoulder, "Annie! Come here at once."

She came, almost slower than me, and we stood restless and wary before him.

"As God is my witness," Mr. Gillentine said, "I am a reasonable man. Job was too, and Lot, the Bible gives us to believe; very patient, even with boils on Job's neck and Lot's wife turned into a pillar of salt and all kinds of petty annoyances."

I'll get it now, I thought. *When he talks Scripture, that's when he's the meanest.* But we hadn't done anything. Not ever, really, I mean. I'd kissed her once, but that was all.

"Even a reasonable God-fearing Presbyterian has limits, though, young lady and young gentleman." His eyes began to get glassy like the owl's in the Gillentine parlor, and his voice trembled.

"We didn't do anything," I said.

With the back of his free hand he clubbed me across the face, a kind of knuckly slap. It was cleverly and quickly done. I never saw him do it just like that. I hadn't been expecting it from that quarter, but I'd remember next time.

"Speak when you're spoke to." He pointed to my hand. "What's that rag you've got tied round your wrist?"

I'd make a mistake there. He knew what it was and so did I—one of Annie's cambric handkerchiefs her Aunt Rhoda Follett had given her last Christmas.

"I—I cut my hand."

I didn't mean to, but I think I started to cry a little. Not from fear, though I was scared, but mostly from sheer exasperation that I was used so, and Annie too. Then, when I remembered she was standing next to me, I blinked hard and thank God the tears stopped, if that's what they were. King, indeed! I must just be a common potato-eating Irishman like old Paddy Doolan that curried horses at the Garden House and was always drunk and whining. If the blood was really kingly, then I'm damned if I should cry at being smacked.

"And where did you get that flowered blue cambric handkerchief that sells for over a dollar a dozen in Utica and is imported all the way from the Old World?"

I set my lips in a hard line and stayed on the balls of my feet so I could duck that hard nubbly fist when it came my way. But Annie spoke before Mr. Gillentine could get set good.

"It's mine, Papa."

He turned in mock surprise. "Yours, Lady?"

"Yes, Papa."

"Well!" He sucked at his teeth. "The cat is out of the bag for fair, now, is it? So the two of you were together, eh? Down the hill under the vines? Doing what, may I make so bold?"

I thought he was going to hit her and I stepped forward, my fist clenched. But he didn't even see me. He raised his long arms high over his head, caterwauling like a cat that's got its tail pinched under a rocking chair.

"Sodom! Gomorrah! Babylon! Gehenna! Oh, my Redeemer, right here in my own hop patch!" When he got real mad he had spells, and it looked like one was about to start.

"Papa!" Annie pleaded. "Please, Papa, it wasn't anything."

"No, it wasn't," I said. "And as for Babylon and Gehenna and all those places, I've never been there. Sir, you've got it all wrong. All it was, Annie and I were just talking and wondering if—"

I got carried away with my own eloquence and wasn't careful. This time he backhanded me with the other fist. I felt that bony club smash my lips into my teeth; then I went arse-over-tin-cup into the vines. Hop-poles splintered, vines tore, I could smell warm earth and the rank green spice of bruised hops. Lying flat on my back, looking up at the sun through the tracery of the vines, I rubbed my fingers across my bruised lips. Yes, the blood was still red. Red and thick, and very common. I rolled over and got to my knees, dazed. The sun went behind a cloud and everything got black and my ears hummed like a wasps' nest when you throw a stone at it. I would have fallen back into the vines if Mr. Gillentine hadn't grabbed my galluses and hoisted me up.

"March, you heathen! To the house!"

I must have staggered in the wrong direction, because he cuffed my ear and sent me spinning. Not knowing what I was doing, I struck out with my fist.

"Assault me, will you?" He whaled me across the breeches with the hoe handle; a good lick, that one was.

"No, Papa!" Annie cried. "Please, Papa! He's hurt!"

"I'll hurt him!" Mr. Gillentine bawled.

Ashamed, weeping this time and no mistake, I ran away. I admit it. I floundered through the vines, doing what must have been eighteen dollars worth of damage to come out of the wages I never got in the first place. Mr. Gillentine only beat me harder with the handle of the hoe because of the swath I was mowing. That handle had a real whip to it.

Oh, bitter kingdom! Oh, fleeing royal blood! The coronet brought low, the fires burned out! The queen distraught, our lands ravaged, the enemy aprowl with lance and fiery torch! With rats for company, he locked me in the corncrib without any supper.

That night, more than anything I missed my books. I was a great one for limbering the mind. After a hard day's work in the hop fields I would lie long awake reading the *Compendium of Homeopathic Medicine* or *Ivanhoe* or the *New York State Farmer's Almanac and Planting Guide*. I knew the Holy Bible almost as well as Mr. Gillentine. Annie's Aunt Rhoda (sister to Mrs. Gillentine and no relation to my tormentor) had given me an old stack of *Leslie's Illustrated Weekly*. My blanket shielding the glow of the candle (for Mr. Gillentine complained often of the cost of candles), I read the accounts of Antietam and Chancellorsville and Sharpsburg, thrilling at the crisp woodcuts that showed horses rearing and gallant men clutching their throats to fall in glory. The newest of these was a year old, but concerning events up until that time I was well informed. Someday, after the war was over, I would become rich and buy all the rest of *Leslie's* to find out how the war ended. For now, I lay on a pile of husks, watching the moon paint golden stripes on the floor of the corncrib. Usually I wrote in my journal every night, but not this night. A rat rustled in a corner and I threw an ear of corn, wincing at the knives of pain that lanced my backside. Well, for whatever indignity Mr. Gillentine had wreaked on me, just that much might have been spared Annie. When he worked out his anger he then became only miserly and sanctimonious, which could be put up with though it was not my choice. I sneezed in the dust the thrown ear raised, and felt a salty taste in my bruised mouth.

"Hssst!"

I picked up another ear of corn.

"Hssst!" I threw the ear but something went *hssst* again. It was Follett, Annie's little brother, cowering in the shadows at the corner of the crib. "What do you want?" I growled.

"I'm a messenger."

"You're a what?"

"A messenger." He wriggled in a transport of fear and delight. "You know, like in the story you read me. I'm a messenger from the queen."

As it always did, his nose was running. He had weak lungs, the doctor said. Sticking my arm through the slats, I wiped his nose with my sleeve. "You get back to bed or your pa'll tan your hide."

Impatient and angry, he shook his towhead. "No, Charlie! That's not what you're supposed to say! You're supposed to give me a bag of gold or something and ask me what the queen said!"

How a man's dreams rise to plague him, even when he wakes! I didn't want to hear any more about kings and queens. I was hungry and sore and dishonored, and the king business didn't look promising. It took too much effort to imagine this dusty crib a romantic prison like Chillon. But Follett wouldn't give up.

"Hssst! Where's my gold, old King?"

"That's 'O King,'" I said. "Not old king, for heaven's sake!" I wrapped a few grains of corn in a husk, folded it over, and put it in his hand. "All right, messenger."

"Now listen, King."

"I'm listening."

"The queen is going to come to you when—let's see—when the moon is over yon sycamore tree. That's what she said, Charlie—I mean, O King."

I squinted through the slats. The moon was high already, and white hot—not red gold. Before long it would be over the sycamore tree that sheltered the house.

"You tell the queen to stay in the castle and not risk any more trouble with her pa. He's awful mad."

Follett whistled gravely through his teeth. "He surely is. He whacked me for getting milk gravy on my shirt at supper."

I winced; my stomach grumbled. Milk gravy! Hot, creamy, meat-fragrant milk gravy! On biscuits! Mrs. Gillentine was too scared to say much around the house, but she could cook. More than likely she took out all her love in the cooking.

"You skedaddle!" I said.

"Did I do all right, Charlie?"

"You did all right."

His wraithlike nightshirt flitted away through the shadows. It fluttered palely up the sycamore tree, across the slanting roof of the summer kitchen, and into the maw of the open window. Good night, Follett, and flights of angels celebrate thee in the sycamore tree. Thou didst all right. Or did you say *thee* didst all right? I wasn't sure.

Fearing I would somehow hack my way free, Mr. Gillentine had taken my penknife. I still had my mouth organ, though, and I squatted on my heels in a moon-drenched pool of light and blew a tune. "Maryland, my Maryland," that was a rebel song, *Leslie's* said, but it fit my mood, very mournful and sad. In the house a square of yellow light showed in the parlor. My captor would be sitting in the tufted horsehair rocker, reading the New Testament. About the third chorus of "Ora Lee," however, the lamp winked out and there was nothing but night and the soft wind and the moon rising, a silver boat in a dappled sky. Cloying and sweet, the smell of honeysuckle came from the piazza of the Gillentine house. I wondered how many imprisoned men had smelled the scent of growing things, and languished and died. *Father,* I thought, *did you once smell flowers, and were you young, and did you want to clutch all of life and hold it to you tight?* But I didn't even know his name. Campion, they called me at the orphanage before I was bound out to the Gillentines. That was all I had—a doubtful name and a penknife with a script *C* on the handle.

"Charlie?"

Deep in reverie, I heard a word that sounded strange, meaning nothing.

"Charlie?"

"Yes," I finally said.

"It's me. Annie."

From somewhere she had got the key to the lock; it clicked brassily and the door swung open. Clad only in her gown, white feet bare, she stood on the threshold. "Didn't Follett come to you?"

"He did."

"Follett wanted to come. The rest were afraid of Papa. Follett likes you, Charlie."

Swiftly and gracefully she dropped to her knees, clutching her arms round me, burying her face in the rough stuff of my shirt. "Ah, Charlie, whatever will become of you?"

I knocked the spit out of my mouth-harp. "I don't care."

"But you do! And so do I."

"The hell I care!"

She put a finger on my lips. "Don't swear, Charlie."

When she turned her eyes up to mine I could see a glint of moonlight across tears. I'm a mushbrain when it comes to a woman's tears. All Irishmen are.

"Does it make any difference to you what happens to me, Annie?"

"You know it does, Charlie. I'd—I'd die without you."

"Well, then," I said, feeling pleased. I stroked her hair, and I felt something else too—something I'd read about, though not in satisfactory detail, in the *Compendium of Homeopathic Medicine*. It was a little alarming, in a way, and yet very pleasant. Almost without knowing what I was doing, almost like it was planned, my hand strayed downward from her soft hair to her shoulder. It was warm and round and soft. My hand dropped a little farther, and when it was just short of that intriguing fullness under her gown, she pulled violently away from me.

"No, Charlie! No."

"Why not?" Face in the shadows, she scrambled to her feet. "Are you mad, Annie?"

"No," she whispered. "Not mad. It's just that—that—well, not *that* way."

Stupid, I asked, *"What* way?"

In one quick motion she pulled her gown over her head and stood mother-naked in the moonlight. "I don't want you to pussyfoot around and *take* anything from me like it was shameful. I want to give it to you, Charlie. Whatever you want from me."

The light was poor, but it was clear enough what caused that remarkable fullness about the chest. She was high-breasted, like a true princess, and her legs were long and straight, her hips full and ripely curved. I drew in my breath like someone had hit me in the stomach. This wasn't one of those sneaking things Paddy Doolan and the hangers-on at the Garden House snickered about. This was sweet and noble and great-souled, nothing Presbyterian at all about it. It was a very great obligation for me; when I look back on it sometimes it seems to me I must have been a boy of substance and promise, no matter what happened later.

"Annie," I said, "I love you, I guess."

She flew into my arms, and curled there like she belonged. "And I love you, Charlie."

I kissed her ear. "Nothing harmful will ever come to you through me, Annie. You can trust me for that."

Ah, liar that I was! I was a willful liar, but who could know what the future would bring? There was a sweet wholesome smell to her, like violets in the rain, and her skin was soft and made little galvanic shocks in my fingertips when I touched her.

"Annie!"

"Charlie!" she murmured. "Oh, Charlie, Charlie, Charlie!"

Afterwards we lay for a long time, I don't know how long, holding each other tight. The night went on, and a chill came in the air. I took off my shirt and wrapped it round her, and she roused like a sleepy child.

"Was it wrong, Charlie?"

"No," I said. "For how could it be? Don't we love each other through all eternity and time?" I was arguing, I think, more than stating a fact, for mingled with my satisfaction was a strange feeling of sadness and loss.

"Of course," she said. "For ever and ever."

I remember thinking she must put on her gown and slip up to the house, but it was so pleasant there for a love-starved bound boy. I promised myself that as soon as I counted to a hundred, saying one steam-engine, two steam-engines, three steam-engines, four . . . steam-engines, five . . . five . . . five . . .

I woke with a start. The moonlight was gone. But some kind of light was there. I sat up, blinking, rubbing my eyes.

"What is it, Charlie?" Annie murmured.

The light was a stable-lantern. Mr. Gillentine held it high over his head so that his face was in shadow. But I knew what was in his mind. He had his stock-whip in his hand, and behind him was Mrs. Gillentine, and then in order Grover and Abraham and Cyrus and all the rest.

"Go back to the house, quickly, Mrs. Gillentine!" the old man said. "Take the children with you."

They scampered away with a rustling like frightened mice. Comprehending the horror of our situation, Annie and I leaped to our feet, she holding her flimsy gown before her and me trying to get a leg into my pants and falling flat on my back, thrashing like a trapped coon.

"Papa!" Annie screamed. "No!"

Maybe the whip was meant for me; I never found out. But it missed me and caught Annie across the face. With a tremendous spasm of energy I got my tangled foot free of the trousers, ripping the seat in the act, and pulled them around my waist, cinching the belt tight.

"Damn you!" I screeched. "Give me that whip."

I was small, as I said, but wiry. I don't think he was expecting the fury of my charge. I was on him like a wet cat, spitting and clawing and breathing hellfire. Together we fell over backwards, and his head hit the rotten slats of the crib and splintered them through. I scrambled free, holding the whip aloft, prepared to strip the hide off him.

"Charlie!" Annie put her hand over her mouth, eyes wide and frightened. "Papa! Something's wrong. Papa!"

The old man had fallen with the splintered ends of the slats catching his throat as in a bear-trap. His head was outside, and the rest of him was inside. The long booted legs stiffened, kicked, and then went limp. A horrible gurgling came from somewhere.

"Help him!" Annie cried. "Charlie, help him!"

I dropped the whip and ran outside in the cold morning light. It was cloudy, and looked like rain. Somewhere a cock crowed. With bleeding fingers I ripped at the splintered boards and somehow got him free of that deadly trap. With Annie's help I managed to drag the body into the corncrib, and we stood there, two frightened children, staring down at our handiwork. No, *my* handiwork. I had done it. And I was not a child, either. When you kill a man, then you're a man whether you want to be or not.

"He's dead," Annie whispered.

"I guess so." Frightened, I crossed myself.

The weal on her face was white in the growing light, and her dark hair in disarray.

"Oh, Charlie, what will they do to us?"

I put my arm around her. "They won't do anything to you. You didn't have anything to do with it." I think I grew up that night at the rate of a year a minute. "Here," I said, "put this damned flimsy gown on and get back in the house. And when the sheriff comes from Utica, tell him—tell him I violated you. Yes, that's it. Tell him I forced you to submit to me."

"I won't!"

"Damn it!" I begged: "Promise me, Annie!"

"I won't, I won't, I won't! You can't make me! We loved each other, didn't we?"

I grabbed her arm and dragged her up to the house behind me. The parlor was cold and gray, and the stuffed owl stared at me with glassy eyes. On the marble-topped stand beside Mr. Gillentine's rocker I found my gold penknife. From upstairs I could hear a frightened chittering, like birds stalked by a hungry hawk.

"Mama," I heard Grover say, "she didn't have any clothes on!"

Oh, how I hated to leave my books! But there was no time to stand on ceremony.

"Charlie, what are you going to do?" Annie asked.

"I'm going away," I said. "I always wanted to go find my father and I expect this is about the best time to do it."

She clung to me, but I pushed her gently away and kissed her on the forehead. "Don't ever forget me, Annie, because I'll be back for you some day. We loved each other best of all, and I can't forget that. Nor can you."

"Nor me," she whispered.

I went down the road in bare feet, nothing in my pockets but the penknife and my mouth-harp. The dust was chilly and damp between my toes; a deer watering at the creek looked at me for a long moment and then bounded up the hillside, another frightened creature. At the bend I looked back. She was still standing at the gate in her nightgown, and I am sure she waved. With that troublesome feeling of having lost something I trudged away, the first drops of rain spattering my shoulders.

Chapter 2

I didn't head for Utica—I was too smart for that. Once, when Mr. Gillentine had thrashed me for something I didn't do, I'd run off to Utica and worked for two days sweeping out and emptying spittoons in the Garden House before he found me and took me back. No, I was too well-known in Utica; it had to be the other direction.

On a line all the way from Rochester to Albany, to the south of that line, was the hop country; thousands and thousands of acres of hop vines. The farmers grew them in all sorts of ways. One of the commonest was to plant high poles, twenty-feet tall or more, and string wires down to stakes in the ground like a tent. The hop vines would wind and twirl up the wires; a fleeing boy could go mile after mile in the shade of those tents of hop vines. I didn't really care for hops after what I'd been through, but now I was grateful. Even the drizzle of rain didn't come through too bad. Not that there was much that rain could damage; all I had was my shirt and a pair of torn breeches.

That night I slept in a barn almost ten miles from Gillentine's, but not far enough for me to rest comfortable. The rain had stopped; a red, streaky sun came out under dark scudding clouds, for all the world like a bloody eye staring at me from under heavy brows. I was soaked, and maybe a little light-headed from what had happened and being without food so long too. The barn was a distance from the house, and the farmer and the hands and all the family were at supper. I found a sweaty-smelling old horse blanket and wrapped myself against the chill, but I couldn't sleep. Through the cracks I saw the yellow glow of lamplight at the house; I heard a child's voice call "Here, Hector!" and then laugh. Dishes clinked and some-one scratched a match. The light flared up and down as a man sucked flame into a stogie or pipe. All, all familiar sounds of home—someone's home—though I had only viewed them from a distance at Gillentine's. Finally I could bear it no longer. Stealthy, like an Iroquois Indian in one of Mr. Cooper's books, I tiptoed across the wet sodden meadow to stand in the shadows at the corner of the house.

Something growled at me, and I jumped. A moment later a wet nose pushed into my hand. It was old Hector, or whatever his name was. He snuffled me all over and didn't seem alarmed. "Good boy," I said.

Hector was a fat comfortable old dog, willing to live and let live. He went back to gnawing at a bone, occasionally raising his head to stare at me and hit the porch boards with a few licks of his tail. A person isn't supposed to bother a dog when he's eating, but that bone still had some meat. There was a bowl too with something in it that looked like mush and drip-pings.

"Good boy," I said again. While he was gnawing the bone, I snatched the bowl and walked nonchalantly away like it had been my mush all the time. Hector looked up; this time he didn't wag his tail. But he didn't take it too hard. After a while he came out to the barn and sat for a long time on his haunches, staring somberly at me. When the lights winked out in the house he heaved a long dog sigh and curled up beside me. I was grateful for the warmth of his fat body.

I slept for a while, though not too long, for I was afraid they'd come out to feed the stock in the morning and find me there. Once I woke—it must have been well after midnight—with a sharp cry, having had a bad dream where Mr. Gillentine caught me with his stock whip and was flaying the skin off me. I was afraid someone had heard me, but all was quiet in the house. When old Hector nuzzled me and licked my cheek, I curled up again under the stinking blanket and slept till almost dawn.

* * *

When a man is fleeing for his life he can't afford to be particular. Near Herkimer I stole a coat that a lady had hung out to
air the camphor smell from it. It had been a long while in a
trunk; the creases where it was folded never came out, but it
was a good coat of broadcloth with a lot of handy pockets to
put things in. When I folded the sleeves back so I could get
my hands out, it fit fine. In Fort Plain a merchant had a rack
of boots sitting under an awning, for the weather had changed,
the rain had gone, and it was warm and sunny. I could only
get one boot under my coat at a time without being conspicuous.
The first one was a fine Wellington that looked like it would
be a good fit. I sneaked back for the other one while he was
inside fitting a lady. Then a man that looked like a constable
sauntered down the boardwalk, swinging a mace. In panic I
grabbed the first thing I could lay my hands on. When I got
back to my hiding place in an old dry-goods box at the rear of
Madame Fontaine's Millinery, I found the other boot had a
Napoleon leg on it, and didn't exactly match. But they both
fit pretty well when I stuffed rags in the toes and around the
heels. When a kind lady in Fonda sewed up the rent in my
breeches and gave me a bowl of bread and milk and a piece
of Dutch honeycake, I felt almost like a dandy.

I didn't think of these activities as stealing, of course. I was
a star-crossed fugitive, a romantic figure in a way. Such a one
could hardly be judged by the same standards that apply to a
common thief. Besides, some day I would come back the same
route in reverse order, very well-known and wealthy, and leave
the price of my purchases with a few gold pieces extra for their
trouble.

In Cobleskill I painted a fence and earned fifty cents. In
Schoharie I carried bricks and mixed mortar for a man building
a chimney and made a dollar; he gave me a pair of stockings
and some underpants, too. In Scotland, still fleeing eastward,
I danced a jig ("Casey's Dream," which I whistled as I danced)
and recited *The Destruction of Sennacherib*, for a bunch of
loafers taking the air in front of a saloon. They passed round
the hat and gave me a dollar and fifteen cents. I didn't know
there was so much money in the world.

"Where are you from, boy?" one asked.

I bowed graciously for their largesse, and kept the hat, for
I needed one. "Here, there, and everywhere," I said. "God

bless you, gentlemen, and I will pray for you, too."

That town was ripe for a good theater. I only wished I had time to stay there, but I hurried on. Scotland, Kieffer's Junction, and finally—Albany.

I might say I was a desperate and fear-ridden miscreant, but that would not be true. For the first time in my life I was free— free from work, free from authority, free from the rules and restrictions and don't-do-thisses and don't-do-thats that plague a boy. I knew the blackness of my crime and prayed for forgiveness each night; whenever I had a chance I borrowed a newspaper and scanned the columns for news of Mr. Gillentine's death and speculations on where the murderer had fled. But freedom is a heady thing, especially for a strong lad who has been successively imprisoned in a Manhattan orphanage, a series of upstate foster homes, and finally bound out to a severe man like Mr. Gillentine.

Annie I thought of often. Thinking of her, I would lie awake at night in a barn or shed, or perhaps in a fence-corner with my coat wadded up for a pillow and the deep star-sprinkled July sky for a coverlet. I reconstructed again in my mind the shine in her eyes, the slender womanliness of her body, the clean flowerlike smell of her hair. *We loved each other best of all. I can't forget that, nor can you.* And her reply, soft and tremulous: *Nor can I.*

I wish she had been with me to see the Hudson for the first time. She'd never been away from the farm except to Utica on market day. Standing on a bluff above the river, I felt scared. The broad river, powerful and deep, surging what looked a mile across; the fabled Hudson, looking almost like an inland sea, bordered with grassy dales and forests of trees. Its bosom was dimpled with sloops and barges; a tremendous sidewheel steamer backed out from a landing below, jingled, and drifted down the river like a white swan. A moment later I smelled burning cordwood, and the music of a steam-whistle came to me long after I saw the plume of white vapor rise. All that had gone before was prelude. Here was the reality, the beginning, the fateful step. As I have said, I was frightened. But I took my courage in my hands and ran down the hill to the landing.

When I saw a barge loading limestone, I sauntered up, whistling and careless.

"Where to, sir?" I asked the foreman.

He was a big man in a plaid shirt and bowler hat, drinking beer from a stone bottle. Wiping his mustaches with the back of his hand, he looked at me for a moment, and then said, "Twelfth Street landing; the Novelty Iron Works."

They used limestone to make steel. I remembered reading in *Leslie's Weekly* that the Novelty Iron Works was where they built the engines for the sidewheeler *Arctic* that had rammed the *Vesta*, with three hundred souls drowned.

"Need any help?"

He belched, and threw the bottle away.

"You ain't big enough."

"I'm strong for my size, though."

Pulling out a cabbage of a watch, he looked at it and then yelled at the man on the landing. "Come on, hurry it up! The dark is a-coming and we're not half-loaded!"

There was only one thing to do, and that was to show him. I took off my broadcloth coat, which fell automatically into the familiar creases, and laid it on a piling. The rest of that afternoon I pushed a wheelbarrow back and forth, sweating and panting and straining. When dusk came the barge was loaded, and I had a sprung back and open blisters on the palms of my hands the size of duck eggs. The foreman took off his slouch hat and put on a blue captain's rig with a brass eagle on it.

"I guess I've been of some use to you," I remarked.

"When you grow up you'll be a daisy." He reached in a pocket and handed me a fifty-cent piece.

"It isn't that," I explained. "What I wanted—well, I mean what I really *need* is a ride down the river."

He scratched his chin, and eyed me. "Boy, are you running away from home?"

"No," I said truthfully. After all, it hadn't exactly been home.

"Well, then." He waved me aboard. "Cast off the lines!" His name was Captain Beeks, and he let me keep the fifty cents. Seeing I had nothing to eat, he gave me some bread and cheese and part of a bottle of beer. Wrapped in my fine coat, I slept that night curled up in a coil of hawser. That was how I got to Manhattan, feeling very pleased with myself.

Sister Eudora was the oldest sister I'd ever seen—maybe the oldest lady. Frail, robed in black with a starched white hood, she sat at a rolltop desk in a cubbyhole piled and stacked and jammed and cluttered with papers. Stacks of old newspapers, bundled and tied and yellow with age; boxes of printed forms and cards and ledgers; shelves sagging with books and journals and string-tied packages of foolscap; and over all was the smell of dust and decay.

"Yes," she said, peering at me over the tops of rimless spectacles pinched onto the bridge of a nose almost translucent with age. "Yes, indeed! I keep the records for the Holy Shepherd Foundling Home and School for Indigent Young Persons. And what do you require, young sir?"

Perfunctory and slight as the smile was, it seemed even that slight effort might be enough to make her ivory face start to crack and crumble with age. I would not have been surprised to see the entire birdlike frame join the collapse and shower down into a pile of ancient dust and black habit.

"I used to be a—a pupil here, ma'am," I explained. "My name is Charles Campion, and I was left in a basket a long time ago. I never knew my father, and I'm trying to find out who he was."

She looked at me for a long time. I began to feel her spirit was leaving her body as I watched, and that the pale unblinking eyes behind the shiny pince-nez saw nothing but vistas of heavenly gates and choirs of angels.

"Ma'am?"

"What?"

"Campion, ma'am. Charles Campion."

"Ah, yes! You're the young man who wanted some information about his father."

"If you please, ma'am."

While she blew dust from a dog-eared morocco-bound volume, I went to the embrasured window and looked out at Cherry Street. The crumbling brickpile of the Holy Shepherd Home was in the middle of what they called Sweeney's Shambles, and a shambles it was. Hundreds of tenements teeming with the poor, the sick, the maimed; street beggars, piles of refuse and worse in the streets, waifs searching the garbage barrels for food, fevers and fluxes and drunkenness and death the order of the day and no one thinking but what it was the just lot of the poor. At least the air had been clean at Gillentine's, and the old man had never figured a way to ration me. Here, however, the foul vapors permeated everywhere, even into the Home itself that the sisters kept as clean as they could though soap was dear.

"Campbell," Sister Eudora crooned. "Campanelli—"

Upstate there hadn't been much fuss about the war. Occa-

sionally a soldier home on leave would be seen at the Garden
House, perhaps buying a round of drinks for his friends, and
then be gone, back to his regiment. In Manhattan, however,
blue coats swarmed the streets, especially in the Shambles. For
a hundred dollars or thereabouts a wealthy man could buy a
substitute to take his place in the draft. It was the only way
some of the poor boys could help their families. As I watched,
an irate sergeant with yellow chevrons was trying to form a
gang into some semblance of order so he could march them to
their first barracks.

"Campiglia—ah, I remember him, a sweet child with long
black curls."

"Campion," I said.

"Here it is!" She traced the entry with a waxen forefinger.
"Let me see, now—five years ago a Mr. Casper Gillentine
took you to raise."

"That's right, ma'am."

"How are you and Mr. Gillentine getting on?"

I thought it best to let that go unanswered. "Please, ma'am,
about when I came to the Holy Shepherd. Who brought me?"

"Well, it's very faded. Let me see." She adjusted the pince-
nez but continued to stare over the tops of them. "Sister Agatha,
requiescat in pace, had the records then. Poor dear, she never
wrote a proper hand! But it looks like—yes, it is—a Mr. Regan
from Gotham Court brought you in. You were left in a basket
on his door."

"That's all it says?"

"That's all." As if exhausted from the effort, she sank back
in her chair. After a while she opened her eyes. "You're an
orphan, Charles, but there are many orphan boys who made
their way in the world and became fine men without knowing
their family."

"You don't recall a Mr. Regan from Gotham Court?"

"Heavens, no, child! There must be a thousand Regans in
the city. And that was a long time ago."

Foolishly, perhaps, I had put a great deal of faith in what
I might find in the records. I turned to go, but remembered
my manners.

"Thank you, sister."

"If you'd like to try," Sister Eudora suggested, "I can tell
you what you might do."

"Yes, ma'am."

"The ward bosses know everyone. I'd go see Mr. Dancer,

the head of the Tenth Ward. He's generally at"—she took a deep breath, as if summoning up courage—"at McAteer's Saloon on Second Avenue."

"Thank you," I said, feeling a little better.

"But don't you go in that sinkhole!" Sister Eudora warned. "Ask someone to call him out, and say I sent you!"

I thanked her, and hurried away.

Mr. Dancer was standing in front of McAteer's picking his teeth with an ivory pick. He was a florid man in a hard hat and shirtsleeves; at the time I came up he was passing out sacks of potatoes to the faithful.

"Let's see, now. You're Thomas Grogan."

"Yis, sir."

"Always been a Democrat?"

"Yis, sir."

"How long?"

"Twenty-five years, sir."

"Always vote the Democratic ticket?"

"Ah, yis, sir! Always!"

"What ward?"

"Why, the tinth, sir!"

Clapping him on the back, Mr. Dancer shoved a stogie in Paddy's mouth. The poor fellow shambled proudly away, his vote in Mr. Dancer's pocket for a few mickies and a miserable cigar. When he came to me, Mr. Dancer slapped his thigh and laughed a thick gargling laugh. "Now look at what's voting in the Old Tenth, will you?"

"Please sir, it isn't that," I explained. "Sister Eudora sent me."

"Sister Eudora, is it?"

"Yes, sir."

"And what does the sister want of me?"

I explained my mission. Mr. Dancer stared into space and chewed his ivory pick. "Regan? In Gotham Court? Well, let me see. There was Mike Regan, but they hanged him. Chauncey Regan—no, they sent him to the wars. Last I heard he was killed at City Point; run over by a wagon." Mr. Dancer gargled again. "Wait now! There's a Pat Regan ran a grocery store in Gotham Court. A good man, Pat, and a Democrat. He'd be the kind to worry about a foundling."

"Thank you, sir," I said, and wrung his hand. "That must be the one!"

He called me back. "What was your name, boy?"

"Campion. Charlie Campion."

"You from around here, Charlie?"

"No, sir," I said. "I'm from—" I caught myself in time. "From Jersey City, sir. I work in a livery rental there." Then I ran off to Gotham Court.

It was the most miserable part of Sweeney's Shambles, if one part could be worse than another. Regan's Grocery was on a corner, with a locked bin in front where the poor could get coal at fifty cents the bushel. On stained shelves in the window lay a few wilted and half-rotten vegetables. Fly-specked glass cases held clay pipes, some unmatched crockery, and a small tub of milk in which a valiant fly still twitched. In a dark corner was a barrel that had a sign tacked to it: FINE GIN FIVE CENTS A GLASS. As I entered, a small girl in rags brushed by me; she was holding a wooden tray filled with wilted flowers, and she was weeping. A curtain lifted from an opening at the rear of the store and a lardy blob of a woman rushed out, shaking her fist and bawling curses.

"Now, Lil, you just get along and peddle them flowers, do you hear? No more o' your sass, or I'll beat you within an inch of your life!"

Lil fled, still weeping. The fat woman saw me then; wrapping the dirty shift tighter around her, she shuffled toward me on swollen bare feet squeezed into carpet slippers. "Here, now; what's going on here? What do you want?"

Her concern was justified, for I was no fashion plate. I suppose she thought I was about to steal a withered orange from the counter.

"All I want, ma'am," I said, "is some information."

She looked at me sulkily. "We don't deal in information."

I held up one of my hard-earned greenbacks, and it sweetened the fat lady a great deal. She reached for it, but I snatched it away. "Not so fast," I said. "Is Mr. Regan about?"

"Himself is dead for the past three months and more. A relative didn't leave money, by chance?"

"Not that I know of."

She shrugged and stopped sniffling.

"My name," I explained, "is Charlie Campion. Does that mean anything to you, ma'am?"

She shook her head.

"I'm told Mr. Regan found me on his doorstep in a basket when I was only a few days old. He took me to the Holy Shepherd Home and left me."

Twittering like a bird, she raised a finger and pointed. "You? You're the boy?"

"I am."

Clucking and twittering, she went to the barrel and poured two dirty glasses of whatever it was. Gin, the sign said, but I'd heard it was mostly tobacco leaf infused with camphene water or somelike chemical.

"Here," she said, "Have a little nip! So you're the foundling, eh? My, my—so long ago! You wouldn't think it to look at me now, but I was a nice piece in those days. Himself admitted I could give cards and spades to some of them fancy whoors on Second Avenue!"

At first she had been reluctant; now my greenback loosened her tongue so I couldn't get a word in edgewise. She collapsed into a wicker chair, fanning herself with a dirty China fan.

"I remember the day! Himself had gone to McAteer's for a can of beer, and I was minding the store. Himself was never prompt, and about nine in the evening he came back, a growler in one hand and a basket in his other. 'Look here, Fan,' he said; that was what he called me, though Fanny was only a nickname, my real name being Vera, Vera Casey before I was married, and I was married proper too and have the papers to prove it."

I sipped the gin. The stuff was raw and bitter and made tears come to my eyes, but Mrs. Regan was too busy prattling to notice.

"'Look here, Fan,' he says, 'what I found on the step outside.' And it was a little boy, wrapped in a blanket! 'His name is Charlie,' himself says, though how he could be sure God only knows, for there was nothing in the basket to tell." Her bleared eyes softened. "Himself and me, we could never make a boy; nothing but three girls, and all of them a disappointment but Lil, though she's a trial to me and don't bring home half of what she could make, her being such a sweet-looking thing, though with a temper like himself. Ah, but when I took off the blanket and the gown and saw that little tassel on you, I wanted to keep you, I did!"

I blushed to the roots of my hair and took another drink to cover my confusion.

"There was a penknife, I think."

She sat up and poked a fat finger at me. "So there was! Himself wanted to keep it for his trouble, but I wouldn't let him."

Was she telling the truth, or simply prating and jabbering to earn the dollar?

"Please, ma'am," I said, "this is very important to me! I want to find who my father was."

She pursed her lips and made a great show of pulling the dirty shift over her fat knees. "Now himself was a good man, but he run with a fast crowd. I always suspected Regan knew more about the baby then he let on. Oh, I don't mean it was one of *his;* himself drank a lot, and he used to beat me to get his mind off his troubles, but do you know what?"

I didn't know what, and had another drink to comfort me in my ignorance.

"I always thought the baby was a bastard of one of his flashy friends." She nodded in satisfaction. "Charlie, that's the name he give it."

"At the home he told them to put down 'Charlie Campion,'" I said.

"Campion?" She wiped gin from her fat chin, and pondered. "Why himself used to run with a Ned Campion! Well"—she shrugged—"it's one too many for me."

Excited, I leaned forward and spilled some of my drink. "Do you know anything about Ned Campion?"

She looked immeasurably sad. "If himself was here—"

"But he isn't, damn it!"

"I'll thank you not to curse at me," Mrs. Regan cried.

"But he said my name was Charlie Campion! And if there was a Ned Campion—"

"The only thing I know, Ned was a fast one. Well brought up, himself always said, but a boozer. After the shooting—"

"What shooting?"

"Oh, Ned got into some kind of scrape and killed a man. I think he went out West then." Her eyes became hard and calculating. "Now I think that's a damned good dollar's worth!"

Since I'd run away I had tried to be very careful, knowing they would be looking for me. I never stayed too long in one place, and always made sure when I went in one door there was another way out. But the gin made me careless. Not till I saw the old lady glance at the doorway did I realize someone was behind me.

I'd never dealt with a detective, but something told me this was one—a small man with a square-cut beard, wearing a shiny black coat that fit him tight around the shoulders and glistened like the hide of a prime seed-bull. Most of them were off spying for Mr. Lincoln, but I guess there were some left over to dog poor boys like me. Behind the detective was Mr. Dancer, the ward boss.

"That's him!" Dancer cried. "That's the boy!"

Quick and light on his feet, the detective came toward me, a rolled-up paper in one hand.

"Are you Charlie Campion?"

I didn't wait to haggle, instead I darted past him toward the door. But Mr. Dancer blocked the way and threw his arms about me. I twisted free while the old woman screamed to mind the glassware. Then Mr. Dancer stumbled and fell and knocked over the gin barrel. It bounced on the floor like it was India-rubber, and the staves split and the stuff poured out in a stinking flood. The Pinkerton grabbed at me but slipped on the wet floor and went sprawling. The way was free, and I dashed through the door and into the street. For a moment I paused, looking this way and that, wondering where to run. Behind me I heard squalling and screaming and breaking crockery and heartfelt cursing. The last thing that crossed my mind before I fled up Cherry Street was the realization that in the scuffle I had dropped the dollar bill. At least I paid my just debt to the old hag.

Chapter 3

Thank God for Boyle's Brigade! Fleeing, I bowled pell-mell into a straggling column of recruits for the Brigade. Shabby and unshaven, carrying carpetbags and gunnysacks and paper-wrapped parcels, they straggled up Cherry Street to the music of a band. None of them looked happy about his prospects. Some appeared to be considering whether to bolt and run, but they were chivvied on all sides by a lot of yellow chevrons. A captain in a Kossuth hat ran round them like a terrier, baring his teeth in an unconvincing grin and harrying them on.

"Come now, brave lads! Close up there—move smartly! We'll be late for the cars!" He whacked a shuffling red-nosed man with his walking stick and acted like he had done the poor wretch a favor. "There, now, move along, my man! On the double—one, two, three, four!"

I almost knocked down one of the recruits, a spindly man with buck teeth and a dirty slouch hat. He snarled at me and raised his fist, but I ducked and raised my hands in supplication. "Please, sir, they're chasing me!"

"Who? Who's chasing ye, lad?"

Out of the corner of my eye I saw the Pinkerton, charging back and forth, casting here and there to sniff me out.

"The Pinkerton!" I cried. "There—the man in the black suit! He's after me!"

That was all they needed. Poor men all, and hating the law, they took me in and hid me. To balk the law was something they delighted in, and quickly the word ran down the column that I was a fugitive fleeing from the Pinkerton. Someone took my old hat and clapped a verminous wool cap on me. Another took my good broadcloth coat and swapped me a tattered Chesterfield with a velvet collar that was shiny with grease; he got the best of that deal.

All the while they spun me from one place in the column to another and the word went round in whispers: "The lad's running from that Pinkerton in the black suit! Pass him on! Keep him moving!"

They moiled and moved about and straggled this way and that until the Devil himself would have had a time trying to single out a sinner. Exasperated, not knowing why the column was in such confusion, the officers yelled and cursed and threatened. The captain was in a transport of rage and promised to send everyone to the guardhouse at the first opportunity. The band played on, very off-key, and crowds began to line the street. Some cheered and some jeered, but it all made for more confusion, and the Pinkerton hadn't caught me yet.

"Here, lad!" The red-nosed man pushed me behind him just as the angry red face of the Pinkerton loomed up on our flank. But he didn't see me and moved on down the column, craning his neck this way and that. The captain was with him this time, and I heard him lining out the Pinkerton in a high-pitched voice.

"God damn it, man, I don't give a busted night-vessel for your paper! This is the United States Army you're interfering with! If we're late for the cars I'll hang you from a lamppost by your privates!"

On Second Avenue they bundled us into a waiting line of blue Army wagons. Someone found an old canvas and they rolled me in it and stowed me under their feet; then all fell to looking as innocent as cherubs. After a while the captain came along and stuck his head in, counting. The Pinkerton was with him.

"A hundred and sixteen. Twelve more here—that makes a hundred and twenty-eight. That's the exact number I've got on this roster here, and that's the number I've got to deliver to Camp Chase in Ohio according to these orders!"

"But I saw him!"

"You might," the captain said, "have seen our Lord and Redeemer riding an ass down Fifth Avenue, but that don't make it so!" He brought out a shiny brass whistle and blew a blast on it; the long line of canvas-topped wagons began to move toward the river. "Now, my man, stand aside, or one of these fine U.S. Army horses will mash you flat. Any more fuss from you and I'll put you under arrest!"

As we rumbled away, the red-nosed man kept me informed. "Put him under arrest! Oh, my, that Pinkerton's mad! Put *him* under arrest? He looks like he's going to have kittens!" They all whooped at joy at the prospect of the law in chains. "He's shaking his fist," the red-nosed man reported. "Now he's talking to that other feller, the one with the toothpick and the striped shirt."

"Are they following us?" I asked timidly.

"No," someone said. "And they ain't likely to. That captain is the real hardcase article. He'd run up that feller's ass and snatch him inside out if he made us late for the cars."

There was general agreement. After a while I thought it safe to come out. Drawing a deep breath, I found I was trembling and wet to my skin with a cold sweat. But I was safe—for now.

Go out to Camp Chase in Ohio with Boyle's Brigade? Why not? The farther away from that Pinkerton, the better. And while Boyle's Bastards, as they called themselves, were planning to eliminate Mad Jack Spurrier and his guerrillas from Ohio and Kentucky, I had my own legitimate business in that direction. West was where the mysterious Ned Campion had gone; I, perhaps his son, would follow.

I had read a lot in *Leslie's Weekly* about General Spurrier. His cutthroats roamed the Ohio River valley, a great plague to the orderly plans of General Meade. At Portsmouth and Marietta and Cincinnati, Mad Jack was a name to quiet rebellious children, to make stout men blanch; a monster with long yellow hair and crazy eyes who poisoned wells and burned homes and killed children and violated women. In the woodcuts in *Leslie's* he always wore a wide-brimmed hat with a plume, and spurs with rowels the size of saucers.

But Boyle's Boys would take the measure of Mad Jack Spurrier. Never having been on a steam-train before, I sat stiffly in my seat next to a yellow-chevroned sergeant and listened to their gaffing: men in undershirts and bare feet, sad men, whiskered men, men passing round a bottle, men staring at nothing, men who would be dead soon on some unnamed hillside, and men who would tell their grandchildren how they went out to Ohio in the cars to fight Mad Jack. Over all was the smell of unwashed bodies and cheap liquor and penny cigars and coal smoke and shabby carpet.

"We'll twist his tail and shove it up his arse!"

"Oh, boys, show me that lovely and I'll beat him to death with his own feather, I will!"

The red-nosed man was more clinical in his opinion. "Now to me, fellers, Mad Jack looks like a morphodite!"

"What's a morphodite?" someone asked, and there was a wild whooping and pounding each other on the back and passing a stone jug round. "Did you hear that?" the red-nosed man gasped, weak with laughter. "What's a morphodite? Oh, that's a good one, ain't it!"

I didn't exactly know what a morphodite was either, but I gathered the term was one of derision. A little uncomfortable at grown men acting like children, I turned to the window and watched the late afternoon of a Pennsylvania summer. Neat and orderly, like a well-made quilt, the Dutch country passed by the window. Square-cut solid barns painted with odd symbols in bright colors—stars and diamonds and wiggly lines; parklike meadows where cattle fed; the sun tinting in gold wash the clouds that grazed on the horizon like fat sheep.

"So you're the boy the Pinkerton was after," the sergeant said quietly.

I jumped. The men all knew the story, of course, and would not give me away. But the sergeant represented authority; he might be the kind to put me off the train at the first stop. I decided it was better to be honest.

"Yes, sir," I admitted.

"What's your name?"

"Campion, sir. Charlie Campion."

The sergeant was a lean whip of a man with a wearily beautiful face like you see on old green statues. Tight little gray ringlets wet with sweat pressed against his forehead, and the armpits of his flannel shirt were black with stains. Little as I knew about soldiers, this must be the *real* Army—the regulars. He was educated too, I could tell that, and had a little brogue of some kind—foreign. Slumping back in the seat he propped his booted legs up and lit a long-nine.

"Name's Bregand. Philip Bregand."

"You won't give me away, then?"

"Christ, no, boy! I don't even know what you've done."

"Well," I said, "I'm stealing a ride on the train with Boyle's Brigade and I don't belong to the Brigade."

He flipped a sulphur match into the aisle and put the block back into his shirt pocket. "What's one more or less to the government, eh? Anyway, three of these *cochons* jumped the train at the station before we could get under way. No, what I mean is—what did you do to get that feisty little Pinkerton after you?"

I swallowed. In for a dime, in for a dollar. "I'm wanted for murder."

He swallowed smoke the wrong way and coughed. *"Qu'est-ce que c'est?"*

It was French, I decided. "I murdered a man."

He looked at the stogie for a long time, then threw it into the aisle. "Are you telling me the truth?"

Anxious only a moment ago I would be found out, I was now nettled by his disbelief.

"I guess if you asked that Pinkerton, he'd tell you!"

The sergeant rubbed a hand over his damp curls. "Maybe you'd like to tell me about it."

I would, and did. I always had a way with a story; when I finished, Boyle's Boys were congregated round me in a circle, mouths hanging open. Some, I'd swear, had tears in their eyes. The red-nosed man sniffled audibly.

"Oh, the sadness of it!" he declared, shaking his head and blowing his nose. "Well, you did right, boy. The old coot had it coming the way he beat you and cheated you! Isn't that right, fellers?"

They all agreed. But some artistic soul noted a flaw. "In a way," he said, "it winds up kind of flat. Ain't there a woman in it some place, Charlie? A pretty girl? Come on now—tell us the truth."

I hadn't told them about Annie. That was too sacred, too private. Blushing to the tips of my ears, I lapsed into confusion. I was Sergeant Bregand's slave when he swore at them and promised to put everyone on report if they didn't clear the aisles in case there was a train wreck or fire or some such catastrophe.

"I guess you believe me *now*," I remarked.

"I believe you," Bregand said. *"Voilà!* Remind me to walk wide of you. You're bad luck."

The light faded; purple shadows crept over the land like a coverlet pulled up; yellow winks of light came on in toy houses. We crossed a bridge over a run; the wheels of the cars clattered loud and then hushed again to a monotonous clicking. The car surged this way and that, back and forth, as the drivers bit into the rails. Around Harrisburg, as we crossed what someone said was the Susquehanna, a brakeman came round and lit some of the swinging lamps. Though the light was bad, I spread out a crumpled handbill I found stuffed in a crack in the seat and read it.

> *The cars are so constructed as to combine the convenience and elegance of a private parlor by day and the comfort of a well-furnished bed-chamber by night— clean bedding, thick hair-mattresses, thorough ventilation, etc. Conductors and porters accompany each car to provide for the wants of the passengers, and in the palatial dining-car may be found the finest of viands and beverages prepared by Continental chefs.*

"Here," Bregand said. He handed me a sandwich wrapped in newsprint: a thick slab of fried pork between two shingles of hardtack. "There's water in my canteen. Tank up front's gone dry."

Peril escaped makes for apathy, numbness, a weakness, and craving for sleep that seeps into the bones and loosens the muscles and makes the mind reel. Before I knew it I had fallen asleep. Once (I think it must have been when they changed engines at Pittsburgh) I woke, and found my head on Bregand's shoulder. Embarrassed at this childish weakness, I pulled away and rested my cheek against the cold glass of the window. But Bregand did not appear to notice. He stared ahead at a smoky lamp swinging to and fro. The coal on the end of the stogie flared up, then dimmed; that was all. He sweated quietly and smoked. After a while I dozed off again and slept till morning, and we crossed the Ohio.

Oh, the river! Growing light in the eastern sky, the river a ribbon of burnished copper between banks of stone still pitch-black in shadow. Below us a stern-wheeler spun white lace, and then the sun tipped over the hills. The whole river lay bathed in red light; the Texas windows of the stern-wheeler winked like diamonds strung on a great necklace; the smoke from her fluted stacks lay like gauze along the banks; a covey of waterbirds rose into flight and became jewels against the soft green of the willows and sycamores bordering the giant Ohio.

"Blue Wing," Bregand said.

Not knowing he was awake, I jumped; or perhaps he had never been asleep.

"What?"

"Blue Wing." He pointed out the window with a fresh stogie. "The stern-wheeler. Government's taken her over to ferry troops up and down the river. They mean to get Mad Jack this time for sure."

To Boyle's Brigade the world looked very different this morning. The first flush of excitement, the novelty of the ride on the cars, the strange country—all these had worn off, and most of them had big heads after the passing around of so many jugs and bottles the night before. At every bend in the rails they craned from the windows and looked fearfully ahead as if they expected to see Spurrier and his guerrillas spring out on them from the bushes, pillage the train and slit everyone's throats, and disappear in a clap of thunder. Even the thin gruel and hardtack passed out for breakfast drew only a faint muttering from these recent heroes. Sergeant Bregand had spattered water on his face and drawn a comb through his gray ringlets, though there was still a pepper-and-salt stubble on his chin. When he came back to the seat he put on his uniform tunic and kepi; I saw a flash of colored ribbon and the dull gleam of a medal with some words on it that looked like French.

A corporal and some men came round with a big milkcan full of what was supposed to be coffee. It was lukewarm and black and bitter, and I threw mine out the window. Sergeant Bregand seemed to like it, though. He lit a fresh stogie and sat for a long time sipping the cold coffee and puffing on the stogie and not saying anything. We Irish are sensitive and discerning people, and I didn't say anything to him; he seemed withdrawn, but I didn't know why. Maybe he would be pleased if I told him I had decided to join Boyle's Brigade and play the drum, for I was very musical. But as I decided to speak, he finished the coffee and wiped his mouth.

"Charlie, you're going out in the world."

"Yes," I said, "but I—"

"Don't trust anybody." He held up his finger. "Especially

don't trust women! *Non!* They are harpies, mostly, and un-natural. Always be honest; speak up, tell the truth and shame the Devil, as they say. Stay away from strong drink, for it has ruined many a good lad. And when you've a proper job to do, do it well and make yourself indispensable to whoever you're working for. That's all I have to say, lad. Think on it."

The cars had glided so fast over the level lands of Ohio that houses and factories and churches came upon us, and we were entering Columbus. I wanted to tell Bregand I intended to join the Brigade, but he jumped out of his seat and began to haze the recruits into order.

"All right, there! In the aisle, all of you! Brace up—straighten your backbones. You there, the man with the wen! Put your shirt on—you're a soldier now, my lad! *Vite!*"

The little captain with the walking stick came through the cars looking very severe, and where Sergeant Bregand left off he took over.

"My good Christ, but you're a bunch of beauties! You there with the hangdog look—get your chin off your chest and stand to attention! Sergeant, that man still drinking coffee—put him on report." He pranced down the aisle, little stick tucked under his arm. In response to a warning glance from my friend Bregand, I ducked low under the seat and put someone's valise over my head till he was gone.

The train lurched and groaned and screeched, and we were in the smoke-blackened station. I waited till everyone was out and then left the car. Up and down the worn brick paving, as far as I could see, Boyle's Brigade was strung out in companies. Cursing sergeants tried to whip them into some kind of straight line and didn't do very well at it either. Sergeant Bregand seemed to be making more progress at it than the others. When I saw he had things well in hand I sidled over and spoke to him.

"Eh? What is it?"

"Please, sir," I said. "I'd like to join Boyle's Brigade and go to Camp Chase with you."

"I thought you were going west to look for your father!"

"I was. But there are a lot of men in the Army. Maybe father's in the Army. Maybe right here in Ohio, with Boyle's Brigade."

He turned back to his recruits and said over his shoulder, almost casually, *"Va-t-en.* Get out of here."

"What?"

"I said get out of here! We don't need children in the Army."

"I'm not a child! I'm almost sixteen. I'll make a good soldier. Look, I can read and write better than any of those blockheads standing in line over there—you must need a clerk."

With an oath he pulled me behind a rusty iron pillar that held up the sheet-iron roof of the station. Some of the recruits tittered and looked knowing, but Sergeant Bregand flashed them a sulphurous glance that fired them into pottery statues.

"Let me come!" I begged.

"The hell I will!" Sergeant Bregand cried. "Go away, lad, and be about your proper business! There's no place in the Army for such as you. You're bad luck!"

I was crushed; the Army didn't want me. But I remembered my manners. Even if Sergeant Bregand had scorned me, I would be courteous.

"Well," I said, "thank you anyway, Sergeant. Good luck, wherever you're going. I'll remember the advice you gave me, and try to follow it."

Chewing at his lip, he stared at me, and he was sweating even in the morning cool of the station. The companies were falling into a ragged line, swinging out in fours and marching toward an iron gate at the end of the platform. In a voice so low I could hardly hear him for the hiss of the steam and the clank of steel and the shuffle of boots on the worn bricks, Bregand said, "You'll understand some day."

"Understand what?"

He took a deep breath. The ribbons flashed, and the medal shone. "I'm a dirty old Army man, Charlie, and not fit to give advice to anyone. I've soldiered all over the world; I know a dozen ways of pleasuring a woman, and some tricks with young boys too, God help me. So—"

"Sergeant!" someone called. It was the captain, pounding his little stick into a gloved palm.

"So," Bregand said, "get the hell out of here, you handsome child, before all that bright beauty gets tattered and dingy. Get, now—*vite*! There's hell to pay with Captain Wagner already!"

I went, quickly. Sergeant Bregand was surely a peculiar man.

With so many men gone to the Army I had no trouble getting a job at the Columbus *Journal*, the local newspaper, rushing the growler and sweeping out, and currying the horses they used to deliver bundles of papers around town. Four dollars a week was princely income; the first thing I did was buy a gray clothbound ledger to start my journal again. There was a fascination in newspaper work, though I was only on the fringes of it. But newspapers dealt with words, and I loved words.

The whole state was shaken by Spurrier's raids. Only a few days before he was rumored to have crossed the river into Indiana near the Ohio border, not too far north and west of Cincinnati. No one was really sure where he was, and the *Journal* breathed fire and defiance:

> *This grisly amoral animal who kills and tortures as casually as he draws breath, this relic from a prehistoric age of mindless and unreasoning monsters, must be destroyed. The strengthening of Boyle's Brigade in response to the demands of our Senator is welcome news to the citizens of Ohio. Boyle's Brigade is sure to trim Mad Jack Spurrier's claws and singe his fur if he ventures into the Buckeye State.*

Not being sure what *amoral* meant, I looked it up in the composing room dictionary. It said "not concerned with moral standards," and I guess he wasn't—concerned, I mean.

Columbus was something like Utica—not a big town, but nice-sized and friendly, though the gray pile of the state capitol looked like a soap box with a wheel of cheese sitting on top of it. The *Journal* was a good paper too; when I ate my lunch of bread and sausage, I sat on a stack of newsprint and read every page from top to bottom. Professor Galen Potts and his Shakespearean Troupe were to give *Othello* in the Farmer's and Drover's Hall Tuesday next; admission twenty-five cents for ladies and gentlemen, children a dime. Federal troops, the *Journal's* Washington correspondent revealed by telegraph, had scared Jubal Early's gray-clad troops away from the capital, and Early had escaped across the upper Potomac back into Virginia after his Shenandoah raids. Count Kasimir Blatski, the famed Polish aeronaut, had thrilled the crowds attending the Franklin County Fair with a death-defying balloon ascension, and would appear soon for performances at Greenville and Wapakoneta. Doctor Ainslie's Galvanic Syrup was just the ticket for colds, chillblains, fevers, the ague, and catarrhal disorders, having an electric current from a galvanic battery passed through it, greatly strengthening and fortifying the ingredients. Not only that, but—I stared at page three of the *Journal:*

> *Utica police, the New York State correspondent wired the* Journal, *have advised citizens to be on the lookout for a desperate runaway boy, Charlie Campion. The youth assaulted his master, Mr. Casper Gillentine, who owns a hop-farm near Utica, and attempted to murder him.*

Attempted to murder him! Then Mr. Gillentine was not dead; I hadn't killed anyone! I almost cried out in relief. "After having also attacked Mr. Gillentine's young daughter Annie—" Oh, that was a lie, a black lie!

> *After having assaulted Mr. Gillentine's young daughter Annie, the young criminal fled. He was variously reported as having been seen in Fort Plain and Herkimer, and a Pinkerton's man nearly trapped him in a low dive in Manhattan.*

It had been a pretty low place, although it was not technically a dive; it was really a grocery store.

> *He is suspected to have taken shelter in a draft of recruits for Boyle's Brigade, and to be with them at Camp Chase near Columbus in Ohio. Representations are being made to the War Department in an effort to discover the whereabouts of the young thug. In the meantime citizens are urged to watch for Charlie Campion, a youth of about sixteen, small for his age, with curly dark hair and blue eyes. He is well-spoken—*

At least they had something good to say about me! ". . . well-spoken, writes a good hand, and seems innocent."

Seems innocent? I *was* innocent, being guilty only of the crime of love! After all, what is a man to do when his beloved's father comes at him with a stock whip?

In a sudden silly gesture I stuffed the newspaper away under a pile of inky rags as though there were not thousands of them already on the streets, available at a penny apiece. Well, at least I had changed my name when I asked for a job at the

Journal; I was not Charlie Jones. But I was also obviously a rootless boy, small for my age, with blue eyes and curly hair. Whether I seemed innocent or not I didn't know, but I guess I was well-spoken, and I did write a good hand. How long would it be until someone discovered me? Had I ought to flee now, or would that cast suspicion on me and sound the alarm?

The decision was made for me that afternoon. Well-spoken? I was really too-damned-much-spoken—that is, I talked too much. I could not abide errors in spelling; when I found *abysmal* spelled with two s's in the next day's editorial, I called it to the attention of the foreman.

"Pretty smart, ain't you?"

Modestly I said, "Anyone could have done it."

"The editor sent it down like that." He took a folded sheet of notebook paper from his pocket. "That's the way *he* spelled it."

"But it isn't right!"

"Not only that! I proofread the column. What do you think of that?" His face began to get red.

"Well. . ." I squirmed. What was it Sergeant Bregand had advised: *Make yourself indispensable.* I was trying. *Always tell the truth.* That cinched it.

"No matter who wrote it, or who read it, it's wrong, that's all!" I went to get the composing room dictionary; when I came back with it he boxed my ears and threw me out of the newspaper business into the street.

"And don't come back!" he bawled.

The *Journal* still owed me a dollar and eighty cents wages, but I was too scared to go back for it.

Chapter 4

On the National Road west of Columbus all was confusion and rumor. Wtih my valuables in a bundle on the end of a stick I trudged westward in the August heat; no one would give me a ride. A stranger got short shrift in Ohio. He might be an advance agent for John Selby Spurrier and his ruffians, searching out the land and cataloging fat sheep and stocks of grain and marking mayors and village officials for hanging.

At noon, parched and footsore, I knocked at the door of a solid brick house that sat back from the road at the end of a lane bordered by poplars. This was a prosperous-looking place; surely they couldn't refuse a poor boy a drink of water and a crust of bread. The door opened—a tiny crack I wouldn't have known was there had not a rusty hinge creaked.

"Who—who is it?" a voice quavered.

"Please, sir," I said. "Or is it madam? At any rate, I'm only a poor orphan boy that's tired and hungry."

The door opened another fraction of an inch; glassy eyes stared at me from the interior gloom.

"I'll chop wood or whatever you want."

Below the doubtful eye a pistol-barrel emerged, a good twelve inches of it, it seemed. I never saw one so wide a bore.

"G'lang with ye, now! Don't be abothering peaceful citizens that never done anyone harm."

I was tired and hot and exasperated. "But I never did anyone harm either! Please, can't you—"

I heard a hollow metallic click, and the yawning pistol barrel became three calibers larger.

"If'n you don't g'lang, I'll shoot!"

"All right!" I shouted. "If that's the way you treat homeless boys in this state. But let me tell you—"

Clenched in a bony fist, the old gun poked out through the crack and weaved back and forth like the head of a snake trying to locate a prime target. I didn't tell the man, or woman, or whoever it was, anything. I ran as fast as I could and stopped behind the trunk of a big sycamore. From that distance I saw the pistol withdraw; the iron-strapped door squeaked shut. What an inhospitable neighborhood!

Hobson's Federal Cavalry had pickets out along the road. At least a dozen times that day a vedette stopped me and asked questions. By late afternoon, what with my thirst and fatigue and my natural Irish temper, I was growing very tired of Hobson and his horsemen. I gave short answers to a burly corporal with a jaw full of chewing tobacco, and he got down off his big bay and demanded to see what was in the sack I carried.

"Just my own personal belongings."

"I want to look at it anyway."

"All right," I said, and untied it for him.

"What's this?" He wet a dirty thumb and began to riffle through my clothbound journal. "By God, it's poetry, fellers! And to a girl! Listen to this—'Annie, my love, Annie my queen—'"

"Give that back!" I yelled, and snatched it from his hand.

"Well, now," the corporal said. "What have we got here, boys, a little Romeo?" They all guffawed. "Now be giving it back to me, for it may be a kind of a cipher that the captain would want to puzzle out."

"No."

The corporal brushed his stained mustaches with two fingers, and rested his fist on his big Colt revolver. "Will you give it to me, boy, or will I spank your didie with the flat of my saber and take it anyway?"

"You touch this book," I said, "and there'll be a new face in hell in the morning!"

A horse started to caper and dance in the dust; saddle leather creaked, and someone said, "Come on, Grady. He's only a boy—Mad Jack don't trust his spying to infants."

The corporal continued to preen his mustaches; then he shrugged and laughed and put a booted leg over the saddle. "What's your name, boy?"

"Charlie."

"Charlie what?"

Unmollified, I said, "None of your damned business." He wasn't a bad sort. Before he spurred away with his patrol he shared half a canteen of water with me, and told me I'd better stay off the National Road or someone with sensibilities not quite so delicate as John Grady's would read the rest of my poetry.

In that late afternoon of an August day I wandered into a swampy place near a lake and sat on a rotten log, cursing my fate. Overhead the hot blue of the sky filtered down through the arrows of the reeds that sheltered me; yellow-banded wasps sizzled in and out of a mud nest on the other end of my log. I pulled off my boots and let my burning feet sink into the foam-flecked mud. Oh, I was hungry! Why hadn't I the common good sense to buy a loaf of bread when I left Columbus, or hook a stone water bottle to my belt? I scooped up a handful of the water but it was green and sickly-looking, and filled with water bugs and trailers of moss. Instead of drinking it, I strained out the scum and rubbed it on my sunburned face. Well, at least it was cool among the reeds and willows.

My prospects didn't look very prime. True, I had four dollars and a pretty good suit. But my boots had holes in the bottoms, though I had lined them with several thicknesses of cardboard. If only I had something to eat! Thinking to restore my spirits, I took out my mouth-harp and breathed into it a few chords. Something rousing was needed, but all that came to mind were sad and doleful melodies like "The Turtle Dove" and "Poor Miss Maude" and "The Unfortunate Rake." What was it the printers at the *Journal* had sung? It was a catchy tune—"The Copperhead," that was it! They had a lot of Copperheads in Ohio—that was what they called people that favored slavery. There was a snake in Ohio called the copperhead, a shiny black snake with coppery skin.

He wired in, he wired out
Leaving the people still in doubt
Whether the snake upon the track
Was going South or coming back.

Only a buzz came from one of the holes. There was probably dust or spittle in it, or something. I knocked it hard on my knee, and a rivet popped out of one end. The whole instrument sprang apart in a shower of tiny brass reeds and crumbs of wood. *Oh, damn, damn, damn!* I was in a black mood.

Ned Campion. Who was Ned Campion? Was there a Ned Campion? I knew myself for a silly child, ever to think I could pick a Ned Campion out of all mankind and claim him for a father. Charlie Campion and his fine talk about king's blood! I sneered at myself and wiggled my toes in the mud. West, ever west; why in God's name should I think to go west? Because a mysterious Ned Campion had disappeared in that quarter of the compass? This West that I was journeying through appeared to be a very hard place for a young man. Man? In my piteous state I sneered again at my grand pretentions. *Spank your didie*, the corporal had threatened. Maybe he was right.

Sometimes a person can see better out of the corner of his eye than straight ahead. Slumped on my log, weeping and trying not to and then thinking again that it was all right—I was after all only a mewling infant—I saw several times a disturbance on the fringes of my vision. Something deep in my brain took awareness of it, and tried hard to warn me. Deep in despond, I refused the warning, and wept unashamed maudlin tears. *There is something very odd going on beyond the screen of reeds; something is passing by, dimly seen, like a black dog padding behind a picket fence.*

I wept on, wallowing in my misery, cursing my fool Irish luck. But all along a little voice tugged at my thoughts: *You're a damned stupid Irishman if you don't pay attention to that dark shadow passing behind the reeds. And by the way, poor Charlie Campion, what in hell is that sucking sound, like a horse pulling muddy hoofs out of the bog, and the jingle of harness, and the flat slap that might be a whip on a horse's flanks?*

Come to my senses at last I sprang to my feet, staring this way and that like a sleeper awakened. Where the reeds were thin, I saw a man on a big chestnut. He wore a tight-fitting black suit; in one fist he held the reins, in the other a whiplike branch from which he had trimmed the leaves and sprouts. Paralyzed with fear, I saw with dreadful clarity the little white scars where the knife had lopped off the branches. It was the Pinkerton!

I stood for a moment, heart in my mouth, feeling the drumbeat of my pulse in my ears. He had reined up the chestnut and was peering this way and that, his face red and sweating under the big drover's hat he had put on against the heat.

Perhaps he would not have seen me if nature had not betrayed me. Standing motionless in the muck, my bare feet in the ooze, I felt myself leaning unaccountably to one side. Desperately I tried to keep my balance. In a kind of daze I realized the mud was giving way and I was about to sprawl headlong. For an eternity I balanced on one foot, trying to right myself, holding out the hand clutching the bag farther and farther in an effort to preserve my balance.

He still had not seen me, still sat motionless in the saddle, head swiveling this way and that to search the reeds and willows. In a last frantic effort to preserve my stance I leaned far over; I tightened the muscles in my near leg and tried to draw the bare foot clear of the clinging mud. It came, too free and too fast. I toppled into the green ooze with a splash.

"Who's there?" the Pinkerton yelled.

I didn't care to discuss it; instead I floundered away, slipping and sliding and falling and picking myself up and floundering deeper into the reeds.

"Charlie! Charlie Campion! In the name of the law, stop or I'll shoot!"

The reeds sawed at my face and hands, but I plunged deeper, my breath coming in sobbing gasps. The mud sucked and pulled at my bare feet, and a smell like rotten eggs came from the depths. If I stopped running, just lay quiet in the water like a crocodile in the Nile, maybe he wouldn't find me. Anyway, I had to stop and catch my breath; my face and nose and ears were full of molasseslike mud, and I couldn't breathe. I propped myself on all fours, dirty water up to my belly, and pawed at my face to clear my nose. But my hand was dirtier than my face, and I choked and coughed.

"Stop! In the name of the law, boy! Stop or I'll shoot!"

Horrified, I saw him again, holding the reeds aside and waving a pistol. He must have abandoned the chestnut, thinking to get around better on foot. Though he hadn't yet located me

in my dim bower of reeds, I was panting like a switch-engine.
It was only a matter of time till he had me centered with that
long-barreled pistol.

"Oh, there you are, damn you! Stand up, boy, and put your
hands over your head."

I stood up, but only to flounder away again. Through the
lacy screen of willows I could see blue water and a peaceful
small cottage and a man hoeing in a garden. There would soon
be no more reeds, and I would be trapped between the Pinkerton
and the lake.

"For the last time, boy, stop! Stop in the name of the law!"

For the moment I was hidden but my last refuge was running
out. I stood at the edge of the reeds, a walking ball of mud,
completely winded. My legs turned to India rubber, my chest
heaved, the whole universe turned upside-down, hung there
for a moment, and started to revolve like a pinwheel. Was this
the end, the end of all the great dreams, the muddy end of
Royal Charlie Campion? The man in the garden stopped hoeing
and looked up, shading his eyes. Tomatoes, that was what he
was hoeing. Tomato plants.

A ball whistled over my head. I was too tired to duck. Well,
the Pinkerton had been fair enough. He'd given me every chance
to surrender. But I wasn't going to surrender; I'd never go
back. They'd never take me. Slowly, painfully, I dragged one
muddy foot forward and pulled the other one after. Let him
shoot me! I was damned if it made any difference.

"Stop!"

That was when I saw the snake. At least I thought it was a
snake. A half-inch in diameter, brown and hairy, it wriggled
through the fringe of reeds. I didn't care. What harm could a
snake do to me now, even a copperhead? Let it sting!

But it didn't sting. It wriggled on and on, a foot, three feet,
ten feet. How long was this snake? I laughed. I had been shot,
that was it, and was not in hell. The snake was the beginning
of eternal torment for a vicious and wicked boy. As if to confirm
this theory the sun faded and I stumbled in a cold shadow.

"Now I've got you!" the Pinkerton cried.

Suddenly I knew what the snake was. And the shadow too.
And I knew what the man with the hoe had been looking at.
It was a balloon—a tremendous, gay balloon fifty feet or so
over my head; the snake was a rope that trailed from the pendant
wicker basket. If there had been time to think I would probably

have acknowledged the thing for a balloon—an unaccountable balloon flying above the fringes of a lake in Ohio—and turned to hold out my wrists for the Pinkerton's manacles. But there was no time to think. I grabbed the rope and held on. Away I caromed, spinning this way and that, while from the basket overhead awful curses rained down on me and the Pinkerton and the innocent man with the hoe. The great silken bulk dragged me through the man's garden; ass-over-tin-cup I went rolling and scraping and plowing furrows this way and that.

"Stop!" the Pinkerton yelled, and fired his pistol.

I knew a good thing when I saw one. The balloon was pulling me away from the Pinkerton faster than I could navigate on my own. I splashed into the shallow fringes of the lake, still holding on, while a shower of what must have been sand ballast poured down. Well, I'd go the lot! Frantically I wrapped the loose end of the rope around me, passing it through my legs and about my middle and over my shoulder and any way I could, knowing that in my weakened condition I wouldn't be able to hang on much longer. My only chance was to snarl myself like a fly in a web and hope for the best.

The rope jerked at my webbed body; I was borne up, up, up into the sky. Below me the Pinkerton stood openmouthed, and his red face got smaller and smaller until it was only a pink dot. The man with the hoe dwindled also, and his cottage became a toy for children. It was a mistake to look down, though. I clenched my teeth and shut my eyes and gripped the rope harder. Then my head bumped something. It was the rim of the wicker basket. A small hand grabbed me by the collar and helped me into the basket. I was safe, at least for a while.

Winded and dizzy I hung to the rail of the basket, astonished to see that somehow I still clutched my bundle with all my possessions. That was wonder enough, but the balloon basket beat anything I ever saw. In the middle was a kind of a sheet-iron stove with a tall chimney that went up through the network of cords and ropes to a hole in the bottom of the silk bag. The rest of the basket was cluttered with what looked like scientific instruments—shiny brass tubes and lenses and glass dials—and a kind of hand-cranked winch the small man must have used to haul me up. There was a large cardboard speaking trumpet, too—I suppose to hail people on the ground. The aeronaut fizzed and sparked at me like a catherine wheel, but he was too busy stoking the fire with straw and twigs to do a proper job of cursing. He was a small birdlike man in a linen duster and goggles—tiny, spare, with sharp features and a dainty beak of a nose.

"Brszwy polzkcerz!" he roared, or something that sounded like that; then he went back to stoking the furnace in an effort to keep us out of the lake. It was a hot-air balloon and seemed to take a lot of fuel.

"Yes, sir," I said. "Thank you."

My knees gave way, and I sagged down on the littered floor of the basket. What was this on my hand? Dirt, mud—sure enough; but red? I stared fascinated at my forearm. I had been pinked, winged, in fact shot by the Pinkerton. Across my arm, a hand-span above the wrist, was a rough-edged gully where one of his bullets had plowed.

"Brszwy polzkercz damn damn damn no business at all *krplop!"* the aeronaut shouted. He shook his fist at me but I was busy contemplating the outrageous violation of my hide by the Pinkerton's bullet. My arm, I suddenly discovered, was numb to the shoulder. Though the wound had stopped bleeding, it was ugly and caked with dirt. When a man is shot for the first time, it gives him a great deal to reflect on.

The aeronaut saw me staring at my arm; he worked his way round the roaring stove and pulled a lacy handkerchief out of an interior pocket, wrapping it around my wound.

"Brszwy too bad, *rakczy,* sorry," he said.

I was beginning to get the hang of his language. I finally decided it was English, but swamped—a heavy accent like syrup oozes over griddle cakes. Then I slumped too far down and burned my knee on the red-hot stove and let out a great squall of pure agony.

"Oolciki brzasta own damned fault," my rescuer said. "What in *pokrasti szentsenyi* you do in my *wieczlinsza* balloon?"

He was little, smaller than me, with a grizzled beard combed in two forked tails and a kind of uniform cap on his head held on by a scarf tied under the chin.

"I'll explain later," I said.

"Merde!" I didn't know what that meant, but it seemed to be disapproving. Anyway, he peered over the side, watching. Something brushed against the bottom of the basket, and then tree branches poked up round us. The limbs pricked and tore and pulled at the basket, but the great silk bag pulled away. In another moment we bumped on the grass at the far side of the lake, and the aeronaut jumped out and tied his long hairy

rope to a tree. At the same time he jerked and tugged at a
dangling chain with a red-painted wood handle; the whole great
bag collapsed like a dying prehistoric monster. The breeze
carried it away from over our heads, and slowly, gracefully,
the hundreds of yards of varnished cloth lay down to windward.

"Fini," the little man said. "Well-done, eh, *pzsti lacsi?"*

It was neatly done, all right. While he was drawing the fire,
I staggered out of the basket and collapsed on the grass. I felt
sick and suspected I was dying. After a while he came over to
me and squatted beside me with a flask.

"Drink."

I grabbed it and gargled some down. It wasn't water—it
was some nameless fiery liquid. It snatched me back from the
heavenly gates or wherever I was headed for just in time. The
fuzziness faded, and I blinked my eyes and took a tentative
breath.

"He chasing you."

I coughed, and nodded.

"The man in black."

"Yes."

"You are a—what they call it?—a criminal?"

"No," I said.

"But why he—this man—why chase you?"

I could understand him fine; maybe it was the liquor. But
it was hard to marshal my brains and say anything intelligent.
"Annie," I said thickly. I don't know exactly what I meant,
but I had Annie on my mind. How she would pity me, seeing
me in this sad condition! It gave me mournful satisfaction.

"Annie?" the little man sucked his lips and fingered the
forked beard. "Ah, a woman! No?"

"Yes," I said.

"You did for love, whatever was?"

I nodded again, and reached for the flask. He shook his
head, and stuffed it into the pocket in the linen duster.

"Ah," he said. He seemed satisfied. "For love! Beautiful.
A Pole understand this. Whatever was—for love." He nodded
and got up, peering across the lake. "Well," he said. "Well,
merde!" He scratched his small nose with a gloved finger.
"That man—the black man—is coming fast. On a horse. Oh,
a very muddy horse. But he be here quick."

I tried to scramble to my feet, but I was too weak. The
Pinkerton had watched us soar over the lake and then had
remounted his chestnut and galloped after us.

"For love," the Pole said. "Touching. Here in America. Of all places. For love." Very touched, he put his arm under mine and helped me to my feet. When I started to wobble off with some very impracticable idea of running again, he pulled me back by the shirttail. "No. In here."

I closed my eyes hard and opened them again, trying to clear away the gossamer veil that was enveloping me.

"In where?"

He pointed to the sheet-iron stove.

"But I'll cook!"

"No. Is cool now."

I still must have looked doubtful, for he said, "You know better place hide?"

"No," I admitted.

He helped me wriggle through the door at the bottom of the stove, and then pushed it to with a clang and latched it.

"You all right, *svzczy dobrin?*"

It was hot in there, and the soot made me sneeze.

"Yes," I said. Remembering my manners, I added. "Thank you very much."

There was just enough room to stand erect. Through the hole at the top I could see a circle of blue sky and an occasional spray of leaves as the breeze stirred a tree. A moment later I hear thudding hoofs and the angry voice of my nemesis, the Pinkerton detective. Oh, but he was a persistent man! Why was it so important that he catch me? And why pursue me all the way out to Ohio?

"Where's the boy?"

"Boy?" The aeronaut's voice was languid. "Oh. Boy."

"Yes, damn it, the boy! He's a fugitive from justice."

"He fell off."

"What?" The Pinkerton's voice broke shrilly, unbelievingly.

"In the lake. In the water. Very sad. Probably drown. Go clear to bottom. All for love."

"What the hell are you talking about?"

"Very sad. Have a drink."

My aeronaut must have handed him the flask, but the Pinkerton was not to be put off.

"You've got him hid someplace!"

"Then we drink. So. Very good. We call *slivovitz*. Plum brandy."

The Pinkerton was irate. "Now listen here, you—"

"Blatski. Count Blatski. Polish royalty. Address me very careful, with respect, eh?"

"I don't give a hoot for royalty. All I say is you're harboring a fugitive, and that's against the law."

"So where harbor, eh? Look for yourself."

There was a long silence. I imagined the Pinkerton pussy-footing round the balloon, lifting folds of silk. The wicker of the basket creaked and the stove swayed a little, or was I just dizzy? No, he was in the basket. I spread my legs wide, hoping that if he looked in the little door he would not see my feet.

"Look, cossack," the count said. "You got a—what you call?—a *papier*, eh? A warrant?"

The door opened and a shaft of sunlight came in. But the Pinkerton did't see me. I swallowed hard and thought of a long string of Hail Marys. The door went shut again.

"Warrant? Of course! The boy's wanted for attempted murder."

"We don't believe," the count mused. "Such a nice boy. Well, too bad. All drowned. Very sad."

Another pause. Then the Pinkerton said, "There's something fishy about all this."

"Fish. Interesting. In Polish we say—"

"I don't care what you say. I think I'll take you in for questioning. You know a lot more than you're telling, Count."

"We are too busy. No time."

"You'll have time. A lot of time. In the Springfield jail."

Another pause! Good Lord, would the Pinkerton never give up? But there came a sudden and dramatic change in the conversation.

"Don't you point that pistol at me!" the Pinkerton cried.

"We have killed three men," the count said. "Two with sword in duels, only one with pistol. But we are magnificent shot. Go way. *Heraus!*"

"But—"

"If you still here to annoy us in one minute—look, we start now counting by watch—in one minute we shoot you in heart."

"Now, wait a minute—"

"Fifteen seconds gone. Maybe we shoot your horse too."

"You've not heard the last of this!"

"Thirty seconds already."

The last thing I heard was the drumming of the chestnut's hoofs as the Pinkerton galloped away. The heat was stifling.

Even allowing for the dimness of my hiding place, everything got black as the inside of a cow. I folded up as a telescope collapses and fainted away.

═══════Chapter 5═══════

I never knew exactly when I rejoined the world I thought to have lost. I had no body, no arms, no legs, nothing but one open eye that saw a little patch of something blue. After a while I figured it must be the sky, a late afternoon sky, because a small puffy cloud, its belly washed with gold, drifted across the span of my single eye. I opened the other eye; something in my numbed brain shifted back and forth and there was depth to the sky, meaning and substance that relieved me.

Very tired, I was content to lie in the grass. I knew it was grass, all right. That was good. I didn't think they had grass in heaven—more likely everything was paved with mother-of-pearl. A bug crawled up a blade of this grass, and as I watched him he came to the end and dropped off. There were no bugs in heaven either. Very good.

"Kara?"

From a great distance someone was calling. Kara? What an odd name.

"Kara! Kara!"

Let him call; I didn't care. Experimentally I tried breathing. I was a pair of eyes and some lungs, at least, along with a remnant of a brain. Where was I? What had happened? I ran my tongue out and licked at the corner of my mouth. It tasted like mud.

"We require another bottle of wine, Kara."

Apparently Kara had the custody of the wine. Gingerly I willed a toe to move. It wiggled. Well, no use rushing into things. I would rest for a while before trying any major moves.

Suddenly I was drowning. A Niagara of cold water poured into my face. Spluttering and gasping, I sat up. With more speed than I had planned I moved back into the world of real things.

"You've come round," a female voice laughed.

I spluttered again, and gargled, wiping at my eyes.

"I told him you'd be all right," the female said. "All it took was a bucket of lake water."

She stood over me, holding the empty pail and smiling, a big blond girl with yellow plaits pulled back in a knot. Over a fine bosom was buttoned a red uniform coat with big braided frogs, the kind of coat an animal trainer wears in a circus. I had never seen a grown woman with so short a skirt—it barely covered the calves of her sturdy legs, and she wore a pair of scuffed brown boots.

"Who are you?" I croaked.

"Kara."

"Yes, Kara." She was the one who had the wine. Suddenly my memory fizzed like a galvanic spark. The Pinkerton! I scrambled to my feet.

"Don't worry," Kara said. "Everything is all right. The count will take care of everything."

"The detective—"

"The count frightened him away."

I took a deep breath. "That was very good of him."

We were in a grassy glade at the edge of the lake. The sun was low, and shadows of sycamores and elms lay long in the grass. A few yards away a mule grazed, and another drank from the wind-riffled surface of the lake. A gaily painted wagon stood under the trees, bright red and purple and yellow. A cloth banner tacked to the side said:

THE RENOWNED COUNT KASIMIR BLATSKI
Leading Aeronaut of the Entire World

In the lee of the wagon sat my late rescuer, napkin tucked into his collar, dining at a deal table spread with a white cloth. On it was a tall bottle, a bowl with fresh roses, and what looked like fine china and crystal and silver.

"So," the count said. "You wake up, eh, boy? *Prszy kwicz solowny.*" That was what it sounded like. "We are pleased." He gnawed at a chicken leg.

"Yes," I said. "I—I guess I'm all right now. I have you to thank, sir."

He waved negligently with the chicken leg. "Nothing. Nothing at all. We kill many men. An American detective—poof!"

"But if he comes back—"

The count threw the gnawed bone into the weeds and wiped his hands on the napkin. "He not come back, not for a while." Chuckling in a small dry way, he poured another goblet of wine. "He get help—a lot of help—before he try again. You see?" He lit a thin pencil of a cigar, and got up to stroll around the envelope of the balloon, which lay like a great dead animal at the edge of the trees.

"We must wash some of that dirt off you," Kara said. She had her sleeves rolled up and was stirring a pan of water over the fire where the chicken had lately broiled.

I rubbed a hand over my cheek and looked down at the muddy smear. I needed a bath, that was sure.

"And that wound on your arm—we'll put a clean cloth on that and have you decent again in no time. What was your name?"

"Charlie."

She soaped a rag in the hot water and came at me.

"Now just a minute! I can wash myself!"

"Don't fight so, Charlie! Will you look at that boy, now! Stand still! I declare, the mud is an inch thick on your neck."

Kara was a tremendously strong girl. I wriggled feebly and protested, but she put an arm like a wrestler's around my neck and clamped me helpless, scouring at my ears and eyes till I thought the skin would peel off like an onion.

"God damn it!" I cried. "Let me go, will you? I'm not a baby!"

Well, I was small for my age, and greatly weakened by my experiences. While the count puffed at his cigar and made rasping amused noises, she skinned me out of my shirt and washed the top half of me. Finally I squirmed free and ran into the bushes. But she only laughed, a childlike laugh for so big and rough a girl, and let me take the basin and the rag behind a thicket for privacy. Afterwards, she loaned me one of the count's old shirts and a pair of woolen trousers, and tie^d a neat bandage around the gash on my forearm.

"There," she said. "You look like a different boy!"

"Good," the count said. "Very good."

While he sat in a canvas chair, fondling the twin forks of his beard and staring at the twilight, Kara and I folded the balloon. It had to be done quickly, she explained, lest the dew fall on it and cause mildew. It was hard work and I was awkward, but we finally worried it into a big square package and threw a canvas over it. By that time my stomach was rumbling with hunger. Before I had to ask, Kara got out a sack of hardtack and some cold sausage, and shared a jug of thin, flat beer with me. The moon rose as we ate, a giant Ohio moon like a disk of orange paper pasted on the horizon.

"How," I asked, "did Count Blatski happen to come over the lake when I was running from the Pinkerton?"

She wiped her fingers on the tails of her coat, and reached for the jug.

"More beer?"

I shook my head, and she drained the jug. She ate and drank a great deal, but she was an Amazon.

"He made an ascension at the Springfield Fair. Always, for the grand finale, he lets the ground rope go and floats away waving the Polish flag in one hand and the Stars and Stripes in the other, singing the *"Marseillaise."* In the wagon, then, I follow him and try to be there when he lands. Only this time the wind carried him too fast. I had to go around the lake, so he landed before I got there."

"Are you his helper?"

"I am his daughter. Kara is my name. Kara Blatski."

I buttoned my shirt collar against the evening chill. What a wonderful life! To soar here, there, everywhere, with a gaily painted wagon to follow!

"He must be very famous," I said. "Very rich, too."

"Not so famous as such a great man should be. Not so rich, either." Kara sighed, and wiped her lips with a sleeve. "It costs us a great deal to live. The mules eat a lot of hay and oats, and the count must dine well. Silk and thread to patch the balloon come dear, and the balloon is getting old. Someday"— she looked fearful—"someday it will burst, right down the middle. Oh, I shudder to think of it!"

"But the crowds—the people? Don't they pay?"

"I pass the hat. Sometimes a man will want to take a ride

for a dollar, and I hitch the mules to a pulley and run the balloon up and down. But everyone is too excited over the war. No, times are not good for us." Still looking into the red eye of fire, she sighed; her strong fingers played with a heavy gold earring. "It is a shame that a great man—my father—comes to such an end, a clown at fairs. And he is getting old. Sometimes I have to help him out of bed. He shouldn't eat rich foods—he has the gout—but he will have his port and his beef and his walnuts; turtle steaks when we are along the river."

Women were always cautious and inclined to worry about things.

"Well," I said, "I guess that Pinkerton didn't faze him!"

"He is brave," Kara said. "But it takes more than that, Charlie. You are young. Some day you will know how it is to see a fine man—your father—grow old."

"You don't look like him," I said judiciously. "He's very small and dark, and talks with an accent, and—"

"My goodness!" Kara said. "It's late! Now where has the time gone? Charlie, be a good boy and take this jug down to the lake and rinse it for me, *ja?*"

"Is that Polish?" I asked.

"What?"

"Ja, or whatever you said?"

"Lord, what a curiosity the boy has got! Now hurry, while some blankets I get!"

At the edge of the lake something splashed in the shallows. The rising moon laid a ladder of yellow light across the water. Holding the jug upside down to drain, I looked back at Count Blatski's camp. What a peaceful scene: the wink of the fire, the gay wagon, mules grazing in the moonlight, the count sitting under the stars. I could see the glow of his cigar. It was so . . . why, it was *homelike*, that was what it was! Even way out West under the Ohio stars, this was home. I swallowed hard, and took the jug back to Kara. She had set up a folding canvas cot under a tree for her, and there was a pile of blankets and a pillow with a Dutchy kind of embroidery for me under a tree.

"It's getting a little cooler," I said, handing her the jug.

"Eh?" The count roused, and looked at me as if he too had been thinking about something. "Oh. You." He stubbed out the cigar and fondled the twin forks of his beard. "What's your name, boy?"

"Charlie."

"*Oui*—Charlie. Sometime I forget. *Alors*—"

He got to his feet, and stretched. "Tomorrow we go to Xenia, eh, Kara?"

She laughed, wiping the jug. "What a funny name!"

"I look on map. Is Xenia, all right. We make a lot of money there, *hein?* Masons or Baptists or somebody have there—what you call?—a collection."

"Convention?" I asked.

The count eyed me fondly, and put his hand on my head. "Is convention. *Tak.*"

"He speaks Danish, too," Kara whispered.

"We go to bed now," Count Blatski announced. From beneath the wagon Kara produced a small wooden step, and the count mounted it. "Goodnight, Kara," he said. "Goodnight, Charlie."

That was the end of a very trying day for me, but a momentous day, too.

When I woke in the early dawn, it was chill for an August morning. The eastern sky was washed with all kinds of soft color, and the dew was heavy on my blankets. Kara was already about, stoking the fire and frying sausages and eggs; the table was again neatly set. A moment later the count emerged in a flannel nightcap and a tattered dressing gown, yawned, and stroked the tails of his beard. I hurried to rise, but my body seemed to be one yowling ache. Stiffly I edged out of the blankets, put on my shirt, and folded the blankets. It looked like rain.

"*Bonjour*," the count said. "You sleep well, boy?"

I knew what *bonjour* meant. I was already picking up a little language.

"Yes, sir," I said. "Thank you."

When the count had finished breakfast and started his toilette with a straight razor and a basin of suds, Kara and I ate what was left of the sausage and some fried potatoes. Neither of us talked much. They were going to leave me and I was sad. Kara bustled around scouring the frying pan and packing the table and the linen and the silver as if she didn't want to think too much about anything.

I helped get the balloon and the stove and the wicker basket atop the wagon and lashed in place, and rounded up the mules and harnessed them. Dan and Beersheba, their names were;

Dan tried to bite me, though Beersheba was ladylike and only nuzzled me looking for sugar or an apple.

"Here, boy." The count tossed me a pair of worn boots. "To big for me. You wear, and remember Count Blatski."

"Yes, sir," I said. "Thank you." I would remember. I would never forget. I had left my boots in the swamp yesterday. Was it only yesterday? It seemed I had known Kara and the count for a long time.

"Where you go?" the count asked.

"Where I go?"

"Now. Where you go when we leave?"

"I don't know." I waved vaguely westward. "Out there."

Count Blatski climbed on the wagon. Kara was already sitting on the high seat, reins in her hands.

"Goodbye, Kara," I said. "Thank you very much. And you too, sir. I'll never forget what you did for me."

Kara smiled, her lips set tight and a glint in her eyes that could have been tears.

"Goodbye, Charlie."

I was damned if I was going to beg. Here it was going away from me, all of life, it seemed—romance, adventure, good people, even a kind of home, and a man I would have been glad to call Father. I set my lip, too, and waved. The gay wagon trundled out of the clearing and onto the south fork of the road—the one that went to Xenia and a collection of Baptists or Masons or something. I picked up my mud-caked sack and my stick and watched the wagon go. It paused at the road, the count stood up and yelled at me.

"Gardez-vous contre le Pinkerton!"

His voice came to me thin and faraway. A few drops of rain spattered my shoulders.

"What?"

"The detective. Watch out for him, *hein?*"

I nodded, and waved. When he sagged out of sight behind the bulk of the balloon my courage broke; my pride shivered into a thousand glassy fragments. I ran after the wagon, calling out.

"Please, sir! Wait!"

Kara reined up; they both stared down at me. I was breathless and frightened and utterly, completely humble.

"Don't go away! Don't leave me! I'll work for you. I'll help with the balloon and the mules and the cooking and everything.

Just take me with you. Please take me with you!"

The count looked pained. He blew out his breath in a long sigh, his veined cheeks rounded like apples and inside of his lips, red and wet, pressed against the grizzled thicket of beard.

"Please!" Kara said. "He's a good boy, Papa!"

The count took a well-polished violin out of the wagon. He adjusted one of the pegs, not looking at either of us, and plucked a string.

"Good." He tried another string, and tightened another peg. "I know. Good. That is not question." His voice was kind. "What we do with a boy, eh? Money is few. The *prszylinicz* mules eat so much. Times are not good."

I cast down my eyes. It was not fair to impose on them. But I liked them so. I felt again that awful sensation of having lost something, something needful for life itself; I remembered the feeling when I trudged away from the Gillentine farm that terrible morning.

"I'm sorry," I said. "Excuse me. I—I shouldn't have begged."

Kara was crying, no doubt of it. Shiny tears rolled down her cheeks and onto her chin and dropped into the bosom of the man's shirt she wore under the uniform coat. *God damn it,* I told myself, *don't you cry, Charlie Campion! You're a baby if you do!* It was all right to talk about an Irishman's feelings being so near the surface, but I would be disgraced if I cried now.

"Go away," I muttered. I waved my hand in what must have looked like an angry gesture, though I didn't mean it that way, being only confused and bewildered and lost. "Now. Go on! I—I'll write you a letter some day if you let me know where you are."

The count scratched his chin, and smiled a wry smile. "Yes," he said. "First you let us know where to write you—tell where to write us." He looked at Kara. "It sounds very queer, *n'est-ce pas?*"

"Papa," Kara said, "I'll just put more water in the soup! Charlie won't eat much, and God knows I eat too much already and get fat. Besides, he can pass the hat while I play the drum. And the balloon is so big and hard to handle. Please, Papa!"

If I ever saw a man besieged and desperate, it was the count. He tuned the violin, he looked at the sky, he smiled and then frowned. He played with the tails of his beard; he looked at Kara and at me as if we were strange creatures from another world whom he had never laid eyes on before. *"Merde,"* he said thoughtfully.

"No," I cried. "It isn't fair to devil the count. Good-bye and good luck to you—and to Dan and Beersheba, too, though Dan did try to bite me."

"Well," the count scowled, "No pay, *bien entendu!* Times are very hard."

I blinked hard, not believing I had heard aright.

"You help," the count said. "You help much, eh? Feed mules, pack balloon, stack hay for stove, patch balloon with special thread I show you how, pass hat, eat light, eh?"

I tossed my bundle and stick high into the air. "You mean I can go with you?"

Kara threw her arms around the count.

"Is all wrong," the count grumbled. "Shouldn't be. But is. Climb on wagon, boy. Hurry to Xenia where collection is."

"Convention!" I shouted, climbing up on the bulk of the balloon. "Yes, sir! Thank you—you'll never regret hiring Charlie Campion!"

The count fiddling a foreign tune, we trundled away for Xenia. The rain had stopped; it looked like it might be a fair day.

═══Chapter 6═══

I learned about balloons from Count Blatski. Not that he let me ascend; that was a glorious experience reserved for Ohio farmers who had a dollar to pay their way. But the technique of ballooning, the way the great sacks were built, the precise style to sew up a rip with silk thread and to compound the black pitchy stuff the count invented to patch the fabric—all these things and many more I became expert at in that golden autumn. I thrilled at the physics of the hot-air balloon, learned Archimedes' principle, and gaped openmouthed at the beautiful simplicity of the dragrope in traveling by balloon. That was the reason for the count's rope dragging across my path and rescuing me.

"For you understand," the count explained, "it it necessary to—how you explain me?—*stabilize* the balloon as to how high up, eh? *Alors,* we don't want to go too high up, and not too low down, either. So we drag long rope. *Petit Géant* get too low—weight of rope carried by ground—we go *en haut*—up! *Petit Géant* too high—carry all weight of long rope—go down! *Magnifique, n'est-ce pas?*"

Happily I agreed, feeling myself a secret sharer of the riddle of the universe. Like most people with little knowledge I began to fancy myself an expert and would have contracted to build and navigate a balloon if anyone had desired me to.

That was the trouble. No one seemed to want one. Even less did they desire to pay for the privilege of inspecting the *Petit Géant*, as the count called our balloon, or hand over a dollar for a ride. The Confederate General Jubal Early roamed the Shenandoah Valley, and Washington was fearful. Casualties in the war mounted every day; there was not a home in Ohio, I think, that did not have its sad news from the front. When there is a war on, people do not have time for a gay painted balloon.

There were, of course, other sources of income from owning a balloon. At least, theory said there were such ways. The count assured me these latter techniques had been very successful in York, Pennsylvania, in Lancaster, Ohio, and other locations where he and the *Petit Géant* had traveled. He instructed me thoroughly and when we reached Xenia I was eager to do his bidding.

As advance man for Polish royalty, I looked very brave in a swallowtail coat of the count's and a striped cravat with a diamond stickpin. I think it was a diamond; it sparkled to hurt your eyes in the morning sun. Kara wanted to inspect my ears, but I put her off with a magnificent gesture. After all, was I not the established agent of Count Kasimir Blatski? I buckled the satchel with the literature and papers the count had given me, and shook hands all round.

The count clapped me on the shoulder. "We are men, eh, Charlie? We talk—how it is said?—men to men. We trust you. You are good boy. *Kochany moj ciepla*. Poland shall be free! Bring back a lot of money."

"Yes, sir." I waved, and walked away down the dusty road. Alexander the Great never had more confidence.

The first place I tried was a general store on the main street crowded with Saturday customers. I leaned against a cracker barrel for a while, waiting for the proprietor to finish with an elderly lady who was very particular about a fat hen.

"Don't smell fresh to me," she said, holding it by the blue horny feet and sniffing.

"Just killed it myself," the grocer said. He was a skinny man with a long nose that almost met a long chin over a straggly gray moustache. "Couldn't be fresher."

"There's all sorts of diseases fowls catches," the lady said. "This one looks poorly."

The grocer sighed.

"Eight cents a pound?" the lady asked.

"That's right, Miss Tate."

"Well—" She fished in her reticule and brought out a change-purse, opening it with as much care as if it had been the vault of a bank. "Seems mighty dear to me."

"The war," the grocer said. He wrapped the hen up in a sheet of newspaper, tied it with string. "Thirty cents exactly. Will that be all?"

The lady banged the change-purse shut. "I couldn't afford anything more at *your* prices, Mr. Eyler."

After that, the grocer probably wasn't in too good a mood. But I had already spent ten minutes of my valuable time waiting on him. I strode up to the counter, plunked down my satchel, and started to take out the postcards, folders, and banners.

"What do *you* want?" Mr. Eyler growled.

"Let me introduce myself," I said. I reached for his hand, finding it clammy and wet with recent chicken fat. "I am Charles Campion, Mr. Eyler, associated with Count Kasimir Blatski, late of Lwow, Poland. You've heard of the count?"

Mr. Eyler wiped his hands on his apron. "Can't say as I have. There used to be some foreigners lived over near Yellow Springs—Blatz or Blotz or something like that."

"Count Kasimir Blatski, the world's premier aeronaut." I got out one of the count's hand-painted postcards and showed him. "That's the count's balloon, the *Petit Géant*. That means little giant in French. The count speaks several languages."

Behind me a lady poked at a pile of carrots and looked impatient. A man in a straw hat went behind a counter at the front of the store, took out a plug of tobacco and tossed a nickel on the glass.

"What in Bethlehem does a balloon mean to me?" Mr. Eyler said. "Now look, sonny, this is a Saturday! I ain't got time to—"

"You ain't got time?" I demanded. When in Xenia, talk like the Xenians. "You ain't got time to make a hundred dollars? Mr. Eyler, you mean to tell me you ain't got time to consider the most marvelous opportunity a grocer ever had? You mean you ain't got time to—"

"What was that you said about a hundred dollars?"

"Let me explain." I leaned confidentially on the counter. "How many grocery stores in this town?"

"Why—" he scratched at a hairy wart on his chin—"there's

Willard's down the street, and Jake Fasnacht's place over on Diamond Mill Road. There's Kleber's over on Dayton Road, but he don't handle much but dairy stuff—cheese and milk and eggs."

"Exactly," I said. "That's why I came here. You run the best grocery in town. And you're a man knows opportunity when he sees it. Now look here." I smoothed a handbill flat on the counter. "We make our grant aerial ascension tomorrow at the Fairgrounds. For two dollars I can arrange to have a hundred handbills like this printed up, advertising Eyler's Fancy Grocery, and the count will shower them down over the city."

From the stony look he gave me, I don't think the proposition appealed to him. Another lady came in with a basket under her arm, and looked around as though she might take her custom elsewhere.

"I didn't think such a modest proposition would appeal to a man of your merchandising ability," I said. I grabbed one end of the long silk banner and dragged it the length of the counter, across a barrel of pickles, and halfway out the front door. "Now here's a rouser—an elegant banner, bearing the name of your establishment. When the count goes up precisely at two in the afternoon, this genuine silk banner with EYLER'S GROCERY lettered in gold a foot high, dangles from the basket of the balloon. Can you imagine the excitement it will create? Why, all southern Ohio will be talking about Eyler's Fancy Grocery! People of taste and discernment will flock to your store—it will be the fashionable place to buy coffee and beans and candles! What do you think of that!"

Mr. Eyler transfixed me with an obsidian eye.

"Only a dollar for the banner," I said warmly, "and we use real fourteen-carat gold leaf for the letters. Can you imagine?"

The grocer's long chin drew closer to his long nose. "I can imagine," he said, "that you better get out of here quick so's I can wait on trade. I got all the business I can use. What I need is stock, not trade." He waved to a man standing in the doorway. "Got your order all boxed up, Mr. Scheer. Be with you directly. Have a lemon drop from the jar there!"

"How about a dozen of these attractive handpainted scenes of the count and his balloon as gifts to your customers? For every dollar of goods they buy, give 'em a handpainted souvenir."

Mr. Eyler came round the corner, wiping his hands on his apron and looking purposeful.

"Or a gross of these colorful plaster-of-Paris replicas of the count in his cavalry uniform in the 1863 uprising against the Czar of Russia, where he was a hero and was forced to flee Poland for his very life?"

"Get out!" Mr. Eyler yelled. "Out! Out! Out!"

Hastily I gathered my traps—the banner, the handbills, the cards, the plaster statues. In my hurry I dropped one of the statues and it broke into fragments that crunched under my heel as I retreated. Mr. Eyler reached for a broom. Since it extended his reach so greatly I conceded the loss of the battle; he only used it, however, to sweep up the plaster debris.

"Balloons!" he complained. "Statues! Painted cards! Banners! Oh, the things a man has to put up with when he goes into service to the public!" Seeing me loitering on the steps, he raised the broom. "Get along with you, now, and don't be bothering me again!"

"I can give you a special price on a short gross of the statues," I said. Then, when he swung the broom at my head, I left quickly, in fairly good order except that the banner was still spread out in the store, and I had only one end of it. As I heard a horrendous crash from the store, I had gotten to the middle of the street, my arms full of my samples. The other end of the banner had apparently caught on something. While Mr. Eyler shouted for the police, I stepped behind a livery stable to fold the banner and pack my satchel. There was a rent in the end of it, but it still looked impressive. When the furor in the street died down, I emerged again, this time intending to try Jake Fasnacht's place on the Diamond Mill Road that Mr. Eyler had mentioned.

Mr. Fasnacht was even more unpleasant. When he found that I had come to sell rather than buy, he led me personally to the door by the ear.

Kleber's was no better. Then I tried the Farmers' and Drovers' Saloon, even singing three choruses of "The Harp that Once Through Tara's Halls," and doing a clog dance. Some of the loafers threw pennies, but the proprietor wasn't interested in making his saloon the fashionable watering place of Ohio. I worked two more saloons, a millinery store, and a feed and grain place. No one was interested in our proposition. By then it was late afternoon. My feet hurt, my shirt was plastered to my back under the scratchy wool of the coat, the satchel weighed a thousand pounds. In desperation I tried the Granger's Hall where the Church of the Redeemer apostles (for that was what the convention was) were holding an afternoon session. They didn't think they needed a balloon for their missionary work, and told me so. I didn't think religious people could swear so.

Well, I was defeated. Not permanently, of course; I would retire from the field only to return strong and refreshed on the morrow. But it *was* discouraging. Why were people so dull of soul, so insipid, so unimaginative? No wonder they were groundlings, who could fail to be captivated by a painted balloon, soaring gay and delicate in the sky?

Unfortunately, Xenia was only first of many debacles; for that reason, though, I probably remember it best. Kara played the big drum; I stoked the fire in the stove and monitored the gradual swelling of the *Petit Géant;* the count sat in formidable grandeur on a bunting-draped chair, a pen in one hand to deliver autographs for ten cents each. But at two in the afternoon only a few idlers were on hand, along with a drunk who kept bringing me handfuls of green grass to put into the *Petit Géant's* boiler. He liked to see it smoke.

"Where are all the people, eh?" the count asked.

I wiped my sweating brow. "A man told me the Redeemers scheduled a real brannigan this afternoon. All kinds of shouting and rolling and speaking in tongues and laying hands on the sick and such."

Indeed, it was true. From the grassy plot at the Fairgrounds we could hear hymn-singing and cries of exultation and a lot of groaning and wailing. The Redeemers were a live bunch, all right.

"Kismet," the count said. He smote himself on the forehead with the back of his hand. "I am born under an evil star, *vous voyez*. Ah, it is to be discouraged!"

Kara hoisted the drum into the wagon, and looked sadly down at the two drumsticks in her hands. Her fair brow was spangled with perspiration, and her cheeks pink with exertion. "These people," she said. "Ah, such dumbheads! Isn't it?"

"Isn't what?"

"Isn't dumbheads?"

She had a queer way of using "isn't it" to mean almost anything.

"Sad," the count said. "Very sad. I am ahead of my time."

"No, you're not!" I spoke with spirit. "It's just the people. Like Kara says—dumbheads! Someday they'll be sorry they missed such a great opportunity. You wait and see!"

He sighed and stroked his beard, looking very old today.

"In meantime, what we live on, eh, young spirit?"

"Well," I said, "I've got four dollars saved from when I worked on the *Journal*. You're welcome to that."

"I don't take money from you. *Non!*"

"But we're all, well, all one *family*, aren't we, in a way?" I took out the money and tried to hand it to him. "Aren't we?"

The count smiled, but pushed back my hand.

"*Danke*," he said. "One family, *bien entendu!* One for all and all for one, *hein?* One family. But a family come on evil days, too."

I protested. "Not evil. Not with a balloon like the *Petit Géant!*" I pointed to the trembling bulk, the ground rope taut, waiting only for a word of release to soar into the sky. "As long as there's our balloon, nothing can hurt us!"

"Charlie, almost we believe you!"

"Of course. I'm right. You'll see!"

Kara blew her nose and brightened up too. "*Ach*, you're a tonic, Charlie!"

"We are a family," the count said. "You Irish. Me—they call Poles 'Irishmen of Europe.' You know that, eh? We are two crazy Irishers, *n'est-ce pas?* Kara here—she is family, too. All family, eh?" He got out his fiddle and played a tune, and I danced while Kara clapped hands in time.

The drunk stood stock-still, both hands clutching sprouts of grass he had pulled up. I guess he thought we were crazy. But things turned out better than we hoped. The drunk had a dollar, and the count took him up for a look over the city. The only trouble was that he got sick in the balloon basket, and I had to clean it out. But that was all right. I would clean out the Augean stables every day if I could be with the count and Kara and our little giant.

Well, if Xenia was not a success, there were a lot more towns to try. But they all turned out to be distressingly alike: preoccupied with the war, busy with reaping and threshing, and very slow with a dollar. In Eaton we made three dollars, and spent six for mule feed, ten yards of silk, a dozen eggs, and a bottle of Lake Erie Catawba wine for the count. In Greenville we made eight dollars and a half, but the judge fined us ten dollars when Beersheba broke down a man's fence to get at some peony plants; she was very fond of peonies. In Richmond, Indiana, we did well but Kara came down with a toothache that swelled out her whole cheek. She didn't want to spend money for a dentist, begging me to pull it with a pair of the count's pliers. But when it got so bad the count noticed it, he insisted she have the dentist do a proper job on it, and there went our profit! She was a brave girl, though, and bore the pain for a long time so there would be money for the count's viands.

"For," she said, "he is not a common man, and does not eat like us, Charlie. Fried brains and buttermilk and spoon bread would upset his digestion something awful."

Well, they didn't do mine any good either, but I was young and resilient; besides, a balloon was all I required to sustain me.

On we traveled through Indiana: Connersville, Greensburg, Vienna, Henryville, Galena. Threshing crews worked in the golden-stubbled fields; the days were hot and clear with an occasional dark thunderhead on the horizon; dusks were hazy and lingering with a smell of smoke in the air. Nights became chill and the stars were icy stabs of light in a dark mantle.

September came—my birthday. I was sixteen, and growing—even I noticed it. The old boots hurt my lengthening feet; my shoulders widened so I bid fair to burst out of my old shirt. Kara had to sew three inches of new length to my jeans. The material almost matched and did so when I rubbed a little dirt into it. Even my voice, which had been light and flexible and well-adapted to Irish ballads, joined the rebellion; I started to croak and squeak and make the most ungodly sounds. And while I had almost reconciled myself to being slight in build, I became rapidly on the gangling side, awkward and slung together with India-rubber bands.

Ah, it was a good life, though! Poor as we were, we shared everything. Camped in a grassy glade along the river, snug around the fire after catfish I caught and cornmeal dodgers fried in the grease, we made a self-sufficient family group: the count, booted feet spread out to the fire, telling us wonderful stories of his adventures; Kara the dutiful daughter darning socks, her bun of golden hair catching the firelight; Charlie the son with mouth open and eyes wide at visions of glory.

"—and so," the count said, "we spit in his face—*pah,* like that! Right into the face of Alexander Second, Czar of all the Russias! *Gowno,* we say to him." That meant the same as *merde,* only it was Polish. "They take us away to prison then—ha, *us* in prison! The Polish Eagle in prison!"

Kara dabbed at her eyes with the toe of a sock, her woman's pity always ready. But I was excited. "What happened then?"

The count looked very stern. "No prison hold *us!* Not the leader of the Poles! We dig out of prison, just as they come in morning to hang us. Fast horses, good friends, a—what you say?—bribe here, bribe there; we get away. Go Paris, go London, go"—he rose, throwing out his arms in the firelight—"go America! Go freedom! Ha!"

It was magnificent. After he had gone to bed in the wagon, Kara and I sat for a long time beside the dying fire, talking of life and great enterprises and the wonder and glory of this best of worlds. I had not for a long time thought of the mysterious Ned Campion.

"The count is a great man," I said.

Kara nodded, and bit off a thread. "So very great."

"And you're his daughter." I wound my arms around my knees and propped my chin on my arms. How wonderful to be blood of his blood, flesh of his flesh!

"You call him Papa," I said. "But he never calls you daughter."

She shrugged, and looked away.

"Why not?"

For some reason she was annoyed. "That's his business." Then, seeming to think better of the edge on her tongue, she said, "I'm proud to call him Papa. But why should he be proud to call me daughter?—an ugly, big, ignorant girl like me."

"But you're not ugly! You're—you're—" My unreliable voice failed me again. I croaked like a bullfrog, my voice unaccountably deep and strong. "You're beautiful!"

"I know what I am, Charlie."

She wasn't very much on reading and writing and ciphering; on the other hand, I could testify Kara was simple and cheerful and kind and generous and lots of other things—including attractive in a Junoesque way.

"Maybe you don't know what you are," I hinted.

"How old are you, Charlie?"

"What's that got to do with it?"

"I just wondered, that's all. You talk so grownup."

"How old are you?"

"Nineteen."

"Well . . ." I pondered for a minute. "I'm sixteen. Practically sixteen, anyway. My birthday is—let's see—the twenty-fifth of September."

"If you are a foundling, though, like you said, how do you know it's the twenty-fifth of anything?"

"I don't," I said. "The nuns figured that was close enough."

She finished darning the last sock and put her sewing away. Then she yawned, and bent over to give me a sisterly peck on the forehead. "Good night, Charlie."

"Good night," I said.

Before I went to bed in my pile of blankets under the trees, I lit a candle and sat cross-legged, back against a friendly elm, writing in my journal with a stub of pencil. I had been remiss in keeping my journal up to date, and there were many wonderful things to record. But my mind was too full to concentrate on writing. I sketched fantastic animals and whirls and Greek symbols and geometrical friezes that belonged on the Parthenon. Kara. The count. The *Petit Géant*. Where was the Pinkerton? Why had it been so important to the law to chase me all the way out West? Old Mr. Gillentine—was he entirely recovered? And Annie. I closed my eyes, thinking of her slender body, her dark hair, the fresh scent of her flesh. Was she thinking of me, this September night and hundreds of miles away? I wrote her a poem, or started to. But trying to think of a rhyme for "lady fair," I suddenly realized Annie wasn't fair at all. She was dark, with brown eyes and a ribbon in her hair. Angry and uncomfortable, I realized that fair Kara Blatski had been in my mind all along. I was vile, to write a love poem to my eternal love and let someone else intrude! Ashamed, I threw the journal away from me to sprawl in the starshine.

Mauckport, a little town on the Ohio River, was no better stand than any of the others. The citizens came, gawked, and then drifted away when the hat was passed. We took in three dollars, but the constable made us pay five for a permit to hold a public exhibition. We had no more money, we were penniless, except for the four dollars in my wallet I had saved so long.

"Here," I said to the count. "Take it. We're all in this together, *n'est-ce pas?*"

Looking undecided, he tugged at his beard. Then, suddenly, turning on his heel he walked away.

"He is very proud," Kara whispered. "His feelings, maybe, you have hurt."

"But I just wanted to help!"

"*Ach, ja,*" she nodded. "He knows. You are a good boy, Charlie."

The day was not a total loss. With so little balloon business the count permitted me to go up with him while Kara drove the mules. It was a concession on his part, since the balloon and its instruments and trappings were a kind of sacred enclave to him; to let groundlings ride in it for a dollar was, he declared, a sacrilege that he would not have countenanced if his Polish estates had not been confiscated by the Czar.

True, I had been aloft once before, the day he pulled me out of the lake with his gear-driven winch. But I had been nearly insensible at the time. Now I could float over Indiana and Kentucky, see the sunlit ribbon of the great river, almost reach out and touch the glossy banks of foliage, play chess on the fields of new-cut grain, see the plume of smoke from a threshing crew over near Laconia.

"Look!" I cried, drunk with revelation. "Over there! And look down that way! And the boat on the river!" A bird flew near us, dipped under the basket, and rose on the other side. "Look," I cried.

The count smiled indulgently, chewing his stogie.

"Another world, eh?"

"Yes!" I cried. "Oh, it is!"

The highest I had been until I met the count was the top floor of the orphanage. That made me dizzy, to look down at Cherry Street from there. But this didn't make me dizzy; instead, it exalted me. Maybe the difference was that we were soaring free, connected with the earth only by a threadlike cable. When the count leaned over the side and signaled Kara, I was not ready.

"Do we have to go down?"

The count's stogie had gone out. He dusted off the ash and slipped it into his breast pocket. "All comes to end, boy. *Sic transit gloria mundi.*"

At supper that night I was still jabbering like a magpie. It was a skimpy supper, right enough. And it was my birthday, too, though I had forgot. Kara had bought a cake, though how she managed it with no money, I don't know. There were candles on it. The count brought out his last bottle of French brandy, and poured me a cup. I protested, knowing he would perish without brandy, but he waved a hand.

"One is sixteen only one time in the life."

"A wish make," Kara whispered, "and blow out the candles."

What other wish could a boy make—except that this should

all go on forever and forever? The candles went out at once, as if a cyclone had hit them. I was sixteen.

The next day was a Sunday. The count was taking a nap in the wagon, the mules were peacefully grazing, Kara was somewhere down by the river washing clothes. I was busy patching the pesky small holes in the balloon fabric the sparks from the boiler always caused. Sew them up with needle and thread, smear the India-rubber compound on, set and smooth a silk patch, put a weight on to dry; hundreds of little holes, so it seemed. It was tedious work, but it was balloon work!

Suddenly I had a magnificent idea. We were out of food, except for flour and lard and a few greenish-looking sausages. But the count loved his delicacies; what finer treat than turtle steaks! I would go down to the river and snare a turtle with a noose of thread, provided I could find a tardy one that had not yet burrowed into the mud for the winter.

I called softly into the wagon. "Please, sir."

The count stirred. "Eh?"

It would be a surprise. "I'm going down to the river for a while."

"Bien." He sighed, letting out a deep wheeze.

"Are you all right, sir?"

"Yes. But we feel today nine years older than the Lord God."

"Don't worry," I said. "Everything will come out all right."

He was silent for a moment, and then said, "People we fight, Charlie. But circumstance . . ."

I let the flap fall, and stole away. I'd make him feel better. At the water's edge I got out my little gold penknife and cut a pole. Fastening a noose of thread to it, I pushed aside the screen of bushes, scanning the mud and ooze for a nice fat turtle. But I fell back in embarrassment, gulping. Who was there, bathing in the sun-warmed brown water, but Kara! A mother-naked Kara, singing a little song and soaping her arms and breasts and thighs!

"Charlie!" she cried. She didn't seem modest at all about her exposed body, but annoyed instead. "Now get on with you, right away! Can't you see I'm washing?"

It was like a scene etched on a photographic plate by Matthew Brady, dreadfully clear and detailed; the full thighs, the jutting high breasts crowned with soft pink-brown nipples, her yellow hair tied up in a plume with a scrap of ribbon, even the soft fluff of down where—let's say where her limbs joined her body—and a delicate golden curl under her upraised arms.

"I'm—I'm sorry," I croaked, transfixed.

Damn it all, she should have screamed, at least, and put her hands over—well, over *something!* You might have thought I was a troublesome child, a small brother, someone to spank and send home crying!

"Well, go *on,* now!"

My mind was in a whirl, startled and confused and angry and guilty all at once. I *was* her brother, wasn't I? Wasn't that what I wanted, Kara and me at the feet of our wise and understanding father, our valorous father, our common father? On the other hand, I was sixteen years old, and good as a man. A passion stirred in me that was not at all brotherly.

"God damn it," I yelled. "Go put on some clothes, will you?"

She smiled, a knowing tolerant female smile that made me turn red. "When I finish bathing."

I could have beaten her with my fists. No, I couldn't, either! She was gentle kind sweet Kara. . . .

"Do as you like!" I shouted, flinging away into the underbrush, breathing hard and feeling as if I'd been taken advantage of. Well, what was it to me if she wanted to bathe? Yet it was a great deal to me, it seemed, or why was I baffled and angry?

Crashing through the willows like a lost steer, I stopped stock-still. Barring my way the ugliest face I had ever seen stared at me from a frame of sun-dappled leaves. The face was grinning, and a pair of shrewd blue eyes looked me over under a thatch of uncut blond hair. The chin sprouted a kind of billy-goat beard, and a tattered slouch hat drooped over the whole unlovely countenance.

"Who—who are you?" I quavered.

The owner of the ugly face stepped out from behind the bushes, holding a long-barreled rifle dead center on my belly.

"Just stand there a spell," he said. "Don't flinch, 'cause I'm a mite edgy today. Got any grub on you?"

That was how I came to be captured by Mad Jack Spurrier and his ruffians.

~~~~Chapter 7~~~~

General Spurrier was all that the articles in *Leslie's* made him out to be. There was a flickering light in his blue eyes that scared me, and he laughed a lot in a high-pitched voice, though the laugh seemed mainly to happen at the wrong places.

"So!" he said. "A balloon! How about that, fellers? We done captured a balloon!"

They guffawed, hundreds of them, it seemed. Where they came from so quick and so quiet, I didn't know. One minute Kara and I were talking by the river; the next minute we were captured and the count, too. Mean-looking men they were, ragged and wiry-looking, but with guns and pistols and bandoliers of cartridges that looked well-cared for.

"Now do you all know what we're going to do with that balloon, fellers?" Mad Jack raised his gloved hand, forefinger pointing to heaven. "Can anyone guess?"

He was the only one that looked decent; I mean, that was *dressed* decent. His long yellow hair had a slouch hat jammed over it, with the brim pinned up and a feather stuck in it. He wore a white shirt with a ruffle, and a long-tailed coat with brass buttons.

"Ty skorwy synie!" the count shouted. That was Polish, and

71

meant "you son of a dog" or something like that. Two of the
biggest ruffians had him pinned by the arms, and he fought
and struggled against them. *"Idz do diable!* You don't do anything to balloon, you pigs! Let us loose, we kill you—kill you
all!"

Someone slapped the count in the face, and blood spurted
from his nose. Gasping, he fell back dazed. They were holding
me too, and Kara. All Kara had on was a blanket they let her
wrap around her nakedness. We both struggled to pull free and
defend the count, but it was no use.

"Well, ain't you the little firebrand!" Mad Jack grinned, the
wild light flickering again in his eyes. "Boys, this here is a
real Spanish cock! He's going to kill us all. You heard him,
didn't you?"

They giggled, and poked each other with their elbows.
"Gonna kill us!" somebody snickered.

"Let me go!" Kara cried. "You ought to be ashamed of
yourselves, you bullies, picking on such a little one!" Her
golden hair was wet and scraggly-looking and the blanket was
muddy and stained, but there was true queenliness in her manner. "Let him go!"

I don't know whether the count was more infuriated at the
threat to the *Petit Géant* or at Kara's calling him such a little
one. "You give me a pistol—any pistol—and we take you all
on at fifty yards! Saber, *epée,* knife, anything! We charge you
all and cut you to pieces, ha! Like sausages we chop you up!"
He lunged at Spurrier again; this time the fury of his rush almost
disengaged him. But someone got him by the coattails, and
others pinioned his arms. I struggled to get free, but the man
holding me knew his business. He twisted the neckband of my
shirt so it cut off my air, and I quit fighting pretty quick.

"Now what was I saying?" Spurrier strode up and down in
the glade, hands clasped behind his back, the famous Chinese
beheading sword trailing at his booted heels. "Oh, now I recollect! The balloon!"

Whatever I thought of Mad Jack Spurrier, he had these
scoundrels in the palm of his hand. They stared at him as if
he were a patented miracle, and hung on every word.

"Tell us, Jack!" someone yelled. "What we do with the
balloon?"

Lighting a stogie, Spurrier put one foot on a stump and
gestured with the cigar. "You all know that damned Boyle and
his cavalry are chasing us."

"Yes! Yes, Jack! Sure thing!" they nodded to each other. "Damned Yanks. Chasing us."

"And we got to get across the river."

Another chorus of agreement.

"And we're all tired and hungry, ain't we?"

"We sure are!"

"Then," Spurrier said, "I'll tell you all what we're agonna do. We're agonna sit here, in this pleasant little grove of trees, and have us a good rest that we ain't had for a month. We're agonna barbecue us a mule, and have a smoke, and rest easy till the *Blue Wing* comes down to the river."

"The *Blue Wing?*" someone muttered.

"The very same." Mad Jack dragged deep on the stogie, and flickered ash away with an elegant gesture. "The Federals' paddle-wheeler. We'll signal her to the landing below. When she ties up, we'll swarm all over her, and claim her for Jeff Davis. Now don't that sound fine, fellers? We'll ride down the river and go home thataway."

A swaggering little man with a bugle slung over his shoulder stepped forward, putting a finger to his brow in salute. "Beg pardon, sir!"

"What is it, Ben?"

"General, we can't hang around here! Boyle's after us, and headed for Mauckport. Ain't it better to light a shuck out of here and try to cross down by Cincinnati somewheres?"

"Ben," the general said, "that's why you're a corporal and I'm a general. We got a balloon, ain't we?"

The little man scratched his head. "Sure, but—"

"This fighting cock here is agonna join the Confederate States of America—him and his balloon. He can see all over Indiana with that thing. We'll put him up in the air to watch for Boyle's Brigade. In the meantime, we take our ease down below—wash up, have a smoke, sleep. We're safe as if we was in Richmond, because our little rooster is agonna crow and warn us when he sees Boyle coming! How's that for a plan?"

They cheered, and slapped each other on the back.

"I could shore use a little sleep," one man said. Another scratched himself and commented, "Me for the river to drown some of these lice!" A third sharpened his nicked saber on a rock, and looked hungrily at Dan and Beersheba. "Dibs on the tenderloin, boys!"

"But suppose this foreign feller double-crosses us, general?

Suppose he sees Boyle and don't give the word?"

That mad light flashed in Spurrier's eyes. "We'll send some-one with him to keep him honest. Nothing to worry about there, boys; no one double-crosses Jack Spurrier!"

"Never!" the count howled. "We never use *Petit Géant* against our country! We set fire to her first!"

Spurrier gestured, and the scoundrels beat the count un-mercifully. The slapped him, they whipped him with the flat of a saber, they knocked him to the ground and kicked him. Kara screamed in anger and pity; I twisted and squirmed until the twisted band of my shirt choked off my voice. Spurrier finally waved off the bullyboys, and squatted beside the pros-trate count.

"Well?" he asked.

The count huddled small in the grass.

"Well?"

The count didn't answer; Spurrier grabbed him by the beard and pulled his face up close.

"Well, rooster?"

The count took a deep breath. It sounded like wind through a tattered November shock of corn.

"We—we do."

"No tricks, now!"

The count swallowed hard, an agonizing spasm of his throat. He was weeping—not with the pain, I knew, but with the humiliation—the Polish Eagle handled so! I wanted to call out to him, to tell him I understood.

"No—no tricks," he wheezed.

In response to a gesture from Spurrier, one of the band threw a bucket of water on the count. Gasping for breath, he struggled to his knees.

"Get the damned balloon up," the general said. "Quick! Boyle was in Connersville last night. I've got a hundred men depending on me, and I'll stop at nothing to bring them home in good order. You understand that?"

The count nodded, wiping his bloody nose with a sleeve.

"Let's go! It's almost sundown." Spurrier motioned to the swaggering little man. "Ben, take two of the boys and keep an eye on him. Give him a hand if he needs help. Hurry, now!"

The count staggered to his feet and stood swaying for a moment. "We need wood for the boiler," he croaked.

General Spurrier put Kara and me in the wagon, with a guard to see we didn't cause trouble. I don't know what we could have done surrounded by a hundred rebs. Through a rent in the canvas I watched them getting the *Petit Géant* ready for flight. It was dusk and the scene one that Mr. Winslow Homer would have liked to sketch. Cooking fires winked red against the dark wall of trees, men squatted around them, frying meat and boiling coffee; under a canvas fly Mad Jack Spurrier chewed his cigar and stared at a map by candlelight. Horses on the picket line wrenched up grass with their big white teeth; three men started a card game using a tree-stump for a table; a boy with a bandage around his head winced and swore and yelled when a comrade tried to peel it off and wash his wound. Even in the open among the trees and grass and coming night, I smelled men and sweat of horses and the sweetish odor that might have been a wound going bad. Over it all drifted a gentle pall of wood smoke.

"Damn it," I said. "They don't know how to handle a balloon! Look there—they'll burn a hole in it before they get it off the ground!" I pushed aside the flap and started to climb out, but the sentry stuck his musket into my ribs so hard I cried out.

"I was just going to help with the balloon."

He spat brown juice into the grass.

"Gin'ral says you stay in thar, bub, you and the gal."

"But—"

He whacked me on the shins with the barrel of the musket and I tumbled back into the wagon, mad and hurt.

"You be careful, Charlie," Kara said. "Those are bad men. They'd kill a body."

"Rats!" I glowered. "That fellow with the gun—he isn't any older than me, nor bigger."

"But he's got a gun."

"Well—" I said, forced to admit a point.

She had put some clothes on—a skirt and a ragged blouse— and had tied her hair back with a ribbon; now she huddled in the blankets on the floor of the wagon, knees drawn up and bare arms wrapped around them.

"Is Papa all right?"

"I guess so," I said, peering through the hole.

The fire roared in our balloon's boiler; in the waning light I could see the folds of the *Petit Géant* rolling and surging as the hot air crept through them. Around the circumference a dozen men held the fabric up and joked and laughed as the balloon started to fill.

"Looks like your old woman, Tom, last time she got pregnant!"

"Oh, my, but don't irregular cavalry get mixed up in some funny didoes!"

"Who's going up with the professor? Not me, shorely—I gets giddy standing on a stepladder."

If there was only some way the laws of physics could be repealed; if only *Petit Géant* that particular night would refuse to fill, if she would lie there and pay no mind to Archimedes and the hot air, if only—oh, disaster!—if only she would catch fire and burn! But slowly, steadily, her bulk grew. She heaved up in little bubbles and globules and spherical protuberances; the air rushed this way and that, a mound collapsed only to grow into two other mounds that were larger, the fabric rustled and strained and pulled with the urge to fly.

"Charlie?" Kara said.

"What?"

"I want to talk to you."

"Go ahead."

She pulled at my trouser leg. "Not like that. Come down here, beside me."

Impatient, I crouched beside her. "What?"

She bowed her head and looked away from me. "I'm so ashamed."

"Ashamed of what?"

"A long time now I've been meaning to tell. But I just couldn't put myself up to it."

Mystified, I asked, "Up to what, damn it? Don't talk in riddles!"

Her eyes were swimming in tears. "Now that we're all in mortal danger, I remember what Pastor Stoltzfuss said. 'Tell the truth,' he said, 'and shame the Devil.' Charlie, I—I'm not the count's real daughter. I couldn't go to the heavenly mansions with a lie on my conscience."

Well, I guess I never thought she was his own daughter. But it didn't really make that much difference. Not enough to get upset over, anyway.

"That's all right," I said awkwardly, patting her hand.

That was a mistake. She clung to it, pressing her lips against my knuckles and crying harder. "Oh, I'm a wicked, wicked girl!"

I swallowed, wondering what to do. "No, you're not either."

"But I am!"

She was crying all over my hand, and my sleeve was getting wet.

"My real name is Ellie Schwabacher, and I'm from Lancaster, Pennsylvania. Amish we were, house Amish. My folks was real strict, and never let me do anything. When Papa—I mean, the count—when he came to town, I sneaked out to watch him go up in the balloon. My pa was real mad. He whipped me and made me stay in my room. So I ran away with the count."

I felt funny listening to her little sins. I had a few of my own on my conscience.

"Well, that isn't so bad," I said. "I ran away too, didn't I?"

She shook her head. "I was *wicked!* I stole sixty-eight dollars from Pa."

What in the devil could I say? I wasn't qualified to hear confessions. Sixty-eight dollars was a whopping lot of money, though. And what was that she said about running away with the count? I didn't like the sound of that. Had I been gulled? Was she my sister, or something else? A hideous suspicion crossed my mind.

"Look here, now—you don't mean you—you don't mean you and the count—"

She slapped me hard in the face. "Well, I guess *not!*"

Well, Kara seemed like she was in better spirits, anyway. Or Ellie, or whatever her real name was.

"What kind of girl do you think I am, Charlie Campion?"

"Well," I grumbled, "you didn't have to hit me so hard! I was just asking."

It took a long time to get the balloon clear up. Sometimes it's that way, dampness in the air, or a rip in the fabric you didn't see, or green wood that makes mostly smoke and no heat. It was dark now, full dark. I was tired and hungry. The excitement was beginning to wear off.

"Kara?" I said. No answer. I looked down. I guess she was asleep. I touched her shoulder. "Kara?" She didn't move. I heard soft deep breathing, and then a funny little catch the way a child does after it's been crying.

I took one more look out of the hole. The balloon looked the same as it did an hour ago. I squatted beside her, wishing I had something to eat, but all our traps were spread out beside the wagon. The canvas lightened for a moment as our guard lit his pipe and sucked in the flame. No use asking *him* for anything. *Captured,* I thought. *Captured by Mad Jack Spurrier*

and his ruffians! What a story I'd have for my journal! But
now I'd just close my eyes for a minute and rest.

Much later, I woke with a start. Someone was in the wagon,
grubbing around.

"Who's there?"

No answer. But there *was* someone there, and it wasn't
Kara! She lay beside me, breathing heavily. The dark form
went on grubbing and searching. At last, satisfied, it raised the
flap.

"Who's there?" I called out, frightened.

The form paused, silhouetted in the starshine.

"Is only us. Count Blatski."

I scrabbled to my knees. "Are you all right?"

"Tais-toi, boy! Speak soft."

"Are you escaping?"

He laughed a short hard laugh. Now that my eyes were
adjusting, I saw he had on his long linen duster and his uniform
cap with the shawl tied around it, ready to go up. The guard
was behind him, covering him with his musket.

"Naw," the guard said. "He ain't escaping."

"We just come back for a few things," the count said.

"Can I get anything for you?"

He moved away into the blackness, and the guard started
to close the flap.

"Wait a minute!" I said. "Count, are you all right? Kara
and I—we've been worried about you! Look—let me go with
you! Wait a minute—please wait!"

The guard pushed me back. "Ain't nothing you can do, boy.
Git back in thar!"

"But—"

"Dang it!" he said. "Git!" He pushed me sprawling over
Kara and closed the flap.

"What is it?" Kara asked sleepily.

"I—I don't know."

She sat up. "But I heard someone talking!"

"It was the count."

In her eagerness, she clutched me. "Is he all right? They
haven't hurt him or anything?"

"No. He's all right. He was just getting ready to go aloft."

I guess he had been all right. But there was something
wrong. He hadn't seemed to want to talk to me. And why was
he rummaging around in the wagon? He could have waked me
and I would have helped him look.

"He's had a cough lately. And he hasn't had his supper, either. Oh, I hope he doesn't get sick!"

"I don't think any of us has to worry about getting sick," I said. "What we have to worry about is getting shot or something."

"You don't think they'll hurt him, do you, Charlie? I couldn't *live* if anything happened to him."

I shook my head. "He's pretty smart. Don't worry."

"I can't help it."

I went back to the rent in the canvas and watched. Dawn was on the way; the eastern sky was a delicate blue-pink, the color of some celestial Easter egg. Some of the guerrillas slumbered in the grass; others were up and boiling coffee. A patrol of a few men straggled in, bone-tired, and reported to General Spurrier. He wasn't putting all his eggs in one balloon-basket, that was sure.

"They're about ready," I said.

Kara joined me at the slit, and I ripped it a little wider so she could see too. Through the wider hole I could see that our guard was still keeping an eye on us. The *Petit Géant* was fully inflated now, tugging at the ground ropes. The count stood, a silent and lonely figure, beside the basket, one hand on the wicker rim. The boiler glowed, and I could see little heat waves ripple around it. Dan and Beersheba were hitched to our block-and-tackle rig for raising and lowering the balloon, and our longest length of rope was coiled neatly beside it—the five-hundred foot piece. As we watched, General Spurrier sauntered over and joined the little knot of men around the balloon.

"Ready to go, are you?"

The count only inclined his head.

"Ben!"

The little man with the bugle saluted.

"Get in the basket."

Ben was thunderstruck. "General, that ain't fer *me!* I got a weak liver, the doctor says. Heights don't do it no good."

"Get in the basket. Take your bugle. One blast to go up. Two blasts to come down. Three means danger, look out! You've seen Boyle's troops. Understand me?"

"God damn it, General, I don't belong in no danged balloon! I'm forty-three years old and married and got a wife and children in Raleigh. Why can't someone else go?"

Spurrier was a real hard-case. He took a big pistol out of his belt and pointed it at Ben. "Get the hell in the balloon basket and don't sass me none! Your mouth is too big, Ben. Mind me now—keep your eyes open and your mouth shut, and watch our little Spanish cock here. Don't let him pull no didoes, you hear?"

Count Blatski smiled grimly, and held his hands out in a gesture that seemed to say "I have no weapons, gentlemen."

For all their bragging, no one really wanted to go up in the balloon. When Ben had been picked, it relieved the feelings of the rest of them, and they jeered him unmercifully.

"Better take the chance, Ben. It's as close as you'll ever git to heaven!"

"Give my regards to Saint Peter, Ben!"

"Mind the birds, now!"

Unwillingly the little man climbed into the basket, and the count followed him.

"It ain't fair," Ben grumbled. He twisted his bugle around in front of him for easy use, and took out a long-barreled pistol, too. "All right," he said. "But when I joined the damned army, I didn't contract fer no balloon rides."

The count signaled, and the men paid out the rope through the pulley. Slowly the *Petit Géant* rose into the morning sky; at first it seemed only to drift upward through the mists and woodsmoke. Then faster and faster the rope paid out. The balloon dwindled in size, lost reality, finally became a tiny golden speck tethered at the end of a spiderweb of cord.

"Look at that!" I said, marveling. I could never get over the mystery, the beauty, the soul-wrenching spiritual experience of going up, up, up in the sky. "I've never seen it go so high!"

"I hope he's all right," Kara said. "I wonder if he had a good breakfast first."

Well, that was that. The balloon was up. I was hungry, too—and Kara must be. I combed my hair in the cracked mirror, hitched up my pants, and buttoned my shirt collar. I would ask the guard if we could have something to eat, and maybe walk around to exercise our cramped limbs. I opened the little wooden cabinet where we kept our valuables at night: my wallet with its four dollars, Kara's earrings that had belonged to the count's mother, my goldy penknife. The door came off in my hand. The moldy leather hinges had given way. Or had they been *ripped* off? Stupidly I looked at the scrap of wood in my hand. I felt around inside. Nothing was there. The cabinet was empty.

"What's wrong?" Kara asked.

For a minute I couldn't answer.

"Charlie, what is it?"

I motioned. "Someone pulled the door off. It's all gone. Everything's gone. My knife, your jewelry, my wallet and the four dollars. Everything."

"But it can't be. I remember—" Kara put her hand in and felt round. Then she knelt and peered into the cabinet. "Someone took everything!"

"That's right."

"But who?"

We looked at each other in the growing light that filtered through the canvas. A patch was lit with purest gold where the sun had peeked over the trees. Somewhere a bird sang.

"But who, Charlie?"

The guard? But the cabinet was midway of the wagon. Even if he knew it was there, he'd have had to climb over Kara and me to get to it.

"But who, Charlie?"

I remembered the count in the middle of the night, rummaging softly around the wagon, acting so queer and all, not even wanting to talk to me. Then he'd gone away quick, never looking back, and the guard had pushed me back in the wagon. But why? What would the count want with our few dollars and a pair of old earrings and a maybe-gold penknife?

"I don't understand it," Kara said. The rising sun picked out the gold of her hair, lit the incredulous look on her face.

"Well," I said, "I—"

No one would ever know what I was going to say. The heavens were split with the most fearful scream I ever heard. It was a long-drawn out quavering scream that made my hair prickle and stand up, and it ended in a weird bubbling.

"Dear Lord!" Kara cried. "What was that?"

I didn't know what it was. But it seemed to come from way up high, over our heads. . . .

~~~~~Chapter 8~~~~~

I tumbled out of the wagon, Kara after me. The guard didn't stop us; he was running, too, toward the big pulley and the mules and the rest of our rig. Everybody was running and yelling and pointing into the sky.

"What is it?" Kara gasped, stumbling and falling in the wet grass. "Charlie, wait for me! What's happened?"

I looked up. The *Petit Géant* was a lot higher than the five hundred feet it was supposed to be, and gaining altitude. General Spurrier was swearing and shouting orders, and everyone started shooting at the runaway balloon. Dan and Beersheba thrashed around in the coils of rope that enmeshed them, and all was confusion.

"Shoot down that balloon!" the general yelled. "God damn it, stop him! He's getting away!"

A ragged volley scattered through the grove and then stopped as suddenly as it began. Mouths opened, eyes gazed in horror, someone cursed softly as a tiny rag doll plummeted down from the basket. At first it was only a dot in the clear morning sky. Then it showed arms and legs and spun this way and that as it fell.

"Look out!" a man yelled. "It's going to hit us!"

Some ran for cover under the trees. Others only stood, gaping into the sky. The rag doll spread out flat for a moment, arms and legs spread-eagled, and then it tore through the trees with a force of an explosion. There was a great wet smacking sound as it flattened the grass and lay still. It was Ben.

No one said anything for a minute. I looked up at the *Petit Géant*. A strong wind was blowing it north or maybe northwest. I blinked my eyes, and then lost it. Was it gone? Could I still see it? I squinted, and my eyes blurred. Maybe I was crying; I don't know.

"He's gone," Kara said.

"He sure damn is." Trembling with a kind of fierceness that had come into me, I walked over to the mules and tried to pull some of the tangle of rope off them. Dan tried to bite me again, and I hit him hard in the nose with my fist. "Stop that, you bastard," I said.

Somehow or other I had the end of the rope in my hand, and I kept looking at it. It was cut, clean cut. My little penknife had been sharp, all right. My own knife had betrayed me.

"He shouldn't have done that," I said. "Why did he have to do that?"

Kara looked dazed. Her fingers kept going to her ear where she always wore the gold earrings. "He's gone. He's gone away."

"Why?" I demanded. "Why didn't he tell us? We should have known, shouldn't we?"

Someone grabbed me from behind and whirled me around, and a man tied my wrists with a piece of cord. "Well, we got *you*, anyway. Git along; the gin'ral wants to have a little gam with you and the girl." The ruffians gave me a push that sent me sprawling, then dragged me to my feet and pushed me ahead of them with their muskets.

"Don't you hurt him!" Kara screamed.

One of them doffed a ragged cap in mock humility. "Oh, we ain't gonna *hurt* him, ma'am! Jest cut off his privates for what he done to old Ben."

"But he didn't do anything!"

The man spat. "Ah, you're all in this together! Spies, that's what you are! There ain't anything lower than a dirty goddamn spy! Get along there—you too, ma'am!"

Spurrier squatted beside the body. He seemed casual, and his voice was almost courteous. He pointed with a gloved finger. "Cut his throat from ear to ear. Then he threw old Ben out of the balloon and soared away. Neatly done, I must say."

I shook my head. There was a lump in my throat, and I couldn't get any words round it.

"It was a plot, wasn't it?" the general asked, very nice. "Ah, don't try to make up any stories now, boy! You planned it together, didn't you—how the old man would get away and bring Boyle's Brigade whoopin' and hollerin' down on us? And you—or maybe the girl—slipped him the knife to do the job, eh? Wasn't that about the size of it?"

I could hear him talking and knew I was in peril. But somehow or other, that didn't matter. All I could think of was that cut rope, the mute evidence of the count's betrayal of me. Maybe Mad Jack Spurrier was going to draw and quarter me or whatever they did to spies in wartime; I didn't care. What mattered was that Count Kasimir Blatski, the Eagle of Poland, the closest I'd ever come to a father, had spurned me as a son. I loved him, honored him, basked in the sun of his approval. I had been dutiful and obedient and hardworking and anxious to learn. No one could have wanted a better offspring. I had given the count everything I had, even wanted to give him the four dollars, but he wouldn't take it. Now he had it and the gold earrings and my knife and all the rest.

"We didn't plot anything!" Kara cried. "You are dumbheads, all of you, to think such a thing!"

What an unnatural father to flee and leave his son to battle the enemy! That wasn't the way things were supposed to be! If he had stayed, he could have commanded me to charge them, the whole gang, with a willow switch, and I would have done it gladly! My blood was his to command, my honor, my life— everything!

"Where did he get the knife?" General Spurrier asked. The blue light was in his eyes again. "He didn't have a knife before— we searched him! Somehow he got a knife, and slit Ben's poor old throat and cut himself free, too. Where did he get the knife?"

What a fool's paradise I had lived in these past months! What an idiot I must have seemed, so naive and so innocent, prattling and chirruping, running and fetching and bowing and scraping! All the time it had meant nothing to *him!*

"Answer me!" General Spurrier drew the shiny long Chinese sword, and in a fit of anger hacked it deep into the trunk of a sapling. Cut almost in two, the tree swayed and then wheezed leafily down. Some of the men looked at each other, and it seemed to me that they were afraid of him too. "By God, will you tell me the truth, boy?"

I swallowed hard, and the lump bobbed aside enough for me to mutter, "I don't know."

"What do you mean, you don't know?" His voice was high-pitched and mean. He raised the Chinese sword again, and Kara screamed, "Don't you dare touch him!"

Someone tugged at his sleeve, and he dropped the sword, staring balefully at me.

"What is it?"

A raggedy barefoot man said something in his ear. At the same time I saw a mounted patrol come through the trees. Their horses were flecked with foam.

"All right," General Spurrier said. "Keep an eye on the two of 'em, boys, while I see what Tom John and Ocie got on their minds."

Slamming the sword back in the black-enameled scabbard, he went over to the horsemen. They scrambled down and began to tell him something they were excited about, waving their arms and pointing north, though they were too far away for me to hear more than an occasional word.

Weeping, Kara clung to me. "Oh, Charlie, whatever is to happen to us!"

I patted her hand. "There, there. Nothing's going to happen. We didn't do anything."

"But the general thinks we did."

I looked round at the menacing faces, the leveled guns, the businesslike look of war. They weren't parade-ground dandies, that was sure; they were some of the toughest soldiers around. *Leslie's* said so.

"He's just trying to scare me," I said, and didn't believe it too much.

What in Lucifer was I doing in a fix like this? I hadn't ever harmed anybody, or meant to, anyway. I felt like an amateur actor thrust into Hamlet's togs and pushed onto the stage to deliver a soliloquy. I didn't really belong here. They must have had someone else in mind.

"Do you know how to pray?" Kara whispered.

I hadn't prayed for a long time; I was practically an infidel. But, damn it all, if the count hadn't run off and left me, I wouldn't have to be here in a lonely grove, ringed by hard and desperate men, trying to think of a prayer.

"He shouldn't have done it," I muttered. "Oh, what a das-tardly thing to do to someone that trusted him!"

Kara hugged me tighter.

"Don't blame him, Charlie."

"Why not?"

She was crying again. "He was old and sick and tired. His rheumatism was bad, and he never had his wine and brandy anymore. It was hard for an old man."

"It's harder for us, left behind."

"He'd have taken us if he could, you know that. But there was no way. He had to go alone."

I put my arm around her shaking shoulders, which was a little hard to do because she was taller than me. The circum-stances called for something noble; imperishable words that would be read in a history book a hundred years from now, in nineteen-hundred and sixty-four. But I couldn't think of any.

"He was so ashamed," she murmured. "I could see it. The way they beat him and humiliated him. In front of us. In front of you, especially."

"Me?"

"Of course, silly. Me he paid no mind, but you were his all, Charlie. He was so ashamed, for you more than for him."

I swallowed hard. The lump was still there. "A fine way to make it up to me—running off and leaving me behind!"

"He left me behind, too," Kara said, "and I forgive him for it. He made me real happy while I was with him."

"Well," I said, "I—"

A man poked me in the ribs with his gun. "Stand up straight. The gin'ral's coming."

For a minute Mad Jack Spurrier stood and looked at me, chewing his lip, as though he'd forgotten who I was. His eyes no longer had that weird flickering look. Instead they were hooded and flat, like a snake I'd seen once in the hop vines and almost stepped on.

"Change your mind?"

"No, sir," I said. "I don't know anything."

He turned to the barefooted man behind him. "Tom John, get a rope."

Tom John scratched a large Adams apple. "'Scuse me, gin'ral?"

"You heard me. Get a rope and tie a noose. Put this lying whelp on that old mule, and throw the rope over that low limb there—the elm tree."

"You—you ain't wantin' me to—"

"I'll hang him!" the general yelled. "Hang him by his damned Yank neck for a lesson to spies! Hurry now—Boyle and his cavalry are all the way to Willow Creek and coming fast." He made his hands into a cup, and bellowed out a command. "Saddle up! Feds are half an hour away! Don't carry nothing you don't need. We got to travel light."

The barefooted man looked at me. One of the other men stepped up and saluted.

"General, I didn't volunteer into this war to hang no children."

Spurrier stared at him with that flat look.

"Billy, are you about to argue with me?"

"No, sir, but—"

—"Good! For that would be mutiny. And I could shoot you, right here and now, like a dog." The general took out his big revolver and spun the cylinder. "Is it mutiny, Billy? With the Feds just down the road?"

"No, sir," Billy said sulkily. He shook his head and walked away. Tom John took me by the arm, not ungently, and pulled me away from Kara. They had to hold her and stuff a dirty rag in her mouth, because she fought like a wildcat.

"I'm sorry, bub," Tom John said. "Oh, what a damnable war! I never knew it was agonna be like this."

"It wouldn't be," I said, "if I hadn't been a damned fool."

"You mean you're sorry for being a spy? 'Cause if you are, and you tell the truth about what you all planned, maybe the gin'ral—"

"No," I said. "I didn't mean that."

He gave me a hand up on old Dan. Someone threw the rope over the branch and dropped the thick noose over my head and round my neck. Kara tried to scream and break away from her guards, but all she could do was to make a muffled gasping sound, and she finally sank back swooning in their arms. General Spurrier stood beside me, leaning on the long Chinese sword.

"I'll give you one more chance, boy. Are you ready to tell the truth?"

For the first time I began to get scared. They were really going to hang me! It was a crazy scene out of a crazy play, and I didn't belong on this unreal stage.

"I—I've told you the truth," I quavered. "I don't know anything, honest I don't!"

"Well, then. Got any last words?"

Around me, the sun spattering light and shadow on them, Spurrier's guerrillas were saddled up, watching. More than one face was sad and unbelieving. A horse shied and whinnied; the rider cuffed it on the nose, like when someone creates a disturbance in church. I guess they weren't bad men really. That was just the way a war was.

"No," I said, "except I'm a poor boy that never did anything except look for his rightful father and be taken in by a rascally old man and a balloon."

"All right, then." The general raised the sword. "Slap the mule on the rump, Tom John!"

What happened next I never rightly knew. But I guess when you're hanged you're not supposed to know the time of day on this earth anymore. There was a hell of a noise and commotion, and I swung into the air, feeling Dan's broad back run out from under me.

Dark. Dark. Dark. I swam in a dark sea, gliding and dipping and soaring like a bird, a small bright spark bobbing on the Stygian deep. So this was death! Well, not at all uncomfortable so far. But St. Peter and the heavenly kingdom were surely somewhere on the rim of this sable ocean; there would be the Devil to pay when my soul docked at the alabaster shore. In the meantime, this must be Purgatory.

Above my sea hung misty dark vapors, drifting aimlessly. As I watched a swirl arose and funneled into a queer black shape. A bull it was, a feisty little bull with ruby eyes and sharp-pointed horns. Pawing and tossing his head, he dared me to cross his path. But over there, beyond him, were fields of pink and white and yellow flowers. Ned Campion stood knee-deep in them, jeweled crown on his head and sceptre in his hand, smiling and nodding and beckoning me to join him. I had never seen his face, but this was Ned Campion; it had to be. I ran toward him, but the little black bull tossed his head and hooked me, wounding me in a hundred places so that I gushed thick fountains of blood. Mortally struck, I saw Ned Campion fade into the dark vapors. At last there was only a pale hand beckoning, and then it too dwindled and disappeared.

I was falling deep into night, falling off the edge of the world, screaming and spinning. But I was suddenly borne up in strong arms, and a face bent over mine. It was Kara, painted and bedizened like Jezebel. Her yellow hair fell over my face in a perfumed cascade. Holding me in her arms, she crooned a lullaby and nuzzled me as if I were an infant. *Stop it!* I yelled. *God damn it, I'm not an infant! I'm sixteen, and a man. I'll show you! Go away, or I'll do something awful!* I wept with indignity, and yelled and fought. But the calm strong arms only held me tighter, and the song grew louder and louder so it made my ears ring. The golden hair filled my nostrils; I drowned in a golden tide, and screamed for help, and I floundered and kicked and twitched.

"He's all right," someone said.

That was a familiar voice.

"Hold him down. He'll hurt himself, kicking like that."

A man's voice.

"Charlie! Stop it! You're all right. Everything's all right."

It sounded like Sergeant Bregand, my friend on the cars coming out to Ohio. Was Bregand dead, too, and talking to me while our souls tarried in Purgatory? Killed, no doubt, in the theater of battle.

"Slap him," a harsh voice suggested.

I cringed, but a leathery palm cracked against my cheek. In angry defense, I struck out and opened my eyes. I wanted to complain at such unfair treatment, but all I could do was make a furry croaking sound.

"There—he's come round."

My eyes strained, trying to focus. Finally I got them adjusted and saw a leafy screen above me like a canopy. It looked suspiciously like the real world. Faces, too—many faces. Sergeant Philip Bregand. The cocky little captain—what was his name? Wagner, that was it, Captain Wagner. A lot of soldiers. Boyle's Brigade. Oh, but my throat hurt!

"Lie quiet," Kara whispered. "It's all right, Charlie, *liebchen.* All is right, now. Lie quiet."

"But—"

"Don't try to talk. *Ach,* your poor throat!"

Sergeant Bregand knelt alongside me, leaning on a saber that had crusting red stains on the blade.

"They tried to hang you, but I guess you were too tough and gristly for them."

"Here." Someone held out a skillet with warm bacon grease in it. "Rub some of this on that rope burn. It'll ease the smart."

Gently Kara rubbed the grease into my bruised neck. I smelled like a country breakfast. "Those devils!" she muttered.

"I want to get up."

"Don't hurry it," Captain Wagner said. He slapped his little stick into his palm. "There may be a bone broken somewhere."

"But I've got to get up!"

With a lot of help I rose, tottery as a new colt. These weren't my legs, they were some ridiculous stilts I was propped up on, and they wouldn't do my bidding. Bregand took one elbow and Kara the other. With them aiding me I took a few halting steps and looked round. The sun was high, and the flat light threw into a dreadful relief a scene of carnage and desolation. A pall of gunpowder smoke hung over the clearing, dead bodies lay among the bushes like rag dolls flung aside by an angry child; from the distance came the ragged popping of musket-fire.

"Did—did you capture General Spurrier?" I croaked.

Sergeant Bregand shook his head. "Not yet. We got a lot of 'em, but the general and a few of his dandies are still holed up along the river, trying to break out."

"Did—did you see a balloon when you came from Willow Creek?"

"A balloon?" He looked at me as if I was crazy.

Kara told him the story of the *Petit Géant* and the count's escape.

"No," Bregand said. "I didn't see a balloon."

Before me lay a body. I knew the face. It was the red-nosed man from the cars, the one that had laughed and joked so about Mad Jack Spurrier looking like a morphodite. Only he wasn't laughing now. The poor man's eyes were kind of half-open and squinted, like he was staring at some too-bright star, and his once-red nose was pale and blanched, drained of all blood. His head was fastened to his body only by a stalk of gristly cords that grew out of his neck.

The ragged popping came from farther away now, up the river toward Evans' Landing. Was Mad Jack Spurrier getting away after all?

"E and F Company are on his tail," Captain Wagner said. "They'll skin him and nail his hide to the wall."

"I hope so," I said.

"You, boy, seem to attract incident, violence, and confusion."

Nettled, I snapped, "Well, I'm sorry!"

"Not too long ago I had to throw off the post a Pinkerton agent claimed you'd tried to murder some poor old farmer in

New York State—Albany, was it? No, near Utica."

"He's told me about that," Kara said stoutly, "and he's not to blame."

"Dossey," the captain said, chewing on his little stick and looking at me. "That was the Pinkerton's name. Lemuel Dossey. One of their best. I guess you outsmarted him. The story went that you took off round the corner in a balloon."

"That's right," I admitted. "Do you—do you know where Mr. Dossey is now?"

"Well, I understood the farmer that hired him ran out of money. Those Pinkertons come high, you know. Most of 'em are in the Army nowadays. The last I heard of Dossey, he went back to New York City empty-handed."

I heaved a sigh of relief. "Thank God!"

"What will you do now?"

I didn't know. The count always made our plans for us.

"Well," the captain said, "we'll be pulling out in a few minutes to join up with the rest of the regiment."

The rattle of musketry was only a faint disturbance in the autumn stillness. A fat bee buzzed in my ear, then lurched drunkenly off to bob like a pendulum on a pollen-rich bloom. Leaves hung dusty and flat on the trees. On the western horizon mounds of black cloud rested; a thunderstorm looked likely.

"Captain," I said, "I want to thank you. I'm beholden to you for my neck, I guess. I'll never forget."

"Glad to do it," Captain Wagner smiled.

Later on, when the bodies were buried and the debris picked up, Sergeant Bregand took some men and got Dan and Beersheba hitched up and all our gear packed in the wagon. There wasn't much now; the balloon and most of the count's things were gone. Maybe a dozen or so of Wagner's men sat their mounts casually in a column of twos, Bregand at their head, waiting for the captain. I wished Bregand would come over and say good-bye, but he didn't pay us any attention. He was looking off toward where Spurrier and his guerrillas had fled, carefully examining a folding map.

"Well," the captain said, "it's good-bye—for now, anyhow." He stared at me, scratching his nose. "I wonder what commotion you'll get into next."

I didn't know whether he was joking or not, but I pointed vaguely westward. "I guess we'll go that way."

West was where Ned Campion had gone. It was as good a

direction as any. But I wasn't too sure I wanted to find him anymore. Fathers had turned to Dead Sea apples in my mouth— all ashes and precious little sustenance.

"Good luck." He touched his little stick to the brim of his cap, and nodded to Kara. "Good-bye, ma'am."

As we drove out of the clearing, I looked back. Bregand and the captain and the little column were already gone into greenery, upriver.

A blast of cold wind riffled the canvas wagon-top and blew heavy, fresh-smelling drops into our faces.

"Where are we headed?" Kara asked, snuggling next to me and pulling a shawl around her shoulders.

"I don't know exactly," I said. "I'll figure something out."

"Whatever you decide, Charlie, is all right by me."

Her trusting manner made me uneasy. Damn it, I needed some love and guidance myself; I wasn't prepared to give it to a nineteen-year-old girl!

~~~~~Chapter 9~~~~~

I was used to winters up in New York State, but, this prairie cold was different. It was hard and sharp and painful, like a nail driven into you. It seemed we would never get warm again. Across southern Indiana we went, picking up an occasional odd job hauling feed or coal, Dan and Beersheba plodding into the sleety winds, breath coming in foggy puffs and their hoofs crunching on the earth. The sun set red and streaked early in the afternoon; the mercury dropped to the bottom of the glass and huddled there, afraid to come out. Kara and I slept in the wagon, wrapped in sheets and comforters and sweaters and coats and rags and scraps of canvas. It was perfectly moral; Kara and I were passing as brother and sister making our way in the world. Besides, it was too cold at night to do anything but shiver and blow on our fingers and wish the winter sun would rise again.

November, December. Ranger, Buffaloville, Yankeetown on the ice-rimmed river; Straight Line Junction and Hovey on the Illinois border. At Hovey a man let us stay in his livery stable for the night and gave us a dollar to haul a load of manure. After that the wagon never smelled quite the same.

In Illinois the coldest winter in twenty years thinned our

93

blood and reddened our noses. Sherman's Army had arrived before Atlanta, a week-old paper told us. We couldn't afford to buy one, but a nice lady wrapped some biscuits and a piece of ham in it for cleaning out a shed and hauling an old stove to her sister's.

"Balloon?" Slicing the ham, she looked at me over the tops of her spectacles. "No, I ain't seen no balloon! There ain't been no balloons around here." She threw in a piece of preserved-peach pie, too, saying, "You both look starved, and the girl's a pretty thing."

Mill Shoals, Belle Prairie, Bluford, New Minden: the middle of December. In the towns there were candle-lit Christmas trees and gifts in the general store and warm-bundled people pressing through the snow to attend holy services. Yellow-paned windows in the dusk, smell of woodsmoke, jingle of sleighbells from a passing cutter, an almost unbearable odor of baking mince pies that wafted to us through a kitchen door.

"I never doted on mince," Kara said. "Too rich."

"I guess you're right," I said, and slapped the reins over the mules' bony backs. They were hungry too.

I was like a man after a long illness. Some of the childishness had been amputated from me, and the scar still hurt. I had seen the elephant, and he was a frightening beast. But even as the scar healed, some measure of strength and balance returned. It seemed to me I was somewhat more mature, and on the long nights huddled in the wagon with Kara, things looked different.

One night we camped in a brake of willows alongside a frozen stream. I broke the ice for the mules to drink, and then turned them loose, hobbled, to wrench mouthfuls of frozen grass from the bottomland. There was no wind, and the dusk was bitter still. It's funny the way an iron tire on a wooden wheel acts. As I stood there, slapping my arms across my chest to warm them, I could hear the cracking and popping as the cold metal compressed the wood tighter and tighter. A late duck flapped across the sinking red eye of the sun. Kara knelt at the blaze of frozen twigs to warm the coffee and fry a piece of fatback, spreading her skirts wide to catch and trap what warmth was left over.

"I wonder where he is," I said.

She handed me a tin cup of the bitter stuff. Coffee was in short supply, and dear; this stuff was mostly ground chicory and sawdust.

"I think on it a lot," she murmured.

Her face was thinner and sharp-cut. I guess we'd both lost weight. But she never complained.

"I suppose you were right," I said.

She drained the last of the cup and held her hands tight around it.

"About what?"

"About why he had to go. I was mad then, but things look different now. Maybe I understand."

She took my hand and pressed it between hers. "*Ach*, I'm so glad! You should never think bad of him, Charlie. He liked you so much, though he didn't say so."

"I wonder if we'll ever see him again."

"That is for the Lord to decide. But we pray for him, isn't it?"

"Yes," I said. "We pray for him."

In the wagon I lit our stub of candle. Kara hung the old gray blanket from the bows and undressed; that is, she took off her skirt and blouse to keep them from wrinkling and pulled on an old sweater and a velveteen coat of the count's.

"I'm ready, Charlie."

I retired behind the blanket and got ready for bed. Not being so dainty, I didn't take off anything, just wrapped myself deeper in whatever I could find. I started to blow out the candle, but Kara stayed my hand.

"Do you know what night this is?"

I pondered. "Why—let's see—last Tuesday was the twenty-second. I remember seeing the date on the Staunton *Herald and Eagle*. That must make it—"

"Christmas Eve!"

"Christmas Eve?"

"*Ja.*" Coverlet pulled up under her chin, Kara's blue eyes danced in the candle-glow. "Dumbhead, you—to forget Christmas Eve!"

"Now how could I forget Christmas!"

Of course, it hadn't been too hard. In the orphanage Christmas was an orange and some sticky candy, with maybe a warm muffler or a pair of socks. The Gillentines weren't much on Christmas, either, especially for a bound boy.

"Well, *I* didn't forget." Reaching under the coverlet, she brought out a package wrapped in paper and brown string. "Merry Christmas, Charlie!"

Touched, I opened it. She had made me a watch-fob from leather, polished to a dull sheen and whipped with brass wire

from a spool the count used to repair his scientific instruments.
I knew where the leather had come from too. It was one of the
count's belts he had left behind, a belt from his trousers. But
the fob was delicately and beautifully fashioned. Kara had skill
with her hands.

"Thank you." I held it up in the candlelight. "It was a nice
thing to do, to remember me."

"Of course," she said shyly, "you haven't got a watch. But
someday, Charlie, with that brain in your head you'll be a great
man and have lots of watches. Maybe you'll wear it then, for
me."

With my sense of the theatrical, I waited just long enough.
Then I said, "I didn't forget, either."

Clutching the coverlet over her breast, she sat up. "You
didn't? Oh, Charlie, don't plague me so! It isn't nice!"

"All right," I said. I took out my package, wrapped in a
scrap of balloon-silk.

"Oh, Charlie!" She was like a little girl, picking hastily at
the string, trying to open it. "Whatever could it be?"

When she got it open she laughed in delight. I had seen the
possibilities of the count's old belt, too. I had taken off the
buckle, polished it till it looked like silver, and wrapped it here
and there with the same brass wire to make a heavy and costly-
looking ornament, topped off with a scrap of scarlet ribbon.

"A barrette," Kara murmured.

"For your hair." I touched the heavy gold tresses, feeling
the weight and silkiness. "And—and remember me, when you
wear it."

I kissed her. There was nothing carnal about it, I felt sure.
Besides, it was Christmas Eve.

"I'll keep it always."

"Me, too," I said. "And I'll have a gold watch soon. You'll
see."

We watched the winter moon paint the thin wagon-canvas
with shadows. From a far-off village came the faint shimmering
of church bells on the frosty air. Old Dan and Beersheba whuffled up to the wagon and stood close, maybe trying to get
warm. Or—it was a nice thought—on this bitter Christmas
Eve they might have been trying to share their animal warmth
with us.

"Good night," Kara said. "And a merry Christmas, Charlie."

"And a happy New Year," I said. "It *will* be, too. You'll
see. We'll *make* it be."

*   *   *

In January I wrote a letter to Annie Gillentine, being careful not to put a date on it or address or anything that might help to trace my whereabouts.

"Dearest Annie," I wrote. "Oh, but I have had the most amazing experiences since I left last summer!"

Well, *that* was certainly true.

"I barely escaped from the Pinkerton detective your pa hired to catch me. Once in Manhattan, and once out West here."

That was vague enough so far as geography was concerned. The West was a big place. I went on to tell her about my adventures:

> *For a while I thought about joining the Army, but came to think better of it. I don't think I will ever fit too well into anything that is organized. But I ran into this Polish count and his balloon, and had a grand time for a while. I was captured by Spurrier's irregulars, though, and the count flew away in his balloon and left me to their fury. (That was nice literary touch.)*
>
> *They tried to hang me for a spy, which I wasn't, but friends of mine from Boyle's Brigade rescued me in the nick of time. Maybe it was in the papers. Did you see it? Anyway that all happened in Indiana and I'm far away from there now. I'd like to tell you where to write me—I know you wouldn't betray me—but this letter might fall into the wrong hands so I've got to be careful.*
>
> *I think of you often, and of little Follett, and of summer under the hop vines, and that night we pledged our sacred love in the corncrib. I hope your pa is all right. I never meant to hurt him, or anybody.*

I closed with a flourish, making a lot of loops and whorls. "Your heart of hearts and devoted friend, Charles Campion." Adding a PS, I said, "I am traveling with a very nice girl named Kara. Don't doubt my love, though—ha ha!" Then uncertain about the impact, I added a PPS: "She doesn't mean anything to me, being more like a sister. I will tell you all about it someday when I come back."

In one of those perverse and ill-timed spurts that plague a boy, I was growing again. My arms became long and skinny, with awkward big-knuckled hands. My legs lengthened so alarmingly Kara had to sew a kind of awning to the bottom of my jeans to cover my ankles. We looked like a pair of gypsies—Kara done up in old rags and bright-colored swatches; me long and gaunt in whatever came to hand; Dan and Beersheba thin and harness-sore. Dan was so hungry that most of the meanness had gone out of him. The old wagon swayed and lurched on this road and that, looking for hauling jobs, firewood to split, whatever would pay a dollar; it was a marvelous complex of nails and improvised braces and fence-wire and patches that defied nature. But on we rumbled westward, like a sick man in a delirium.

Kara was really a surprising girl. Maybe she had been that way all along, and I had been too inexperienced to notice. Many times she would say things that were close to being profound. In the long winter nights we talked a lot in the dark, not being able to burn expensive candles. Talk, I guess, is the luxury of the poor.

"When I was a child," I mused, "I used to think a lot about kings and such. Did you?"

"No. I never knew much about kings."

"Didn't you *read* about them?"

"Pa didn't hold much with books, except for Holy Scripture."

"Well," I said, "there's kings in *there.*"

"*Ja,* but the Bible was in the parlor all the time. Us kids couldn't go in there."

"Oh," I said.

"Besides, who cares about kings?"

"Well, it wouldn't be a bad life. Of course, kings go kind of cheap. But royal blood is more than just blood, you know. If you've got royal blood in your veins, you're apt to be a special person—very brave and kind and willing to die for your people and especially for principles." Modestly, I added, "I have royal blood in me, That's a fact. Ancient royal blood—the blood of Irish kings."

For a long time she didn't say anything. After a while I began to suspect she was having some king of bronchial trouble. Or—or was she giggling under the ragged quilt?

"You're laughing," I said stiffly.

"No, I'm not!"

"What *are* you doing, then?"

"Just thinking."

"About what?"

"What you said about kings and all."

Mollified, I said, "Kings are important in history, you'll have to admit that!"

"Yes, that's true."

"I wonder," I said, "what it's like to be a king."

"Oh," she said, "I don't think the king knows."

"What?" I cried.

"I don't think a king *knows* how it feels to be a king."

For a long time I thought about it. Then, when I wanted to talk over certain points, I found she had fallen to sleep. Women, I began to appreciate, could actually *think*, in addition to their other interesting properties.

We crossed the river at St. Louis on a ferryboat. The river was choked with ice, and the captain said it was a long time since he'd seen such a bad winter. Prices were high there, and no work, so we went on. February and March. The Federals captured Fort Fisher in North Carolina, the papers said, and the Thirteenth Amendment had been passed that abolished slavery and freed the negroes. There was even talk of a "Freedman's Bureau" to care for the negroes. I wish there had been some kind of a bureau to take care of Kara and me. We were cold and hungry.

How we ever survived the winter I don't know. And the spring was late coming. Along the Missouri we went, picking up an odd dollar here and there in towns called Pacific, Boon, Brunswick, and St. Joe. What unaccountable weather! Out of the south would come a warm wind, and we thought about spring and green shoots pushing through the damp earth and the song of birds. But the next day the bottom would fall out of the thermometer and the mud would turn into black glass that cut the mules' hoofs and made the wagon sway drunkenly on the road, if road you could call it.

Old Dan got tired of the whole thing too, and his normally evil temper turned dastardly. He tried to bite me every time I came near him with the traces and often succeeded. I tried to sell him to a farmer, but the man only looked at him and laughed.

"He's a mean one!"

"Well, he never took any prizes for sociability," I admitted, "but my sister and I need the money, and he *is* a good stout mule."

"Kind of thin, ain't he?"

"For ten dollars," I said, "you can afford to fatten him up."

"Nope. Ain't interested."

"Well, have you got any work we can do? Hauling or plowing or anything?"

"Ground's too wet to plow."

"Anything!" I pleaded.

"Times are hard, boy." Shaking his head, he turned away. Then almost as an afterthought he said, "You and your sister might try Bugtown if you're headed that way."

"Bugtown?"

He grinned, chewing on a thin stogie. "Guess folks there calls it a different name. New Concordia, or something like that. A passel of religious simpletons up the river. Don't pay any money—feller told me they think money is evil—but they swap a lot, and they set a good table. Maybe you and your sister could finish out the winter there."

It didn't sound promising.

"Well, thanks anyway," I said.

"Think it over. Maybe they can use you and your mules."

Kara's pinched face looked down at me from the seat of the wagon. "What did he say?"

"Bugtown."

"What?"

"Nothing," I said. "We were just talking. Anyway, there's no work around here. Maybe if we come back in a couple of months..."

She shivered, and drew the old coat tighter around her.

"Cheer up!" I said. "The winter's bound to break soon. Look!" I pointed at a puffy cloud in the hard blue sky. "That means spring's coming, sure as anything! Back home we could always tell when clouds like that showed up."

The spring did come and suddenly. Neither of us was prepared for it, in more ways than one. The sun shone, and thousands of little clouds sailed in the sky; the frozen ground thawed into black soup, and shoots of green misted the trees. A thousand miles from home, and a thousand years separated from the disasters of Spurrier and his guerrillas and the count's hasty flight, we watched with delight and wonder. Trickles and rivulets and rills and then bank-high creeks and the great churning of the river; wet mud steaming in the sun, the soft green of willows, a smell of wood smoke and growing things and a lingering warmth of the spring sun on our backs.

This was the edge of buffalo country. Small herds of the humped beasts, skitty and touchy with their calves, watched us pass, and an old bull bellowed a challenge. This was the edge of Red Indian country too, and I was excited to see an old wrinkled buck sauntering along wrapped in a blanket, his squaw plodding behind carrying a heavy gunnysack load.

Slapping the reins on the mules' broad backs I yelled out in sheer delight. "Don't it smell good?" Even old Dan capered a little, and Sheba smiled a mule smile.

"I guess we made it," Kara said. "Oh, sometimes I thought I couldn't go on! But we made it, Charlie. You brought us through the winter, you and your bright mind."

"I don't know about that," I said. "Anyway, it's still too wet to plow."

The farmers began to come out of the general stores where they'd spent the winter with their boots up on the stove, and it was an encouraging sign. But they only yawned, and looked vacantly around, and scratched their backsides. No one was ready to go to work yet.

One of them opened a toothless mouth and advised me I might try Bugtown, up the river.

"I've heard tell of it," I said.

"Mighty curious place. Holier 'n hell. I hear all the men sleeps in one place and the women in another. Onct a month the Lord High Bishop or whatever he calls hisself lets 'em get together. Then"—he slapped his thigh—"look out!"

"Are they Baptists or Holy Rollers or what?"

My informant loaded a corncob and set a match to it.

"German people, mostly. Good farmers. I can't take that away from 'em. They got their own brewhouse and a granary and a steam-engine. Oh, they're a lively lot, all right!"

"Very strict, eh? Make all the women stay away from the men?"

He nodded solemnly, chawing on the willow stem of his pipe.

"God's truth!"

"Well," I said, "it takes all kinds."

"Sure does."

At White Cloud, I plowed a farm for a man, and he paid me eight dollars and an old banjo. That night we celebrated with fried beefsteak and potatoes. I bought a bottle of corn whiskey too and put some in our coffee.

"What makes it taste so funny?" Kara asked.

"It's medicine. Medicine to make you feel good and forget the winter."

Together we sat on the high wagon seat, watching a new moon come up over the ragged horizon. A south wind stirred the new leaves, an animal rustled in the brush, an early owl flitted across the face of the moon and disappeared on silent wings. I marveled at the ageless ways of spring and strummed a C-chord on the banjo.

"Isn't it wonderful?" Kara murmured. "*Ach,* I feel all new again!"

I played a chorus of "Green is the Vine," singing very softly and feeling her warm body against me, the press of her thigh against mine. My singing voice was rusty—after all, there hadn't been much to sing about of late—and I took another nip of the whiskey.

"Now," I said, "we are delivered from the winter of our discontent. Spring sets his verdant touch on the land. All things blossometh. The rude swain casts roguish eyes on his maid and feeleth her—"

She smacked my hand. "Now stop it, Charlie! You behave!"

"All right," I grumbled.

"But it did sound so pretty! It's poetry, isn't it?"

"I made most of it up," I admitted. "But it's true." I tried to pour more whiskey into her cup, but she wouldn't let me. "You're still in the winter," I complained, "but I'm in spring. Glorious spring!"

"You better not drink so much."

"Well," I said, "there really wasn't much to begin with. It was only a little bottle." Holding it up to the disk of the moon, I peered through the bottle. "Are you sure you don't want any more?"

"No, and you'd better not either."

"Alcohol," I explained, "is very volatile. It evaporates if you don't use it up. I'd better finish it before it's all gone." With this illogical statement I turned the bottle up and drained it.

"Oh, Charlie!"

"Now," I said, "I'll sing two or three choruses of 'The Little Drummer Boy.' It's a very sad song about a poor child who was slain in a border war in Scotland a long time ago." Midway in the song two of the banjo strings snapped, but I went bravely on. In the last stanza, however, I was overtaken by grief at the plight of the drummer boy. Putting my head on Kara's shoulder, I started to weep.

"Now you stop!" Again she slapped my roving hand, and this time she was good and mad. "I declare, you're a case! Why did you waste our money on that rum?"

"It's whiskey," I said with dignity. Good Lord, didn't the woman know anything? "It's prime whiskey. Have a drink."

"There isn't any more; you've drunk it all, and I'm glad of that. Now you just settle down, Charlie Campion, or I'll put you to bed!"

That was the wrong thing to say. "Let's do!" I cried.

That was when she jumped down off the wagon. Baying the moon, I pursued her, whooping and hollering. Round and round the wagon we went, while Dan and Beersheba stopped their grazing to stare at us in mule amazement.

"Charlie, stop it! My land, the boy's roaring drunk!"

"Kara!" I screeched. "Come back! Wait for me! I won't hurt you! I just want—"

"I know what you want!"

Becoming a little dizzy, I stopped in the shadow of the wagon to get my bearings.

"Where are you?" Silence. "Kara?"

Treacherously, she hit me from behind with a board. I went down like a slaughtered steer. With a weird zitherlike sound the banjo fell from my nerveless hands. Not content with mayhem, she poured a bucket of cold water over me. The little drummer boy never had such grief as I did that night.

"Now will you stop?"

Broken, but still defiant, I tottered to my feet.

"What did you have to do that for?"

"To protect my—my maidenhood, that's why!"

Worried, she moved closer to me, but not too close. "Oh, Charlie, that bump on your head! Did I hurt you?"

"How," I said, "could you hurt a man by hitting him over the head with six feet of oak plant?"

She giggled. "You smell like a brewery! And you tore your pants."

She certainly did sober me up. Twenty-five cents worth of corn liquor, gone like a snap of the fingers! But in the cold light of reason, I began to get scared. What had almost happened? Why, almost I had overpowered her and—This was no good! Conscientious as I knew myself to be, maybe I'd have had to marry her! Distraught, I could see myself as an old bearded man of twenty or so, surrounded by bawling infants while Kara toiled at the washboard. Gone, gone, gone, the shining hopes of youth, the promised adventure, the flying gay and light as a bird on strong young pinions! Gone, all gone, on the altar of an unwanted domesticity! I shuddered.

"Are you all right, Charlie?"

I took a deep breath. "Get everything packed up,"

"Tonight?"

"Tonight."

"But where are we going?"

"I am going," I said sternly, "to get you to a nunnery. It's no good, this wandering about the country and pretending you're my sister. It's bound to cause trouble, like tonight. I wonder I didn't see it before."

She was doubtful. "What's a nunnery?"

"Up the river," I said, "is Bugtown. They're very religious and moral and the men and women have to sleep in separate places. I think that's what we need. We're going to Bugtown as fast as I can get there."

~~~~Chapter 10~~~~

It wasn't fair to call it Bugtown. Of course, that wasn't its real name; it was really Concordia-on-the-Platte, and one of the prettiest and best-kept places I'd ever seen, religious simpletons or not. Pleasant whitewashed frame buildings with dark green ivy and new pale-green speckling it; a solid-looking granary made of fieldstone below and bricks above, with slits in the wall that made it look like a fort; fresh-faced sturdy people in rough clothes in the streets and lanes, all busy at some task; and everything surrounded by rich black fields neatly stitched with rows of new green corn. Thick woods surrounded the town, nut trees and maples and sycamores proud in their bright new leaves. The violets were the bluest, the jack-in-the-pulpits the tallest, the May-apples the most delicate; juicy mushrooms grew in the shade of the elms. Over all was a canopy of bright blue sky and warm sun. If ever all was right with the world, it was here on the banks of the Platte at Concordia. Concordia meant "agreement," I knew, and here nature and man had obviously agreed.

I pulled up the mules at a fine whitewashed barn where a
—man was milking a cow. A line of cats sat alongside him, and every once in a while he would upend a teat and squirt a fine

stream of milk at the next cat in line. It was comical the way they sat up, sparring with their paws to keep their balance, opening pink mouths wide to receive the squirt.

"Excuse me," I said.

"Eh?" The farmer peered at me through thick-lensed spectacles.

"I'm Charlie Campion from New York State, and this is my sister Kara. I'd sort of like to leave my sister here at Bug— I mean at Concordia for a while. Who do we talk to?"

"Kind of had a hard time of it, ain't you?"

"We sure have," I said.

He left the cow and peered up the dirt lane toward one of the main buildings. Then he opened his mouth and bellowed a lot of German-sounding talk I didn't understand.

"Henry," Kara whispered in my ear. "Fat Henry. He's calling *der Grosser Henner*. That means 'Fat Henry.'"

A man crossing the open plaza looked our way and then hurried toward us. He was fat, all right; face like a winesap apple, tight-skinned and shiny, with little tight-slitted eyes and a bald head. He was apparently some sort of official. He wore a long brown robe of rough stuff, and a gold chain around his neck with an ornament on it, and carried a kind of mace.

"I'm Charlie Campion," I said, "and this is—"

"Knew you were coming," the fat little man said. He took off the broad-brimmed felt hat and bowed to Kara. "Glad to meet you, Charlie."

"This is Kara. My—sister."

"Knew that too." The little man laughed and dug the milker in the ribs with an elbow. "Didn't we, Mr. Schiller?"

"Ja," the milker said. "I guess we did all right."

"Now you just let Mr. Schiller take your team and wagon and the both of you come in to the *Speisehaus* and have a bite with us. Nothing fancy, you understand. We're plain people. But first maybe the lady'd like to freshen up a bit."

"I would," Kara said. "I'm awful rumpled, from traveling."

While she freshened up in a washhouse set off to one side, I doused my face and hands in a pail outside and tried to smooth my hair down. It was long, and needed cutting. Maybe they had a barber here. Cautiously I felt my upper lip. Maybe I needed a shave, too.

"After supper," said Fat Henry, "we'll see if we can talk to Brother Adrian."

"Who?"

Fat Henry chuckled. "I guess we know more about you than you know about us. Brother Adrian is our spiritual leader, and Governor of Concordia-on-the-Platte. A remarkable man, Charlie; a great man, I might say. Imagine—carving out a paradise like Concordia from the wilderness and making it *work* too! Ah, we're all very happy here!"

"I guess that's remarkable enough," I said, "but what's more remarkable, how did he know we were coming?"

He looked at me roguishly, eyes disappearing into fat pink lids, and chuckled again. This was the chucklingest man I'd ever met.

"That's Brother Adrian's secret!"

We had supper in a communal eating-house with a hundred or more of the citizens of Concordia; husky, bearded men in rough shirts and heavy clodhoppers, the women mostly spare and angular, with plain faces and their hair drawn back in a bun. But they all seemed happy, laughing and visiting back and forth, though the men sat at one table and the women at another. I remembered what the farmer down the river had told me about them sleeping separate too. I was about to ask *der Grosser Henner* if they went to separate heavens when they died, when Fat Henry rapped on the table with his mace and everyone stopped talking like they were shot.

"Now praise Omnipotence for all this good provender," Fat Henry said. He raised his fat arms and closed his eyes. "Mighty World Being, Great Maker, Everywhere-in-Being Intelligence that sees our heart of hearts and knows all, understands all, punishes transgressions and makes our hearts pure and loving, hear our thanks! Know our good will and honest intentions that often go astray." Taking a slice of coarse bread from a plate, he broke it into bits and flung the pieces in the air. "We share our bread." He poured some milk from an earthenware pitcher into his hand, and spattered it all around the table. "We share our drink." Finally, he put his hand on my head, and I felt like a damned fool. He said, "We share our love as well with this here Charlie Campion and his sister Kara from back East. Now let's eat."

It was a pretty gamy kind of grace. I never heard one to compare with it. But the food was good, I'll say that. After a winter of being starved, it was like being let into heaven on a pass. Pink home-cured ham, thick fat-marbled slices of it in a spicy gravy; candied sweet potatoes in a bath of butter and brown sugar; crunchy breaded onions, new spinach in a cheese sauce, crackling-crisp corn fritters. Platters of home-baked bread and plates of fresh yellow butter and pitchers of clotted cream. To top it off there were flaky cuts of custard pie and big tin pitchers of hot coffee brought round by the bustling women that served the tables.

"Might be I'm going to be sick," I said to Fat Henry, "but do you suppose I could have another small piece of that custard pie?"

He clapped his hands, and the lady came round again.

"Pour some cream over it," Fat Henry said. "Pie sets easier on the stomach with a little cream to tamp it down."

After supper *der Grosser Henner* took us on a tour of the settlement. The days were longer already, and we walked in a smoky red glow from the setting sun. People strolled the streets, nodding and smiling to one another; birds sang evensong in the trees; an old dog on a porch yawned as we went by. From the kitchen-house came a pleasant clatter of dishes. Fat Henry took us in the sprawling clutter of lean-tos, porches, and sheds.

"All is prepared and cooked here, you see. The womenfolk take turns."

There were long flat-topped woodburning hearths of brick, and scoured oak troughs for sinks, fed by spring-water through a pipe. While the dishes and cutlery were being washed, preparations were going on for the next day. Doughnuts fried in hot grease; a group of bright-eyed children were helping by poking the holes with their thumbs. They laughed and giggled when they saw Kara and me. Aproned women made noodles, rolling the dough tissue-thin and slicing it into extra-fine slivers. At Fat Henry's invitation we went down into the cellars below, lit by a candle he carried. There were dozens of small rooms carved out of the earth and filled with shelves and bins. Shelves of glass jars and stone crocks: dark red beets, yellow peach-halves, white pears; barrels of kraut with caked overflowing brine; apples, troughs of cold water to cool milk cans; carrots and salsify in earthen mounds, and overall the sharp smell of fermentation, rootstuffs, decay; the endless processes of earth.

"No one ever goes hungry here, eh?" Fat Henry dug me in the ribs.

"It reminds me of home," Kara said. "Those women upstairs—they *schnubbel* up the noodles just like ma used."

Taking a jug from a shelf, Fat Henry poured liquid into tin cups. "Brother Adrian don't hold to liquors, but some of us put up a little *peistengl.*"

It was fruity and a bit sour, but good.

"Rhubarb wine," Henry said. "Prime, ain't it?"

Even without the *peistengl*, I was already convinced. At first I had thought to leave Kara here and go on about my business. Now I wasn't so sure. Maybe I'd better stay for a while and see how she got on. My, that custard pie had been good!

"Maybe," I said, "we could see Brother Adrian and sign up, or whatever you do." Fearing I had been too hasty, I looked at Kara, but she nodded. From the look in her eyes she needed this kind of settling down as much as I did—for a while, anyway.

"You wouldn't be making any mistake," Fat Henry said, hiding the jug behind a sack of potatoes. "But there's lots of details to be settled, you know. Brother Adrian will have to talk to you. If he likes you, he'll nominate you and your sister to the Blessed Kingdom."

"The what?"

"On the surveyor's plat it's Concordia, but in the eyes of the Great Omnipotence it's the Blessed Kingdom. The Hidden Books of the Bible—Tarsh and Menharsin—they speak about the Blessed Kingdom."

I didn't remember reading the books of Tarsh and Menharsin, but I suppose that was reasonable, them being hidden.

On our way to Brother Adrian's temple, as they called it, we passed odd little houses, whitewashed with a kind of blue tint. Rose-vines and ivy and stuff climbed all over the roofs, and there were no windows—only a door with fancy hex-like designs painted on. Somebody was moving about in one of them, and I heard a woman laugh.

"What's in there?"

Fat Henry pulled us along with him. "Brother Adrian will explain how the society operates. Hurry now. It's almost time for his meditation!"

We didn't want him to miss his meditation, I knew how important meditation was, so I didn't press the point.

The temple was a big house with tall wooden pillars in front. A man in a white robe sat on the porch playing a harp. For me it would have been kind of cool with no pants, but he didn't seem to mind. Fat Henry wrote out a sort of pass from a notebook he carried in his pocket. The man put down his harp, took a long time reading it, and finally gestured for us to go in. He kept the pass, or whatever it was. In the candlelit gloom of an anteroom inside we heard him banging away at the harp again. He wasn't very good at it, I didn't think.

"Wait here," Fat Henry said, and rustled away up a stairs.

"Charlie," Kara whispered, "I'm kind of scared."

I patted her hand. "I guess lots of times in the wagon we were scared."

"But this is different!"

"Trust me," I said. I was enjoying it, it all being romantic and mysterious. Soon as I could, I'd have to read Tarsh and Menharsin.

Fat Henry materialized from shadows, and I jumped. He put a finger to his lips. "Come quietly! Miss, you'll have to pull that shawl over your head. Brother Adrian has graciously consented to an audience."

He opened two big doors. There were thick carpets, candles flickering in iron brackets, a smell that was old and thick and dusty. At the far corner of the chamber sat a man at a table, leaning back in a relaxed pose with one hand supporting his chin and the other on a big book. An oil lamp cast heavy shadows, and I couldn't see his face too well. But I knew who it was all right. I felt a fountain of ice water spurt through my chest, and my knees got weak. It was the figure in my dream— the shadowy hooded figure of Ned Campion, the figure that beckoned me to him across fields of pink and white and yellow flowers. Here in Concordia-on-the-Platte I'd found him!

"It's you!" I cried, shaking off Fat Henry's hand and running forward across the thick carpet. "I've found you!"

Well, it wasn't, of course. Maybe I'd only seen what I wanted to see. When he pulled down the hood, he wasn't Ned Campion at all. I didn't know for sure what Ned Campion looked like, but this wasn't my father. This was Brother Adrian, a small, monkish-looking man with gentle eyes and sunken cheeks only partially hid by blond side-whiskers.

"Come back here, you!" *der Grosser Henner* shouted. "Don't go rushing up on him that way!"

Brother Adrian didn't seem bothered. He smiled and nodded, and said, "I must resemble someone you know, my son."

Flustered and confused, I looked down at the carpet. For a minute I had been so sure—I had *known*. Something, somebody had played a trick on me. "No," I said. "I guess not. For a minute I thought—"

"You thought what?"

I didn't want to get a reputation for being crazy. They

weren't likely to nominate any crazy people for the Blessed Kingdom.

"Excuse me," I said. "I—I was kind of mixed up."

Fat Henry brought Kara forward. "Gracious brother, this is the boy's sister. Kara. Kara Campion. And Charlie. They're good folk, even though the boy may be a mite forward."

"I can see they're good children," Brother Adrian said, his voice remarkably deep and resonant. "The Blessed Kingdom is happy to have you visit."

"Well," I said, "begging your pardon, it's more than a visit." I told him all about our long winter, and the troubles we'd had. "Kara needs a proper home, a place where she can be with womenfolk and knit and cook and do what women do. It isn't natural, roaming around the country and all. For a boy, it's no great harm. But a female is different."

He was one of the nicest men I'd ever met. Oh, he wasn't my father, of course, and he couldn't match Count Kasimir Blatski for style and dash, but there was something gentle and holy about him, I could see that. Even Fat Henry, who was a kind of bossy type, was awed by him, uneasy like a long-tailed dog in a roomful of rocking-chairs.

"I honor you for a man's mind in a boy's years," Brother Adrian said. "It is very honest, and very touching. But we have to be careful who we take in here, you understand. Not all people think the way I—the way *we* do. There are trouble-makers. A person's motives and background have to be investigated thoroughly, for our good as well as his."

"Oh, I know that!" I cried. "But you'll find sister very reliable and dedicated, if that's what you need! And if it's all right, I'd just as soon join up too!"

He got up and paced the floor in his long robes, hands locked behind his back in an attitude of thought. From the porch below came a sour note on the harp. In a dark corner glowed a bowl with incense in it, and the smell was sweet and spicy.

"I'm scared," Kara whispered. I pressed her hand, watching Brother Adrian pace the floor. Finally he stopped, and looked keenly at us.

"You'd have to sign over all your worldly goods, of course. That's one of the conditions."

"Well," I said in a burst of honesty, "you'd be getting the worst of *that* deal. There isn't much, except a wagon and two middling mules and some odds and ends."

"You'd have to sign an oath renouncing worldly vanities."

"I never was much on them."

"Nor me," Kara said. "Pastor Stoltzfuss used to say I was one of the plainest girls in his church."

"You'd have to dedicate your lives to the Great Omnipotence."

That was all right, being apparently just another word for the Lord. I had a queasy feeling for a moment, wondering what the sisters at the orphanage would say, but then I'd never be going back there. Anyway, I was old enough to know that men call God by a lot of different names.

"We understand," I said.

"Well, then." He sat down, scribbling words on a scrap of paper with a long goose quill. "I'll recommend you to the Elders, and we'll see what happens."

"You won't regret it," I said warmly. "We're hard workers, both of us."

In closing, he made us kneel down, saying some words over us while Fat Henry mumbled along after him. They didn't seem exactly Christian to me, being more kind of general and moral than strictly religious. I'd have to read those Hidden Books soon as I had a chance.

When we got up, Brother Adrian drew a slow circle in the air with his finger. "Unity!" he said. He punched a hole in the circle with his finger. "Purpose!" Then he came out from behind the table and shook hands with us. "You're provisional members. The Elders meet on Tuesday next. Bless you, my son, my daughter." He gestured to Fat Henry, and he took us out and closed the doors softly behind him. He was sweating.

"I never seen it done so fast," he said, seeming a little put out.

"Maybe he had a vision," I said helpfully.

"Maybe." He swung his mace and pondered.

"Great men like him don't have to wade through a lot of logic like we do. It just comes to them."

"I guess so," Fat Henry said. "Well, it's full dark. We go to bed with the birds around here so as to get up early and do the work the Great Omnipotence has in mind for us."

At the door of the women's house he rang a bell. A motherly-looking woman in a calico dress came to the door.

"Sister, this here is a new provisional member approved by Brother Adrian."

"Wait a minute," Kara said.

"What's the matter?" the lady asked.

"I—I just want to talk to Charlie a minute before I go in."

The lady made a shrugging motion and waited in the doorway with a candle. Inside I could hear a lot of women gossiping and chattering the way they do.

"All right," I said.

"Not here." Kara looked at Fat Henry. "Over—over there, by the lilacs."

I followed her. The spring night was soft as velvet and lit by starshine.

"Charlie, I'll never forget you."

I stared at her.

"It'll be different now. People all round us. No being together in the wagon, just you and me, talking and all."

"Well, it was fun," I admitted. "But it wasn't right. This is better. Much better, you'll see."

"Maybe." She sighed, and twisted her shawl into a knot under her chin, staring at the lilac bush.

"It's more—more proper."

"I guess you're right. You can always think things out better than me."

"Besides," I said, "a person just has to trust Brother Adrian. He's a good man."

For the first time that day she smiled. "I know."

"Now," I said, "you just go along and—" With a violence I didn't think possible in her gentle nature, she threw her arms around me and kissed me hard on the mouth. Then she hurried away, hiding her face in the shawl. The door of the women's house went shut. Fat Henry stared at me, and scratched his chin.

"Your sister is real affectionate, ain't she?"

I took a deep breath. "She's very loving. We—we're close, the two of us."

He took my arm, and we sauntered down the silent street. The doors and windows were closed and shuttered against the night air, and I could smell lilacs strong—or was it Kara?

"In here," Fat Henry said. "This is where the men sleep."

There were rows and rows of cots with huddled forms, here a snore, and there a creak as someone turned over. It smelled like men, and not half as good as Kara. But it was a bed—the first real bed I'd had for almost a year. Gratefully I took the rough blanket Fat Henry handed me.

"Buffalo wool," he said. "Make 'em ourselves in the factory. Finest blanket there is."

Long after he had gone, leaving me in the men's house, I lay with hands locked behind my head, too excited and wound up to sleep. In the awesome presence of Brother Adrian I'd forgotten to ask how they all knew we were coming. Tomorrow I'd have to investigate that. My mind raced and teemed, but slowly wore itself out. I dozed, I remember once waking in the middle of the night. I guess I did, anyway, and finally slept. Maybe it was all a dream, I was never sure. A commotion was going on outside the men's house. Someone cursed; a man started to cry out, then the sound was bitten off sharp. But I was so excited and wrought up by fall that had happened that day that perhaps I only dreamed the whole thing.

══════Chapter 11══════

Until the Elders could get around to deciding whether we would make good converts, they put me to work in the fields hoeing corn; Kara worked in the *Speisehaus* peeling potatoes and making pie crusts. I didn't have much time to myself, they kept everybody pretty busy. But I did find a few minutes before bed to start writing in my journal:

> German people from Illinois founded this place on the Platte twenty years ago. It was real wild Indian country then, and that's why the granary was built like a fort. They use it now for a jail, I guess. At any rate there's a guard, though no one seems to want to talk about who's kept there. Anyway things were pretty hard, and they scrabbled along for years until Brother Adrian came. That was a great occasion, because things got better once he took over. He was what they called a Vorläufer. I don't know enough German to figure out exactly what that means, except it's some kind of a holy messenger from the Lord that appears on the face of the earth and has got the Divine Word right from on High.
> Mr. Schiller says there are ways you can tell a Werk-

zeug, *but it wasn't too clear to me. Brother Adrian started right in organizing things and planning and getting everyone to forget their squabbles and work together. The* Erdspiegel—*that was the best part. He brought along an* Erdspiegel *when he came. That's a kind of spiritual looking-glass that a* Vorläufer *can see all kinds of things in. Brother Adrian could look in the* Erdspiegel *and tell what crops to plant, how to cure the quinsy, who to appoint to the board of Elders—all kinds of things. As a matter of fact, that was the way they knew Kara and I were coming, or so I was told; Brother Adrian looked in the* Erdspiegel. *It sounded spooky to me, though Mr. Schiller said there was mention of such things in the Bible.*

I wanted to look it up, but Brother Adrian keeps the holy books of Tarsh and Menharsin locked in the Temple. That is where the Erdspiegel *is too, in a special room with a twenty-four hour watch of Wise Virgins over it.*

That was all I had time for that night. I blew out the candle and tucked the dog-eared journal under my pillow in the men's house. What a wonderful place this was, with all sorts of interesting features! Everybody in New York State knew about the Oneida Community up in Madison County and the outlandish way they carried on, but they couldn't hold a candle to Bugtown, I mean Concordia-on-the-Platte. There was a kind of nobility to this place; something like the old Greek city-states.

Morning came before I was ready, but after a *Speisehaus* breakfast of mush and ham and fried eggs and bread and jam and about a quart of milk I was ready to start hoeing again. On the way out to the fields with Mr. Schiller, I saw Kara from a distance and waved to her, but she didn't see me. She was going into the temple on some kind of business.

I liked old Mr. Schiller. He was an honest and kindly man, wiry and hardworking for all of his years, and liked to talk about the farm he used to have in Illinois and how his daughter married a shoe drummer and lived in New Jersey.

"Killed in the war," Mr. Schiller said. *"Ach,* it pains me so to think on it! Jacob was such a fine young man. About your built, Charlie, and very dependable. Poor Emmie—left alone with her three kids! I send her money when I can spare it, but there ain't much. Food we got to eat here—plenty of it—but precious little cash."

"Well," I said, "maybe when the war is over—"

He peered at me through his thick spectacles. "When the war is over?" Straightening up, he leaned on his hoe and stared at me. "The war is over, Charlie. In April the war is over!"

"Well," I said, "traveling around the way we did, I didn't get to see a newspaper often."

"The President dead—"

"What?"

He nodded soberly. "Killed by an assassin."

I felt like a three-ply stemwinding idiot! All these things going on, and Kara and me not even knowing! There were advantages to traveling, but keeping informed didn't appear to be one of them. Right then and there I knew I'd made the right decision; to settle down here on the Platte and set a few roots.

"I don't suppose you ever heard of a Confederate general named Mad Jack Spurrier?" I asked.

Mr. Schiller huffed on his spectacles and polished them with his shirttail. "Seems to me was in the Des Moines paper. Spurrier! Now as I recollect he was the one raided into Indiana."

How well I remembered!

"They caught him." He put the spectacles on, and picked up the hoe again. "Put him in the big prison at Columbus. Might be he was the one that broke out and escaped back to Kentucky last winter."

I'd had some bad dreams about Mad Jack Spurrier. That was all over now.

"Well," I said, "the war's finished. Thank God for that."

We saw *der Grosser Henner* coming, and got back to our hoeing. Fat Henry was a sort of straw boss, and took his duties very serious. I didn't mind the work, though. It felt kind of good to sweat in the fields, to match your strength against a physical task, to be in the hard rough company of men and feel one of them, united in a physical task of wresting a living from nature. But something was missing. I missed Kara. I think those men missed the company of their wives too. Oh, there were the little vine-covered cottages where they could go once a month in private when they got a pass signed by Brother Adrian. But love shouldn't be scheduled like that. Maybe it was hearsay, but I mentioned it to Mr. Schiller one day.

"It's the way the Blessed Kingdom works," he said. "It's

all writ in the Hidden Books. Besides, laying with a woman too often weakens a man. That's a historic fact."

Mr. Schiller was pretty old to be laying with a woman, but somehow I got the idea he missed being around his wife too.

Of course, I was glad to see Kara getting along all right without me. Once the board of Elders took us in as regular members, it wasn't any time at all till Brother Adrian appointed her one of the Wise Virgins to tend the *Erdspiegel* in the Temple. It was quite a recognition, though it did set some tongues to wagging. One of the Elders raised a lot of sand about it, though most people thought it was just because he thought his daughter ought to have the job. His name was Vogel, a peppery little man with furry dark eyebrows and a raspy way of talking. One morning I heard him grumbling while he was setting out tomato plants.

"It ain't right, that's what! A young girl like her in the Temple! They was all supposed to be mature women that tend the *Erdspiegel*—maiden ladies, not unattached young girls. I tell you, there's bound to be trouble!"

Someone agreed with him, and said they didn't like certain things that seemed like went on in the temple. They didn't remember any authority in the Hidden Books.

"That's right," Mr. Vogel complained. "If you ask me, Brother Adrian is making up some of the things he says are written."

"Well, you're an Elder," someone else said. "Why don't you speak up in meeting?"

Right then Fat Henry came up and wanted to know why we were all leaning on our hoes and talking. "Don't no tomato plants get set out that way," he said. "Besides, the Devil finds work for idle hands. What was you talking about?"

No one spoke. I don't think they trusted Fat Henry.

"Well," he said, chuckling his apple-faced chuckle, "don't make *me* no never mind!" He ran a fat hand up and down the polished wood of his official mace. "Only I'd advise you fellers to mind your tongues. I heard a little bit of what you was saying, and it sounds to me like you're making trouble in the Blessed Kingdom. Now we don't want no trouble here. This is the work of the Great Omnipotence we're called on to do. And he sees and hears everything, remember that!"

Still smiling and chuckling in a friendly way, he sauntered off.

I didn't know how much the Great Omnipotence saw and

heard, but I had an idea that *der Grosser Henner* saw and heard quite a bit. Maybe he told the Great Omnipotence about it. After that, I was pretty careful what I said. And Mr. Vogel somehow or other resigned from the board of Elders, so I heard. He didn't work in the fields anymore, either. Maybe the Great Omnipotence had some other job for him; I wasn't going to stick my nose into theological matters.

The buffalo-wool factory was the Blessed Kingdom's great enterprise, the way they hoped to bring in hard money. We could set out tomatoes and plant corn and milk cows all day long, but all that did was fill our bellies. Hard money was what the Blessed Kingdom needed, dollars to buy building materials and wagons, tobacco for the men and new silk dresses for the Wise Virgins on account of them being in the temple all the time and needing to look proper. But the buffalo-wool factory wasn't doing well. Alarmed at all the settlers moving in, the buffalo were moving westward. The original idea had been that the Blessed Kingdom buffalo-wool factory would pay top prices for prime hides from the commercial hunters and the Indians. But when the buffalo wandered west, the Indians and hunters went too and didn't care to bother with selling hides to the Blessed Kingdom. There were too many cash buyers right on the spot. Now all the people that were supposed to soak the hides and heat them and pull the wool, and all the workers that were to card the wool and spin and do all the rest just sat around the factory and looked out the windows. I thought about what Fat Henry said about the Devil making work for idle hands. *There* were a lot of idle hands, all right! One of them was an old buffalo-hunter Brother Adrian had hired, hoping he could bring in a few hides. Ike Coogan had a six-month contract; he showed it to me.

"It's a shame to take their money, though. Hell, I ain't brought in but three skinny bulls in the last week!"

He sat in the sun, tilted back in his chair, stained old hat over his eyes, drowsing in the sun. He was about fifty, a solidly-built man with shrewd eyes in a weathered face and a shock of unkempt gray hair and a grizzled beard. I never saw a dirtier man, though. He wore greasy buckskins with long fringes on the arms and legs, and there was a crusty ring round his neck and wrists and ankles. If you stood downwind of him, it kind of took your breath. He never ran out of stories about when he used to trap down on the Picketwire, or the time he killed three buffalo-bulls with one shot from his old Sharps rifle. His favorite story was about the winter he lived with the Utes and had a fight with a buck named Bad-Eye. He said he ended up cutting off the Indian's privates and making a sack out of it to keep gold-dust in.

"That Injun was quite a ladies' man," Ike explained. "After I tanned that article, and had one of the squaws stitch it up and put a drawstring to it, would you believe it?" He leaned forward and looked me straight in the eye. "That bag would hold a good twenty, thirty ounces of prime dust."

"What did you do with it?" I asked. "The bag, I mean."

He leaned back and shoved his hat over his eyes. "Lost it up on the Yellowstone one winter. Gold and all. Hell, I didn't mind, though. The thing was kind of creepy. Used to get gooseflesh onto it when the weather turned cold."

"Ike," I said, "I never know whether to believe you or not!"

"It's God's truth!" He held up his hand. "Why should I tell a lie about a thing like that? Hell, it wasn't no joke to that Ute, was it?"

"Well," I said, "I wish you could bring in some hides as easy as you tell those damned lies."

He spat, and hit an unsuspecting fly dead center. "They ain't *all* moved out. There's plenty of 'em up the draws and down the coulees. But they're scattered, and a man can ride hisself to the nub chasing those critters." He shook his head. "There's six months work for the factory if I could lay my hands on what's left, but I ain't about to kill this coon doing it."

He was always calling people "coon" or "old hoss," and talking about the way his stick floated. I guess that meant fate or something.

"There ought to be a way," I said.

"Well, if you find one, you let this hoss know, because I swear my behind is one big boil by now."

A couple of times he went to church with me, but he didn't have the right frame of mind for it. I had a hard time keeping my attention on Brother Adrian's sermon when Ike Coogan was sitting next to me. I think he just went along for the company. I was about the only one in the congregation would come near him. He'd sit there, solemn as a judge; all of a sudden, he'd dig me in the ribs with a bony elbow and whisper, "Do you believe that, old hoss?"

"Believe what?"

"All that palaverin' about the Great Whoop-te-doo?"

"The Great Omnipotence?"

"That's it!"

"I don't know. It's real interesting, though. Hush up and let me listen!"

Brother Adrian was a powerful speaker. Small and wispy as he might look with his blond side whiskers and sunken cheeks, he seemed to be ten feet tall in the pulpit. He would start slow and quiet, almost in a conversational tone.

"The world has known many great religious leaders, my brothers of our Blessed Kingdom. Gautama Buddha was one such. There was Moses. Our Eastern brothers knew and revered Mohammed, the Prophet of what they thought was the One God. There was Jesus, the Nazarene. Many men, many religions, many faiths. The Jains, the Quakers, the Swedenborgians, the Gnostics, the followers of Thomas Erastus, the Ancient Abyssinian Church."

Maybe it was my imagination, but there seemed to be uneasiness in the congregation. I don't think some of them liked the way he casually threw Jesus Christ in with the Ancient Abyssinian Church and Gautama Buddha.

"Many men, many leaders, many faiths." He went on and on. In a way it was like a chant and hypnotized you. "Down the musty paths of history, man plods from one century to the next, hoping, seeking, searching, groping—seeing in his mind always the dazzling vision of the *one* leader, the *one* philosophy, the *one* religion, the *one* god."

Well, that was fair enough.

"But *is* there only one?"

Someone coughed. The sound was loud in the stillness. Ike Coogan woke up and looked mildly around.

"*Is* there only one?" Brother Adrian's voice rose. He pounded on the pulpit. His eyes filled with a luminous radiance, and I would swear that a glow enveloped his head. "I ask you, brothers of our Blessed Kingdom, *is* there only one?"

No one spoke. I guess we were all waiting for the answer. But Brother Adrian was too expert an orator to break the tension. He went on, building to a climax that no one yet understood.

"Accompanying man on this search, the handmaiden of his efforts, the constant companion of his questings, has been—what?" He raised his hands high, and the sleeves of the robe fell back to reveal his thin white arms. "War, brothers! Famine, pestilence, plague, deceit, violence, trickery, and blood-lust. Wickedness. Corruption. And why? I ask you—why?"

His fist on the lectern sounded like a thunderclap, and I jumped. I wasn't the only one who had stumbled down through history looking for the one true faith and finally finding myself called to account. All the brothers were uneasy.

"I'll tell you why!"

There was a collective sigh from the congregation, a blessed relief from strain. He was going to tell us why! Now we would know and understand and feel better about the whole thing. But it didn't work out quite that way.

"It is because," Brother Adrian thundered, "there *is* no single way—no unique faith, no final and ultimate religion that is the answer to man's search! I tell you, brothers of our Blessed Kingdom, I have finally put my finger on the cause of all man's ills! I have labored and studied and worked and agonized in my temple—all this for you, brothers—and I have found the answer. Why it was right there all the time for anyone to see!" He threw out a hand in a magnificent gesture of discovery. "All these so-called faiths, all these fumbling religions, all these ramshackle philosophies—they are *all* false, *all* wicked, *all* destructive, *all* a sham and a delusion! Yes, our Christianity, too, that we—you and I—believed in."

Someone stood up and shouted something, but I didn't quite make it out. There was a scuffle in one of the back rows, and a woman cried out. When I turned to look, it was quiet again.

"But there is hope! There is still hope!" Brother Adrian leaned forward, luminous eyes sweeping the congregation. "And I have found that hope, brothers. I have marked it! I have singled it out, and made it the cornerstone of our Blessed Kingdom! Yes, after long and painful and tedious study and meditation, I am ready to announce our new creed!"

More scuffling in the congregation. Ike Coogan leaned close to me, and whispered, "I mind a fight in a saloon in St. Looie once that started out just like this. Fellers was arguin' about religion too. Burned down the building before they was done."

"Be quiet," I said. "I want to hear this."

"Through all man's sorry history," Brother Adrian shouted, "through all his gropings and searchings and hope for better things, there is one thing that stands out. One thing alone. One great principle. One Great Omnipotence. And do you know what it is?"

Nobody knew.

"It is that Great Omnipotence that comes of man's concern for his brother. It is that Great Omnipotence that says love your fellow-man. It is that Great Omnipotence that says do ye have regard one for the other. That is all there is to it, brothers. Obey that Law, and do not fret about how many days it rained before the Flood, or whether Hell is stoked with wood or coal, or if an angel is bigger than your thumb. Oh, my brothers, do not think on these things! Forget them all! Forget old ways, old times, old leaders, old philosophies, old religions. Sweep them out, and let in the bright new light of freedom! Dare to be *men,* dare to be *thinkers,* dare to be the New Believers! Come forward with me on this new crusade! Love your neighbor! That's easy enough, isn't it? Love me, love Fat Henry, love the Twelve Wise Virgins, love Concordia-on-the-Platte!"

It seemed to make a great deal of sense when you thought about it. And I could do it all, except maybe love Fat Henry; I'd have trouble with that. I stood up and cheered, carried away by Brother Adrian's great vision. Others stood too, and cheered and applauded. A lot didn't though, and there was milling around and shouts of protest. After church, knots of people congregated outside and jawed and argued, and a fistfight broke out. Brother Adrian left by the back door. But I could still see in my mind's eye his luminous gaze, his graceful gestures, hear the thunder of his voice, great and compelling.

"That was an experience," I sighed.

"I guess so," Ike said. "I ain't strong on experiences, though, Charlie. I done had me enough already to last for a long time." He hurried away, looking uneasy.

Brother Adrian's sermon set off a real brannigan in Concordia-on-the-Platte. People formed into two groups: the New Believers that loved everybody and the Old Believers that thought Brother Adrian had gone too far, and wanted a return to the Bible and the good old religion. Mr. Schiller was a leader of the Old Believers, and he said some things that were real critical of Brother Adrian. Knowing about the jail and what had happened to Mr. Vogel, I was afraid for him, because he'd been a good friend to me.

"I don't know why you should raise so much sand about it," I said. "The New Belief makes sense. And it's the only way of reconciling all religions, isn't it? I mean, they can all agree we ought to love each other, though we might differ about whether God should be called Jehovah or Allah or what-ever."

I couldn't discuss it with him, though. He got mad and red in the face, and yelled.

"I'm not about to reconcile my God with any African voodoo god! Why, it's the most *immoral* thing I ever heard of! And to think"—he took off his broad-brimmed hat and fanned his sweating face—"to think he's been leading us down the garden path all this while—him and his Hidden Books of the Bible and the Great Omnipotence and all the rest of that rubbish! We trusted him for a *Vorläufer*, and now he's trying to destroy us!"

I looked around for *der Grosser Henner*, and was relieved to see there were only the two of us amid the tomato vines.

That was a good year for tomatoes; the vines were higher than my head and loaded with prime fruit.

"You ought to be careful what you say," I urged. "Anyway, Brother Adrian wouldn't destroy anybody. He's a good man, and smart. He knows what's best."

I couldn't talk to Mr. Schiller, that was certain. And I had to talk to somebody or burst like a balloon. Not only a *some-body*, either; I needed a *woman* to talk to. I needed Kara.

Of course, no one was allowed in the temple without good reason and a signed pass. Now that there was all this trouble between the New Believers and the Old Believers, there were extra guards at the temple. They didn't play harps, either, but carried clubs like Fat Henry did. Oh, why did there have to be so much trouble! But it was an old, old story. Brother Adrian was just ahead of his time, that was all. The forces of evil and reaction were trying to drag him down like the jealous Sanhedrin did to Jesus Christ. I grieved about it, and thought a lot, and finally I just had to talk to Kara. At last, on a dark moonless night in July, I took the chance.

Everyone was asleep, snoring peacefully. It had been hot during the day, but now—well after midnight—the Nebraska air was cool and soft, like velvet in the nostrils, and I could smell a honeysuckle vine. Taking a roundabout way through the trees, I slipped out and made my way to the temple. Two guards were sitting on the front porch, talking in low tones. Unseen in the bushes, I made a quick circuit of the temple. No other guards. And a light was on in the back room where Kara tended the *Erdspiegel*. I'd just shinny up the drainspout and across the back-porch roof and scratch at the window.

Heart pounding, I climbed up, scratching my face and hands on a climbing rose bush that straggled across the metal pipe. I tiptoed across the rustling shingles and found the window open. The white curtains hung straight down in the still air.

"Kara?"

No answer; the room was bare except for the draped bulk of the *Erdspiegel* in the middle of the room, and a flickering candle on a stand. She wasn't keeping a very good watch, I'd say that! Carefully I climbed over the sill and sneaked into the room. Silence. All silence, and cool candle-shine.

Curious, I tiptoed over to the *Erdspiegel* and lifted a corner of the draperies. It was rich brocade, so stiff and worked with gold that it crackled in my fingers. Fearing someone would hear, I dropped it. After a while, when nothing happened, I raised the cloth again.

The *Erdspiegel* was nothing remarkable, only a wood-framed mirror a foot square and set on trunnions rising from a polished walnut base. Mrs. Gillentine had one something like it. Some of the silvering was even gone from the *Erdspiegel,* and it looked old and shabby. But of course that didn't matter. It was what you could *see* in it that counted.

When I heard a creak in the boards outside the hall door, I dropped the brocade in panic and crouched for flight. But the handle of the door turned, and the door was opening. The candle flickered in a gust of air from the hall. Trapped! I was trapped in the Temple. How would I explain what I was doing here, profaning the *Erdspiegel?*

But it was only Kara, dressed in a long white robe and sandals, a circlet of gold binding her high-piled golden hair.

"Charlie!" Closing the door behind her, she hurried over to me, face perplexed and concerned. "You shouldn't be here! Oh, you foolish boy!"

I didn't like to be called any kind of a boy, let alone a foolish one. Anyway, she was only a couple of years older than me.

"You're not watching the *Erdspiegel* very good," I muttered. "I could have walked right off with it."

She had a mysterious smile on her face I didn't like.

"Oh, that's all right! Brother Adrian knew I was close by."

Not only that; she had some kind of spicy perfume on and paint on her cheeks and lips. Even through the white robe I could see she didn't have much on underneath.

"Where in hell were you, then?"

She put a finger on my lips. "Don't swear, Charlie. It's not right, especially here in the temple."

"That isn't all that isn't right here in the temple," I growled.

"Whatever do you mean?"

I touched her cheek, and red came off on my finger. "You look like a damned whore done up that way! Look at that!"

"There's nothing wrong with that," she said mildly. "Brother Adrian likes me to look nice." Starry-eyed, she went to the window, leaned against the jamb, and toyed with the lace curtain. "Oh, he's such a wonderful man, Charlie! You'll never know how he loves everybody."

"I don't doubt that," I said. And I didn't either. But she seemed so happy, so content. Who was I, to bring up ugly suspicions? I kept my lip buttoned with an effort, although I would damn well have liked to know where she'd just come from, half-naked and smelling like some Turk's harem-girl. "Are you happy?" I asked.

She turned to look at me. "So happy."

"That's good," I said awkwardly.

"How about you?"

"Working hard. Studying to be a New Believer."

Squatting suddenly on the floor beside the open window, she pulled at my trouser-leg. "Sit down here and tell me all about it."

Uneasy, I allowed myself to be pulled down beside her.

"Is it safe? Where's Brother Adrian?"

"Asleep. He'll be sound asleep until morning."

I locked my arms around my knees and stared moodily at the shrouded *Erdspiegel*. "By God, you seem to know an awful lot about his sleeping habits."

"Now I don't want to talk about Brother Adrian. I want to talk about *you*." She put her arm in mine; through the filmy robe her thigh was warm against me. I remembered that day I had seen her bathing mother-naked in the river.

"He likes you, you know."

"Who?" I asked.

"Brother Adrian. He says you're a very bright boy—I mean a bright young man. He predicts a wonderful future for you here in the Blessed Kingdom. He sees a lot, you know, and knows a lot. He knows you're all for the New Belief. Oh, isn't he a great man, Charlie?"

"Thought you didn't want to talk about him," I sniffed.

"I didn't mean to. It's just that he's so good and kind. All day long I find my thoughts falling on him."

She was in love! And Brother Adrian was supposed to be celibate, according to the Hidden Books. Anyway, that was what Mr. Schiller had told me. This looked like trouble!

"It's right, isn't it, Charlie?"

I parried for time. "What's right?"

Exasperated, she pinched my arm, and it hurt. "For being such a bright one, you're a real dumbhead every once in a while! I mean Brother Adrian and loving everybody like he said. Isn't that all right? What could be wrong with that?"

What to say? I felt responsible for her; I'd brought her to Concordia-on-the-Platte. And I believed the New Belief myself. How could I make any case against loving someone?

"Kara," I said, "I—I—" My voice squeaked alarmingly and shifted an octave higher. "Damn it all," I said, trying again, "what I mean to say—"

She put a finger on my lips. "Hush! I thought I heard someone." Kneeling at the window, she peered through the curtains into the yard below.

Fat Henry? Nervously I joined her. In the faint starshine there was only the carefully kept yard, shadowy bushes, a mockingbird starting a preliminary trill.

"I'd better go," I whispered.

"So soon?"

"Soon enough. You never know who might be watching. This New Belief is a touchy business around here."

She clung to me, laying her cheek against my shoulder. "I miss you, Charlie."

"I miss you, too. But I've got to go."

"I'll let you know when's a good time to come back. You will come again, won't you?"

"If you want me to."

"Of course I want you to."

"All right," I said and kissed her cheek. Then I stole out of the window, across the roof, and dropped into the yard. The mockingbird squawked and flapped away. It looked like I was home free, but I was sweating; my shirt was wet and clammy in the night air.

I was skulking past the back of the old granary when someone hissed at me. I turned, betrayed.

"It's me, Charlie."

There was a pale white face at the barred window.

"Mr. Schiller."

"*Ach,* it's me, all right."

"What are you doing in there?"

He sighed. "I guess I'm an enemy of the New Believers. Oh, that ain't the reason they gave me, but I'm in jail just the same."

"Why, they can't do things like that."

"Well, maybe not, but me and Vogel and a lot of others are in here, you bet. For our own good, they said." He passed a piece of paper out to me. "Could you maybe sneak this out and get it mailed for me? It's a letter to my daughter in Jersey. If she don't hear from me, she'll be worried. Once a week I write, always."

"I'll take care of it," I promised. "Now don't you worry, Mr. Schiller. Everything will work out, you'll see. These things happen sometimes, but I'm sure Brother Adrian will straighten it out."

"I hope so," the old man groaned. "*Ach,* my joints ache so! It's damp in here, Charlie, so damp."

Still with the pesky feeling that someone was watching me, I decided to put a bold face on it. If I was being watched, I'd have to make up a story. Waving good-bye to Mr. Schiller, I walked around the granary to the front where a guard was on duty.

"Good evening," I said.

He raised his lantern, looking at me sourly.

"It's after midnight. You got a pass to be roaming around at night?"

"I didn't know one was needed," I said truthfully. "I couldn't sleep, that was all, so I got up and took a stroll."

"It's a new order," he grunted. "Need a pass after sundown. There's been all kinds of trouble. Not git along and go to bed before I arrest you for suspicious behavior."

"Yes, sir," I said. "Yes, *sir.* Thank you, sir."

I hurried away, and slipped into the men's house unnoticed. Ordinarily an adventure like this would have left me excited and thrilled. Now, though, I was gloomy and depressed. Concordia, indeed. Why couldn't people get along together? There were serpents even in Eden.

~~~~~Chapter 12~~~~~

Much as I hated to confess it, Kara was my responsibility. Oh, she was older than me, that was true! A case could be made that she knew what she was doing. And Brother Adrian might not take kindly to me sticking my nose into theological matters. But still and all, she appeared to be in love with him. That could cause all kinds of trouble for her and for him too. That clinched it. I'd have to speak to Brother Adrian man to man. I'd go the lot.

One day I didn't ride out to the fields with the rest of the hands. Instead, I left the *Speisehaus* after breakfast, not having eaten more than a couple of eggs and some biscuits and a little fired *panhaas* with bacon. I had a dish of stewed peaches too, but my stomach was too nervous and upset to finish the crullers.

Club across his knees, one of the guards on the porch of the temple sat smoking his pipe. It was a fresh clear July morning, and a spiderweb across the climbing roses on the porch sparkled diamonds. The sun was barely up, and slanting shafts of orange lit the temple in bold relief. I took a deep breath and went up on the porch, making the sign of the circle for unity and then punching a hole in it with my finger for purpose.

"I want to see Brother Adrian."

The guard measured out three or four puffs on his pipe, and the blue gray smoke curled upward in the sun.

"That so?"

"Yes, it's so. I've got business to discuss with him. Important business."

"Got a pass?"

"No. I don't even know where you go to get one."

He shook his head. "Can't see him then."

Exasperated, I burst out, "But I've got to! It's important!"

He started rocking again. "That's what they all say."

"What the hell is this?" I demanded. "The Blessed Kingdom, or a damned jail? Why can't I see him?"

The guard was a New Believer—I remembered he sat next to me at supper one night and told me all about Philadelphia, where he used to work in a ropewalk down at Chestnut and the river—but he was getting a little put out.

"Get along now, boy! I got my orders, and I'm swore to protect and defend Brother Adrian. Besides, you got to have a pass, and you ain't got one. So git!" He raised his cudgel, pointing down the path to where the rest of the field workers were getting into the old Studebaker wagon.

"All right!" I snapped. "If you won't let me in peaceably on legitimate business—" I went into the wet grass and around to the side of the temple, hailing an open window. "Brother Adrian! It's me, Charlie Campion! I've got to see you!"

The guard rushed around, yelling and waving his club. "God damn it, boy, leave off that hollering! You want me to get in trouble? I declare, there ain't no reasoning with young folks nowadays. Now you git, before I tan your britches!"

He swung at my legs, but I hopped over the arc of the stick, still yelling at the top of my lungs for Brother Adrian.

"I've got to see you! Please, Brother Adrian!"

It was a sacrilegious thing to do, all right. Everyone was running this way and that, upset. The people getting into the wagon paused, staring. Fat Henry ran toward me, gathering his long robe up about his knees and yelling. The guard got an arm around my neck, but I still kept roaring in a strangled kind of way. Just as my eyes were about to pop out of my head, Brother Adrian looked out of the window. He had a sort of Hindu turban-looking thing on and seemed very calm and peaceful in spite of the ruckus going on in his back yard.

"Who is it, Herman?"

The guard loosed his grip, and I gasped in a lungful of air. "It's me, sir! Charlie. Charlie Campion. I've got to see you, Brother Adrian. It's very important."

Huffing and puffing, *der Grosser Henner* galloped up. "Put him in the granary, Herman, and let him cool off a bit! Young jackanapes!" He raised his sweating face toward the open window. "I'm sorry this happened, Brother Adrian. Troublemakers all round anymore. I'll just—"

Brother Adrian raised a hand. Then he signed to Fat Henry. "Let him come up."

Fat Henry goggled. "Let him come up?"

"Yes."

Shaking his head, Fat Henry motioned to the guard. "Search him first, Herman. He may be carrying weapons."

"Weapons?" I howled in disbelief.

"That's right." Fat Henry helped Herman look. He slapped me on the rump and stuck his fat fingers in my shirt pocket but didn't find anything but the rattles off a snake I'd killed and a petrified bug Ike Coogan had picked up in the Arizona Territory. There was a piece of string too and a mashed cruller and a stub of a pencil and the butt of an old stogie I'd been sneaking drags on but not liking much. In the Blessed Kingdom only the grown men could smoke tobacco.

"I guess you're satisfied," I said. "Unless maybe you could figure out a way I could hurt someone with a cigar butt."

Fat Henry glowered at me, his eyes hard, glassy pebbles in the folds of flesh, but he turned me loose. With great dignity I shot my cuffs, dusted the seat of my pants, and walked away—onto the porch, into the musty interior of the temple, up the dark stairs, and I knocked at Brother Adrian's door.

"Come in," he called.

I was scared; my palms were wet and my knees trembled. But Brother Adrian was smiling. Sitting at the big table spread with books and papers and documents, he motioned to a chair.

"Sit down."

"Thank you," I said.

That first night it was all kind of spooky and scary, but this morning was different. Sunlight came in the window, a breeze ruffled the papers, Brother Adrian's face was kind and concerned.

"Now what is it, Charlie?"

I took a deep breath, and swallowed hard. "Please, sir," I said. "What—what are your intentions toward Kara?"

He looked surprised, and pursed his lips.

"Your . . . sister?"

"Yes, sir."

His pale face seemed cut in stone. *Now I've put my foot in it,* I thought. Charlie Campion, world's premier blatherskite! I'd been a fool, as I often was. But it was too late to back out now; I was fair caught.

"You know," I mumbled on, "we've always been very close, Kara and me. You—you can understand how I feel, us two being alone in the world together. Mama always made me promise to take care of her, even though I was the younger by a year."

Lightning would probably blast me right where I stood. I hoped the sisters at the orphanage could spare an occasional prayer for me. How much did Brother Adrian know or suspect? I had a frantic mental picture of him bent over the *Erdspiegel,* discovering in its glassy depths my duplicity.

"Do you know," Brother Adrian said in his deepest voice, "that I am sworn to celibacy? That the leader of the Blessed Kingdom must live on a plane far above the carnal world of men? That I dwell in the pure air of spirit and intellect only?"

"Yes." I gulped. "I've heard that. But—"

"But what?"

Rashly I blurted out my suspicions.

"Well, you're still only human, too. So am I. So are we all. And Kara is a handsome girl and very loving. I wouldn't give you much for the rest of the Twelve Virgins—if they're virgins it isn't hard to see why. But Kara is different, Brother Adrian! You can see that!"

The stern lines of his face relaxed, and it looked like he was going to smile. "Yes, I can see that, Charlie."

"Well, then—"

He got up and went to the window, staring out at the Blessed Kingdom: the black fields high with corn, the freshly white-washed buildings, the pastures where cattle grazed. Out of respect I rose too. Finally he turned toward me with a sigh.

"Youth is always worth listening to. Young people haven't yet grown handy with duplicity and cunning, and they speak a noble truth out of habit." He sat down, chin in hand, the soft luminous eyes fixed on me. His voice was soft too, mesmeric. "Charlie, I'll put it this way. Kara will never have cause to regret at my hands."

How could I ever have doubted him? How could I ever think he would betray Kara?

"I knew it," I said.

"I've convinced you, then?"

"Yes, sir. You wouldn't knowingly hurt her or me or anyone. I know that now."

"I wish the rest would believe that. Their own good—that's all I have in mind. And with the great responsibilities I bear, it's hard to press forward with all the gossip and trouble and recrimination." He spun the globe with his finger. "They can't see what I'm trying to do. They're too hard, too set in their ways, to have a dream anymore. Look"—he pointed to some place in Europe—"here they cross themselves with the whole hand. Religious wars have been fought over the difference—homes burned, armies locked in combat, women and children slaughtered."

It did seem silly.

"Here." He pointed to Asia. "These people won't eat cows. The people next to them won't eat pigs. They kill each other over the difference."

How childish my fears about Kara had been! I felt mean and ignoble. This great man was above all that; he was locked in combat with the Prince of Darkness himself!

"Form, they seek, not substance. Theology they beg for, not religion. Ceremony they desire, and they smile and prance while Old Nick feasts on their souls. Charlie, do *you* see my grand scheme? Do you see how we must make a start at rooting out all the claptrap and superstition and ignorance and pomp and deceit? Love, that's all we need! Love is the answer to it all! Love alone will conquer man's soul and prepare him for whatever hereafter may be! The rich emotion of love, so cheap, so available—love of man for woman, parent for child, brother for sister, mother for son—love is all!"

Spellbound, I nodded. Love! Love! Love! O magic word, O great discovery, O heavenly love! I was ready to roll on the floor in ecstasy but restrained myself. Brother Adrian, I knew, loved old Mr. Schiller and peppery little Mr. Vogel and all the rest too; that was why they were living a protected life in the granary.

"You—you'll win out," I predicted breathlessly. "You've just *got* to! Once people understand—"

"It's a hard road I travel, Charlie. I wish I could convince them all the way I have you. But your mind is fresh and young and open. Those people—" He gestured toward the buffalo-wool factory; through the open windows I could see people sitting idly, talking, visiting. "Idleness breeds discontent. I fight it every day, all day. Oh, how my great plan is brought low!"

Buffalo . . . Buffalo-woo! . . . Something Ike Coogan had said came back to me: *Plenty of 'em in the draws and coulees.* Then I had said, *There's got to be a way.* Suddenly the idea hit me like a box of stove-lids.

"A balloon!" I shouted.

Brother Adrian was startled.

"A balloon!" I insisted.

Oh, what a marvelous idea! My brains swam with the shock of it. I remembered the day the count took me up along the river near Mauckport. We could see all over the state! Towns, fields, threshing crews way over toward Laconia; why, it was like the whole state of Indiana laid out at your feet! Why wouldn't the same thing work in Nebraska? I could spot buffalo for Ike—for a whole crew of hunters! The buffalo-wool factory would hum night and day; people would be busy and contented; the Blessed Kingdom would prosper both materially and spiritually: much of the great burden would be lifted from Brother Adrian's frail shoulders.

"A balloon!" I shouted. "We'll build a balloon!"

Quickly, words falling all over each other in my eagerness to explain, I told him about Count Kasimir Blatski and my apprenticeship in ballooning. I may have blown up my part a little bit, but most of it was true. Especially the part about how far we could see from the dizzy elevation of the *Petit Géant.*

"And it will work the same way here! Imagine—it's the greatest thing since railway cars! We'll hunt buffalo by *balloon!* Why, it's bound to revolutionize the buffalo business and make the Blessed Kingdom a household word!"

Frowning, Brother Adrian tugged at a side-whisker. "But do you know how to *make* a balloon?"

Well, I didn't know *everything,* but I wasn't going to let a few details stand in the way of the spiritual health of the community.

"Count Blatski gave me all his secrets—how to cut the cloth in gores and sew it, the formula for balloon-varnish, the secret mixture for the cement to fix holes and rips—the whole thing!"

Brother Adrian closed his eyes and sat motionless for a long time, rubbing the bridge of his nose. "It might be a diversion; something to keep their minds off troublemaking and gossip."

"It's more than that," I pointed out. "It's salvation! It's success!" Feeling him waver, I drove in the clincher. "It's almost like some Great Omnipotence chose me as the instrument to deliver us all!"

"Eh?" He looked sharply at me.

"I'm filled with love," I modestly admitted. "The Great Omnipotence has come on me and given me a vision." I made the ritual circle in the air. "Unity." I punched a hole in it with my forefinger. "Purpose." I was going to have a balloon or know the reason why. "Praise be!"

"Yes," Brother Adrian murmured. "Yes, indeed. Praise be. Well, all right. I—I'll arrange the details. Help, material, a barn to work in. We've got a few bolts of cotton sheeting—"

"Can Ike Coogan help me?"

"If you want him. He's not doing anything for his money right now, that's for sure!"

Oh, rapture! We might even get a patent on the idea! Dizzy with vision, I rose to go. But Brother Adrian called me back.

"Just a minute, Charlie."

I paused. "Sir?"

His voice had a sudden hardness. "Fall is coming on, and the buffalo are prime right now after a summer on the range. If your balloon idea is a success, we stand on the threshold of a Golden Age in our Blessed Kingdom. So I wouldn't want anything to go wrong."

What did he mean? "No, sir," I said. "I'll work hard."

"I think you will." His voice was sharp as an iron nail. "Perhaps you will work so hard you will have no time to shinny up rainspouts into the temple at night to visit the Virgins! There will not even be time to mail letters for our erring brothers who are in protective detainment. Do you understand?"

I gulped. Someone *had* been watching me that night! Or did Brother Adrian see me in the *Erdspiegel?*

"Yes, sir," I said. "I understand."

From just an ordinary field hand, I became an important person in Concordia-on-the-Platte: the Boy Who Was Building the Balloon. Brother Adrian set aside an old shed for the balloon manufacture; I supervised the activities of a doubtful Ike Coogan; sewing ladies; a tinsmith; an old sailor named Mr. Jimson, who knew all about ropes and rigging and cordage. No longer did I sleep in the mens' house, having instead a pallet in a partitioned-off cubbyhole in the shed, where I also drew elaborate construction plans with the aid of instruments and a T-square. Us being so busy, Brother Adrian sent down an order to the *Speisehaus* to deliver our meals to the balloon-shed, although we were still required to eat separately; Ike and Mr. Jimson and the tinsmith and me at one table, the sewing ladies at the other.

Some people weren't too happy about what we were doing, and there was muttering about us being favored. One angry lady stuck her head in the doorway and sniffed scornfully.

"A balloon, my lands! If man was meant to fly he'd have been given wings, *nicht wahr?* Answer me that, now." She didn't appear to be addressing anyone in particular, but an Irishman doesn't need much excuse to strike up a conversation.

"Mrs. Winkelman," I said, "for a long time I've ridden out to the fields with your husband in a wagon. If we were meant to get out to the tomatoes that way, wouldn't we have been given wheels?"

Her nose came up in the air like a shiny battle-axe, and she glared at me.

"It's against nature, that's what it is! Devil's work. There'll be trouble, you'll see!"

"But Mrs. Winkelman—"

She turned her scorn on my sewing ladies. "You, Effie! And Violet, and Emmie Neiswander! Shame! Shame on all of you! My stars, I don't know what this wicked world is coming to."

"Ma'am," I said, "we're awful busy—"

"Don't threaten me!" she cried. "Beelzebub, that's what you are! Fire and brimstone! I smell it on you!"

It was probably just some flowers of sulphur I was mixing into the secret patching cement. But I couldn't have her disorganizing my workmen, so I had to close the door in her face.

"Well, I never!"

I heard her gasp and then stomp away. Ike looked relieved, and the sewing ladies went back to stitching the gores of cloth I'd laid out from a paper pattern.

"Don't mind her," I said.

One of the sewing ladies looked up at me and then quickly away.

"They said the magnetic telegraph was evil too. They thought the steamboat was wicked. A preacher even spoke out against

Mr. Brady's photographs, said they were graven images, and an abomination to the Lord. Wasn't that ridiculous?"

I wasn't at all sure they agreed with me, but they kept on sewing and that was what counted. Thousands of tiny stitches. Tens of thousands of tinier stitches. It seemed like we would never get done.

Ike Coogan wasn't convinced, either. He worked hard enough, pumping the bellows for the smith who was making the brass stove, helping old Mr. Jimson with the cordage, smearing cement on the seams, but he was melancholy.

"Ike," I said, "don't you believe in balloons?"

He scratched his crotch thoughtfully.

"Well, *don't* you?"

"You sure there *are* such things, Charlie?"

"Of course. I rode in one didn't I?"

"What holds it up?"

I tried to explain Archimedes' principle to him, but it was like trying to tell a hog about Sunday.

"I can see how it works in water," he conceded. "Hell, that's all a boat is, ain't it? But—"

"But what?"

"Well, air ain't water!"

"Of course it isn't!" I cried. "But the principle is the same!"

"Well, if you say so, Charlie. You're a bright boy, and been to school."

"You still don't believe it!" I protested.

"Birds fly," Ike said mildly. "They flap their wings, and that's how they stay up. But I never seen no bird just stand still and float right up in the air."

"That's different!"

"Besides," Ike said, with the air of a parent humoring a troublesome child, "I can float in water. I don't cotton much to water, but oncet I did it on a dare. But how come me not to float in air, if it's the same principle? Answer me that, old hoss!"

So exasperated with his obstinacy that for once I couldn't say a word, I spluttered like fat on a hot griddle.

"No," Ike said sagely, cleaning dirt out of his nails with the old Green River knife, "this child has got to be showed. Of course, I ain't saying it ain't *possible*. Lord, I seen many a sight *you* wouldn't believe, Charlie. Did I ever tell you about this old Shoshone woman I seen up on the Yellowstone? Believe it or not, she was born with two heads! My, it was comical;

she'd hold long palavers with herself, and take both sides to an argument. Oh, I tell you—"

"Get out of here!" I cried. "Go help Mr. Jimson or something. Why I don't go out of my mind I'll never tell you, with all the liars and idiots around here!"

Not that I was so sure myself that the *Petit Géant II* would fly; I was beset by doubt and not nearly so confident as I tried to appear. When everyone else was gone I would slump over my latest batch of plans, sustained only by a flickering candle and a pot of sour black coffee. What in the hell had I gotten myself into, with my flannel-mouthed dreams? Count Blatski had been the world's premier aeronaut, and he'd taught me himself. But Count Blatski wasn't here to help me. This was my project, my undertaking. If the balloon didn't fly, it was on my head.

Eyes bleared from lack of sleep, bone-tired, shaken by unaccustomed responsibility, apprehensive at the growing pile of neatly-stitched cotton panels, I dozed at my worktable. I don't know how long I slept, but I awoke with a start, trembling from a nightmare in which Archimedes' principle had been revoked by the Congress and no one had told me about it. I tottered out into a rose-streaked dawn, sloshed water from a pitcher over my head, and shivered wetly. *Lord,* I thought. *Great Omnipotence. Love! Whatever Your Name Is. Make it work. Make it fly. Please take it in your hands on that day and draw it up into your sky!*

Brother Adrian trusted me, though, far more than I did myself. His trust led to complications, however. Count Blatski's balloon had been a two thousand meter balloon; on a moderately cool day the original *Petit Géant* had plenty of lift for an aeronaut and a passenger, scientific instruments, even lunch in a hamper and a few bottles of wine. But my little *Petit Géant II* was only one thousand meters displacement, about thirty-five feet in diameter. To cut down weight I had figured everything to the ounce. Where Count Blatski's balloon had a roomy wicker basket, mine had a tiny wooden seat like a child's swing, with my feet left to dangle. The boiler was not good stout iron, but paper-thin sheets of brass riveted together. Even the cloth was flimsy—thin cotton with only the lightest film of varnish. But my balloon *should* fly, especially if I followed my plan of eating and drinking nothing for three days prior to the flight. I didn't weigh too much to start with and by this last stratagem hoped to lose five pounds. But then Brother

Adrian made a state visit to our balloon manufactory, bringing disaster with him. The first I knew of it was two heavenly harpers plinking away down the road, followed by the Twelve Virgins carrying that *Erdspiegel* on a kind of sedan-chair, Brother Adrian bringing up the rear.

"How do you like it, Charlie?"

He had the sewing ladies hold it up, all fifty feet of it, an ornate embroidered banner that said LOVE LOVE LOVE LOVE LOVE along it, appliquéd white silk letters against a field of green velvet, all stitched in gold thread.

"Quite a surprise, isn't it? I've had the Virgins working on it for a week!"

"But—but—"

"Right around the middle of your balloon, where everyone will see it! Oh, I know there's been grumbling about the balloon idea, but they'll forget that when you soar into the sky with this lovely banner catching the sunlight!"

"It's awful heavy," I said.

"Silk. And gold. Fitting materials for a heavenly sentiment."

"But—"

"Don't you see, Charlie? It makes the whole thing right! It was a masterstroke. It came to me right out of the *Erdspiegel!* I looked and saw you soaring into the sky—oh, so high! And there was this beautiful banner shining in the sun. Love, Charlie! Love, love, love!"

Well, who was I to argue with the *Erdspiegel?*

"Yes, sir," I said helplessly. "It's a beautiful banner."

After he and his party had gone, I spent a long time figuring weights all over again. The *Petit Géant II* might—it just might— stagger into the air if the day were cool, if there was no wind, if I could get the boiler fire hot enough without melting the thin brass plates ... if ... if ...

I dropped the pencil and chewed my nails for a while. It looked like I'd better stop eating and drinking today—right now. I wasn't hungry anyway.

Chapter 13

When Kara and I first came to the Blessed Kingdom, Sunday church was an impressive and soul-stirring experience. The sisters at the orphanage would never have approved of me going there, but it was Christian, it was devout, and it filled a void in my unchurched hide. Now, with the unrest and trouble, Sunday church was more like a battlefield than a time of grace. Each Sunday Brother Adrian became grimmer and shouted louder; each Sunday the congregation grew surlier and more uncooperative.

"I am grieved," Brother Adrian shouted from the pulpit, "that you do not, or will not, understand! Love! All faiths have glorified love, unselfish, unquestioning love such as I bear for you stubborn misguided lambs. Cast away suspicion and bickering, and politicking; forget worldly vanities; abandon hate and suspicion and mistrust! Love, instead, do you hear? Love, *love*, LOVE!"

He made it plain they were going to love everybody or he'd bash some heads. That didn't go down well with the brothers. One got right up in church and demanded an accounting of the Kingdom's funds.

"Understand," he said, "I ain't claiming there's been any crookedness; we all know you love us, Brother Adrian, and wouldn't hurt *anyone.* But I say we deserve, we *demand* an accounting of the money and property we all turned over when we come here." He turned to the congregation. "Ain't that right?"

Some called out "For shame!" and were indignant. Others—the majority, it seemed to me—cried "He's right!" and nodded and whispered among themselves.

"This," Brother Adrian yelled, out of all patience, "is a house of worship! It's sacrilege to speak of money-changing in a church of a Sunday! Why, the Devil has got into you folks, and I must cast him out!" Folding his hands and glowering skyward, he took off on a long prayer for their stunted and blackened souls. Bit by bit the muttering and complaining stopped. Only he could have done it; I never heard a man with such a gift of persuasion. It had been a narrow squeak, but he made it. Looking ashamed, the congregation straggled out. But their contrition wouldn't last. The trouble was growing. I had to get the *Petit Géant II* in the air for Brother Adrian as soon as possible. That was the best way for me to help.

One hot September noon Ike Coogan walked into the shed with a shrouded bundle and a mysterious look. He wouldn't tell me what was in the bundle, only rolled his eyes and smirked.

"You'll see."

"When?"

"Come dinner time, I reckon."

The sewing-women seemed to be in on the secret too, for they giggled and sneaked glances at me while they were setting up the boards and trestles and putting out the plates and cups and knives and forks.

"Ike," I asked, "is this some special day?"

"I expect somewhere in the world it is."

"Something unusual for dinner, then?"

"I guess you could say that."

"Why do you have to be so damned mysterious?"

Grinning, he fondled his mangy mustache. "Some is given to know, Charlie, and others to find out."

I'd get nothing from *him,* that was apparent. And dinner from the *Speisehaus* was very ordinary—green beans boiled with ham hocks, a pan of cornbread, sliced tomatoes, and a galvanized pot of strong black tea.

"Well," I said, pushing back my chair, "time to get back to work! Mr. Jimson, I've changed the plans for the cordage a little. This afternoon I'll show you how—"

"Just a minute," Ike interrupted. He got to his feet, and placed the bundle before him. "You just sit tight, coon. I got a little palavering to do before the whistle blows."

There was a spatter of giggles.

"Now there's a lot of important days in a man's life." Ike folded his hands under his coattails and preened himself like a turkey gobbler. "There's Christmas time and Easter and Independence Day—oh, just *lots* of important days!"

They all applauded this stirring sentiment.

"But today is the best day." Ike unwrapped the package. A cake! A birthday cake, frosted green and yellow and pink and white, with seventeen candles stuck into it. "Happy Birthday, Charlie, from us all!"

Oh, I was moved! To think—all the way out here on the Platte River, good thoughtful people remembered my birthday. I could hardly talk for the lump in my throat. Ike lit the candles, and they all cheered when I blew them out.

"It was really Kara's idea," Ike whispered, handing me a note. "This comes with it, old hoss."

After I'd shook hands all round and acknowledged the congratulations and good wishes, I found time in a corner of the shed to read the dainty note:

> *Dearest Charlie:*
>   *Happy, Happy seventeenth birthday! I'm sorry I couldn't be there, but Brother Adrian doesn't like for me to leave the temple. But happy birthday anyway! I only hope you are as contented as I am, for I have you to thank for bringing me here where all is love. Bless you, Charlie, and have many more happy birthdays.*

Such fine friends: Ike, Kara, Brother Adrian, all the rest! Such wonderful people here in the Blessed Kingdom! I don't know why I was so uneasy, but I was.

As the proper medicine for worry, I literally threw myself into the balloon work. My fingers became raw from sewing, my knuckles burned from the heat of soldering brass, my hands swelled from the stickery bits of hempen rope that worked their way into them. My eyes grew red and bleared from the forge smoke and lack of sleep, my body turned into one great throbbing ache, each muscle contributing a twinge. We all worked long and late; they grumbled and complained, and Ike threatened to go and live with the Brule Dacotahs, but we finished on time. Tomorrow was the day, the Great Day. The first of October, to go down in history. A majestic free levitation to a few hundred feet, the gradual dissipation of the balloon's lofting powers, a dignified sinking—back to earth accompanied by the cheers and huzzahs of the astonished brothers. Balloon Day!

I couldn't sleep. Sometime before dawn I rose and dressed and heated leftover coffee on the forge. Though it was cold and dark, I went outside and stood trembling till dawn came.

There it was, all my work, all *our* work. This was the scene of—triumph? Or failure. Clasping my hands round the warm tin cup, I shivered again. Before a next dawn, I would be Charlie Campion, aeronaut, or That Boy Who Built the Balloon That Wouldn't Go Up.

The gray light heightened, then came hints of pink. A pale yellow wash suffused the sky, and turned to gold. The scene lost some of its stark line-drawing aspect and took on fullness and roundness, tangibility, another dimension, even hope and promise. At last a shaft of sunlight slanted through the trees and warmed my back and shoulders. I began to feel better.

There was the rough wooden dais where Brother Adrian and the Virgins were to sit. Over to one side was an old stove with a hand-cranked blower fitted to it, and a canvas tube leading to the appendix of the balloon. It was my idea—a quick way to bring about initial inflation of the *Petit Géant II*.

I'd had another idea too. Rather than let the collapsed balloon lie on the ground, I suspended it from a rope that ran between two tall elm trees. The theory was that, thus suspended, the balloon would take hot air more readily and fill faster. I never lacked for ideas; telling which were the good ones was my trouble.

Hanging from the limp bundle of balloon was my trapeze-perch, with a trail-rope tying it by a slipknot to a stake driven into the ground. Above the swing-seat was the little brass stove within easy reach and a burlap bag of dry twigs to keep the fire stoked. All was ready. All, that is, except the aeronaut.

In spite of the cheering sun, in spite of the neat workmanlike appearance of the balloon, a clammy hand enfolded my heart and clamped the vital pulsing to a murmur. Suppose it didn't work! Suppose the *Petit Géant II* just hung there from the suspending cable and blandly refused to take me aloft! And with all those people watching!

I looked wildly around. I could still get away before the fateful hour. No one was yet on the scene. I could run away. I *would* run away! In panic I stumbled from the awful scene and ran headlong into Ike Coogan.

He grasped me by the arm and peered into my face.

"Charlie, are you sick or something?"

"No," I lied, avoiding his gaze. "What makes you think that?"

"You look funny."

I pushed him away, trying a joke. "You're no work of art yourself."

"Maybe so, but I don't look like no case of the consumptions, either."

"I've been up all night. I'm just tired."

He took a stone flask out of his possibles bag and uncorked it.

"Anyway," I asked, "what are you doing down here so early?"

"Here, take a sip of this." He held the flask out to me, and his hand trembled a little.

"What is it?" I sniffed; it smelled rancid. "Rum?"

"The best. Paid a dollar for a gallon. This is the last."

I waved it away. "I'm all right, Ike. Besides, I need to keep a clear head."

He shrugged, and took a swallow himself; then another, another, and three more. Finally the rum was gone, and he threw the bottle away and belched. "Well, *I* feel better, anyway! I tell you, this balloon business is hard on an old man. It will go up, won't it, Charlie?"

"Yes," I said. "It will."

He nodded, with a deep sigh of relief.

"That's good. I trust you, Charlie. You're a smart one."

A little off-center in his gait, he walked away to inspect the dangling balloon. Suddenly the tight-wound spring in my chest seemed to come loose and run down. Ike had been as scared about the balloon as me! It would work, of course it would work! Who could ever doubt it? I felt almost gay and danced a little jig.

At nine in the morning I had old Mr. Jimson start a coal fire in the big stove, and he and Ike spelled each other cranking the blower. Impatient, I stared at the *Petit Géant II,* watching for the least ripple, a swelling, a disturbance of the folds of fabric. Nothing! The thing hung limp and dead. The ascension was scheduled for noon, when all the hands would be allowed to come in from the fields.

"Faster!" I ordered. "Crank faster! Mr. Jimson, put on more coal."

People began to straggle into the stands. The sun rose higher, while I begrudged every golden ray. The cooler the outside air, the more lift my balloon would have.

"Faster!" I urged Ike. "Crank faster!"

"God damn it!" Ike complained. "My pore old back is broke already, and I got a blister on top of a blister!"

Mr. Jimson wiped his brow. "Charlie, the stove is red hot. We'll burn her up!"

"Don't worry about that," I said. "Here—let me crank awhile."

The sun grew hotter, and the damned balloon hung like wetwash on a line. Would it ever fill?

Ike whispered in my ear. "Here comes his High and Mightiness and his court."

Down the road marched the Virgins in stately procession, carrying the *Erdspiegel*. Brother Adrian followed, wearing his turban and carrying a kind of ornamented shepherd's crook. Kara brought up the rear, carrying the train of his long state robe.

"Here, take the handle," I said to Ike, and went over to greet Brother Adrian.

"Everything all right, Charlie?"

"Yes, sir," I said.

"I hope all goes well."

"I hope so too."

He touched my arm with his jewelled crook. "I don't need to tell you how important this is to me. To *all* of us. Do you love that balloon?"

"Oh, I do, indeed, sir. It's everything to me."

"That's good," he said and made the mystic circle, and pushed his finger through it. "Unity. Purpose. And *love*. Love, love, love!"

"Yes, sir," I said. "You're absolutely right."

The crowd made a quick incredulous noise, a sort of gasp or sigh. I wheeled round with a premonition of disaster. Brother Adrian, excited, pointed with his crook. "There! Look at that!"

I gulped in relief and knew what had happened. I'd seen it

before, with Count Blatski's balloon. The pressure had built up in the *Petit Géant II,* which was so twisted and folded back on itself that it stuck together obstinately and would not fill and round. Finally the stuck-together folds had freed themselves with an audible popping sound; hot air rushed in, and already my creation was half-rounded and pregnant-looking—pregnant with fire and smoke and heat, tugging at the anchor-rope. Around the equator hung the green and white and gold LOVE LOVE LOVE banner, looking very pretty in the sun. I hurried back and sat in my little trapeze-seat. Thump! My weight pulled the balloon down hard. That damned banner! But by shoving off with my foot, I could tell there was lift—considerable lift.

"Faster!" I ordered. "More coal!" I lit the twigs in the brass stove over my head so as to add to the lift. "Crank harder, Ike!"

He wiped his dripping face with a rag, howling with the indignity of it all. "God damn it, how come me to get mixed up in such a crazy business? I swear, I must have caught softening of the brains!"

"Don't talk," I urged. "Crank!"

He and Mr. Jimson both had hold of the crank now; the two of them were winded and seemed to be using the handle for support instead of turning. But aided by the brass stove over my head the *Petit Géant II* drifted upward, and tugged at the anchor rope.

"Keep cranking!" I implored. "Don't stop now! She's going up!"

I pulled the slipknot, and the balloon shot into the air. Unaccountably it stopped again, quivering and surging; my legs dangled ten feet off the ground. The cheering of the crowd died to a perplexed murmur.

Ike waved his hands and shouted. "Keep going, God damn it!"

"Something's wrong," I said. "I—I'm stuck!"

Mr. Jimson's white-fringed face stared up at me. "How could that be?" Bewildered, he scratched his head. Then he brightened. Good old Mr. Jimson! "Why you're probably caught under the rope that runs between the trees!" He ran back for a look and nodded vigorously. "That's it, all right! Here, Ike, give me a hand!"

Together they tugged at the trailing ground rope, dragging the plump bulk of the balloon out from under the rope suspended between the trees. I swung in my perch like a clock pendulum and hung on for dear life. Suddenly the *Petit Géant II* pulled free and shot like a bullet into the clear October sky. I was off—and away!

With all my big talk, I was petrified. Up, up, up I soared! Too frightened to look, I grabbed all the ropes I could find and clutched them to my breast, screwing my eyes shut. Would this dizzy ascent never stop? I could feel the seat pushing hard against my bottom, and knew the balloon was still accelerating. Count Blatski's balloon had never acted like this! It had always furnished a sedate, comfortable ride. In panic I reached over my head and scattered the twigs out of the brass stove, burning my fingers but not caring. That should slow down this crazy balloon.

After a while it seemed I was not rising quite so fast. Cautiously I opened my eyes. Fearing what I might see, I did not dare to look directly down. Instead, I squinted off into the distance and gradually willed my eyes to open full-bore.

There was the whole Blessed Kingdom off to the east— tiny houses and postage-stamp-sized fields; black antlike dots that must be people! I could see the balloon-shed, the wooden stands, and a stippled tide of the antlike dots streaming across the prairie in vain pursuit of me. The great muddy curve of the Platte wound like a brown snake in the distance. Ribbons of road, patches of trees like a nubbly rug. I was aloft, thrillingly aloft, suspended in space like the eye of God!

Carefully I looked down, straight down, between my dangling feet. It would not have been so bad if a nosy crow did not at that moment flap squawking below me—far below, and he was a *bird!* My senses reeled, my stomach writhed; I became giddy again and hung on for dear life, clamping to the ropes like a leech.

After a while the dizziness passed. Now I could look down again, framing the green earth by my dangling boots, and enjoy the view.

Judging from my speedy westerly progress a wind was blowing aloft, though traveling with it as I was there was no sound, no sensation of movement. Away to the east, Concordia-on-the-Platte sank below a tree-studded rise. A whole new world wheeled into being under me. I was ashamed of former doubt. Fly? She could never fail to fly! All fire and vapor and pulsing spirit, my balloon was a creature of the air, drawing sustenance from the heavens!

Buffalo? There were plenty of them. One here grazing in a sunlit valley; over there, half-hidden in a thicket, three more. A dozen, at least, at the edge of a leafy grove; several more up a narrow draw. From my vantage point they were clearly all over the place! Ike Coogan was right. Now, with my magic balloon, I would direct the campaign of the buffalo-hunters— six, a dozen, maybe even companies and regiments of buffalo-hunters. We would scour Nebraska clean of the shaggy beasts; not one of them would escape my probing aerial eye. Thrilled with the prospect, I screamed a warning at one fat bull directly below me, cocking my finger and yelling "Bang!" So far did sound carry from my aerial cockpit that he tossed his head, looked wildly round, and galloped away.

When I planned my glorious flight I had not intended to travel so far. Now, faintly alarmed, I scanned the racing earth and wondered where I was. Shadows lengthened, the air was cooling, my balloon was losing lift. The great plain could not be more than a hundred feet below. Where was I? What should I do?

I was no longer elated. Instead, I stared at the wind-stroked grasses and felt lonely. In the first flush of my aerial odyssey nature seemed benign and courteous; now the lowering clouds, the wind-rippled plain, the purpling shadows, all these awed me, taking on new and frightening significance. They were no longer landscape, they were threatening presences, individual and mighty. Lost on the prairie! Why, oh why, hadn't I thought things through! At the very least I could have ascended on a rope and been pulled down again in safety. It was after all only a demonstration. But no, I wanted to fly like a bird, and now here I was, God knew where! I felt suddenly cold and afraid. Indians, too—there might be bloodthirsty Red Indians down there, hidden in the tall grass, marking my progress and waiting only till I brushed the earth to rush on me, riddle me with arrows, rip off my scalp!

Below me more woolly buffalo grazed in a tree-shaded meadow. Spraddle-legged on a knoll, a great bull saw me; he bellowed a challenge and pawed the earth as I drifted not a dozen feet over his wet black nose. At noontime these beasts had seemed picturesque toys in a fairy landscape; now they were dark and menacing. The guardian bull was a black troll, daring me to trespass on his shaded and lowering world. Trembling, I clung tightly to my ropes, waiting for the moment of contact—and reckoning.

Lower and lower sped my *Petit Géant II,* the stiff breeze driving it scudding over the plain. Now my feet almost touched the grass. How would I stop the force and energy of the balloon? Over my head the bulk of it towered, an enormous sail. I was an unlucky mariner blown toward a wild and desolate shore.

The decision came sooner than I cared to make it. Still in my seat, I hit the earth in a wild skid, and was dragged into a thicket of willows. Branches caught at me, stabbed me, finally combed me free of the balloon and its dangling ropes and cordage. The balloon rolled on, bouncing and heaving, a giant's plaything.

Frantically I disengaged myself from the trap of willows and ran after my balloon. I seemed not to be too damaged; no bones were broken, else I could not have run so fast. On the balloon rolled, surging and bounding, flinging high in the air its cordage as it revolved. "Wait!" I howled in desperation. The LOVE LOVE LOVE banner tore loose and unrolled in the grass. A gust tossed it high and blew it in my face, wrapping me like a shroud. "Wait!" I commanded. "Stop! Damn it, stop!"

Next time I would plan my descent. Now I could only stumble and curse and lose ground in the race. Only an accident stopped the chase. The network of cordage snagged in a thicket of stumpy bushes; the balloon tugged hard, tugged again, and lay spent and heaving, reined in by its own ropes.

Nevertheless, I still had a problem. The wind was strong, and the *Petit Géant II* continued to pull at the ropes. To prevent further damage, I ripped the trailing appendix light with my hands, letting warm light air spill out. Then I floundered up on the stranded whale, pulling myself along by the netting so that the weight of my body helped force out more air. Slowly the bulk dwindled; the balloon shuddered and gasped, and tossed dying about.

For safety I tied an extra line to another clump of bushes. Then I threw myself on the last great bubble of fabric near the crown of the balloon. Riding the bubble down, I suddenly blanched and let out a squawk. Until now hidden by the bulk of the balloon, a band of silent painted savages watched me with interest. There were a dozen or more, carrying lances and muskets and war-bows and skin shields. Indians! Merciless Red Indians!

Chapter 14

Gently the expiring balloon laid me down on the wrinkled fabric. For a moment I lay motionless, waiting for the lance-thrust, the blast of a musket, the steel chop of a hatchet. Or did they scalp you first? The skin on my head tingled with anticipation of the encircling gash, but nothing happened. I stared glassy-eyed at the ring of moccasins, bare brown toes, braceleted ankles.

"Aaargh," one of them said. I winced as something hard prodded my ribs, but it was only the leather-wrapped butt of a lance. "Aaargh!" the man insisted, and gestured to me to rise.

Weak-kneed and clammy-handed, I did so. My mouth seemed filled with cotton, my throat was dry and constricted; the very air I breathed tasted old and funereal.

I raised a hand, palm out, and croaked, "How!" Wasn't that what you were supposed to remark? "How! How?"

Silently they circled, looking me over from head to toe. One felt my upper arm and grunted. Another made me open my mouth and looked in. A third felt the homespun stuff of my breeches. Then their interest turned to the flattened corpse of the *Petit Géant II*. One of them stepped on it gingerly, slunk about it for a while, and then suddenly jumped in the air as if the fabric had burned his naked feet. Muttering, he drove his lance again and again into the fabric. Another went jaunting down the slope and returned trailing the LOVE LOVE LOVE banner. Wrapping himself in the silken folds he tried several styles, and was not pleased with any of them, it seemed.

"Aaargh!" the principal man said again, gesturing. He appeared to be some kind of a chief, and had a fur hat with a set of polished buffalo-horns, and a wrinkled sagging face like a bloodhound. In response to his gesture, I sat down, cross-legged like a Turk, wondering what was to happen to me. Did they eat people? Or was that the black cannibals of the Congo?

They squatted round me in an impassive ring. The sun went smokily down in the west, the bloody rays lighting their bodies in odd and bizarre ways. Not being dressed for a Nebraska October, I wore only a thin shirt and a pair of cotton pants, and shivered from the cold. No, I might as well be honest; most of the trembling came from fear. I was scared, scared out of my wits. What did they want of me? What must I do?

"Aaargh!" the chief rumbled. I jumped guiltily, but his attention was apparently not on me. Instead, one of the party rose and drew off a little distance where he made a fire from twigs. Drawing a half-dozen furry blood-spattered rabbits from a bag, he gutted them, skinned them, and spread them on a rack of green twigs over the fire. Somewhere in a copse of willows a horse whinnied. That must be where their mounts were. After a while the man came back and said "Aaargh" to the chief, who said "Aaargh" in return. So far their speech appeared to be very simple and without embellishment.

I was glad to see those rabbits roasting. At least now they did not appear to intend to eat *me*. My squatting position was cramped and painful, though. I squirmed and found a more comfortable seat. Though they continued to stare stone-eyed at me, no one objected. Perhaps they were waiting for the moon to rise before slaying me.

A man can't stay scared indefinitely; it's too hard on the constitution. Though still in grave peril, I found myself wondering if there wasn't some way to comm.nicate with these people. For a starter I could say "Aaargh" with the best of them. But more was demanded. How to explain I was only a homeless Irish boy that meant no harm? It was a delicate p int to make, especially since my balloon was meant to decimate the buffalo they believed their property. Maybe they understood some English.

"My name," I said, "is Charlie Campion."

This created a remarkable amount of disinterest.

"I don't mean to harm anyone, never have, as a matter of fact, except for an evil old man who came at me with a whip, and even then I was only defending myself, you might say."

They passed around a charred rabbit and pulled off bites of it, still staring at me.

"All Gaul," I said, "is divided into three parts."

Was that a flicker of interest in the chief's glazed eye? No. He only belched and spat out some rabbit fur, wiping his mouth with the back of his hand.

I tried "Horatius at the Bridge" and did no better. At any rate, they hadn't lifted my hair yet, the way Ike used to describe it.

"Abou ben Adhem," I said. "May his tribe increase—"

It would be satisfactory if *this* tribe would decrease, or disappear, or something.

"Awoke one night from a deep dream of peace."

The better to declaim, I got to my feet. No one seemed to object. The chief picked his teeth with a splinter of rabbit leg-bone. It was the first human gesture I had seen him make, and it encouraged me. A man plotting murder does not engage in such homely gestures, even if he is a Dacotah. With growing confidence I went on to the parting of Marmion and Douglas, and then sang a poignant tenor chorus of "The Little Drummer Boy," marching back and forth in the firelight and beating on imaginary drum.

The night grew colder. A half-slice of moon rose in the eastern sky, slanting golden rays across the plain. I might, I just might, drum a final flourish and leap out of the ring. I was fleet of foot, and might thus escape. But no, I had read Mr. Cooper's *Deerslayer* and knew that Indians were faster. Better to keep talking, at which I was expert, and hope to divert them until—until what? I didn't know. But as long as I talked, they didn't seem disposed to harm me.

After a while I began to get hoarse. The moon rose higher and was silver now. They ate the rest of the game and passed round a battered canteen of water. How to move this hostile audience? I sang "Poor Miss Maude" and recited all I could remember of "The Rime of the Ancient Mariner." Legs crossed, arms folded on bare chests, they continued to stare at me. Were they only bored? Had I not touched them? Were they only waiting till I ran down to slit my throat and rip off my hair and disembowel me? My voice cracked into a screech and I broke out in a cold sweat. How long could I keep this up?

I was well into "The Harp That Once Through Tara's Halls" when one of my captors rose suddenly. I saw him wraithlike in the glow of the moon, and then he slipped into a ravine and was gone. What was the meaning of that? Where had he gone?

"Love, love, love, love, love," I said, fearing the worst. I had been saving this sentiment as a kind of clincher. Love, Brother Adrian said, moves all, moves everything, moves everyone. Might it not move them? "Oh, love everyone, brothers! Love your chief, love the buffalo. If you can find a little time, love me, because I never meant any harm to anyone! I—"

On the frosty air I heard a faint tinkle, a creak, a jingle; familiar sounds, but in my distraught condition they made no sense. What tinkled, creaked, jingled?

"Love," I said uncertainly, "is the secret of the ages." I quavered and paused. The sounds grew louder. Something whuffled like a—like a horse, or mule! A wagon was coming up the draw.

"Indians!" I screamed. "Indians! Red Indians! Get away! Save yourself!"

Panic-stricken, I bounded over my circle of captors and fled toward the sound. Ahead of me an old wagon was rising ghost-like out of the draw, the tattered canvas chalk-white in the moonlight.

"Go back!" I shouted. "Indians!"

Whip in hand, Ike sat on the high seat, and beside him sat the painted savage who had lately slipped away from the circle.

"Whoa!" Ike shouted. He peered down. "That you, Charlie?"

"Indians," I said faintly.

"What in hell did you think they were?"

His feathered companion said something to him in a guttural tone, and Ike whooped with laughter.

"Well," I said, "I don't see what's so damned funny! Here I've been in peril of my life this whole blessed night, and—"

Ike dug his Indian friend in the ribs. Even the red man seemed to be enjoying my discomfiture.

"It's only old Yellow Bird," Ike said. "Hell, he wouldn't hurt a fly! He's a nice old man. He can sing 'Rock of Ages' all the way through; I heard him once over at Fort Jackson."

"You mean he's a *Christian?*"

Ike wiped his eyes, still chuckling.

"Oh, my pore ribs hurt from laughing!"

Feeling angry and foolish, I climbed on the wagon too, and we rumbled into Yellow Bird's camp. They all greeted Ike and shook hands like it was an unfamiliar but pleasant ceremony. While the rest of the braves helped me fold the balloon and get it into the wagon, Ike held a long discussion with Yellow Bird. Afterwards, I sulked in the wagon, waiting for Ike to finish his endless gossiping in the Dacotah tongue or whatever it was.

The chief gestured a great deal—a sign language, I suppose—hands fluttering like birds, very pretty and graceful in the firelight. He wanted the LOVE LOVE LOVE banner, and when Ike asked me if it was all right I nodded grumpily, glad to get rid of it. But that didn't take long to arrange. What was Ike arguing about now?

"Ike!" I called. "It's a long way back!"

"Only be a minute, hoss."

Yellow Bird opened a brassbound purse and took out some coins. Ike refused them, grinning, and pushed the old man's hand away.

"Ike!" I called. "It must be nearly midnight!"

He held up his hand to the savage in a gesture of farewell and climbed on the wagon-seat beside me. Unwinding the reins from the brake, he cracked the whip. "Ho, there! Giddap, you brutes!" Old Yellow Bird wrapped his new LOVE LOVE LOVE finery around him and waved good-bye. The rest of the band sat around the fire as if they had neither seen us come or go.

As we rumbled away I bit my lip and vowed never to say another word about the whole embarrassing incident. I had been made a fool of by a psalm-singing Indian and a drunken old buffalo-hunter. But curiosity got the better of me.

"What was he offering you money for?"

Ike giggled. "Yellow Bird was real took by you, Charlie. He wanted to buy you. They never saw the beat of you."

"Oh," I said, mollified.

"A dollar and thirty cents. That was every cent he had."

So that was it! A dollar and thirty cents! At that, it was more than I was worth, after being such a damned fool.

"Well," I admitted, "maybe they liked my singing."

Ike howled with glee. He even reined up the wagon so he could slap his damned thigh and hug himself and yell all the louder.

"Well," I said frostily, "what in the hell is so damned funny?"

"Charlie—" He tried to talk, and only exploded again into fits of gurgling and wheezing.

"Whenever you've sufficiently recovered—"

"Oh, my!" Wiping his streaming eyes with the tail of his buckskin shirt, he finally ran down enough to talk. "Charlie, it's the funniest thing I ever heard tell of! Yellow Bird and his people had been out hunting all day, and they were tired. They wanted to go to sleep, but you kept up such a goldarned racket they *couldn't!*"

I gulped. "You mean they—you mean I—"

"They was just being polite! They kept hoping you'd shut your trap, but you just kept blabbing away!"

"Ike," I said, "are you telling me the truth?"

He crossed his chest with a bony finger.

"God's truth!"

"Well," I said, "it's the damnedest thing *I* ever heard of. They must have thought I was an idiot."

"Oh, I don't know," Ike said kindly. "They was willing to buy you."

"For a dollar and thirty cents!"

"That's all they had! A dollar and thirty cents is a lot of money to a Dacotah. Probably sold some prime beaver pelt for that much cash!" He laughed again and whipped up the mules. Even so, it was almost dawn when we got back to the Blessed Kingdom.

"Ike," I said humbly, "you won't say anything about this to Brother Adrian, or anyone?"

"Why, no, Charlie."

"Because..." I said miserably, "because, well, there's a lot to learn in this world, I'm finding out. And sometimes it's kind of hard going."

"Hell, I ain't never been worried about you, Charlie. You're smart!"

"Too damned smart, sometimes."

He put a hand on my shoulder. "Time'll take care of that. But you got the real stuff, Charlie. Inside, I mean. You'll proof real good when you're growed."

"You're not just saying that to make me feel good?"

"No, by God, it's the truth!"

"Thanks," I said and meant it.

* * *

Thus began the great days of our aerial buffalo-hunting. Proud as a jay, I wrote all about it in a letter to Annie Gillentine:

> *Dearest Annie:*
> *Well, you will be pleased to know I am making my mark in the world! I am in the Far West, that is all I can tell you right now. But the rest of the world will hear of me soon, and my patented Aerial Balloon Buffalo-Hunting Rig.*

I went on to tell her about the great balloon ascension on the first day of October and my subsequent narrow escape from the hands of the Dacotahs. Annie was such a gentle and loving girl; I felt pleased and proud at what I knew would be her concern for my safety. In my mind's eye I could see her pale, clutch at her bosom, weep for my perilous condition, thank God for my deliverance. Well, perhaps I put on a little; after all, the Indians were not so bloodthirsty as I had believed, and Ike *did* rescue me, and I *had* been scared witless. But I knew how to compound a dramatic scene, and did so, taking so much effort in craftsmanship that I did not have time to boggle at details:

> *. . . and so the chief wanted to take me into the tribe as his son, but I refused, having a greater mission at this time—the hunting of the buffalo and the economic restoration of the Blessed Kingdom of Concordia-on-the-Platte.*

I went on to explain the mechanics of the Campion Aerial Balloon Buffalo-Hunting Rig:

> *Sometimes, out on the prairie, I go aloft tethered to a long rope and spy out the country. At other times, wind and weather permitting, I drift high across the plains, managing my height and speed by a careful stoking of the small brass stove, and a trailing drag rope as Count Blatski taught me. In either case I have a system of signals for the hunters on the ground—a dangling strip of colored flags, as on a man-of-war, by which I signal to them the direction and distance of the herd. My good friend Mr. Ike Coogan watches with his spyglass and sends off parties of hunters to run down the beasts and*

despatch them. Annie, it has been the most marvelous success! The first day we got only three buffalo; the next day, as our system improved, we slew eight. Now we are getting twenty to thirty a day. The wool-factory is humming, buyers are already coming from Omaha and Kansas City to contract for our prime buffalo-wool articles, and much meat is being dried and smoked and otherwise preserved for the long hard winter to come.

There, too, I suppose I was a little overenthusiastic. The wool-factory was busy, the good brothers were gainfully employed. But the success of the *Petit Géant II* somehow had only hardened the schism between the New Believers and the Old Believers. The first saw our success as an omen for a purposeful and united future; the latter believed the Love Balloon to be a tool of the Devil, a golden calf introduced by Satan to lure them away from old loyalties and old beliefs. Besides, the Old Believers said, where is all that money Brother Adrian is taking in? We haven't seen any of it—we're poor as ever! When will there be an accounting?

I guess they had all forgotten the mystic sign of unity and purpose and love. I drew the circle and dot at the bottom of the page and for lack of a better symbol enclosed the whole thing in a carefully-drawn heart:

This is a mystical sign, Annie. Some day I'll tell you what it means. For now, though, all you need to know is that my heart [and here I drew an arrow pointing to the heart] *beats only for you. Somehow or other, no matter where I go, what I do, who I meet and know, you are always in the back of my mind, like the sweet smell of flowers or an old chord on my harmonica that I forgot for a while.*

And it was true, too. I even forgot how elegantly I said it, marveling instead at the trueness of it. I closed my eyes, seeing her again in the moonlit corncrib. *Charlie, I want to give it to you.* Two thousand miles and a year or more away, the thought warmed me like a fire.

PS You remember that girl I told you about. Well, you don't need to worry about her anymore. She's in love with somebody else, I guess.

Ike posted it for me when he went to Blair for fresh supplies of black powder and ball.

The edge of winter came, with powdery snow and the ground frozen blue and hard like chilled iron. Wind swept across the plain, and bit the flesh like the teeth of a saw. Then, almost like a reprieve, summer came again—Indian summer, though out here they called it Dacotah summer. The world lay hushed in a golden light; a few late bees buzzed about, the air smelled rich and pollen-dusty, lassitude settled on the earth before its long sleep. But the buffalo crews were busy. The *Petit Géant II* soared night and day; the stillness of late October was made for free-ballooning. It was our last chance and we made the most of it before winter—the real article—set in.

"Charlie," Ike complained, "you're a tough boss! I swear I got saddle sores the size of pie tins on my pore old butt. How come we got to work so hard? There'll be buffalo next year too, you know. Don't want to kill 'em all, do we?"

"Brother Adrian's talking about building a new temple. That costs money."

"What's the matter with the temple we got?"

We were out on the plain west of the river, hauling the balloon from the wagon in preparation for inflating it. The sun was just rising. Dacotah summer or not, it was cold that time of the morning. Slanting rays sparkled on the river, turning dun mud into sheets of diamonds.

"Well," I said, "the old temple is kind of shabby."

"It looks all right to me."

"You're not Governor of Concordia-on-the-Platte, either. Here, give me a hand with these ropes."

He grumbled. A lot of the brothers were grumbling these days. But it was none of our business. Brother Adrian was our spiritual head; he had an *Erdspiegel* and we didn't.

"Hey!" Ike said.

"What?"

He held up a fold of the balloon. "How come this to be?"

The cloth had been cut, several times, in sweeping slashes.

"Now who in hell did that?" I cried. Holding the mutilated cloth in my hands, the slashes hurt as if they had been in my own skin.

"I dunno," Ike muttered.

At night we had been storing the balloon in the shed. Someone must have got in and cut the fabric. With no one there to watch, it would have been easy enough.

"Some of the Old Believers is pretty feisty," Ike said. "They don't hold much with balloons."

"But—but to *cut* it this way!"

"Hell," Ike said, "it ponders me some there ain't been throats cut already, let alone a danged balloon!"

Furious, I packed the balloon back in the wagon and called off the hunt. Ike and I went back home. While he and some of the women patched the cuts, I called on Brother Adrian and told him the story.

I was so damned mad the guards didn't argue with me but let me in right away. There were four of them on regular now, two on the porch and two around in back of the temple, and they carried guns.

Brother Adrian was bent over the big table upstairs, counting money. I'd never seen so much money—piles and wads and string-wrapped bundles of greenbacks, and gold coins in a sauerkraut crock. When I told him about the balloon-slashing he rose wearily and took to pacing the floor. His face was lined and gaunt, and he walked like he was carrying a heavy pack, head bent forward and hands clasped behind his back. Either he was smaller than I first remembered, or I'd grown some more these past months.

"Who could have done such a thing?"

"I don't know," I said. "Anybody, I guess. There's a lot of feeling against the balloon. The shed was wide-open so anybody could have sneaked in and done their dirty work!"

Sighing, he shook his head. "So much trouble, so much bickering and unpleasantness! Charlie, I wonder if it's all worthwhile!"

"Of course it is," I said. "You'll win out, Brother Adrian, I know it! All great schemes have their dark times. But somewhere the sun is coming out to shine on us. I believe that. I believe love conquers all. Isn't that what you said?"

He sighed again, and riffled through a roll of greenbacks. I began to wonder if I'd done right in bothering him with my little troubles. After all, I could have sewed up the rents, and Ike and I could take turns standing guard of a night. I didn't need to bother him. But I did need reassurance.

"Isn't that what you said?"

"Yes. That's what I said." With a violent gesture he threw

the wad of bills down. "Yes! And I believe it too. But we've got to give love a chance, don't we? I'll put Fat Henry in charge of guarding the balloon at night."

I didn't like that too much. "Isn't there anyone else?"

"What's wrong with Henry?"

"I don't trust him."

His eyes weren't gentle any more, and his voice got rough and strained. It was the first time I'd seen him get mad, like other people.

"Charlie, that's enough!"

"But—"

"Not another word! There's been too much gossip and troublemaking already! Henry's a little crude and sometimes violent, but I have no reason to doubt his loyalty. He took the sacred oath to keep order in the Blessed Kingdom, under my authority and direction."

"Well," I said sulkily, "maybe that will do for the balloon, but look out for yourself, Brother Adrian."

He shook his finger at me. "Charlie, I love you, but you push me too far! Henry is sworn to protect and defend me."

I could see I wasn't getting anywhere. "Yes, sir," I said. "May I go now, sir, and work on my balloon?" Feeling miserable, I paused at the door.

"What is it?" he barked.

"Kara—is she well and happy? I—I haven't seen her for a long time, you know."

"She's well. She's happy." Then, as if regretting the curtness of his words, he got up and came over to me, pressing my arm. "Love, Charlie. Remember that! Sometimes things seem strange and unaccountable, the way they seem to be working out. Things, happenings, events. They make a mockery of God. But love, love is all. It cannot be refuted, it cannot be repulsed, it cannot be conquered."

I bowed my head. "Amen!"

"Love, Charlie!"

"Yes, sir," I said, and withdrew feeling like the Pope himself had touched me on the arm.

Chapter 15

Der Grosser Henner was as pleased as I was vexed. Smiling his apple-cheeked smile, he sauntered round the balloon-shed, poking into corners with his mace of office and humming under his breath.

"Been having a little trouble, eh?"

"Someone slashed the balloon."

"That so?" Lifting the hem of his brown robe, he stepped delicately over a bolt of balloon-cloth, his two underlings dutifully following him. I don't think any of them knew what they were looking for.

"They could have killed me!" I said. "And what you're all doing traipsing around like a pack of worthless hounds, I'm blessed if *I* know."

Shifting his big Sharps rifle to the crook of his other arm, Ike grinned toothlessly. "Ring around the rosie, that's what they're playing at. Fat Henry is winning, I reckon."

Henry only smiled demurely. "Just investigating the premises, that's all." He became suddenly businesslike. "You're in charge, Mr. Obendorfer. You and Jake bunk down here, and take turns patrolling. It's understood, *nicht wahr?*"

"*Ja,*" Mr. Obendorfer said stolidly.

"Any snoopers, challenge first, then shoot."

"*Ja.*"

"Charlie here and Mr. Coogan are the only ones allowed in." He turned to me. "Now I'll just report back to Brother Adrian and tell him to rest easy."

"You do that," I muttered.

At the door I called to him. "Ike and I are armed too."

His apple face looked wrinkled, like a bad one left in the bottom of the barrel all winter. "What do you mean by that?"

"Just this," I said. "If Ike and I see anyone poking around, we reverse the procedure. We shoot first and challenge afterwards."

He didn't say anything, only closed the door and walked away, brown robe swishing the frost-killed weeds.

"That," Ike said, "is a mean 'un. If a dog grinned at me like that I'd know he was measuring my ass for a swipe of his jaws."

I shook my head. "I don't trust him, but I can't prove anything. All I know is we're got to be real careful from here on in."

The balloon having been repaired, we left early the next morning for what might well be our last hunt. The air was heavy and metallic with the smell of approaching snow. Our little procession of wagons and hunters went unnoticed down the principal street of Concordia-on-the-Platte. The hour was scarce six, the eastern sky dull and gray. Lights appeared in the *Speisehaus* where the women were frying mush and side-meat and boiling coffee. Behind the barred windows of the granary were ghostly white faces, some new to me.

When we passed the temple, it was dark too, except for an upper window where a lamp burned. Brother Adrian was sitting behind the curtains, turbaned head on hand, doubtless meditating. He had much to meditate on these troubled days. I hoped he would look up and notice our passing—maybe even wave—but he didn't.

Each day we had to hunt farther and farther afield. This morning we were fifteen or twenty miles from the river before we found a promising location to set up our traps. Shortly before noon the sun broke through. There was no warmth in it, only a lemon-yellow glare. The air remained still and cold, ideal for ballooning. By early afternoon ten or twelve prime hides were stacked in the wagon. I had even got one myself. Borrowing Ike's old Walker Colt, I drifted low over a galloping cow and calf, and shot her in the neck. She ran off a little way, tottering and bawling; finally her legs doubled under her, and she lay down and died. For a while the calf nuzzled at her, and I could have shot him too, easy as pie. But the poor runt was that day as perplexed and disconsolate as I was, and I forebore to shoot.

It was early morning since we last ate. When I landed the balloon on a knoll feathered with waist-high grasses, Ike was broiling a liver over a fire of buffalo-chips and making coffee. After eating something I felt a little better. We were in no hurry; our hunters were scattered over leagues of plain, skinning and butchering. It would be dusk before we were ready to return. Ike lit a stogie and we sat in the lee of the wagon, bathed in a thin sunlight.

"I wonder," I said, "how it'll all come out."

"Don't do no good to fret about it, coon."

"I can't help worrying," I said. "And me too—am I doing right? The New Belief is the greatest thing since the magnetic telegraph, but then there's old Mr. Schiller and Mr. Vogel and the rest locked up in the granary. What about them?"

Pondering, Ike drew deep on his stogie. It was funny; he used to smell so awful, and now I scarcely noticed him. After a while, he said, "Now I'll tell you about that. It's *people*, that's what it is."

"People? What do you mean?"

"One man is the best arrangement. Just one man all to himself, like old Ike Coogan. Trap, eat, smoke a little 'baccy, live alone, don't mix. It's when all these one-men mix up and make *people* that there's trouble."

"That's crazy," I said, biting off a chunk of hot liver. "People can't just go off and live separate all to themselves. We've got to get along together."

Ike spat. "All I know is I trapped the Yellowstone one whole winter and had me a prime season. Never saw a human face for six months. Then I went into Fort Buford with a load of beaver pelt. Inside of three days I went broke, owed sixteen dollars for liquor, got married to a lady, was shot at three times"—he took off his hat and showed me a hairless furrow in his skull—"caught me the drips, and was chased out of town by a husband this here lady didn't mention at the time of the ceremony. No, I tell you it's *people* causes all the trouble. Stay away from 'em, Charlie!"

There was a kind of left-handed logic to what he said. Still, I objected.

"There just isn't enough room in the whole world for everyone to go out and set on his own square mile of land! No, Ike, people have got to live together, and learn to get along. That's why wise and good kings come at such a markup. They know how to make people get along. Like Brother Adrian. He's wise and good."

Ike pinched out the stogie and wadded the dead butt into his mouth for chewing. "Maybe he's wise and good, but I remark he ain't getting very far. No, Charlie, kings and such can't do it either. It's people, that's what it is. *People* causes all the trouble." He thought for a moment, and then said something very deep. "Now you *take* kings. Kings ain't such a much. There's more than one kind of king, you know."

"How do you mean?"

"Well, there's kings over people, and they're born into the king trade and wear goldy crowns and move in society and fight battles and such."

I didn't see what he was driving at.

"Then there's what you might call kings of *places*. Hell, when I was up on the Yellowstone, I was king of the Yellowstone, wasn't I? No one near me—just old Ike Coogan and winter and mountains and fat beaver and the sun and the sky. That's kinging for *me*, hoss."

It opened up a whole new philosophy.

"Why, that's right!" I cried. "And there's kings of *doing* things too. Like my balloon. When I'm up there, no king can hold a patch to me! No king over people in history ever saw what I can see. I'm so high over kings' heads—why, they've got to look up to see me!"

"That's right," Ike said.

"Even *Irish* kings. Think of it, Ike, even *Irish* kings!"

I was dumbfounded at my discovery. It seemed to give me a status, a purpose, a meaning to my wild and checkered life. A king of *doing* things! That was the genuine article, the real royalty. Nothing would do but that I go aloft one more time to strengthen and confirm my new philosophy.

"It's too late!" Ike protested. He looked at the sun, low and smoky in the southwest quarter, and sniffed at the hard still air. "Snow's a'coming too."

"Just one quick ride," I promised. "After all, it's probably the last of the season."

"Well—"

I was already away, stuffing wood into the stove, loosing ropes, anxious to be in the air again, high in the November afternoon. I dropped my moorings, and the *Petit Géant II* drew me silently and powerfully aloft. That was when it happened— disaster, or so near disaster I do not care ever to come closer.

At a height of perhaps a hundred feet or so, I heard a tearing noise over my head. Looking quickly upward, I was just in time to see one of the ropes that supported my seat give way. A good half of the strands broke, and because of the stretching of the remainder I was at once sitting askew, hanging on for dear life. My weight slid to the weak side, and then the rope parted company altogether. There was no time to shout, to cry out, even to feel the full danger of my case. I fell, but in desperation managed to catch hold of the dangling seat.

"Ike!" I yelled. "Help! Help me! Ike!"

What I expected Ike to do I don't recall. Although he was almost directly below me, he might as well have been on the moon.

"Help!" I yelled. "Ike!"

A breeze was pushing the balloon along, and by craning my neck and looking down I could see Ike gawking aloft, mouth open. The balloon was still rising at a moderate rate. How long could I hold on? I remembered the man Ben that Count Blatski had murdered, and the flat broken body in the grass.

"Ike!" I shrieked.

Crooking my arm over the seat and locking it in position with my other hand, I kept a death-grip on the seat. The board cut cruelly into my arm, but that was a small matter beside my ultimate survival. Swinging at the end of the rope, I felt giddy and was afraid vertigo might overcome me. All that empty air below my dangling boots! What could I do?

Ike's voice drifted faintly up to me. "Hang on, Charlie! I'm coming!"

How could such a stout rope have parted? It swung uselessly from the netting overhead, and as I stared at it I noticed, or seemed to notice, that it was discolored where the break had occurred. There it was somehow stained and yellowish-looking. And the other rope, the one that still supported me—I blanched, and my laboring heart almost stopped its pounding as I saw an identical stain. Even as I stared, a strand of the remaining rope parted and the severed strands twisted back slowly and omi- nously on the main span of the rope like hideous worms. Someone had tampered with the ropes! Vitriol, perhaps? Oil of vitriol, to burn and weaken?

"Hang on, hoss!" Ike yelled. "I'm a'coming! Sit tight and hang on!"

Great Omnipotence or no, love or not love, Brother Adrian and the New Belief regardless, I found myself muttering *Hail Marys* one after the other. *Hail Mary full of grace, The Lord is with thee....* Suddenly my mouth was full of *Hail Marys*. It was not a conscious supplication.

When the first blast of the big Sharps came, I jumped like a marionette on a string. What in hell was Ike doing? Did he want to put me out of my misery? I looked unwillingly down, and an orange flower blossomed below me. In a cloud of smoke Ike reloaded and pointed the muzzle upward again.

"Ike!" I screeched. "What in hell are you doing?"

Well, he had missed me again. But it was not like Ike Coogan to miss at that range. Still and all—

I think that was when I wet my breeches. In the full horror of desperation I had so far managed to hang on, to remain fairly rational, even to think and consider a little. Now, with Ike Coogan blamming away at me, my bladder collapsed entirely. With every boom of the buffalo gun I druzzled anew. Not only to die, to lie smashed and broken in the high grass, but to approach the Heavenly Gates with sodden breeches— this was the final blow. My hands slipped on the rope, and I knew I could not keep a purchase on it much longer. *Hail Mary full of grace, Hail Mary full of grace, Hail Mary—*

"She's comin' down!" Ike whooped.

Why, it was true! The balloon *was* sinking lower! I was no more than a dozen yards aloft, enough to break my neck, but even as I looked down, the *Petit Géant II* sagged a little lower. Not till then did I realize what Ike had done. He had been shooting holes in the balloon with the big Sharps. That was it, all right! I could see a dozen jagged rents—buckshot, perhaps—and for every one that I could see there were more where the shot came out on top.

"Keep shooting!" I yelled, suddenly hopeful. "Keep it up, Ike!"

If I could only hang on till I reached a safe height, and then drop free! My crooked arm was numb and lifeless where it encircled the seat.

"Hang on!" Ike howled. "Another minute, old coon! Hang on!"

The Sharps boomed again. I peered earthward. Thirty feet? or twenty? I couldn't tell. My senses reeled.

"You're almost there!" Ike yelled, and pulled the trigger again. I don't know whether I lost my grip, or dropped intentionally. At any rate I was falling free, ass over teacup, the ground coming up at steam-car speed. I hit on my back with a crash that drove all the air out of me. For a moment I lay flat, gasping terribly for breath. Ike's grizzled face swam into my view.

"You all right, Charlie?"

I tried to answer, but all I could do was to gasp long rattling wheezes. Ike turned me over and pounded me on the back, which didn't help any. Finally I managed to roll away from his buffeting and got to my knees, still gasping for breath.

"I'm—I'm all right!" I said in strangled tones. "Just—just leave off whaling me!"

Ike was hurt. "Ain't that what a body does when somebody is choking to death?"

"That's different. I wasn't choking."

"Well, you was blue in the face! That's good enough for me."

I looked for the balloon, and saw it rolling along the horizon like a gigantic tumbleweed.

"I better git after it," Ike said, throwing a leg over his mottled pony, which had been standing by, reins thrown over its head, with an air of patient astonishment.

"Let it go," I said. "It damned near killed me."

"But—"

"Someone," I said, "soaked the ropes with acid."

Ike goggled. "They didn't!"

"The first one broke, and I could see where it was all yellow and burned. Then I could look up and see the other one breaking too, and it was all burned and eaten like the first one. Ike, someone tried to kill me!"

We looked silently at each other. There was no need to go into details.

"Maybe I'd better go after the balloon anyway," Ike said. "We'll need the ropes to make a case." But before he got started one of our hunting parties flagged down the balloon and brought it back, dragging at the end of a rope like a fractious steer. I showed Ike the ropes. The strands were like hay—dry and yellow, and they crumbled under my fingers. The vitriol was still working. In a spattering of snow we packed the balloon

in the wagon and went back to Concordia-on-the-Platte to have
a reckoning. On the way, I was grateful for Ike's understanding.
All he said was (and that very diffidently), "I'd change those
britches, Charlie, before going out in public."

Dusk fell as we drove into the Blessed Kingdom. The snow
came down more thickly, so that the lights of the village shone
in halos of radiance. Behind us the great bulk of the folded
balloon was hidden and rounded under a mantle of soft white
snow, and Ike and I looked like snow men. His mustache was
dusted thick with it, and when he spoke some fell off, but not
much.

"Might be a good idea to get the balloon under cover first."

I nodded in agreement, but then put my mittened hand on
his arm. "Wait a minute!"

As we passed the street that led up to the temple, I had
caught a glimpse of some kind of turmoil—people milling
about, bobbing lanterns, a murmur of distant voices against
the rising wind and muffling snow.

"Something's going on down at the temple!"

Ike reined up and peered. "Sure is."

"Let's go up that way."

We were not halfway to the temple before our way was
blocked by the crowd.

"What's going on?" I called to a man hurrying by with a
bull's-eye lantern.

"We're settling his hash, that's what!"

"Whose hash?"

He waved his lantern. "That damned Adrian. That *Brother*
Adrian!" He spat into the snow. "Calls hisself Brother. Hell,
he ain't *my* brother—no more, anyway!"

Still perplexed, I called after him but he only hurried away
toward the temple, holding his lantern high and shouting.

"There's sure-enough trouble." I jumped down from the
seat. "I've got to get to Brother Adrian!"

Ike set the brakes and wrapped the reins around the handle.
"Wait for me, Charlie!" But I was already away and running,
pushing through the crowd to the torch-lit temple. All of Concordia ringed the porch, or so it seemed; even Mr. Schiller and
Mr. Vogel and the rest had been got out of the granary-jail,
and were shouting and shaking fists and gathering up rocks to
throw. On the porch stood a big man in a slouch hat and a
sheepskin coat with a star on it. He had a paper in his hand.

Beside him stood *der Grosser Henner,* apple face shining with triumph.

"What's going on?" I asked Mr. Schiller.

His mouth dropped open. "Charlie!" Taking my arm, he pulled me to one side. "You shouldn't be here!"

"Why not?"

"They're in a very feisty mood, Charlie! They might harm you."

"Harm me?"

"They figure you and Brother Adrian are friends—good friends, maybe *too* good friends! And that girl, too—what was her name?"

"Kara?"

"Ach, that's it! Such a nice girl to be mixed up in this!"

I grabbed him and almost shook him. "Where is she? What's going on here?"

"My letter, Charlie! You remember my letter you mailed? Well, it got to my daughter, I guess. Anyway, the federal marshal came and let us out. And he's got a paper for Brother Adrian's arrest."

"Where is he?"

"Who?"

"Brother Adrian!" I cried, impatient.

Mr. Schiller gestured toward the Temple. "He's up there, and won't come out. I saw him sitting by the window. He won't even look this way."

"And Kara?"

"I guess she's up there with him. The rest of the Virgins left when all the commotion started, but she and Brother Adrian locked the door and won't let anyone in."

Fat Henry was on the porch directing several men carrying a log for battering-ram. I grabbed him by the sleeve and spun him round. His torch-red face wrinkled.

"It's you, eh? Come back, did you?"

"What in hell are you doing with that log?"

"Going to break the door down, if it's any of your business!"

The man with the badge tapped me on the shoulder. "Stand back, son. We are going to break the door down."

I shook my head. "You don't have to do that. Let me go up and talk to him."

The marshal was doubtful. He turned to Henry, and said, "Who is this boy?"

"He's one of 'em, marshal! He's in it with the rest of 'em—Adrian and that girl! They're all in it together, scheming and conniving to cheat us! Sowing trouble and discord, that's what! Liars, crooks, schemers—Adrian, the girl, and especially this boy here. Why, the Blessed Kingdom ain't been the same ever since they came!"

I would have hit him in his gloating face but the marshal caught my arm. "Here, now! Take it easy, sonny! You're interfering with a federal officer in the lawful performance of his sworn duties!"

"He's a bastard!" I cried. "A fat bastard, and a sneak! He took an oath to protect and defend Brother Adrian, and here he is trying to break the door down and harm him!"

Fat Henry's tight-skinned cheeks split in a grin. "Then why won't he let us in?"

The mob started bawling and shaking their fists at me now. Someone threw a snowball, and the way it dazed me when it hit me on the cheek, it had a rock in it.

"He's in it too!" someone called.

"Well," I said, "I wouldn't let a mob like this into the temple either. But I'll shinny up and talk to Brother Adrian. Just give me a minute, will you?"

Henry smirked, and said, "Don't trust him, marshal! He's up to some deviltry. He was always a tricky one."

"Speaking of tricks," I said, "I've got one to talk over with you when there's time." I turned to the marshal, "Please, I know a way up to his room. Let me go and talk to him!"

"Well . . ." The marshal rubbed his stubbled chin. He was a good man, I think; a fair man, trying to do his duty in an awkward situation. "Won't do no harm, I guess." He looked at his watch. "Five minutes, that's all I'll give you. If you ain't down by then we'll bust down the door."

"Thanks," I said. "You won't regret it."

I ran round to the back and shinnied up the drainpipe to the roof. The vines that had covered the roof in the summer were dry and dead, and half-buried in new snow. The window where I had gotten in to visit Kara was locked. I tapped on it and waited; nothing happened. I made a fist and drove it through the windowpane and reached in and undid the catch. My hand bled and dripped on the musty carpet. I wiped it off on my shirt as I peered round the dark interior. Somewhere upstairs a lamp was burning. In the faint yellow light I could see that the *Erdspiegel* was gone from its table, and the brocaded cover lay on the floor. I picked it up, feeling it heavy and scratchy in my hands, and then threw it from me and went into the hall.

Lamplight streamed through the open door of Brother Adrian's office. He was still sitting by the window, turban on his head, in the same attitude of reflection as I had seen him in earlier that morning.

"Brother Adrian!" I called.

There was no answer. The figure sat unmoving, head turned away from me, shoulders slumped.

Something made my flesh crawl on. In that instant the dying lamp guttered, and then flared briefly up. In the hot new light I got a better look. The thing was not Brother Adrian. The thing was a roll of blankets cunningly shaped into an approximation of a human figure, clothed in Brother Adrian's robe and turban, and propped in a chair near the window. A dummy— a lamp-lit dummy!

Aware of the rising babble of voices from below, I raced from one empty room to another, crying out his name. "Brother Adrian!" And, "Kara—where are you?" They only echoed back a dusty reflection of my voice. Gone. They were both gone!

Where was all the money? The drawer of the table was half pulled out, and empty. A bureau gaped open. I threw a closet door wide. It, too, was empty.

Unnoticed at first in my haste, a sealed envelope was propped against the porcelain base of the oil lamp. On the face, in a slanted feminine hand, was written *Charles Campion;* then, heavily underlined, *Personal.* I tore it open.

Dearest Charlie:
  By the time you read this we will be gone, far away. Don't blame Brother Adrian too much, for he is a dear and wonderful man, and has thought this all out very carefully. In his Erdspiegel *he saw trouble coming, and in order to carry out his work in a more congenial atmosphere*

More congenial atmosphere! Kara didn't know words like that. This was Brother Adrian talking!

he is leaving Concordia-on-the-Platte to found a new Kingdom. Wish us luck, Charlie, and remember we both love you very much.

Through eyes half-blinded by tears of fury and despair, I read a postscript: "PS I am going to have a baby. If it is a boy I will call it Charlie."

They were gone! They had probably already been gone this morning when I had passed the temple with the buffalo-hunters. I looked down at my hand. It was bleeding—sticky red drops of blood that spotted my breeches and spattered the toes of my boots. Numbly I wrapped a handkerchief around my knuckles and stuffed Kara's note into a shirt pocket. "Call it Charlie," indeed! That was irony for you! I hoped little Charlie would know more humane treatment than big Charlie ever got.

As the lamp guttered again and went out, I came downstairs and let them in.

"Where is he?" the marshal asked.

"Gone."

"Gone?"

I nodded. "They made up a dummy and left it in that upstairs window. He and Kara are both gone. Probably have been since last night sometime. Everything's gone—the money, the *Erdspiegel*, everything."

There was a chorus of dismay and anger. Fat Henry grabbed me by the arm. "Are you telling the truth?"

"Let go my arm," I said, "or I'll wallop you!"

The marshal pushed Henry away and asked, "Wasn't there any clue or anything? No letter or statement or anything like that?"

"No," I said. "Nothing. It's all gone—everything."

There was jeering and catcalling from the mob. Someone threw a rock and broke a window of the temple. For a moment the shattered pane hung there, cracked and sightless; then it fell back inside with a tinkling like tiny metal bells.

"Now wait a minute, folks!" The marshal held up his arms. "This is all going to be handled legal. Now just a minute!"

Like a giant wave the crowd pressing against the porch rolled over him, waving torches, screaming, cursing, men and women alike, anxious to get into the temple to vent their fury. Old Mr. Schiller ran past me, mouth forming obscenities I had never heard. Old Vogel ripped a hanging lamp from its support and stamped it into shards of glass and mangled metal. Others ripped curtains from the windows, kicked in doors, mutilating and destroying everything they could lay their hands on.

The Blessed Kingdom, I thought. *Where had it gone?* Ike was right. People were the trouble. When men became people, that was when the trouble started. They had never gotten along with each other, never would. That accounted for wars and all. I went down off the porch and climbed up on the seat of the wagon. "Get along," I said to Dan and Beersheba. "Hup! Get, now!"

As they plodded off, their backs heavy with snow, I took one last look at the temple. Torchlight blazed from every window, and flickering red shadows lay on the snow outside. People streamed in and out like ants, fighting over chairs and tables and bits of curtain and carpeting. Some were quarreling and fighting with each other. One man carrying a chamber pot leaped through a broken window, another in close pursuit; they rolled pummeling and gouging in the snow. Finally, a sinuous tongue of flame licked out a broken window and tasted at the eaves. They were burning the temple.

⁓⁓⁓⁓Chapter 16⁓⁓⁓⁓⁓⁓⁓⁓

Sad and bewildered, I drove back to the balloon shed, not really knowing where I was going or what I was doing, but only in response to a need to be in a familiar place, among familiar things. I didn't know where Ike was; probably drunk somewhere with his buffalo-hunting cronies. They knew as well as anyone where the barrels of *peistengl* were kept in the cellar of the *Speisehaus;* in this sudden breakdown of all order and discipline, they had probably headed like homing pigeons to the rhubarb wine.

The balloon shed was dark and cold, and smelled of cordage and varnish and chemical fluxes. Lighting a lamp, I stared unblinkingly down at the flame. Why had they done this to me? I believed in Brother Adrian, believed in what he was doing, believed in his New Belief, swallowed it all, hook, line, and sinker. And all the while he—he and Kara, that is, were plotting to steal the money and run away. She was going to have a baby, was she? Kara, that was so virginal and hoity-toity with me, Charlie Campion! Oh, damn her, damn him, damn the whole damned world! Ike was right. It was a pretty tolerable world if it wasn't for people. Something itched my cheek, and I blinked, and wiped at it. Maybe it was a tear. I didn't know. I didn't want to know.

All right then. That was the way life was. That was that. What to do now? Where to go? Or to go anywhere? Sad as things had turned out, maybe my future was still here. It was getting colder outside, and I had left Dan and Beersheba hitched to the wagon. A Nebraska Territory blizzard appeard to be on its way, and I'd heard about *them;* the dreaded white blindness that turned your directions round and made you giddy, three and four and five feet of snow so that even fence posts and outbuildings were buried, people and stock frozen stiff only feet from the barn they couldn't find. I'd better get the mules inside.

Carrying the lamp, I went out into the storm. The swirling flakes were tinted pink, and a rosy glow lit the sky. The temple must be burning good by now. Let it burn, and with it all the silly childlike notions that had once filled my head. I backed the snow-mounded wagon into the shed and had only started to unhitch the mules when Fat Henry broke a trail through the snow, red faced and puffing. He was carrying his mace of office and looked mean.

"I thought I'd find you here."

In no mood for small talk, I said, "You thought right."

"What are you doing with those mules?"

"It's none of your damned business!"

"Oh, yes, it is! They're the property of the Kingdom, all signed over legal. By order of the federal marshal all assets have got to be reported and counted up to settle the lawful claims of the brothers against that thieving Adrian!"

"They're my mules," I said. "I drove them over a thousand miles of land to get here, and I made a contract with Brother Adrian, not with any federal marshal. He's gone, and so now they're my mules and my wagon and my balloon. I'll drive them the hell out of here when I so please and kiss my ass to the likes of you, Fat Henry."

He smiled his red-cheeked smile, and I thought of what Ike said about the grin meaning he was measuring me for a swipe at his jaws, like a cur dog.

"You're in enough trouble already, boy! If I was you, I wouldn't be so smart. A lot of folks is willing to testify in court that you was thick with Adrian and that—that—"

"Mind your tongue when you speak of her," I warned.

"Oh, it wasn't my intention to offend." He followed me

into the shed, and I hung the lantern on a nail. "I can do a lot for you, boy. A word from me could be a great help. This balloon idea of yours, now there's millions to be made from it, I can see *that*, though at first I didn't hold with it much. Now why don't we just sit down and talk?" Beaming, hands on his fat thighs, he sat on an upturned box.

"What's that on your hands?" I asked.

"Eh?" Startled, he looked down. "What do you mean?"

In the circle of cold lamplight I could see the blotched yellowish stains on his fingers. "Those stains. Like maybe you were handling chemicals or something."

"Oh," he was thoughtful. "I don't know." He rubbed his hands together in a preparatory kind of gesture. "About the balloon, now, I'm sure we can come to a useful arrangement, Charlie. I—"

"Yes," I said tightly. "About the balloon. Someone put acid on the ropes, and if it hadn't been for Ike Coogan, I'd be dead. I think you did it, you son of a bitch!"

His face got red as a ripe pippin. "Don't call me names, you young pup! You're in no situation to call anyone names! You and that—that girl—that *slut*—"

He probably outweighed me by a hundred pounds, but I was on him like a bobcat, clawing and spitting. It was like a lot of things I'd done and regretted—act fast and repent slow. The force of my attack bowled him off the wooden box, and I heard him grunt as my knee dug into his middle. But the advantage was short-lived. Fat men can be powerful, I found. Two arms like tree-limbs clamped round my back fit to snap it, and with a growl Henry rolled me over and was on top, crushing the breath out of me. I tried to yell, but nothing would come. Desperate, I raked at his jowls, and my long-uncut nails raked livid tracks in his red face. Howling, he dropped his grip on me, but I was still pinioned between his fat knees.

"You little devil!" Making a hamlike fist, he drove it down, but I twisted desperately to one side, and he missed. Trapped as I was under his huge sweat-smelling body, he could hardly miss me again. I thrashed desperately, and one outflung boot caught a corner of my workbench. I had been meaning to fix it, but never got round to it. The rickety leg collapsed and nuts and bolts and wires and wrenches and tools showered down. My scrabbling hand found something heavy, with a good heft to it. I grabbed it, and flailed out. It was a heavy soldering-copper, and I hit Henry a good lick on the skull.

The fierce light in his eye dimmed. Still holding a hand to his torn cheek, he blinked, then tottered a little. Desperately he reached for my weapon and did manage to get me briefly by the wrist. But my arm was already driving forward again, the weight of the heavy copper behind it. It mashed his fingers against his face, and pressed through to crunch on bone. Moaning, he toppled off me and huddled on knees and elbows, feeling his battered face and whimpering. For good measure I hit him again, swinging the copper like a maul. It hit him in the back of the head, and he jerked like a pole-axed steer and then sagged flat on the dirt floor.

Breathing hard, I stood over him, still hefting that murderous soldering-copper. Hit him again? Why not! But something stayed my hand. So still, so flat, so broken. Again I remembered the dead man Ben, back at Mauckport, a year and more ago. *Der Grosser Henner* looked that way now.

Frightened, I dropped the weapon and bent over him, listening for breath. Nothing. No movement, no sound. I tried to turn him over on his back, but he was too heavy. Laying my ear to his broad back, I strained to hear a heartbeat. Nothing. Nothing at all! In the snow-shrouded quiet of the balloon-shed, I sat back on my haunches in horror. He was dead! I had killed him! Even as I stared at the lifeless body a gout of thick blood rolled down the fat neck and stained the earth darkly, then another oozing globule, and a third. He was dead. Fat Henry was dead.

I reeled to my feet, panic-stricken. Old Dan, still hitched, looked at me and whuffled in disapproval. What had I done? What should I do now? Where should I flee?

Flee, that was the ticket, all right. I'd have to run for it now. The decision had been made for me. I didn't have many belongings, but I collected them quickly—another shirt, some woolen socks, a handful of the scattered tools, a coat, a coil of rope, an axe. Blowing out the lantern, I threw the plunder in the back of the wagon, and climbed on the seat.

"Giddap!" I yelled.

Gentle Beersheba looked round. The mules expected to be unhitched and to have their grain and water and spend a bitter night indoors.

"Get along!" I yelled, cracking the whip over their backs. "Hup! Get, now!"

Resigned, they leaned into the harness and pulled the wagon out into the snow. The swirling flakes had a hard edge to them now, and stung my cheeks.

"Whoa!" I yelled, sawing on the reins. This way or that? Left or right? The only road led to other towns—Blair, Kirby, and eventually Omaha. If I went that way, they'd find me. No, there was only one way; west, that was it. Across the trackless prairie, into the teeth of the storm.

"Gee!" I howled. "Get along with you now! Hup!"

Mules don't like to head into a storm, but I drove them to it, flailing with the whip till my arm ached. Behind me the pink glow of the burning temple dimmed and faded, then was lost. It was dark and cold, and the gale almost blew me off the seat. But all that was nothing, really nothing. The real fact—the important fact—was that Charlie Campion was absconding with federal property. Not only that, he was a murderer, once again a murderer, at only seventeen. Maybe old Mr. Gillentine had been right. I was just no good.

I don't know how far west I drove the wagon that night. In a blizzard one place looks much like another. Through the night we rumbled and swayed, tacking across the snowy waste like a lost ship, depending only on the good sense of the mules— better sense than *I* had—to keep us out of rocky draws and snow-mounded thickets. Even dawn was not much different from night, except that the black void became a gray void, and the wind blew harder. Finally, even mules can be driven no longer into a storm. They only stood heavily, snow-crowned heads down, refusing any longer to answer the lash of the whip.

"Move, damn you!" I cried, and hurt my arm with the force I put into the whip. Old Dan started, and trembled at the bite of the lash on his flank—then settled back again, dumbly miserable.

"All right!" I cried. "Stand there and freeze!"

We'd all freeze, that was the rub. Half in exasperation and half in panic I jumped down and was instantly to my knees in snow. How we had ever come this far I didn't know. Clutching my arms round me for warmth I peered this way and that. There was no point of reference—no horizon, no sky, nothing but an iron gray light that permeated everything. I was cold and scantily clad, having driven away from Concordia in only shirt and pants and a homespun woolen coat. The gale-force wind sucked the marrow from my bones, and when my hand touched my ears, those appendages felt wooden and dead, and I knew they were going to freeze.

Maybe I could make some sort of shelter from the balloon. In the pearl gray light, bullets of wind-driven snow stinging my cheeks, I climbed on the wagon and tried to pull out a flap of cloth. The fabric was stiff as parchment, and I would damage it by pulling too hard. Finally I worried a few yards free and the rest came more willingly. Stumbling through the snow, dragging the balloon-cloth after me, I ran into a copse of frozen willows near the wagon. Well, that was more luck than good sense. By draping the cloth over the branches, I managed a kind of cavernous lean-to. Hearing the snow tinkle on the varnished cloth gave me a feeling of accomplishment. When I had unhitched the mules and led them inside, and started a small fire from willow-twigs soaked with balloon-cement, it was not half-bad. We had no food, though, and Beersheba nuzzled me gently in reminder. But it was cozy and passing warm, and we might yet survive the Nebraska blizzard. At any rate, no federal officer could track me in the new snow. If he had any sense at all, he'd stay in Concordia and toast his shins till the storm blew itself out.

Hunched over the tiny fire, I stared into the red eye and saw the face of a fool, a triple-winding brassbound patented fool. For so long now I had prided myself on being a man— on being seventeen and almost a half and shaving every few days—yet now that I had a chance to think on it, I realized that I had not acted the part of a man. Hurt by Brother Adrian's betrayal of me and the Kingdom, stung by Kara's easy leave-taking of me, I had only wanted, childlike, to run away from it all. I should have stayed and seen it through; I realized that now. But in my blind pride I had run away and compounded my shortcomings by stealing government property, they said, and leaving Fat Henry battered and lifeless when he tried to stop me. So do our difficulties mount and multiply when we refuse to stand and face them! Even after I had bludgeoned Henry, I could have stayed and confounded my accusers. Henry was the only one that knew I was running away with the wagon; after all, he had been trying to kill me too and outweighed me by a hundred pounds. And I certainly had not been involved in Brother Adrian's embezzling and flight, else why would I have come willingly back to the Kingdom that day to find Brother Adrian and Kara and all the money gone? No, I had acted the fool and must now pay the fool's wage. Glumly I stared into the fire and poked it. Frozen to death in Nebraska, with two mules for company! I muttered a small prayer and then broke off, uncomfortable. The Lord, I was positive, no longer wanted to hear from Charlie Campion, the world's biggest idiot.

Unabated, the storm went on, whistling death across the plain and tearing with icy fingers at our little tent. My stomach rumbled, and I thought longingly of the *Speisehaus* with its good warm smells—roasting fat pork and cinnamon-spiced applesauce, fresh-baked crusty bread, mounds of sauerkraut laced with caraway seed, the incense of boiling coffee. Taking a few of the precious twigs, I tried to feed them to old Dan, but he only nudged them away and tried reproachfully to kick me. I melted snow in a can over the fire and drank it, trying hard to imagine it was chicken-broth, but fooling no one. Would the brawling storm never stop rattling the tent? I melted more snow for the mules, but not enough to satisfy them. Heat was too precious to waste twigs.

A night passed, I think, and another day. The storm still blew. When I tried to lift a flap of the tent to see out, it was so weighted with snow I couldn't budge it. I lay down again near the warmth of the mules, wrapping myself in a fold of balloon-cloth. It was stiff and cold, but better than nothing.

Time passed—I don't know how much time. Perhaps I was delirious. I don't know if mules get delirious before they freeze to death, but they were both in sad shape. Old Dan lay down, something I had never seen him do. Beersheba just stood, head hanging. When the mules staled an acrid smell filled the tent. I crawled near them and huddled over the steamy ammonia-smelling vapor. What time was it? What day? What month? I didn't know any of the answers. When would I die? The question vexed me. It seemed hard to die, not knowing when—or where.

I had lost all capacity to reckon minutes, hours, or days. In fact, I lost even sensation—no longer was I cold, but rather numb in my body and in my mind able only to think very slowly and in the simplest terms. I was freezing to death, and starving, too, and it was not unpleasant. Wrapped in the balloon-cloth, I stared unseeingly at the roof, only half-hearing the gale striking out at our shelter. If I had been able to rouse myself from apathy, I might have slaughtered one of the mules and preserved myself with warm blood and meat. No, that was unthinkable! Dan and Beersheba were good friends; I had gotten them into this by my foolishness, and I could not betray them now. Besides, I was so tired.

There is in man a grudging awareness of death, but coupled with it a resolve to let future generations know he was once here on this planet, breathing and speaking and acting out his part. This accounts for monuments and most wars. Even in my extremity I could not give in without some record of my passing. Summoning what little strength remained, I reached for the dog-eared journal which lay next to me. In that last clear flame before the candle of life gutters into smoky extinction, I would write my last will and testament.

My fingers could scare clamp the pencil, and my eyes were hazed so that the scrabbled characters hardly made sense after I had set them down, but I did the best I could:

> To whomever it may concern, on finding me and the mules:
> My name is Charlie Campion, and I think my father was a certain Ned Campion, although I have never been able to find him. There is a possibility I am of royal blood, although I now leave all such worldly things behind me. The wagon I bequeath to the Holy Shepherd Home on Cherry Steet in New York City, near what they call Sweeney's Shambles. I hope some kind soul will sell it and give the proceeds to that worthy organization.

This exhausted me, and I lay back, a dreadful apathy softening my bones and turning my muscles into pudding. Well, wasn't that it? What else did I have to leave anybody? Nothing, nothing at all. I was penniless, at seventeen and almost a half. What a misspent life. Ah, what might have been! But my writings didn't satisfy me. It didn't seem like much of a final testament, being very sparse. Doggedly I struggled on in the fading light:

> I loved Annie Gillentine, of near Utica, New York, how much she'll never know. But I now leave to her the residue of that love, to be delivered however the Lord thinks best. And I leave also, to anyone that can use it, my foolish trust of people. It got me into a lot of trouble

and caused me to be used and exploited by rascals. But it's good and shining as new, even now, and I'm not ashamed of it.

What a foolish, willful thing to say! My mind must be freezing, too. As if to trust people was anything but a foolish vanity! I wrote no more, only lay in a stupor, the journal sprawling in a flutter of white pages.

Some time that day or night the snow stopped. No longer the needlelike clatter on the tent; instead only a muffling silence. The mules no longer stirred. Were they dead? Was I dead? I didn't know. I didn't care. It was so quiet and peaceful. And that was when I saw this enormous bird peering at me round a flap of the tent. Oh, what a monstrous bird, plump and feathered, with great splay feet and a round furry body! What kind of a bird could this be, out here in the Nebraska Territory?

Breathing hard, I reached for my little axe. Was this deliverance? It seemed very likely. In response to my confessions and a humbled heart, this great bird was sent to save me.

Tottering to my feet, I went after it, swinging wildly. The bird squawked and jumped nimbly aside on its great flat feet. I swung again, slavering at visions of the huge drumsticks turning on a spit. Maybe even the mules, although normally vegetarian, would relish roasted meat. I chopped madly, again and again, and the bird flapped and screamed and blundered from the tent into the sunlit whiteness outside.

With eyes long accustomed to the dimness of the shelter, I blinked in the strong white light. White, glittering dazzling white in all directions! The world lay buried under a thick alabaster coverlet, with only an occasional mound to mark a copse of willows.

A dozen feet away the huge bird stood spraddle-legged in the snow, chattering and scolding. Clumsily I lurched after it, plunging and falling in the thigh-deep snow and brandishing my axe while the great bird chirped and scolded and flapped its wings and retreated ahead of me.

"Stop!" I begged. "Wait! Here, bird!" Craftily I formed my hand into a cup, as if it held grain, and made little chirping noises. "Come here!"

Try as I would, the bird evaded me. Finally, spent and bewildered, I dropped the axe and stood tottering and winded in a field of white. My brains rolled about in my skull, the sky turned upside-down and appeared again under my boots, the bird flapped its wings in triumph. I sprawled facedown in the snow. Weak and helpless, unable to turn over, I saw the black shadow of the bird pass over me and waited for him to peck out my brains with his sharp beak.

Chapter 17

From a strictly religious point of view a man ought to die in full possession of his faculties, the better to appreciate what is happening and to prepare his soul. Animals, however, I understand to have a somewhat improved arrangement, wherein many of them swoon in the presence of danger and so die comfortably unaware. I longed for some of this animal nature but could manage none. Paralyzed by fear and hunger, I nevertheless seemed to be clearheaded enough and only too aware of the monstrous bird dragging me back into the tent, the better to devour me in comfort. It did not seem at all queer that other noisy brilliant birds joined the first, milling about the tent in anticipation of the feast, speaking a guttural bird language and wearing bright feathers that dazzled my eyes. Birds, great birds, colored birds, squawking birds; suddenly I screamed out in horror. But one of them squatted beside me, pressing a cup of some liquid to my lips.

"Go away!" I shrieked, trying to knock the stuff aside. "Let me alone. Help! Help! Holy Mary—"

The cup persisted; a strong arm encircled my neck, holding me tight while some of the stuff dribbled between my clenched teeth. An arm? A strong arm? Since when did birds have arms?

Brown arms, with bracelets? There was a smell too, a familiar smoky, grass-smelling odor that I had known before.

"*Sha,*" a voice said in my ear. "*Sha.* Good. Drink. Very good."

Well, it was at least warm and didn't taste too bad. Suspiciously I sipped at it, then drank more, finally clutching the cup to drain the last drop.

"*Sha,*" the voice said. "Good, Charlie. Good."

The thing knew my name.

"You cold, you hungry."

"Yes," I muttered. "I sure am." My eyes were watering, and I dragged out my shirttail and managed to wipe my eyes. That face! That craggy face, gnarled and twisted like the curved head of a gentleman's walking stick! A bird, yes. Yellow Bird! Old Yellow Bird! He and his band had come on me in my tomb, and brought me back to this life! Overcome, I sank back on what must have been a buffalo robe, crossing my arms over my face to hide my emotions.

"You sick." Yellow Bird settled himself beside me. "We wait." He gave a short barking order, and a fire was seen going in the middle of the tent; water bubbled, and the air trembled with the tantalizing smell of meat juices.

"You saved me," I said.

"*Hopo!*" He helped me to my feet, and I tottered about the tent on his arm. A dozen or more of the band ringed me, powerful men in furs and blankets, grinning and nodding. More were outside; I could hear wood being chopped and ponies whickering. People called back and forth to each other, and someone came in with a handful of cottonwood twigs and led the mules away. "*Sha!*" Yellow Bird said. "Walk, Charlie."

I did not think my painful chest could contain all the gratitude that swelled in it and knocked against my ribs. And that meat smell; indelicate as it was, I could taste a wet coldness at the corners of my mouth that meant I was drooling.

"I'm hungry," I said unnecessarily.

We squatted in a ring about the iron pot, and Yellow Bird himself speared me a piece of fat meat. Though it was still red and uncooked in the middle, I nevertheless wolfed it down, burning my fingers and tongue but not caring. The Dacotah braves, these savage and untutored children of nature, forebore to eat, and only watched me.

"More," I gestured.

I ate my fill, ending with fingers and mouth and shirt smeared with congealing grease, and drank half the liquid in the pot. Not till my hunger-shrunk belly hurt with swelling did I stop eating and belch and sigh and realize I had played the pig.

"Sir," I said, shamefaced, "I—I didn't mean to eat so much."

Yellow Bird grinned, and signed to the rest to help themselves to the little that was left.

"Friend. God damn friend." He made a gesture, and it would have taken an idiot not to know what it meant. His thumb and forefinger curled over his heart, then his hands swept forward and the palms turned out wide. "Friend. Glad."

"I guess," I said, "that in my present sad condition I'm not worth that dollar and thirty cents you offered for me, but I'm glad you still can use me for a friend." I repeated his gesture, liking the simplicity and eloquence of it. "Glad. Me too. Friend."

Yellow Bird took off his buffalo hat and neatly plucked from his locks what I took to be a nit. Popping it into his mouth, he pointed amiably to a young man repairing a broken thong on a pair of snowshoes; cords strung over bows of willow. *"Iktomi!"* he shouted. *"Ah, Iktomi!"*

The young man's name was Fool Dog, and they all jeered him mercilessly in some private kind of joke. *"Hau!"* they shouted. *Hau!"* Fool Dog scowled and jerked angrily at the thong with his white teeth. His long braids, wrapped in shiny fur, whipped about his head. But finally he laughed, too, and came over to clap me on the back and grin.

Yellow Bird pointed to Fool Dog, and shrieked with laughter. "Kill! Charlie, kill. Axe!"

Finally it came to me. In my delirium, I had taken Fool Dog for a gigantic bird. Blundering on his snowshoes into my camp, probably breaking trail for the wandering band, he had been astonished at being taken for game and chased by a maniac with a hatchet. Oh, it was all too foolish! Screaming in delight, I joined in the general merriment. Finally I staggered to my feet and embraced Fool Dog. Curling my finger over my heart, I swept out my palms and made the *glad* sign again. *My heart,* it said. *All to you!*

I had been lucky, there was little doubt of that. In his few words of English, supplemented by the graceful sign language that so intrigued me, Yellow Bird told me the story. They had been moving westward, late in the season, on a visit to his nephew, Leaning Man, on the banks of the Kettle River. An untimely storm caught them, as it had me; Fool Dog on his snowshoes had seen my half-buried tent.

There was, I gathered, going to be some kind of trouble soon on the banks of the Kettle. Yellow Bird made the *heart* sign, then turned his hand over and over rapidly to indicate excitement or emotion. *White men with wagons coming through Leaning Man's hunting country. Bad, very bad. Too many people.* Ah, there it was again! Ike Coogan had been right. Too many people. *Trouble. Much trouble.* God damn!

I knew Fort Jackson had been recently put at the crossing of the Kettle to protect the emigrant trains.

"But there are soldiers there," I said. Having seen the might of the blue-clad Army in Ohio and elsewhere, it did not seem likely to me that Yellow Bird or Leaning Man or any aborigine was likely to stop the Army and the wagon trains if that was the route they chose. Nevertheless, in that snowbound tent I felt a prickling in the small hairs on the back of my neck when Yellow Bird spoke. His voice was flat and hard, and his rheumy eyes glittered.

"Kill!" His people, Ike had told me, were called the Coup-Gorges, the cutthroats, and I jumped a little as Yellow Bird repeated "Kill!" and drew a bony finger across his wattled throat, making a *tcchhk* sound. He got up, and looked down at me, as if to impress me with the firm purpose of what he had said. Then he wiped one palm harshly across the other. There was no mistaking that sign. *Wiped out. Exterminated.*

The next day a warm wind came from the south. The Dacotahs were uneasy; a south wind, it seemed, meant bad luck. But the wind did melt the snow. Brooks ran full, ice-laden trees sprang erect, the earth squished and sucked under our boots. A warm sun drew clouds of vapor into the sky, and the false spring coaxed buds from the willows and chokecherries. Bad luck or no, the south wind beat off the Winter God for the moment, and the Coup-Gorges prepared to move west toward Fort Jackson and the crossing of the Kettle. And I did not get off as scot-free from my brush with death as I had supposed. Driving the mules and wagon in the muddy wake of the little band and their travois, the triangular lodgepole frames they dragged behind the ponies to carry their possessions, I shivered on the wagon seat and seemed never to get warm. Chills racked me, then fever and ague. When I coughed, a knifelike pain lanced my chest, and I coughed a lot, a rattling phlegm-laden barking. In spite of my protests, Yellow Bird dosed me with evil-smelling herbs mashed into a paste, and then had me tied into a travois.

"Sick. Charlie sick."

"I know I'm sick," I wheezed. "Let me back into the wagon! I'll be all right there."

Indians mistrusted wagons of all kinds. The travois was the only good thing. "No. Travois. Wagon bad."

Out of a disordered eye I saw Fool Dog preparing to cut old Dan's throat. I raised such a ruckus that he dropped his knife, looking to Yellow Bird for instruction.

"Don't you touch those mules!" I squalled. "Make him let them alone!" I tried to break free from the strands of sinew that held me to the travois, but sank back exhausted. "Yellow Bird, the mules are my friends! Don't hurt them!"

Fool Dog, disgusted, raised his skinning knife again, and I thrashed about like a steer in an abattoir. "Don't! Please don't!"

Yellow Bird grumbled, but waved Fool Dog off. Finally he ordered a withered old woman to lead the team and wagon, and we started off again toward Leaning Man and the crossing of the Kettle River. "Mule meat good," Yellow Bird complained. Riding his spotted pony, he scowled down at me, trussed like a chicken in the travois. "You god damn mule too."

"All right," I muttered, "but don't you touch Dan and Beer-sheba."

His wooden face splintered into a grin. "You god damn mule too." He made a sign new to me, pounding one clenched fist into the other. I learned later it meant *stubborn.* "We call you Little Mule."

That was the name I bore from then on among the Coup-Gorges, and with good reason. I had always been headstrong, and secretly was ashamed of it and the troubles it got me into. Now I was officially a mule, albeit a little one.

I don't remember much about that trip to the Kettle River. I guess what I had was some sort of inflammation of the lungs, brought about by hunger and exposure. A Dacotah war party is not the best of infirmaries for a sick boy, but they did the best they could. Day after day we toiled across the frozen prairie, me jouncing and bobbing on the travois, wrapped in furs, beset by raging fevers and bone-rattling chills. For much of the time I must have been out of my head; devils loomed out of the snow and bared their fangs at me, ghostlike apparitions danced in the thin rays of the winter sun; flakes of snow falling on my upturned face terrified me. The medicine man, an ancient named Red Shirt, waved his rattle in vain, and did a dance around the travois, throwing sacred yellow pollen into the air. The treatment did not help.

Lucid for a few moments one winter day, I opened my eyes to see a frozen river. The Kettle. It must be the Kettle river. On the other side were lodges, many lodges, looking at dusk like pale lamps, the skin coverings softly aglow from the fires within. I remember the sudden quiet as the grinding travois poles glided smoothly across the ice, and then we were home. Home? To a stranger from a distant land, who had never seen much of a home anyway, it seemed like home. A silent man with woman-gentle hands bundled me into a pile of furs in one of the great lodges. I don't know whether I slept, or only passed into a catalepsy induced by my illness. At any rate, I knew no more.

Night followed day on the Kettle, and then dawn came again, and another night. I could not reckon time in my enfeebled state. My soul, wracked by the inflammation, fluttered feebly and tried to escape, but somehow or other I clung to it and would not let it go. I *was* stubborn, all right. The rising conical shape of the lodge became my world, that and the shy man who attended me. As rationality returned I would lie pale and spent, racked by coughing, watching him move about to feed the fire or boil broth for me. Was he a spirit? Was this a world of spirits? I pinched myself, and wasn't sure.

I knew the word for *thanks,* and beckoned to him and whispered, *"Hie. Hie."* The effort sent me into a paroxysm of coughing, and he pushed me gently down into the furs, signing that he understood.

No task was too mean for him, and he performed them with a grace and style that made them noble. He bathed me, kept me clean, aired the furs and shook them, and fed me a paste of meat that I suspected had already been chewed to soften it for me.

"Mule," I said one day, pointing to my thin chest. I made the *stubborn* sign, putting my clenched fists together. "Little Mule."

Squatting by my bed, he nodded. "Little Mule."

I pointed. "You? Name?"

His handsome face, framed like a copper etching between the glossy dark braids, suddenly froze into a mask. Almost roughly he plucked the skins higher about my neck, and went off to sit in a dark corner of the tipi. He would talk no more that day. Probably I had broken some tribal taboo. I wouldn't ask his name again, but I was everlastingly grateful.

Slowly strength returned to my skinny body. For a part of each day I sat up, propped on a backrest of red and white hide stretched over a wooden frame. One day, when No-Name had gone to the river with his leather bucket for water, I got to my feet and seesawed dizzily across the lodge. Hanging to the skin flap at the doorway, I peered out. Tall lodges crowded the frozen banks of the Kettle; the Dacotah camp was a settlement of some magnitude. In the light snow people came and went, calling to each other, visiting, gossiping. A small boy led a spotted pony by a cord wrapped round the animal's lower jaw. Hacking with a long knife, an old woman cut chunks from a slab of meat hanging from a tree. On the frozen ice a pack of urchins skidded about on sleds made from buffalo-ribs lashed together with sinew, and laughed and shouted and bickered as small boys did once in Sweeney's Shambles. It was a medieval painting, framed by the green of the pine trees, their sweeping branches dusted with snow like sugar on some winter confection. Why there must be a hundred lodges along the Kettle! *God damn trouble*, Yellow Bird had predicted. That many Coup-Gorge Dacotahs could give god damn trouble to a whole regiment.

Near me a young man was painting symbols on a hobbled pony. With great skill he outlined a sun and its rays, and then drew on the horse's flank a jagged wound, dripping blood. When he saw me, he laid down his paints and brush and came over, holding out his hand. It was Fool Dog, the warrior I had chased with my hatchet.

By a mixture of signs and a few Dacotah words I knew and some small English he understood, he told me he was very glad to see me on the mend.

"*Sha*," he said. "*Sha*. Good."

"Mules?" I asked. "My mules. Are they all right?" For answer, he pointed to a group of small boys leading some Indian ponies down to the river to drink from a hole chopped in the ice. Dan and Beersheba went with the ponies, and looked recovered from their ordeal, hides shiny and even a little fat on their ribs. I nodded, and whispered, "Good. *Sha*. *Sha*."

Calling an old man to him, he gave the elder a few colored beads from a pouch at his waist and gestured round the camp. With a remarkably strong voice for so small and withered a

man, the ancient cupped his hands to his mouth and trotted
bawling about, informing the people that Little Mule was now
returned to health, and that all people should visit him and
congratulate him on his victory over the Winter God. At any
rate, that was the general sense of it. Fool Dog grinned delightedly at me, and put his hands over his ears in mock defence
against the old man's raucous voice.

"Loud," he said. "Oh, loud!"

Then No-Name saw me and scolded me for being out of
bed. The encounter between him and Fool Dog was curious.
No-Name seemed uneasy with Fool Dog, almost frightened
though still pulling at my elbow and urging me into the tent.
For his part, Fool Dog had a kind of sadness in his face when
he looked at No-Name and shook his head and sighed.

"Good-bye," I said to Fool Dog. He nodded, preoccupied,
and walked abruptly away.

As I mended many people came to see me, strange brown
faces made familiar by their obvious good hearts and interest
for my welfare. I was touched by the gifts they brought: a few
grains of sugar, which they called *chahumpskiaya,* folded in
paper-thin scraps of hide; some colored river shells; a bluebird
feather, delicate and iridescent. And one day No-Name informed me that Leaning Man himself was to visit me. No-
Name had taught me many Dacotah words, and under his
tutelage I attained some skill in the graceful and flowing sign
talk. For hours I sat across from him, watching his slender
arms wave about and his fingers flutter like birds.

"It is a great honor!" he said, excited. His dark eyes swam
with emotion. "Little Mule"—he made the sign, holding index
fingers at his brow and wagging his head back and forth—
"Little Mule is honored. I am honored. We are all honored.
Leaning Man is great chief."

"I am honored," I agreed. "We are all honored. *Sha.* Good!"

Arms held above his head, he swayed to his feet and began
a little dance around the lodge. Muttering words I didn't understand, he pivoted this way and that, his moccasins touching
the skin floor as delicately as birds flutter down on a berry-
bush. In spite of all my brashness and bravado and the books
I had studied, there were a lot of things in this world I didn't
understand and was too embarrased to ask. For instance, could
a man be a woman? At the Garden House in Utica I remembered
some coarse talk about that. In Sweeney's Shambles I had once
seen an odd-looking mincing man who was identified to me as

a sodomite, but I had thought that was some sort of religious affiliation. How could a born man be a woman? The physiology of the thing was not clear. Watching No-Name's little dance, enjoying its grace and delicacy, all the woman in him apparent, I pondered the question. At last, not able to stem the tide of curiosity, I pointed to him, looked questioning, and made the sign for *woman,* putting my spread fingers to my crown and raking them downward as if combing long hair.

"You? Woman?"

He stopped dancing, one foot suspended.

"You? Woman?"

With a muffled cry he burst from the tent, weeping. I came to the door and looked out. A winter sun was setting, a smoky ball poised on the tips of the dark trees behind the camp. In the slanting red rays, No-Name's moccasin prints in the snow were black and jagged wells, rough in outline as if a wounded animal had dragged itself away. He did not return to the tipi until the next morning. Composed in face and manner, he did not mention the incident, nor did I. Instead, he worked all day sewing porcupine quills on a buckskin shirt I was to wear on the morrow for Leaning Man's visit.

Looking in a cracked mirror, I was repelled by the goatish countenance that stared back at me. The skin, waxy-yellow in texture, lips cracked, nose thin and corpselike; I looked a caution. At the Blessed Kingdom I had shaved experimentally with a borrowed razor and was proud of the meager evidence of manhood. Now the straggly blond fuzz made me look like the muzzle of a hound that has ventured too near a porcupine. Trimmed, perhaps, it might give some worldliness to my face, but there were no scissors or shears about. No-Name, too, gave me to understand that hair on the chin was a disgusting thing, and sure to be disapproved by Leaning Man. Reluctantly, I let him pull out most of them painfully with a pair of river shells used as tweezers, and to tie back my long-uncut hair with a strip of otter-skin.

"*Sha,*" he said, watching me strut up and down in my new shirt and clubbed red hair. "*Sha!* Pretty!"

The word meant many things in the Dacotah tongue. First of all it meant *red.* To a Dacotah, anything red was fine. Fresh meat, red and dripping was fine. The sun was fine. An enemy's blood was red and fine. All *sha.* All fine. Maybe even my long red hair was fine. The color, at any rate, was unusual to the Dacotahs.

I was sitting cross-legged in the lodge playing a willow flute when Leaning Man, his uncle Yellow Bird, and the rest of the state retinue arrived. The Dacotahs were very odd about time. To state that you would do a certain thing at a certain time attracted devils, they thought. Iktomi, the god who was a trickster and knave, would certainly interfere and try to upset things. It was thought best to keep plans secret; consequently, No-Name and I were caught short by this visit. Dropping the flute, I scrambled to my feet. No-Name fled. Nervously I made the *welcome* sign and drew aside to let them enter.

There were a dozen or more, all big of chest and bowed of leg, dressed in shirts of deerskin and mountain sheep decorated with tufts of what looked like horsehair, dyed red and yellow, and designs worked out in porcupine quills and colored beads. Long ragged fringes trailed from sleeves and leather leggings, and their faces were painted. One man carried a hide shield with a sacred many-rayed sun in yellow paint, and most of them wore eagle-feathers stuck in the scalp-lock at various angles, the angle denoting how many enemies each had counted *coup* on. Several carried lances with pennons of red flannel or dyed hair that might have been human for all I knew. Bronze chests gave back a rich sheen from the fire, and the tipi was filled with that sweet-grass and smoke smell I had grown to associate with the Dacotahs.

"Welcome," I said.

A white man was with them, a fat scraggly-bearded man with an immense goiter that parted his whiskers so that they fell down in two dank tails. I had never seen him about the camp; he was probably an itinerant trapper called in to interpret, none of the Dacotahs having much English.

Not sure of protocol, I smiled and said, "Welcome," again. Leaning Man—it surely must be he—stared impassively at me. I saw how he came by his name. One leg was withered, and the foot turned in at an angle, giving him a leaning crablike gait. His face was cruel as an axe, with a great hooked blade of a nose and somber deep-set eyes. He wore less ornamentation than any of the rest, but there was no doubt he was a chief, or *wakicuaza* as they called it, and had great style and dignity. He gestured to the white man, and the white man spoke to me.

"Name's Albert Quigley. These folks call me Big Throat. Kind of a general trader round the Kettle River country." He bowed and scraped toward Leaning Man. "The chief wants you to keep on playing your flute, boy."

Leaning Man sat down, elbows on knees. The rest stood.

"But it isn't anything," I said. "A little flute—"

"Hop to it!" Big Throat said, a little impatiently. *"Hopo!* Play!"

I didn't like him at all. He seemed a born bully, respectful and toadying to superiors and doubtless cruel and selfish to those of less advantage. Since he appeared to think me wholly ignorant of the Dacotah tongue, I decided to let him continue that line of thought.

"Well," I said, "it was just an old Irish jig."

"Don't make no difference what it is. If the old man wants to hear it, you play it."

Sullenly I played a few choruses of "Clancy's Dream." When I finished that, Leaning Man gestured somberly for more. Obligingly I rendered "The Fiddler of Connemara," warming to my task; I ended with a flourish by performing an aria from an Italian opera, though this latter tune was not suited to a Dacotah willow flute.

I hoped Leaning Man liked my performance, though his face stayed as composed and impassive as weathered granite. Surely Italian opera was never heard in stranger surroundings or by a queerer audience. Finishing with a tricky cadenza, I missed some of the notes from the sheer pressure of dark eyes bearing on me. Sweating, I shook the spittle from the instrument.

"Sha!" Leaning Man grunted. "Good! Excellent!"

"Thanks," I said. *"Hie. Hie."*

He interrupted, jabbing a forefinger at me, speaking in that flat gravelly Dacotah tongue, signing the words at the same time in the *lingua franca* of the Plains Indians. His hands moved so beautifully that I caught my breath.

"Why do white people do bad things to my people?"

I caught it all in the signs, and in a large part of the spoken words. Proud I had done so, I was forming in my mind some words and sign to answer him, pleased also that a great chief had asked my opinion, when Big Throat broke in.

"Chief says—white people are all bad."

But that wasn't what Leaning Man had said! I started to speak out but bit my tongue instead. It could have been an error on the white man's part, just lazy translation. He looked slovenly enough.

"Well," I stammered, "he—he—well, tell him that not all white men are bad."

Making a few signs, he jabbered to Leaning Man. Though

I didn't follow them too well, I got the feeling that his interpretation of my words was no more accurate.

Speaking and signing in short phrases to let Big Throat translate, Leaning Man went on. I followed the chief's thoughts pretty well, and was bewildered and perplexed at the meaning the white man put on them. Either he was ignorant, or he was deliberately playing some kind of game. Even an idiot could hardly miss the meaning of the signs—beautiful, incisive, eloquent, almost a kind of poetry.

"The Kettle River has been our land for a long time. We hunt here. We live here. Why does the white man bring his wagons through our land and drive away the game? We do not bother him on *his* land." He gestured south. "Down there— they can go across there. Where the river forks there is a good crossing. No one hunts there. The land is dry and flat and the water is not deep."

There was a long silence. Big Throat yawned and looked at his dirty fingernails.

"I understand," I said.

Big Throat spoke to me out of the side of his whiskered mouth. "You don't understand nothing boy."

"What do you mean?"

"Don't no white man ever understand a savage critter. I lived 'mongst 'em for thirty year."

Staring into space somewhere beyond me, as if seeing a vision denied the rest of us, Leaning Man resumed his speech. "This is The Moon When the Wolves Run Together. But soon the snow melts, and the land becomes green. The white man's wagons come to Fort Jackson, as they did last year. The soldiers ride with them across our land, as they did last year." He gestured westward. "Last year we were few, and had to let the wagons go or the soldiers would shoot us. But this year"—his dark eyes kindled—"this year they will not cross the Kettle River. Our river. I have called all our people together. We will fight. There will be a big gravy-stirring."

Gravy-stirring. That was what the Dacotahs called a big fight.

"Some wagons come already. No one wants to kill anyone unless he has to. But the soldiers at Fort Jackson want to kill us because we protect our land. Little Mule, you are a white man. Maybe you can tell me why the white man treats us so bad? I would like to know."

Listening to Big Throat's rambling translation, I stirred

uneasily. There was a measure of accuracy in what he said, but he had a sly way of making the Dacotahs sound vicious and warlike.

"Tell the chief," I said, "that most men are good—white men and Dacotahs too. Often whole peoples do bad things when as persons they are good. I don't really know why, but I hope when The Moon When the Ducks Come is here there will not be any bad thing happen."

On hearing my words, Leaning Man grunted, and got up awkwardly, favoring his withered leg. He crabbed his way toward me, and for a long moment his cruel face stared unblinkingly into mine. Then suddenly he hit me a lick on the shoulder, hard; the force and suddennness of the blow staggered me. My Irish came to the top, and I doubled my fist and cocked a swing. But his lean face crinkled into a grin. He pointed to my clenched fist, and laughed heartily. Everybody laughed, except Big Throat. Leaning Man hobbled away, still chuckling, making the sign for Little Mule and shaking his head in amusement. At the doorway of the tipi he paused.

"*Sha!*" he called back to me. "Good. Excellent!" Then he left, followed by his retinue and the shambling white trader Albert Quigley. I would remember him, however, as Big Throat, and already had an idea I would meet him again. As he left, he gave me a cunning and prodigious wink.

⚍⚍⚍⚍⚍Chapter 18⚍⚍⚍⚍⚍⚍⚍⚍⚍⚍⚍⚍⚍

Of course, I didn't hanker to get caught up in any Indian war; that much good sense I had. At the same time, I enjoyed my carefree life with Leaning Man's Coup-Gorge Dacotahs. As a kind of privileged character around the camp on the Kettle River, I hunted with my new friend Fool Dog, raced with the other young men on the spotted pony Yellow Bird gave me, felt the juices of youth and life seep back into my body. On special occasions I was even allowed to sit in a corner of the great lodge and listen to Leaning Man and White Bull and the other leaders argue strategy and make plans and tell stories of the great old days. With growing skill and fluency I listened and studied and imitated, and was stirred by the poetry and imagery of the tongue.

Always in these councils, there was felt the necessity for instructing the young men, preparing them to take their place in the tribal councils. I remember old Turkey Wing one day singling Fool Dog and me out for his admonitions: "When you go on the warpath, look out for the enemy and do something brave. Study all you see, look it over, and try to understand it. Have good will to all people. Keep an even temper and never be stingy with food. Tell no lies. He who lies is a weakling. In this way your name will be great."

Leaning Man, not to be outdone, rose painfully to his feet: "Young men, always take good care of your horses. If you have a mare, keep her till she has a foal. If the foal will make a good gelding, train him for running. But if the foal is a mare, keep her—some day your neighbor may need help and you can give the mare to him. That is the best way to be famous and useful to all people."

The Coup-Gorges admired and tried hard to live by what they called the four great virtues: bravery, generosity, fortitude, and fecundity. In support of this last virtue it was not at all unusual for one of the elders to whip off the blanket draped over his skinny hips and display his private parts, calling attention to their size and boasting of the many sons he had begot. Though this was very serious to Fool Dog, I got taken with the giggles one day when old White Bull, one of the Scalp-Shirt Men, made such a display. Disgraced, at least for the moment, I fled from the lodge and had later to give White Bull my steel axe to calm him down.

There was in these daily meetings a great deal of bluffing and boasting and rhetoric, I suppose. But it would have been a mistake to underestimate the Coup-Gorges and their purpose. At The Moon When the Ducks Come they intended to smash the emigrant wagons and the pony soldiers that guarded them. Blood, much blood, would redden the waters of the Kettle River; there would be a great gravy-stirring. The Coup-Gorges, they said, would win a great victory. How could it be otherwise with their great numbers and their bravery?

During those days I learned much from Fool Dog, in particular the pathetic story of No-Name, or Two Moons, which was his real name. Such women-men were not often seen among the Dacotahs, but I could not help thinking that the Coup-Gorge treatment of them was very kind and humane. Fool Dog explained it this way. When a boy was fourteen or so he usually had a sacred vision, during which one of the Dacotah gods appeared to him out of a cloud or a tree or the sun and handed him the weapons of the warrior: lance and bow and arrow, the tools of the men. But once in a great while, Iktomi, the trickster god, darted in to snatch away the warlike implements and hand the youth instead the utensils of the women: the cooking spoon and sewing needle, the knife for scraping hides. When this happens, it is all very unfortunate, but what can be done about

Iktomi? Nothing. Instead, the name of the cheated youth is never spoken aloud again, so that Iktomi will not be able to find him and plague him further. *All,* Fool Dog sighed. *That is all. Finished.* He shrugged.

"So—" I prodded.

Well, that was the way it was. Too bad. Fool Dog made the sign for *unlucky.* Holding his clenched fists in front of his chest, he moved them down and out fast, snapping the fingers open: *medicine.* Then he followed it with *bad,* the two first fingers held at the temple and then moved upward in a spiraling motion. *Bad medicine. Unlucky.*

"But Two Moons was very good to me!"

Fool Dog would not discuss it further. Iktomi might hear us.

The plains winter waned, and new life sprouted from the winter-killed earth. Lambs-quarters, poke shoots, and wild spinach made a welcome change from our winter diet of meat and a little flour and cornmeal. It was still great fun, living with the Coup-Gorges, but nagging doubt began to assail me. Was this right? Did I belong here? Among the friendly brown faces I searched for a pale skin; in the guttural oratory and slashing signs of the councils I longed for a few words of English, my native tongue: the language of Milton and Shakespeare and the Holy Bible. Fool Dog, feeling my uneasiness, tried to divert me.

"Here, Little Mule. Take my pony. It is a present."

It was the thing most dear to his heart—a big-barreled deer-legged paint with slanting quarters and mulish hocks. The animal's hide was fantastically flared and blotched with white and on this account very lucky.

"No," I said. *"Hie. Hie."*

"Let us go hunt, then."

"I will think about it for a while," I said.

We sat together on a grassy rise overlooking the river. The sun was warm on our bare bodies. Painted as I was, wearing only a loincloth and moccasins, a passerby might almost have taken me for a Dacotah. My hair, though, betrayed me. As the sun came north across the plains and the days lengthened, my long hair seemed to get redder and redder. A few freckles popped out too, which I have never seen on an Indian.

"Agreed," I said. "We will hunt."

Together we flushed a whitetailed deer and chased it into a copse of bullberry where it stood trembling, believing we could not see it. Fool Dog cocked his arrow and drew back the bow. If there was time, the Dacotah always prayed to animals before killing them, and Fool Dog squinted down the shaft, crooning.

"I need you. Please come into my lodge. I will give you red paint, fat little high-jumper!"

The bowstring sang and the arrow pierced the deer, which tottered, fell, struggled to its feet, then fell again, dead. But the arrow might as well have struck me in the heart for at that instant, waiting for Fool Dog to make his shot, I glanced through an opening in the trees and saw across the river the flag of my own country snapping on a staff in the breeze; red and white and a faint smudge of darker blue, standing bravely out in the spring wind. Something caught at my throat. Skinning his deer, Fool Dog did not notice my emotion.

I had not realized we were so near Fort Andrew Jackson. When Fool Dog had stuffed the choice cuts into a folded blanket and tied it to his pony's rump, I rode back to camp with him, very thoughtful.

"You are sad," he said. "Why?"

"A vision," I murmured.

With the courtesy due a man who is having a vision, Fool Dog did not question me further.

That night I lay for a long time on a buffalo hide stretched under the stars. They were all there, sprinkled like bits of diamond on the sable sky: The Big Dipper the Dacotahs called Broken-Back; Mars, the Big Fire Star; the Pleiades they knew as the Bunch. Could the stars tell me what to do? Scenting a skunk or a raccoon, the camp dogs yipped wildly, a shower of needles piercing the night. I was wanted back there, where the moon was rising; wanted for killing Fat Henry and absconding with federal property—the mules and wagon—though they were really mine.

Well, I would go back. I must go back. I didn't really belong out here. Oh, I would miss Two Moons and Fool Dog and Leaning Man. I would miss the fine free life, the eating and the hunting and listening to the oratory in the big lodge. But I would go back. Under that snapping glorious flag there were white faces, English words, American ways. I would go back, and give myself up to the officer commanding. That decision made, I took a deep breath and went quickly to sleep.

In the morning I could not find Two Moons to tell him of my decision, but Yellow Bird and Fool Dog and the rest were aghast.

"Go *there?*" They pointed downriver. "But why?"

I went on hitching up the mules, grown fat now and sleek on the new grass. "I have had a vision."

"But—"

I shook my head. "I must go."

Unconvinced, they went to Leaning Man and White Bull with the story. I was summoned to the Big Lodge. They talked to me for a long time. Finally Leaning Man summed it all up.

"He has seen a vision. It is all up to him. A man must do what he sees in a vision. It is that way with all of us. I understand that." Hobbling forward, he put a hand on my shoulder. "Did your vision say anything about the wagons and the soldiers?"

"I—I don't know. That part was not clear."

He pulled an eagle-feather out of his black hair and looked at it for a moment. Then he stuck it in my hair. "Little Mule, go look for your gods. *Sha.* It is what a young man must do."

I bowed my head in respect. "I honor you. I honor White Bull and Turkey Wing and all the rest of the people. I owe my life to all of you, and I wish good medicine to the Coup-Gorges. I will never forget."

He followed me to the door of the great lodge. Fleecy clouds sailed in the sky, the river sparkled. Leaning Man sniffed the air, and savored it. Then he said, "We do not want to fight anyone. Tell the soldiers at Fort Jackson, Little Mule. Tell them for me. Soon it will be The Moon When the Ducks Come."

I nodded. "Agreed. I will tell them."

As I drove the wagon out of the meadow and down the sandy valley of the Kettle, filled with the melting snowwaters, I saw a shadowy figure dart through the trees. I think it was Two Moons. I stopped once and waved. There might have been the faintest flutter in return, though I was not sure.

I had thought Fort Jackson from its name to be some sort of medieval fortification, built of logs, no doubt, but fitted nevertheless with high walls, crenelated towers, perhaps a moat of sorts. If I had any romantic notions about blue-clad knights sallying forth to do battle, they were soon dispelled. The fort was a very ordinary place, situated on a grassy knoll about a mile east of the crossing of the Kettle River. There was a sprinkling of wooden buildings, a headquarters with a wide veranda, and under a few scraggly trees some long sheds for barracks. Around the periphery of the camp were fresh-dug rifle pits. At one end of the camp was a wooden stockade, no doubt for prisoners, and beyond that a kind of grassy park where some canvas-covered emigrant wagons stood. Even as I looked, more wagons rumbled down the grade into the park, wheels locked and the drivers cursing the terrified oxen. The westering wagons were coming.

The road from the ford to the camp was hub-deep in mud from the melting snows, and Dan and Beersheba had all they could do to drag the wagon and its burden through the sucking bog. Near the headquarters building, however, the earth was sandy and better drained. As I drove up, a few soldiers eyed me curiously, then went back to their job of mending a sinkhole in the road with brush and branches. Suddenly a man appeared just ahead; I saw him between the bobbing ears of the mules, and reined up, hauling on the brake.

"Just a minute, boy!" he called out.

Annoyed and a little unstrung because I had almost run him down, I stood up, crying out, "Why don't you look where you're going, damn it!"

He stared bleakly at me, a formless little man wearing a stained linen duster and a wide-brimmed straw hat. Pouches under his reddened eyes and gray-stubbled jowls gave him the appearance of an elderly basset hound. Setting down a leathern satchel crammed with papers and notes, he stood flatfooted before the mules. Ignoring their huge muzzles almost in his face, he took from some inner recess of the linen duster a patent metallic pocketbook.

"What's your name, and where are you from?"

His words were somewhat thick, and he swayed a little as if taken by a vertigo, but his hand was steady on the stub of the pencil. Indignant, I shouted, "What the hell business is it of yours? Now get out of the way of my mules, mister, or—"

"Allow me," he said, "to introduce myself. George Keeler of *Harper's Weekly*. On a special assignment at Fort Andrew Jackson to cover the Indian uprising."

"I don't know of any Indian uprising."

"There will be," Mr. Keeler said. "Ah, there will be!" Saying this, he peered upward at the spring sun, and ran a finger around his paper collar as if finding it a tight fit. "There will be," he said again in an abstracted manner. Then he pitched forward on his face in the mud, the patent notebook flying from his fingers in a sprawl of pages.

Why, the man was sick! Some frontier fever, no doubt. Hurrying down from the wagon, I got him under the arms. Looking around, I saw the soldiers still patching the road. My call to them elicited no interest. Across the road, on a stoop before the post's sutlery, a chevroned corporal smoked a pipe and grinned.

"Give me a hand, will you?" I called.

He didn't budge, seeming to find the whole thing very funny. Outraged, I dragged the limp body across the road, booted heels plowing furrows in the mud, and into the sutler's store.

It was a dim cavern of a place, even at midday lit with a guttering oil lamp, and smelling of rum and rusty bacon and unclean blankets. Some indifferent canned goods were on a shelf, along with some yard goods and a stock of lanterns and dried vegetables and fruits. In the rear several barrels stood on a rack, and behind a rude bar was my late friend Albert Quigley—or Big Throat, as I better remembered him. Pouring rum into a tin cup for a thirsty private, he corked the bottle with a blow of his fist, and then noticed me.

"Well, if it ain't the little half-breed from the Coup-Gorge camp!"

"Help me with this man," I said. "He's sick! Passed out entirely in front of my mules, and I almost ran him down."

They all laughed—Big Throat, the corporal in the doorway, the private with his tin cup of rum.

"Sick!" Big Throat howled. "Hell, he's drunk as a skunk! Never seen Keeler any other way, did you, fellers?"

"Drunk? But I—" Bending over the reporter, I smelled something kind of sour and acrid—something like a distillery.

"Get him out of here!" the sutler ordered. "I don't want no trash like that stinking up my place of business. Hell, he's into me for eight dollars jawbone already for liquor."

Coming out from behind the counter, Big Throat waved his hands menacingly. "You, too, you god damn little Indian-lover! We don't want your kind around here with decent folks."

In my beaded deerskin shirt and moccasins, hair tied back in a strip of shiny otter-fur, I probably looked the part of a savage, all right. The corporal too waved his pipestem at me and from a cloud of blue smoke bade me begone. "Get on with you now! No Indians allowed on the post!"

Angry and baffled, I dragged the senseless Keeler back on the stoop and down into the street, bumping his ass hard on each step. Big Throat loomed threateningly over me, holding a bungstarter.

"But what will I do with him?"

Wiping his mouth, the private with the tin cup snickered. "Just let him sink into the mud, eh, corporal?"

The corporal, a middle-aged Hibernian, knocked the dottle from his pipe on his heel. "He's got a Sibley tent down by the wagon-park. Dump him there if you've a mind to, and can stand the stink of him. Then get the hell off the post, boy!"

Furious, I dragged Keeler into the wagon and touched off the mules. Who in hell did these people think they were? I was an American citizen! Even out here I was entitled to *some* rights! They couldn't throw me off this post, but I would have to settle that score later with the commanding officer. For now, I had to do something about George Keeler, reputedly of *Harper's Weekly*.

In a thicket of bushes I found his tent, a sagging Sibley with a ragged drainage-ditch worked round it. From a stake driven in the ground hung a scrawled sign: G. KEELER, HARPER'S WEEKLY—OFFICE. I dumped him on the cot and threw a blanket over him. The tent was littered with scraps of food, empty bottles, cigar butts, bits of crumpled notepaper. Before I could get away, Keeler recovered enough to be sick all over his blankets. "Good Lord!" I groaned, and cleaned him as best I could. He rolled his eyes, groaned, and then dropped into a rum-soaked stupor. Leaving quickly, I could not help wonder how a great publication like *Harper's* ever came to hire such a wretch. On the other hand, it was probably not too hard to understand. They doubtless had trouble getting men to cover the Indian wars, most of the good reporters preferring the creature comforts of the civilized East or the European capitals. Well, it was none of my business; anyway, I had to make a visit to post headquarters.

The skinny private from the sulter's store was on duty at the headquarters veranda. Seeing me stride up on the porch he barred the way with his musket.

"Where do you think you're going?"

"In there." I pointed to the sign: A. HACKER, CAPT. USA. "I want to see the captain."

He gave me a little push with the musket across his chest. "Off with you, now! Didn't the corporal tell you to leave the post?"

I gave him a push back, a little harder. "Soldier, I've killed better men than you, and for less! Stand aside!"

My rough looks must have impressed him, for he looked uncertain and shifted his weight on his feet. A good inch taller than he was, and savoring every sixteenth of it, I gave him a real hardcase stare and brushed by him into headquarters. "Sir," I said, "I've come to give myself up."

⎯ Captain A. Hacker was a grizzled mastiff of a man, square-cut and soldierly. Bare to his waist, a towel tied round his neck half-covering a gray-frizzed chest, he peered into an oblong mirror, shaving carefully round the pepper-and-salt beard. He did not look directly at me, but one hard gray eye bored at me from the mirror.

"Who in hell let you in here? Don't you know this is a military post in hostile Indian country?" He swiveled to face me, wiping lather from his chin with a corner of the towel. I got the sudden feeling that a civilian was the lowest form of life in the Territory, three cuts below a squaw. "Well, what do you want?"

"I'm a fugitive from justice, sir. I'm wanted in Nebraska Territory for murdering a man and stealing federal property, I guess. It was all a mistake, but still and all I've come to turn myself in and take my punishment. I'm tired of running away."

He snorted. "You damned civilians and your grubby little crimes! I don't care if you assassinated a congressman and burgled the Mint! I've got an Indian uprising on my hands!"

Bewildered, I said, "But I—I think I must have broken some federal laws! Where can I go to give myself up?"

He put on his shirt, buttoning it with military precision. "That's your problem, boy. Now if you'll kindly get the hell out of my office—"

"But couldn't you just put me in your stockade till the federal marshal can come and get me?"

He stared at me as if I were mad, not because of my insistence on being arrested, but rather for my presumption in aspiring to a military prison. "Why, damn it, the stockade is for *soldiers!* It's full anyway with troublemakers and misfits and guardhouse lawyers, the dregs of the East!" Pulling down his coat, he jerked violently at the hem to straighten it. "How they expect a man to fight a war with pimps and thieves and petty criminals is beyond me!"

Well, that was that. I'd have to take my business elsewhere.

But that talk about having an Indian war on his hands bothered me.

"There isn't any danger of an Indian war. Not yet," I said.

He looked at me as if I were from some strange planet. "What did you say?"

"The Coup-Gorges don't want to fight. Leaning Man himself told me that. All they want is for the wagons to stay out of their lands and cross the Kettle River farther down. The country on the far side of the river belongs to the Coup-Gorges by treaty. Leaning Man showed me a paper."

"Pah! A paper!" The captain prowled up and down the room, hands locked behind his stiff blue back. "Every tribe west of the Mississippi has got a paper some politician gave them, and they're not fit to wipe your butt on. Don't talk to me of papers. This is a time for Phil Cook's *Cavalry Tactics,* not for papers!"

"But couldn't you talk to them, and——"

"I tried that once. No, they don't understand. They're ignorant savages." He went on, ranting about the lower crossing of the Kettle. "Impossible! Out of the question! Fifty miles farther for the wagons, that way—clear round Red Buttes and Saleratus Springs. No, there's no question of it, none indeed. Those people in the wagons are American citizens, and entitled to the help and protection of the Army. That's what my orders say." Going to the window, he looked out at the distant wagon-park. "Those are voters, boy, lots of voters. One of 'em is a Senator's nephew, and another is a distant cousin of President Andrew Johnson. I don't like 'em, but it's a sad truth for a military man that this raggedy-ass peacetime Army depends on voters for its bacon and beans. Why, at Chancellorsville—" Breaking off, he turned fiercely toward me. "Say, aren't you the white boy Quigley said was living with the Coup-Gorges?"

"I guess so."

"Squaw-man, isn't that what they call it?"

"No one ever called me that."

"Well, anyway you're bound to see things different. No, those Dacotahs are a warlike people, and planning mischief. Quigley tells me all about them."

This was too much for me. "Quigley is a scoundrel."

His grizzled brows seemed to discharge electricity. "What do you mean by that?"

"Quigley is a self-important and ignorant man. He hardly speaks their language—at least he doesn't get the real sense of it. I suspect he's got his own fish to fry. *I* wouldn't depend on him; I don't think the U.S. Army should."

Grudgingly, to be sure, he turned a little more rational.

"Well, beggars can't be choosers. This tinhorn War Department don't allow me funds for interpreters. Mr. Quigley has been very helpful, and in return I managed the sutler's contract for him. I trust him. He knows the Dacotahs—lived among 'em for years. Besides, I've got a few tricks up my own sleeve. Let the Coup-Gorges try me out. I'll deal 'em a hand too hot to handle!"

"But there's no need for an Indian war here! If you'd only palaver with them. They're not bad people, really, and—"

He held up his hand. "No more! I've got to lay out a field of fire on my maps. Then I've got to inspect the new rifle pits. Best move on, boy, and stay out of trouble." He gestured toward the door, and unrolled a parchmentlike map, spreading it on the table. As I left he called after me. "Wait a minute. Play chess?"

"No," I said. "Never learned."

"Whist? Any card games?"

"I'm afraid not."

Tracing a line on the map with his forefinger, he appeared to have concluded the discussion. Feeling dismal, I left, pausing only to glower at the newly respectful guard on the veranda.

The sun was setting in the west, and a chill soaked into me as the shadows lengthened on the muddy road. I don't think one man has ever felt as lonely and sad. I had left Leaning Man and the Coup-Gorges, the federal authorities didn't appear interested in me, Captain A. Hacker couldn't even use me for a friendly game of cards! Moodily I slogged toward Keeler's tent where I had tied the mules. *Best move on,* Hacker had advised. But where, and to what end? Sighing, I untied the mules. At that moment George Keeler stuck his head out of the Sibley tent.

"Who's there?"

"No one," I said, "of any consequence. Just mules—three of us, in fact."

Making a face, he spat, and ran a liverish tongue round his lips. "God, what a taste in my mouth!" Beckoning me in, he lit a lantern and offered me some hardtack and a tin cup of hot coffee. "Don't ever go into the newspaper business, boy. Be a swindler or a procurer or rob poor boxes. Anything else. Oh, my head!"

"I don't think the newspaper business had anything to do

with your head. You were just swinishly drunk."

He sipped moodily at his coffee. "Well put! Swinishly drunk! Gadarene swine! Pearls before swine! All that. Oh, the richness of the language!" Suddenly he brightened. His basset-jowls shook and his rheumy eyes flared with interest. "Say, aren't you—I mean to say—you're the white boy that old Quigley said was living with the Indians across the river."

"I guess I am. Charlie Campion."

With shaky fingers he got out one of his patent metallic notebooks and spread it on his knee. "By God, this is fabulous! Now tell me—" Pausing, he pinched the bridge of his nose between his fingers. "Oh, that's right! Now let's see—you were down the road, and I—I—"

"Yes," I said. "You damned near got yourself run over by my mules."

Thoughtful, he nodded. "Have you ever smelled a mule's breath—close up, that way?"

"Then you fell down, and I, like a damned fool, thought you were sick. I carried you into the sutler's store, and they said you were drunk again and threw us both out. So I brought you back to your tent and left you."

He shook hands with me earnestly. "I've been very sick, Charlie. Stomach trouble. Take a little bitters now and then for the stomach. But I'm eternally grateful to you for your kindness. George Keeler never forgets a friend. Ask anybody." Dropping some powders from a folded paper into the tin cup of coffee, he took up his pencil and notebook again. "Now, about your life with the Indians. What a fascinating story! Imagine, way out here on the pimply-assed end of creation I meet a decent human being. Let's see—where were you born?"

"Never mind that," I said. "I'm more interested in the war that's about to break out on the Kettle River. What's the matter with that Captain Hacker? Is he trying to be some kind of a great hero or something?"

Keeler sipped at the coffee and made a face. "Youth is a time of great perception, Charlie. You've struck right to the heart of the matter. Of course he wants to be a hero! Alonzo Hacker was brevetted brigadier at Chancellorsville, and he's never forgot it. Now, of course, he's only a captain, pensioned out on the poor-farm. Of course he wants to be a hero. That's the only way back for him."

"Well," I said, "he'll be a hero all right—a dead hero—if he trusts old Quigley very far."

"Why, of course!" Keeler said joyfully. "Old Quigley wants him to be a hero too—wants a big battle on the Kettle River. Hell, there's no money trading with Indians and selling a few jugs of rotgut and plugs of tobacco at the sutler's store! When the Kettle River route is opened up in a few days, old Big Throat'll get rich peddling wormy flour and moldy bacon and horseshoes and tin lanterns to the wagon trains."

"So that's it," I said. "I might have known. Captain Hacker motivated by ambition, Albert Quigley by greed, the Coup-Gorges by simple trust in a scrap of white-man's paper. What a sad and ominous mixture."

Rummaging under the cot, the reporter found a dozen empty bottles. By draining them successively into one, he managed perhaps a tablespoonful of oily-looking rum. "Only thing settles my stomach when I have these spells!"

"You don't seem very worried about all of Fort Jackson being massacred by a thousand Dacotahs," I said. "After all, how many soldiers are there here? Say a hundred?"

Keeler looked mysterious. "What about the gun?"

"Gun? What gun?"

"Hush!" He put a finger to his lips. Teetering to the tent-flap, he lifted it, peered about at the dusk, and came back to collapse on the cot. "What I need, Charlie, is another small drink to kind of tamp down my stomach for the night. I don't suppose you—"

"I gave up drinking," I said.

"Well, maybe you could slip up to the sutler's and buy a little—say a pint—"

"No. I'm out of funds. Penniless."

"Maybe old Quigley would give you some on jawbone."

"Drink the rest of your coffee," I said cruelly. "Now about this gun. What gun?"

"Oh, well. Don't talk so damned loud. It's supposed to be a military secret. Old Hacker has got a fieldpiece in an emplacement above the river. Got it laid right on the crossing—a twelve-pound Napoleon loaded with canister. If the Coup-Gorges stand and fight he can blast them to bits."

"A Napoleon!"

"Shhhh!" He looked nervously round. "Don't blab it all over the camp! It's a secret—a military secret. Don't anybody know about it but Hacker and the adjutant and a detail that hazed into there. It wouldn't be worth beans, would it, if everybody *knew!*"

Suspiciously, I said, "How do you know so much if it's such a big secret?"

He looked smug. "That's a reporter's business, finding out secrets. On the Washington *Evening Star* I was very good at it, until I got this upset stomach, of course."

"A fieldpiece," I said. My mouth tasted funny, like verdigris. The Coup-Gordes had never seen a Napoleon. A thousand braves, they would mass at the crossing and defy Captain Hacker and the wagons. When they did, they would be cut to ribbons by the shrapnel—torn, shredded, annihilated. Almost unbidden my damp palms slid across each other in the sign for *finished, wiped out*. "A Napoleon," I muttered.

"Now remember," the reporter cautioned. "It's a secret. It would be my ass in small chunks if it was found out." Changing the subject, he spread his notebook on his knee again. "Now just how was it with the Coup-Gorges, Charlie? What did you do there? How did you fall in with them anyway?"

I sighed. "It's a long story, and pretty dull, I guess."

"Just to let me keep my hand in," Keeler urged. "You know—taking notes, narrative skills, the vivid phrase, all that." He grinned. "Hell, it might even sober me up. Think of the stars in your crown for *that!*"

"All right," I said dispiritedly.

I told him the story of my life with Yellow Bird and Leaning Man and Fool Dog and the rest, showed him some of the sign-talk, told him old Dacotah legends about Iktomi and Rock and the rest of the gods.

"But how did you come to be with them?"

One thing led to another. I had to tell him about Brother Adrian and the Blessed Kingdom and Ike Coogan and the hunting of buffalo by balloon and all the rest.

"You mean that big thing in your wagon is a *balloon?* Suffering Moses!" The pencil scratched busily, and he reached for a fresh patent metallic notebook. "Greatest invention in the world, these little things. Sir Richard Burton used 'em in Arabia. But how did you *know* about the balloons?"

Of course, I had to explain about Count Blatski and Mad Jack Spurrier and the rest of it.

"Some of the old Boyle's Brigade are here at Fort Jackson," Keeler said. "A sergeant and two or three enlisted men." He finished his coffee and wiped his mouth. "Now how was this again? Exactly what were you running from when the count's balloon came along?"

Then I had to go clear back to the orphanage and old Mr. Gillentine and the hop farm. When I told him about Annie, he clucked sympathetically. "A fine girl, that!"

"The finest," I said warmly. "Some day, when I've served out my jail sentence or whatever, I'm going back and marry her if she'll have me!"

All night long we talked. I didn't realize it till the lamp went smokily out, and a new day filtered through the stained canvas of the Sibley.

"Well," I said, "I'm ever so much obliged to you, Mr. Keeler. It's been good to talk to a white man after such a long time."

He held an empty bottle wistfully to the new day, tipped it this way and that; finally he tossed it under the cot, sighing.

"Guess I'll be getting along," I said. "Thanks for the coffee and the company."

"Where will you go?"

"Oh . . ." I hesitated. "Maybe the Coup-Gorges will take me back. There's no place else to go." I didn't tell him I was weighing the possibility of getting to Leaning Man and telling him about the deadly Napoleon.

He followed me to the door of the tent. Together we looked out over the valley of the Kettle, the far shore rimmed with dark trees, a mist lying in the bottoms. A finger of smoke curled from a cookhouse fire; a bugler shivered in the chill, holding his instrument to his chest to warm it; two riders walked their mounts slowly down the road toward the wagon-park.

"Well," George Keeler said, "good luck, Charlie." He shook my hand. "It's been—it's been—" He broke off, staring at the riders. "That looks like Alonzo Hacker and the adjutant. What in the devil are they doing up and about so early?"

Slowly the riders picked their way toward us. They passed the turnoff to the crowded wagon-park, where cooking fires were going too, and made for us. I didn't like it. I didn't want to be delayed. But there was no choice. Hacker reined up before the Sibley tent, followed by his adjutant.

"I understand, Campion, that the big package in your wagon over there is a balloon—an observation balloon."

Chapter 19

For a minute I didn't say anything. I didn't know what to say, but something told me to be careful.

"Come, come!" Hacker urged. "Cat got your tongue, eh? Is that a balloon in the wagon or not?"

I couldn't deny it was a balloon. "Yes."

"Man-carrying balloon?"

"Yes, sir. It carried me."

"Good." He slapped a gloved fist on the pommel, and his mount pranced a little. "I need that balloon, and you too, boy. How soon can we get it into the air?"

George Keeler looked at me, his nose twitching a little as if he were smelling something. A story for *Harper's*, perhaps? Or just something rotten?

"Sir," I said, "what do you want the balloon for?"

Captain Hacker stiffened. He was in command here, and evidently not used to being questioned by civilians.

"We won't get into that. Anyway, there's no need to worry about details. I'll submit a requisition to the Department Commander for services of a balloon and aeronaut at five dollars per diem for the duration of the emergency. There, isn't that fair enough?"

"But what *for?*" I insisted.

His face got red above the wiry thicket of whiskers.

"Military business. That's all you need to know, boy."

Suddenly I knew what it was all about. I'd read in *Leslie's* about Professor Lowe and his great four thousand meter balloon filled from the gasometer at Washington, the capital.

"It's about the gun, isn't it? The Napoleon."

He jerked as if a minié ball had struck him. "What are you talking about?"

"The Napoleon. The twelve-pounder you've got hid to turn on the Coup-Gorges. You want me to spot fire for you. Well, I won't do it. I'm damned if I'll do it!"

The adjutant kicked his mount forward and tried to grab my collar. The big dun shoulder hit me and brushed me aside, and I evaded his grasp. "Why, you little whelp—how dare you sass the captain?"

Furious, I yelled back, "God damn it, don't try riding me down again, you nickel-plated monkey, or I'll drag you off that crowbait and—"

Captain Hacker rode between us. "Now just a minute here. Lieutenant! Stand easy!" Reins gathered in his fists, he stared bleakly down at me. "How did you know about the Napoleon?"

Fair caught, I could only stammer and blunder. "I—I just— I found out." I didn't dare raise my eyes for fear they would wander and fix on George Keeler. I waited for the reporter to take me off the hook, but he didn't.

"You found out, did you? Well!" Captain Hacker's words were casual, but there was no mistaking his anger. "I have, then, to remind you that this is a military zone—an area under imminent threat of attack by greatly superior Dacotah forces. There are penalties for spying in a military zone, boy. I'd hang you in a minute if you don't cooperate with the military authorities."

"Meaning you," I muttered.

"Yes, if you want to put it that way."

"Sir," I said, "I won't use my balloon against my Indian friends. And as to imminent attack, all they want is the rights guaranteed them by treaty. If you'd only talk to them, reason, discuss the issues, maybe even work out some kind of a compromise—"

His brows drew together in an iron-grooved furrow. "I have all the information I need as to their warlike traditions."

Quigley. That rascal! But it would do no good to chew that

cabbage again. It would only make Hacker more angry. Instead, I said, "No. I won't do it."

George Keeler fidgeted, and murmured, "Good for you." The captain stared him down, remarking, "When this affair is finished, Mr. Keeler, you and I have some talking to do." Turning back to me, he said, "Won't do it, eh? You refuse?"

"Yes, sir. And I know my rights." I was talking through my hat, which I often did. "I'm an American citizen, and I can't be conscripted into anyone's army."

"I saw John La Mountain and his balloon operate in Virginia," the captain said tightly, "and I know what that balloon can do for me here. I don't intend to be balked. You know, of course, I can confiscate your balloon."

That hadn't occurred to me. Confiscate my beautiful *Petit Géant II?* "Can he?" I asked Keeler.

The reporter appeared cowed by Hacker's bluster, and looked away.

"Can he?"

"I assure you I can, and will," Hacker said. "Military emergency. I need it, and now. You were perfectly correct; however you deduced the information. I want the balloon to lay my Napoleon. With the Napoleon I've managed to even the odds a little here on the Kettle River. With the Napoleon and the balloon, I'm not afraid of the whole Dacotah nation. I'll cut 'em to ribbons." His gloved palm cut like a sword in the morning sun. "I'll break their back for all time. I'll . . ." Pausing, he seemed to regather his thoughts. "Well, Campion?"

"I won't have anything to do with such a shameful undertaking!"

He nodded curtly. "Then we have men who can figure out a way to get it into the air."

I hadn't thought of that possibility either. It was true; Archimedes' principle was certainly no secret. It would be no great trick to build a fire and inflate my balloon for their purposes. She needed a little fitting, of course, some patches and new cordage, but they'd figure a way to do that.

"And as for you, Charlie Campion or whatever your name is, I've put up with enough from you. With all my responsibilities as officer commanding, I can't take chances." He turned to the adjutant. "Lieutenant, put him in the stockade."

"In the stockade?" I blurted. Now that he was willing to put me there, I didn't want to go. "On what charges, sir? Mr.

Keeler, they can't do this to me, can they? I'm an American citizen. I—"

This time the adjutant collared me, choking off my words. Though he was a big rawboned man, I was giving him fits when Captain Hacker called for some soldiers to help. Finally, spent, breathless, and near to weeping with the indignity of it, I was pinned down and my wrists were tied behind me. From the saddle of the chestnut gelding Captain Hacker gave me an agate stare.

"American citizen or not, Mr. Campion, you're a threat to military security. You know too much. Into the stockade you go till I've settled the hash of Leaning Man and his bloodthirsty savages."

"But—"

"Take him away." Now in easy command of the situation, the captain waved toward the distant stockade. "And, lieutenant—"

"Sir?"

"Put leg-irons on him. Take no chances!"

"Yes, sir."

Trussed like a chicken for the spit, I was borne ignominiously away.

The stockade was a rectangular structure of pine logs set side-by-side vertically into the earth, making a wall about ten feet high. Inside were some rough lean-tos of sticks and branches and daubed mud; a gigantic log lay on the ground, spikes driven in to secure leg-irons. A few prisoners lounged about—the sick and the halt, I judged—the rest being out to work on roads and outbuildings under an armed guard. A sergeant with a blue-shaven lantern jaw took over my care from the adjutant, shackling me to the log with a skillet-sized padlock.

"Keep a sharp eye on him, O'Meara," the adjutant advised. "Captain Hacker's particular orders. He's a tricky 'un."

"Never fear, sor," O'Meara said. "He's in the stockade entoirly, sir. I'll give him my personal attention."

When they had left, slamming the log door to and barring it, I sighed and took stock of my surroundings. I seemed to have an affinity for trouble with the law, both civil and military. Each time my persecution had been unjust—I could explain everything, at least to my own satisfaction—but there I was in jail anyway. *Guardhouse lawyers,* that was what they called them in the Army. I could give a dozen unassailable reasons why Captain Alonzo Hacker could not commit me; yet here I was in the stockade, and in leg-irons, at that.

I had, I observed, a companion at the great log. Head propped on his arms for a pillow, the ragged fellow slept sweatily in the dust, unaware or uncaring for the commotion of my coming. He had a kind of worn medal pinned to his shirt, and I thought wryly that the medal hadn't sweetened his case any. Well, there were two of us desperate criminals on the post, it appeared. I wondered what his offense had been. He slept on; the other prisoners did not appear to notice me either, instead gathering in a sunny spot and murmuring to each other some sort of gossip I was too distant to hear. Pondering my sad condition, I eventually dozed too. The sun was warm and soothing, and I had been awake all night talking to Keeler.

At noon the stockade sergeant came round with a detail bearing a pot of bean gruel and a sack of moldy bread.

"Still here, eh?" O'Meara joked, and kicked my sleeping companion awake. "Mess call!" After whistling an off-key bugle-call he supervised the distribution of rations.

My gyved neighbor seemed to be a person of some consequence. Two bleached spots on his shirt seemed to indicate the recent removal of chevrons, and as soon as the mess detail departed, the rest of the prisoners carried the food over to our log and built a small cooking fire to boil some coffee.

"Beg your pardon, Sergeant," one of them said to my neighbor, waving a ragged shirttail to blow away the smoke. "Didn't mean to smoke ye like a ham, did we, fellers?"

The late sergeant yawned and stretched and looked sourly at the greasy porridge and the ossified bread. Finally he took his portion, soaking the bread in the gruel, and ate it indifferently. It was too much for me, however; the stench from the bean-porridge was almost gangrenous. When I didn't eat, he appeared for the first time to notice me.

"New member, *hein?* You don't look like a soldier to me, boy. How did you get in here?"

I told him my story, and he frowned thoughtfully.

"What did you say your name was?"

"Charlie Campion, sir. From New York State."

His mouth dropped open. "Charlie!"

"Eh?" I said, startled. "Yes, sir. Charlie Campion."

"Don't you remember me?"

I stared at the stubbled sweating cheeks, the lean planes of the face and temples, the wary Greek-statue-like sensuality of the lips and mouth. . . .

"Good Lord!" I cried. "Is it—can it be—"

He grabbed me in a bear hug, somewhat hampered by our chains. "Charlie!"

"Sergeant Bregand!" I gasped. It was indeed Philip Bregand, the sergeant I had ridden with out to Ohio on the steam-cars with Boyle's Bastards so long ago. Or was it so long? How long? A year ago, perhaps a year and a half. An eternity of time, eons of time. "It's you—Bregand!"

"*C'est moi-même,*" Bregand said. Pushing me away so as to better examine me, he grinned delightedly. "Charlie Champion! Almost grown."

"Friend of yours, Sarge?" someone asked.

"The best. Oh, the best!" His features wrinkled in mock sternness. "Didn't I tell you to stay out of the Army?"

I told him about my adventures, culminating with the balloon difficulty of the morning. "So you see it wasn't any of my doing. It was more Captain Hacker's idea."

Bregand chuckled. "Balloons? *Mon dieu!* And old Hacker, eh? He's a real hard-case. A good soldier, though."

"What are you in for?" I asked.

"Striking an officer."

"Hacker?" I gasped.

"No, that damned *bâtard* of an adjutant. He provoked me, you could say. It wasn't a soldierly thing to do, but I hit him. As a man, I had too."

"I know," I said. "I had trouble with him too."

Digging at the huge spike that secured his leg-chain to the log, he took out a quantity of what appeared to be mud and ashes, and filled the cranny with hot coals.

"What in heaven are you doing?"

He smiled. "Heaven has nothing to do with it, *mon enfant.* I'm burning my way out of here." He showed me where the coals had charred and consumed the wood so that the spike was loose. "You don't think Philip Bregand intends to go back to Fort Leavenworth and die on a rockpile, do you?"

I looked nervously round. The other prisoners were playing cards with a greasy pack in a corner of the compound.

"Don't worry about them. They've got two of the stockade logs sawed almost in half for me already. Ah, they're small-time offenders—a week or ten days in the stockade at the most. They're not about to break jail. But they're helping me."

Seeing the concern on my face, he clapped his hand over the smoking hole. "You won't give me away?"

"Of course not. You know better than that."

"I knew it. Of course I knew it. *Pardon!* Just jumpy, I guess." Then, hearing boots outside the compound, he quickly plugged the hole with dust and ashes mixed with what was left of the bean soup. "Almost finished," he said, and lay casually back, winking at me. When O'Meara entered with his detail to recover the pots and utensils and see that the cooking fires were put out, Philip Bregand was apparently asleep. In the corner some minor argument had broken out over the cards; otherwise everything was peaceful and quiet, and the puffy white clouds soared high in the sky, occasionally dappling our compound in shadow. The air smelled fresh-washed and clean.

"Ah, you're good boys!" O'Meara said jovially. "Model prisoners. Never give the old sergeant an instant's trouble, do ye? Be sure and be here for supper, lads; there's a marvelous slum a-cooking!"

Chained to a log in a stockade, a man's diversions are limited. Bregand and I talked about old times: Captain Wagner, the battle with Mad Jack Spurrier at Mauckport on the Ohio River, bits and snatches of remembered history. However, I was listless in my participation. I had a great decision on my mind. Bregand, a little nettled, said, "Charlie, you're not listening."

"I am too."

"Then what did I just say?"

"I—I—"

"What's the matter with you? Do you fancy yourself too good to associate with a jailbird? For if you do, you know, you're entirely correct, *bien sûr,* and I'll not further tarnish your young manhood!"

"Don't be a fool!" I snapped. "That's not it at all. I—I was just thinking—"

"Of what, pray?" He was still angry.

"A private matter. I'll tell you—you'll be the first to know when I decide."

"Well, then—" Tipping his forage cap over his nose, he turned on his side, grumbling at the restraint of the chain, and went to sleep.

What to do? I gnawed my knuckles in desperation. I had been in *so* much trouble. Was it worth it to gamble, and perhaps sink deeper? One voice in me spoke loud and clear. *Don't be an idiot. Escape is impossible. Even if you bring it off you're still in trouble. Just sit tight till the Indian trouble is over. Alonzo Hacker can't hold you then, not legally; he'll have to let you go. Charlie, don't play the everlasting fool!*

But another and more insistent voice spoke to me, and it was the voice of conscience and not self-interest.

You're a damned coward to sit here, meek as a whipped hound, and let Hacker slaughter your Coup-Gorge friends. For that's what he'll do, you know. He wants a big battle, and a lot of glory for A. Hacker, USA. If you could only get out of this place and warn them!

Coolly and reasonably, the first voice spoke again. *What then? Do you think the Coup-Gorges will be scared by a twelve-pound Napoleon? Be sensible—they've never even seen one! They don't know what it can do. They'll charge right into it and be slaughtered anyway. What makes you think you can change anything?*

Distraught, I rose to my feet, feeling the damned chain pull to its extreme and hobble me. "I'll *make* them see!" I cried. "I'll explain it to them! I'll work something out!"

It was dusk, and a rind of moon floated in the sky. *The Moon When the Ducks Come.* Seeing a shadowy flicker against the lemon radiance, I could imagine them to be ducks on their way northward. Bregand, smoking his pipe, arms crossed over his updrawn knees, spoke.

"Have a nightmare or something?"

"No."

"You were so quiet. Then—*voilà*—you cried out and jumped up."

"I don't know what happened."

Courteously, he did not question me further. I squatted down again, wrestling with decision. Could I ask Bregand for advice? No, that wasn't the way out. He had enough troubles of his own. This was my decision to make. Try to reach Leaning Man and his band? Sit tight and keep my hide out of further trouble? The two voices raged on in my brain, babbling and contradicting each other, trying to shout each other down. And, finally, when I had had enough of the bickering, I made my decision.

"Sergeant," I said, "I want to escape with you."

His pipe glowed red in the dark. "You can't do that. *Non!*"

"But why not?" I explained my reasons. "It's—it's something I've *got* to do! A point of honor. Please let me go with you. Once I'm out of the stockade I'll take my chances and get to the Coup-Gorge camp myself. I won't bother you anymore."

Bregand was surly. "That's a damned fool thing to do, you know. *Quelle bêtise!* Once the Indian trouble is over, Hacker has got to let you go. All you have to do is wait, and—"

"Damn waiting!" I cried. "They're my friends!"

"But they're Indians, Charlie, savages! Hell, they're vermin, really no better than the Tuaregs I fought in North Africa. It's too bad, but the Coup-Gorges are holding up civilization. They're in the way, they've got to go."

"But they're my friends, like you are! I can't let Hacker turn that Napoleon on them. You struck the adjutant, you said. As a man, you had to! The same way with me. As a man, I've got to warn them. I've got to do it."

He bit down hard on his pipe. "If you do anything to upset my plans—"

"I might," I said coolly. "That is, unless you let me go with you when you escape."

For a moment I thought he was going to strike me. His face was pale, and his eyes hard and cold.

"Besides," I plunged recklessly on, "what are you going to do when you get out of the stockade? You'll need a horse, won't you? I know the Coup-Gorges. I can get you a horse and other help too. Isn't that a fair enough exchange?"

Knocking out his pipe, he stuck it into his bootleg. "You talk so fast, Charlie. Ah, what a talker! You'll talk me to my death someday."

"Then you'll let me go with you?" I cried.

"Tomorrow we'll try burning out your spike the way I did mine. In the meantime, try working at it with your fingers and see if you can loosen it." Angrily he passed me a bent spoon. "Use this to dig with. And keep at it. I've got no stomach for them to come and take me back to Leavenworth just when I'm ready to leave by the garden gate."

"Thanks!" I cried. "You're a true friend."

Pushing my hand away, he muttered. "I'm no friend of yours, and don't care to be taken for such."

"But—"

"Stay away from me. Don't even talk to me, you damned infant! Follow me like a bad penny, will you? Christ, you're nothing but bad luck!"

Stiffly I said, "If you want to back out—"

"Ah, *tais-toi!* Blabber, that's all you do. Blabber, blabber!" Angrily he turned his back and rolled into his blanket. The moon rose high in the sky, and I could still hear him fidgeting under his blanket and muttering to himself.

At Bregand's instruction, a road-gang prisoner named Flannery reported back the next night on how my balloon was faring. A ferret-faced man with thin colorless hair slicked over a bald dome, he relished the importance of his assignment.

"'Ah, they've got the machine all laid out flat on the level plot by the Napoleon emplacement. What a great thing it is, like a dead animal of some sort. The boy here built it, ye say?"

"There were a lot of holes in it," I said, digging at the spike with my sharpened spoon. "What are they doing about them?"

Flannery wrinkled his brows, and smoothed his threads of hair. "Why, now, I was too far away to be sure, but it seems to me—yes, I'm certain of it—they were boiling something in a pot and brushing it on. Smelled like tar to me, bucko."

I nodded, dejected. "Tar it would be." Someone knew what they were doing.

"They're laying on new ropes, too," Flannery said, "and fitting a wee brass stove to the netting somehow."

"How long before they get her up?" Bregand asked.

Flannery shrugged. "I'm no balloonist, Sergeant dear. How am I to know such a thing? The way they're laying to, it won't be long."

Bregand looked at me and my spoon.

"Tomorrow night we've got to leave. I don't relish being spied on from a balloon when I'm breaking clear of this place. Dig! Dig hard with that damned spoon!" His own chain was now free, and mine was all that was holding us up. "Hurry, now, keep at it. *Dépêches-toi!*"

"I am! Look, my fingers are bleeding!"

"Idiot that I am! I'm risking the whole damned breakout just for you. Did you know that?"

"I know it!" I snapped.

Wrapping himself in his blanket he would talk no more.

The next day I worked like a Trojan, picking away at the spike and packing hot coals around it to burn it free. My fingers were raw and blistered; periodically the tin spoon collapsed and had to be straightened. Once O'Meara and his detail nearly caught me and scotched the whole enterprise. Entering without warning they were almost on me and Bregand, and smoke was still curling from the enlarged hole. Only some monumental pipe-puffing by Philip Bregand concealed my work. Even then, I think, O'Meara was suspicious. Fondling his blue jaw, he peered warily about and muttered to himself. When he left he stood a long time in the gateway, rubbing his jaw and scowling. Then he went away, perhaps to double the guard or take some extra precautions.

"That was a close one," Bregand said. "Next time—"

"There won't be any next time. I'll make it tonight or give up, and you can go without me."

That afternoon I asked Flannery how the balloon was coming.

"Looks to me like they got it all patched and ready to fly," he said. "They brought in a big stack of firewood. Something's going to happen pretty quick. That park is jammed full of wagons and the people are raising hell with the captain because he won't let 'em cross the river yet."

"Hacker doesn't want to make his move till he gets the balloon up," Bregand said. "Clever. A good soldier, Hacker." He thought for a moment, then said, "We ought to go tonight. Is the spike free?"

"Almost."

"Two in the morning. Agreed?"

"*D'accord*," I said.

Never did I breathe such a sigh of relief as when I finally pulled that damned spike out. It was well after midnight. I could tell by the pointer stars for the Big Dipper that the Dacotahs used as a kind of clock. Bregand clapped his hand over my mouth. "Shhhh! You'll wake the dead!"

"I'm free!" I exulted.

"Not yet," Bregand cautioned.

He whistled low to the rest, and they stirred out of their rude shelters and scurried over to shake hands all round and say good-bye. Crouched together in the moonlight, we made last-minute preparations and used rags to muffle the noise of our leg-irons—though free from the log, the cuffs were still round our ankles, with a dangling length of chain. Flannery was to lift the sawed logs with Hawkins and let us slip out.

"It'll be hard traveling with that chain," I said to Bregand. "Once we're at the Coup-Gorge camp they'll help us get them off."

"Damn your Indian camp!"

I was mystified. "Didn't you say you were going there with me?"

"I changed my mind," he said sulkily.

"Well, *I* don't give a hang where you go!"

"Good. The less you know, the less you'll have to blab when they catch you."

"They won't catch me."

"See that they don't!"

On this unhappy note we waited for a cloud to drift across the moon. A sleepy sentry called: "Post number three, all's well!" From down by the crowded wagon-park a dog barked.

"Let's go!" Bregand hissed. "Now!"

Little hairs prickled on the back of my neck. As I crawled over to the stockade wall all round me shadowy figures crouched, crawling, murmuring, excited, wishing us well.

"Push away the logs!" Philip Bregand commanded.

Solid enough in appearance, they broke with remarkable ease when the prisoners put their shoulders to them. Still secured at the top with great iron bolts, the logs swung like a pendulum and we scurried through. Bregand went first, carrying a sharpened spoon like a dagger. He pulled me after him, and let the great logs swing silently to behind him. We were out of the stockade.

"Well," I said, "this is it. We go our ways." I held out my hand but he did not take it.

"What's the matter?" I whispered.

"Bad luck. *Mauvais*. That's all you are to me."

"Well," I said, "bad luck or not, we'd best be going. The corporal of the guard will be making his rounds in a few minutes."

A spangle of moisture on his brow glittered in the moonlight. "I've changed my mind. I'm going to the Coup-Gorge camp with you, Charlie."

"All right," I said, "but you change your mind more often than a woman."

"I didn't change it. I was going all along."

"But you said—"

"I said you were bad luck for me, and you are. I said you could talk the feathers off a bird, and you can. But I have a misbegotten feeling I ought to see you safe to the Indian camp before I turn you loose. You can get into the damnedest scrapes."

I was indignant. "I don't need any wet nurse!"

He put a big hand over my mouth and threw me to the ground. In the shadows of the stockade we crouched like two animals, listening, sniffing, alert for danger. A sentry strolled through the moonlight, musket at high port, looked round, then turned the corner and disappeared.

"There!" Bregand muttered. "You see? You damned near got caught already, and not two minutes out of the stockade!"

"But—"

"Tais-toi, and follow me."

Together we crept from the shadows of the stockade into a faint moon-radiance. Hurrying across a patch of gold-washed grass, I felt as if I were caught in a locomotive headlight. From a thicket of juniper we peered out, spying the way ahead. A silver-embroidered cloud edged across the moon; in a window of the headquarters building an oil lamp burned yellow. I could smell wood-smoke. Was it that near dawn? Were they boiling coffee already? Before us, in a greasy clearing, lay the great black envelope of the balloon. *Petit Géant II,* I said inwardly. *Oh, heavenly vehicle! Good-bye, good-bye!* Overcome, I blundered away, and fell headlong over a man. The man squeaked like a rabbit, and it was not Philip Bregand. Bregand was a dozen yards ahead of me, stepping like a ragged lynx through the brush.

"Don't shoot," a voice quavered.

A well-remembered distillery fragrance filled my nostrils.

"What in the Devil—"

"It's me. George Keeler."

"Keeler."

Hearing our voices, Bregand ran back, light on his feet as a deer. Before I could explain, he had the sharpened spoon at Keeler's throat.

"Wait a minute!" I grabbed at his arm. "It's Keeler."

"Who?"

"George Keeler. The *Harper's* reporter."

Bregand dropped his grip on the reporter's collar, disgusted.

"What are you doing here?" I hissed. "How did you know—"

"Remember?" Keeler said delightedly. "I told you. It's a good reporter's business to sniff out the news. My God, what a story this will make!" He had his patent metallic notebook clutched tightly in his hand, and the emerging moonlight gleamed dully on it. Philip Bregand pressed the sharpened spoon against the reporter's throat again.

"Who else knows?"

"Nobody! I swear it!"

"Are you sure?"

"It's God's truth!"

I was still looking at the balloon. I couldn't go and leave her that way, among strangers.

"Give me a match," I said.

Bregand was incredulous. "What in hell do you want a match for?"

He wouldn't give me one, but George Keeler, giggling, pushed a half-used block of sulphur matches into my hand. "Go to it!" he whispered.

"Now wait a minute—" Bregand protested.

As I crawled out toward the balloon, I heard him groan, "Ah, Christ, what else can go wrong!"

The balloon made a lovely fire. At first only a dainty lapping of flame at the edge where I had touched the match, it spread in fiery rivulets that spanned the varnished expanse in the wink of an eye. Suddenly the orange and yellow runnels flashed together in a great whooshing Niagara of fire. A crackling like musketry deafened us, and a wall of heat drove us back into the brush.

"Look what you've done!" Bregand shouted above the roar.

George Keeler shouted through cupped hands. "The blaze'll keep 'em busy for a while. They'll never even miss us!"

Into the night the great smoke-crowned plume rose, higher and higher. Some of the nearby bushes burst into flame, crackling resinously. Swinging dots of light speckled the headquarters building, and a bugle stuttered. The fiery death of my *Petit Géant II* was like the bursting of some great bubble, beauty and dreams and a geometrical perfection vanishing into nothingness. I felt a great pain in my chest and then only a leaden sadness. I was crying. What had vanished? Only a balloon? Or something even more insubstantial—my youth?

"Damn it!" Bregand shouted. "Come on. Let's go!"

It was not the first time I had felt that sad unknowable feeling, but then it was all of a piece. A man loses his youth in small fragments, a bit here, a piece there, until finally, as tonight, with the heat burning my cheeks, the last remnant flies away into the sky, never to know earth again. My eyes were wet, but not with weakness or maudlin sentiment or self-pity. No, they were a man's tears at last, honest and just.

George Keeler was yelling in my ear. Arm in arm, he and

Bregand dragged me through the underbrush till the whipping of the twigs and vines in my face raked me free of my reveries.

"Which way to the camp?" Bregand panted.

I pointed north, indicating a wide sweep to bypass the rifle pits. This precaution, however, proved unnecessary. Probably contrary to orders, the pickets climbed from their trenches to run toward the headquarters building which was already being menaced by a finger of red snaking through the grass.

A little before dawn, scratched and bruised and winded, we stumbled on the Coup-Gorge outpost. The scout, a young man of my acquaintance named Torn Shirt, recognized me and took us directly to Leaning Man's lodge—a drunken reporter, a fugitive from a court-martial, and an almost-eighteen-year-old man who wanted to stop an Indian war if he could.

⁓⁓⁓Chapter 20⁓⁓⁓

On the way to the state lodge, George Keeler followed me like a leech, face fixed in an incredulous grin, eyes shining, clutching his patent notebook. The Coup-Gorge chiefs, alerted by some frontier telegraph, waited for us in the great tipi, and the Fox Society guards were at the door. I had thought they would refuse entrance to the reporter, but he scurried in behind me.

"All right," Bregand muttered. "Where's that horse you promised me? I'm in a hurry."

"Just wait," I said. "I'll get you a horse."

Nervous as a cat, feeling a great fullness in my chest, I stood alone before the smoldering fire. Above me towered the soot-blackened cone of skins. Through the smoke-flap I could see a solitary bright star: Mars, the Big Fire Star. To many peoples it was symbolic of war. I hoped it would not be so, this spring dawn.

Even at this desperate time, protocol must be observed. I waited while the chiefs, squatting in a semicircle around the fire, each took a puff at the big soapstone pipe, blowing smoke upward to Wakan-Tanka, chief of the Coup-Gorge deities. Then, after an interminable time, Leaning Man gestured to me, handing me the pipe.

"Hie," I said. *"Hie."*

Squatting across the fire from them, I dragged deeply on the pipe. It was a new experience for me, a privilege in deference to the important news it was understood I brought. For one horrible moment the rank *kinnikinnick* strangled me, and I feared I was going to burst into a fit of coughing. But I successfully swallowed the tickling in my throat and completed the maneuver, blowing aloft my prayer to Wakan-Tanka in the prescribed four directions.

"Hie," I said again, handing back the pipe.

Even now, it was not courteous for me to speak. The first words must come from the chief, the *wakicunza*. Leaning Man, however, did not seem to be the least interested in me. He stared fixedly into the dying coals of the fire, and he and the other chiefs, cross-legged, were silent. From the corner of my eye I could see Keeler's pale face peering from the gloom, waiting also, pencil and notebook poised. From the forests beyond a catamount screamed, a knifelike sound that made me start and fidget and hope that no one noticed. Finally, Leaning Man spoke. He raised his arm in the gesture of welcome.

"Little Mule has come back to the lodges of the Coup-Gorges on our Kettle River. We welcome him." Elegantly his hands fluttered to accompany the guttural words. "Tonight there was a great fire at the camp of the soliders. Trouble, much trouble, at that camp. We know some of these things from our scouts. But our friend Little Mule knows more about it than we do, friends. Maybe Little Mule will tell his old friends the Coup-Gorges what is happening and what we should do."

I tried hard to speak slowly and thoughtfully, keeping my signs clean and sharp and measured in tempo as the great speakers did.

"Friend, they put me in prison because I was one of you." I showed them my iron-cuffed ankle. "Some men helped me get away, and there was a big fire." I did not attempt to explain a balloon to them. It would only waste time, and they would not understand it anyway. I was going to have a hard enough time explaining a twelve-pound Napoleon cannon to people who had never seen anything bigger than the few old .58-caliber muskets they had traded wolf and otter skins for.

"The Moon When The Ducks Come is here. Many wagons are at Fort Jackson. Soon they will cross the Kettle River, with a lot of soldiers to guard them. The Coup-Gorges are very brave. They will try to fight the soldiers and stop the wagons.

But I, Little Mule, tell my friends they must not fight the soldiers. They must not!"

For what must have been an historic first, I seemed to have broken the composure of a Dacotah council. They fidgeted, looked at each other, looked at Leaning Man, muttered, and grumbled. Some looked puzzled, others uncomfortable, a few became downright hostile. An old medicine-man shook his rattle at me, but Leaning Man raised his hand. Calm was restored.

"My friend Little Mule is not a coward. He does not run away. He does not tell anyone to run away from a fight. That is not the way the Coup-Gorges do, and he knows it. We all know it. So we must listen to Little Mule with a good ear and have him make all words clear to us."

The leg-chain clanking, I scrambled to my feet, seizing one of the old muskets that was propped against a lodgepole.

"This is a white man's gun. The Coup-Gorges know this gun and they know it shoots a long way. But the soldiers at the fort have a bigger gun. They have a great gun that goes about on wheels." I paced off on the skin floor the length of the barrel and with my hands showed them the size of the bullet. "This big gun shoots a very long way. It can shoot all the way to the Coup-Gorge camp. Now it is aimed at the crossing of the Kettle River. If the Coup-Gorges go down there and fight, the big gun will kill them all. The Coup-Gorge women will have to gash their arms and paint their faces white. This big gun is bad medicine, friends. I speak the truth."

There was uneasiness and considerable skepticism. Turkey Wing said, "No one has got a big gun like that." Axe arose, strutted about, and said, "How can they see where to shoot so far?" Yellow Bird shook his old head and commented, "Little Mule does not lie. But what is a gun, friends? A little gun kills one man. So. A big gun kills two men, or three. We are many. Let them try to kill us all. I say we should fight them."

I tried to explain about a canister shell. "First comes the big bullet. Then, when it hits, it comes all apart and a lot of little bullets fly out with great fire and smoke and kill many men." I held up both hands, fingers spread, and waved them back and forth to indicate *this number many times over*.

White Bull snorted in disbelief. "Little Mule is sick in the head! He is trying to scare us. He is white, friends. He is telling us crazy things to scare us. Do not believe these crazy things!"

Dropping all protocol, I cried, "No. No! My friends are brave! I cannot scare brave men! But I know these things are true! I do not want all my friends to die for nothing! I do not want Axe's woman to paint her face white. I do not want Yellow-Bird's sons to sing his death song in an empty lodge. I do not want White Bull's daughter to gash her arms. I do not want these things to happen, and for *nothing*. When great men die, it must *mean* something! It is foolish for all the great chiefs of the Coup-Gorges to die at the river!"

I do not know whether I was properly eloquent, but something in my wild-eyed exhortation stayed them, perhaps even moved them. Leaning Man motioned for silence. Squatting again, they passed round the pipe. Gray light filtered into the lodge. Birds cheaped in the bushes, and outside the lodge the Kettle River, *our* river, flowed on. I dragged on the pipe again and passed it back to Leaning Man.

After a long pause he spoke.

"I think Little Mule speaks the truth. I am a chief. I know things other people do not know. That is why I am a *wakicunza*. A man can look at this thing with two hearts. First"—he held up one finger—"the white men have many things. I know this. They have a big gun. They have many people over there." He waved to the east, and I knew he meant the distant East— places like Cincinnati and Chicago and New York City which he had never seen. "They have great lodges many times higher than ours, great camps with many people, big canoes that run fast on the water without paddles, a magic thread to talk a long way. But do these things make them just and brave and *right?* No. I say no!" He pounded his bare chest. "Those virtues are in *here,* and the Coup-Gorges have more of them than any white man. So we can run away from the gravy-stirring when we are right in *here.*"

"No!" they all shouted. "No!"

"But"—Leaning Man held up two fingers—"there is another way to think. It is a chief's way to think, not a warrior's way. I have sons. They will have sons, and their sons will have sons. If we are bound to die, let us die in such a way that they can live and hunt and pray to Wakan-Tanka and be happy and useful. Let our deaths *mean* something to them, buy something for them. Little Mule thinks like a chief. He is a wise young man, who thinks. So"—he poked the dying embers with the stem of the pipe—"a chief must think of all these things. I know how to fight, friends. But right now I do not know how to fight and die and make my dying mean something to the people. Just to die, that is not enough. If we all die, and the wagons come anyway, what does it mean?"

Anyone else but Leaning Man might have been taunted as a coward for these words, but no one spoke.

"What does Little Mule say?" Leaning Man asked.

It was not the ceremonious way of asking advice, and must have indicated the torment in Leaning Man's brain.

"We must go to their camp and talk with them," I said. "Axe, Turkey Wing, Yellow Bird, the *wakicunza*—all the leaders and the Scalp-Shirt men and the great warriors." In a moment of revelation I thought again of what Ike Coogan said: *People cause all the trouble*. And one of the troubles was that while a man could talk to a man and have a fair chance of understanding, a people could not talk nearly as well to a people. But if I could only get both sides together at Fort Jackson, let the Coup-Gorges see the gun and what it could do, let Captain Alonzo Hacker understand the merits of the Coup-Gorges' case and their determination to protect their river and the lands that it drained—

"Fool!" Axe protested. "We have tried to talk to them. They do not listen!"

I saw George Keeler scribbling like mad. *Great. What a story!* If he only knew how much more was at stake here beyond a story for his damned paper!

"Big Throat told them what we said!" White Bull argued. "They know what we say. Why does anyone need to talk any more. I say we should fight them!"

"Big Throat is a liar and a rascal," I said. "He does not like the Coup-Gorges. He wants them all away from here so he can sell things to the people in many wagons. Big Throat speaks with two voices!" I jabbed out two fingers, forklike. "Let me go with you to the soldier camp. I will talk for you. I will tell the captain what is true and right." I raised my arms. "Will you come with me and do what is right? If they kill all of us, then you did what great chiefs do. You tried to do the right thing, and the people will remember!"

George Keeler was carried away. Though I didn't think he understood too much of what was being said, he nevertheless shouted "Hurrah!" and was stared stonily down by Turkey Wing, who hunkered near him.

"Will you come?" I pleaded.

Slowly Leaning Man struggled to his feet. He looked round

the lodge a long time, studying the face of one man and then the next. Finally he sighed—a thing I had never before heard an Indian do—and crabbed his way over to me.

"This once," he said, "we will come. We will try." He hit me smartly on the shoulder. And at that instant an explosion rocked the camp. The lodge lifted as in a whirlwind and split in two. There was a blinding flash of light, and a split second almost photographic image of torn bodies flung this way and that. Stumbling blinded and deafened from the wreckage of the great lodge, the chain still dangling from my leg, I knew with agonizing certitude what had happened. Alonzo Hacker had brought up the Napoleon and turned it on the Coup-Gorge camp.

The sun was just rising over the horizon, and the slanting orange rays lit a scene of panic and confusion. Across the river, at the edge of a thicket of junipers, the soldiers had set up the Napoleon on a rise and were firing into the Indian camp. No need for a balloon to lay the gun; they were at point-blank range. As I stared, horror-struck, a flower of smoke bloomed from the muzzle, tipped with orange light from the sun behind them. I flung myself flat, and a gigantic hand seemed to press me into the earth. Flying fragments sheared a heavy limb from a tree and dropped it on me. Struggling weakly under the tangle of greenery, I looked transfixed at that deadly battery. Philip Bregand had said that two or three rounds a minute was good shooting for a Napoleon. These men were well-trained, and feared no counterfire. Capable men, in spite of Captain Hacker's complaints, they had dragged the gun up there undetected during the night. Now I could see them like distant toy-soldiers, ramming and swabbing and charging like clockwork. They were doing better than two or three rounds a minute, much better. Seeing the flash from the muzzle, I dived headlong into a root-snarled hollow and huddled sick and trembling, hands plastered round my skull in a useless frightened gesture. *Cr-r-r-umppp!* The earth shook, dirt flew into the air and rained down through the leaves like pattering rain, saplings tottered and fell. Damn them! Oh, damn them!

Powdered with tiny sparks, my deerskin shirt was burning. I beat them out as best I could, and staggered to my feet. Leaning Man's camp was burning. Yellow flames licked at the tipis, now broken and askew. Acrid smoke filled the clearing. A woman screamed, a raw saw-edge of grief that tore my soul. Twisted and mutilated bodies lay round me and a tiny naked child tottered about, weeping, splattered with blood not his own. Some few of the Coup-Gorge warriors were running this way and that, trying to find their ponies and make a stand.

"Stop!" I cried to the gun. Reeling down the slope toward the river, I held up my hands in supplication. "Stop, damn it, stop!" In the shallows I stumbled over a body. It was Fool Dog, head forward facing the enemy. He was cut almost in two as though by an iron knife, and red tendrils of blood curled into the swift clear water. His hand still clutched a bow, and feathered-tipped war arrows floated prettily out of his half-submerged quiver and sailed downstream like painted boats.

Crr-rr-rump! The shell burst on the bank behind me, shattering a tree into splinters that rained down on me. The concussion blew me flat on my back into the mud. For a moment I lay there, wondering if I was going to drown. Drown? How queer, to drown in the midst of all this fire and flame and hell!

Lying stunned and helpless was probably what saved me. Across the Kettle River, raising a vapor of foam and iridescent spray, came Hacker's cavalry. Their lifted sabers sparkled, and then big hoofs splashed and sucked in the mud near my head.

Well, I thought, *this is it. Charles Campion, 1848–1866. Almost eighteen, but never to be eighteen. Annie, I loved you best of all! Our Father which art in Heaven.*

Unaccountably, the big-shouldered big-hoofed wave passed over me. The horsemen thundered up the slope. Their sabers flashed and fell and rose and flashed again. Like fox-hunters they yelled and hallooed and their ground shook with the drumming of their wild-eyed mounts. Feebly, I struggled to drag myself to the bank. "Stop!" I whimpered. "Stop! Don't! Please don't!"

It was soon over. The camp was a shambles; fallen trees, burning lodges, the smell of black powder and fresh blood. Away in the trees up the river some of the Coup-Gorges were apparently still fighting, for I heard shouting and the discharge of pistols, and once, only one, a defiant war-whoop. But the camp was quiet, or relatively so. A wounded woman tried to drag herself into the bushes, and a soldier ran her through with his saber, pinning her to the ground till she ceased to wriggle. A camp dog tore with white teeth at a haunch of venison that had fallen from a tripod; a soldier shot the dog dead and picked up the venison, wiping blood off it with his gloved hands. Broken bodies, ruin, red quick death. Dante might have marveled.

"Charlie!" George Keeler had lost his straw hat. His duster was torn and grimy, his face blackened by smoke, but he was apparently unharmed, a sheaf of notes in one trembling hand. "Are you all right? God, what an opportunity!" He shook the notes high over his head in a gesture of triumph. "A first-hand account from the Indian camp! And it's mine, I wrote it! Why, it's history!"

I would have struck him, but my arm was made of lead. My fingers twitched, that was all. "Go away," I said. "Just go away, will you?"

A soldier with a bayoneted musket prowled up. He looked at me in my Indian clothing, anxious I suppose, for some new triumph, and raised the point toward my chest, something very old and dim in his eyes. I didn't even care. What if he did think I was a Coup-Gorge? It was a kind of honor. But George Keeler pushed him away. "Go on about your business, soldier!" There was a hard edge to his voice that no longer sounded like any comfortable old basset-hound.

"Are you sure you're all right?" Stuffing the notes into his pocket, he helped me to my feet.

"I guess so." How could I tell him I was wounded inside, desperately, where it would never show? Where was Two Moons? Leaning Man? All my friends, all my good friends? "George," I said, "it was murder. Sheer murder!"

I was standing with his arm supporting me, staring down at the body of Philip Bregand, when Captain Hacker rode through the diamond-flecked shallows and up the slope into the camp. Bregand was dead, instantly dead; you could see that from the crumpled appearance of his head under the gallant old forage-cap, and the great jagged rent in his belly. The French medal was still pinned to his shirt. He had been proud of that. *As a man,* he had said, *I had to.* As a man, he had had to do this too. I had never got him the horse I promised.

"Bad luck," I said. "He always told me I was bad luck."

Bregand had died because he thought I needed taking care of. In this topsy-turvy world there appeared to be room for the most absurd extremes of honor and dishonor, cruelty, passion, kindness, hate, love . . . I felt very tired, and sat on a fallen tree to rest.

"Well!" Captain Hacker said in a businesslike way. "There you are, Campion."

"Yes," I said. "Here I am."

Big Throat Quigley was with him, and the blue-jawed Sergeant O'Meara.

"That's the one!" O'Meara cried. "Cap'n, he's the one! Oh, I took him for a clever rascal when he was put into the stockade, but—"

"Shut up," Hacker said. He sat the big horse easily, with the sagging comfortable seat of the cavalryman. "Well, what have you got to say to the sorry mess you've caused?"

"*I* caused!" Sick and giddy as I was, I sprang to my feet. "I caused nothing. But you, sir, are a murderer—a bloody butcher of women and children!"

He flushed and drew up ramrod-straight. "This is a military business you're mixed up in, boy! I'd advise you to keep a civil tongue in your head, for you're in deep already. Breaking stockade, spying out our defenses, burning the balloon, traitorous conduct, giving aid and comfort to the enemy—oh, I could go on and on!"

I sounded terrible, but I didn't care. "Stop calling me boy, damn it! I'm more of a man than you are with your monkey suit and Napoleon cannon and blood all over your hands!"

"Before I throw you back in the stockade," Hacker said tightly, "let me tell you something. I'm a military man. It isn't up to me to ask sticky questions of Washington, or go running to the Department to have my nose wiped. It's just my trade to get those wagons through. When you escaped and burned that balloon, I knew there was going to be trouble. I knew you were here inciting these savages to attack. I knew I had to strike first, or be wiped out—and the wagons and settlers too. You damned lousy civilians, you don't know what command responsibility is! You sit on your fat stupid asses and cry murder every time an underpaid hardworking soldier defends himself! Well, I've had a bellyful of that swill! Murder, indeed!" He swiveled round in the saddle. "Sergeant, put this man under arrest. And if he gets away again, I'll tie you up and flog you myself before the whole regiment!"

Flinging himself off his mount, O'Meara cried, "Yes, *sir!*" and ran toward me. But George Keeler put himself between me and O'Meara. "Just a minute!" he said. He took wads of notes out of his pockets and assembled them neatly into a square little package, adjusting the loose ends like a gambler with a deck of cards. "Captain, I wouldn't detain Charlie Campion if I were you."

Hacker's eyes burned hard and bright. "Why not, pray, Mr.—Keeler, was it?"

"Keeler it was and is. George Keeler of *Harper's Weekly*." For the first time since I'd known him he was dead sober—and in dead earnest too, with a hardness in his voice to match Alonzo Hacker's granite stare. "Let me explain what I mean. This boy—this *man*—did a great thing which *Harper's* readers will want to know about. Great magazine, *Harper's*. Dedicated to the circulation and popularization of the truth. And I've got the truth all here, in this little package, ready to send back east by telegraph soon as I can get to a station."

Hacker drew the reins tightly across his knuckles. "Stand fast for a moment, Sergeant O'Meara." To the reporter he said, "My time is valuable, Mr. Keeler. What the hell are you driving at?"

"Just this. Do you know what the truth is, Captain? The *real* Socratic truth, not the simple and easy *military* truth? Well, I'll tell you." I would swear he pulled himself up three inches taller than his normal basset-height. "Item: You put Campion in the stockade on questionable grounds, him being a civilian. It's doubtful if any court would sustain you."

"Military necessity—"

"Item: he broke out—or at least he walked through a gap in the stockade wall. Anyway, he was wrongfully confined and deprived of his liberty. Item"—Keeler ticked off another on his fingers—"He burned the balloon. Well, it was *his* balloon, wasn't it, illegitimately seized and no payment made?"

Hacker snorted. "I would have prepared a requisition. The War Department would pay the fair value."

"That's for the courts to decide." Keeler was, I observed, making the captain uneasy with all this talk about courts. "This could be a celebrated case in the annals of jurisprudence. It could make you famous, captain—or more likely, notorious. Item—and this is a rouser: Do you know what that boy was doing in the Coup-Gorge camp? By God, it was one of the greatest performances I ever saw! Old James H. Hackett himself doesn't belong on the same stage as this young man. Why, sir, it was magnificent, and it's all right here in my notes! Single-handed, speaking the native tongue, he convinced them, these rude warlike savages, to ride down the river with him and talk to you about the best way of avoiding a bloodletting. After weeks of trouble and tension, in the midst of great personal peril and difficulty, Charlie Campion almost turned the damned tide, like Canute. Do you know Canute, sir? Well, no matter. At any rate this modern-day Seneca very nearly brought it off! And that, sir, was when your damned Napoleon started firing upon a peaceful Indian village! That was when your myrmidons swarmed across the reddened waters of the Kettle River and butchered—yes, I say butchered—human beings whose only fault was a simple faith in a scrap of paper from Washington, and whose chief virtue, which betrayed them, was to believe that some accommodation might yet be made!" He fairly blasted the words at Hacker, and the captain's gelding started nervously, and pranced. "No, sir. I should advise you to sheer off from any further molestation of this young man. *Harper's* publication—the power of the press, some call it—stands behind this man. You, sir, will have enough to do to explain your actions before an examining board." Almost as an afterthought, Keeler lifted the torn tail of his ragged linen duster and examined it. "Ruined, absolutely ruined! Ah, well. Maybe the auditors will allow the cost to legitimate expenses in the field."

"Sir?" O'Meara said impatiently.

Captain Hacker's face was a study. He stared for a long time at George Keeler, who eyed him ferociously in return. I fancied I could see all kinds of thoughts floating past Hacker's stone-hard glare, like actors seen dimly in the wings. Once he clawed briefly at his grizzled square beard, and then he rested his hands quietly on the pommel again, as if they had betrayed him.

"Captain," Albert Quigley said, "this is all foolishness. Hell, you don't have to take that kind of talk! If it was me, I'd—"

"It's not you," Hacker said, and in the tone of his voice I knew we'd won—if you could call this a victory. "No, it isn't you, Quigley. It's me—and the Army." Suddenly he wheeled his horse, shouting, "Let him go!" and dashed away upriver where scattered shots were still sounding. Somehow I felt sorry for him. Quigley looked perplexed, but rode away after him. Sergeant O'Meara spat, and wiped his mouth. "Don't ever let me catch you round Fort Andy Jackson!"

I said a most indecent thing to him, and he got red in the face and swore, but took my leg-iron off and rode away with the iron chain swinging from his cantle.

"God," Keeler said, "I wish I had a drink! I sure *need* a drink."

Only one final thing happened. A soldier staggered blindly from the brush, a white-faced young private leading him. Some of the Coup-Gorges were selling their lives dear; the corporal's skull was raw and bloody, and a few flies had already settled on it, drinking eagerly.

"He's been scalped," the private whispered. "Here. Look!" He had the corporal's hair in a bucket of water. "They said I could keep it alive that way till a surgeon sews it back on. Where's the surgeon? Has anyone seen the surgeon?"

Looking at the dead furry thing floating in the bucket, I became suddenly sick. This time it was George Keeler who had to clean me up.

I got my wagon and mules returned to me and went west with the emigrants. I didn't have anything against them; they seemed mostly good solid people, the kind you make a country great from. Leaving in such a hurry, not wanting to be reminded of anything about the bloody massacre on the Kettle River, I didn't even say good-bye to George Keeler, in spite of all I owed him. He knew how I felt, anyway. I was sick, mentally and physically drained, a failure at eighteen. I didn't even want to *think* about anything, just drive the mules and stare westward hour after hour at the long white-tented wagons snaking ahead, up and down, over streams, through bogs, over mountains, always into the setting sun.

From here on it's not a story, really. Nothing happened: no violence, no great adventure, no important happenings of a dramatic significance. But it *was* funny, the ways things worked out.

Six months later—about September, I think it was—I had me a job in San Francisco, hauling dirt with my team and wagon to fill behind a new wharf at Owen's Shipyard near Hunter's Point. I'd run about as far as a man could go. Then there was nothing beyond me—nothing but the blue waters of the Pacific, a spangling of lace atop the breakers as they rolled in. This was the end of my journey; I'd just have to make my peace with the people out here.

"Injun Charlie," they called me, with my long hair and beaded shirt and all. I didn't care. Mostly it was joshing, and otherwise they let me alone to think and consider. It was rumored I had killed a man. Well, I guess I had. But the pay was middling, though not intended to make me rich, and Dan and Beersheba were thriving. A man has to earn his living somewhere, somehow, and this was as good as anything else.

Once, on a summer evening down off Pacific Street, I saw

a gold-lettered sign that said J. CAMPION, FINE WATCHES. Trembling, I took a deep breath and pushed open the door. I don't know why I should have felt so giddy. Behind a low bench there sat a withered little man who pedalled a whirring lathe.

"Eh?" He looked up, spectacles shiny in the lamplight. "What is it, young man? Watch, eh? Watch not working?"

I shook my head. "No, sir. I—I haven't got a watch. I'm looking for someone."

He came to the counter. "Well, I've lived here for a long time. Know practically everybody around here. Except the sailors on the ships. They come, you know, and go. Come and go."

"Ned Campion," I said. "Please, do you know a Ned Campion? Spelled just like on your sign, only *Ned*. Ned Campion."

He took off his spectacles and polished them with a wisp of cloth. Without the spectacles his eyes were wet-looking and red-rimmed, and he couldn't see much. Finally, hooking them over tufted ears, he stared at me.

"Ned Campion."

"Yes, sir."

He shook his head. "There's a few of our name around here. Seems to me I know all of 'em. Where did you say he was from?"

"Back East. New York City. He was said to have come West."

The watchmaker ran a thoughtful hand over his chin, and the sound was dry and raspy against the neat ticking of the clocks. "No. No, no one by that name. What was his trade?"

"I don't know."

"Well." He shrugged. "I'm sorry. Kin of yours?"

"Yes. Well, maybe. I don't know."

I felt like a fool. Seeing his old hand tremble, and realizing I was making him nervous, I thanked him and left the shop. Well, I'd run out of country to look in. There was no Ned Campion. Maybe there never had been. I'd just have to stop this woolgathering and face the hard facts. When I mounted the steps to my boardinghouse on Manila Street that night, I was relieved, almost happy.

My landlady met me at the stoop. Old Mrs. Duffy wasn't afraid of me. "You're a nice enough boy," she'd say, bringing me up a bowl of soup late at night, or a cruller and some milk. "But my land, Charlie, when are you going to the barber and get yourself a decent shirt!" She didn't know I'd killed a man, and probably wouldn't believe it either. Tonight she was excited. "There's a man to see you!"

Instantly wary, I looked round to ensure escape. "Where?"

"In the downstairs parlor. Ah, he's such a gentleman! An old friend, he said. A Mr. Keeler, from *Harper's* magazine. Imagine!"

I pushed aside the beaded curtains and went in. "Charlie!" The reporter threw his arms round me. "By God, Charlie!"

"It's me," I said. "How are you, George?"

He was freshly barbered and turned out in a pearl-gray cutaway and high collar. Even more, he was sober. All I could smell on him was cologne-water. It was commendable but kind of disappointing.

"How did you find me here?"

He crossed a spatted ankle over his knee, and grinned. "You shouldn't have gone away without saying good-bye."

"I know. I'm sorry. And I'm everlastingly grateful to you But I was all mixed up then. I—I just didn't want to talk to anyone."

"I know. Forget it."

"But how did you find me?"

"Trade secret. It's a reporter's business to find out things. I tol you that once." He pointed a finger at me, and laughed. "Although it shouldn't be too hard to find a redheaded fellow in a deerskin shirt with two mules called Dan and Beersheba, and that's a fact!" Lighting a stogie, he took an envelope from his pocket. "Now, first things first! Here's a letter came for you care of *Harper's*."

I held it dumbly in my hand. Then I said, "*Harper's*? Who'd be writing to me, anyway? And why care of *Harper's*?"

"First things first, damn it! Open your letter."

Perplexed, I did so. It was dated three months back, in Utah Territory. Scrawled across the top it said WRIT BY HAND BY ABE CURRY FOR HIS FRIEND IKE COOGAN. Ike couldn't read or write. The letter went on with Ike's communication to me:

Dear Friend:

   Well, I see in Harper's *magazine a drummer showed me you are quite a marvel.* Charlie Campion Boy Hero of the Plains. *Oh, I tell you it's enough to make a man give up rum! You old coon, I never did think I was dealing with a famous man.*

"Look here, George," I said. "What the hell is this all about? What's this blabbering about the *Boy Hero of the Plains?*"

"You done reading?" He seemed ill at ease.

"No, not quite."

"Finish, then, before you get all upset."

I read on. There was much more, mostly reminiscences of old times at Concordia-on-the Platte. But a scribbled PS made me sit bolt upright.

> *Ike says tell you you gave Fat Henry quite a headache, but he cum out on top aniway—he is rooling the roost in the Blessid Kingdom.*

Then I hadn't killed him! I had tried hard enough, but Henry must have had a skull turned from solid hickory. Anyway, I wasn't a criminal! A load fell from my shoulders. But there were still some perplexing things to be explained.

"George," I said, "I'm grateful to you for bringing me the letter, but how in the hell—"

Mrs. Duffy bustled in then with home-baked bread and some cheese and a pot of tea. "Don't swear, Charlie," she said, turning up the lamp. "Now you and the gentleman just sit and visit! I'll be knitting in the back room if you need anything."

When she was gone, George cleared his throat and hemmed and hawed and ate a piece of cheese and sipped his tea and finally said, "Now don't get mad, Charlie. It's all for the best, believe me!"

"What's for the best, damn it?"

"Don't swear, like Mrs. Duffy said. Anyway—you know that night at Fort Jackson when you told me all about your adventures? Mad Jack Spurrier and the balloon, and hunting buffalo at Concordia, and living with the Indians and all?"

"Certainly I remember!"

"Well, I—I wrote it all up. I wasn't in too good odor at *Harper's* then; they never understood me. But they liked the story. They wanted more; I wrote more. And now you're famous! That's how this Mr. Coogan knew how to get hold of you." He shoved a copy of *Harper's* at me. "Look!"

Good Lord! A full-page spread, and right up in front, too. *Charlie Campion, Boy Hero of the Plains!* There was a woodcut of a noble-looking young man peering across the prairie, but it didn't look like me.

"You rascal!"

"Now don't get mad! Remember what Mrs. Duffy told you!"

"Drat Mrs. Duffy! But I could sue you and *Harper's!* Aren't they supposed to get my consent or something?"

He saw I was joking, and brightened. "Here!" Whipping a wad of bills from his satchel, he pressed it in my hand. "Fifty-fifty, eh, Charlie? They paid me five hundred dollars altogether. There's two hundred and fifty for you."

"For me? I don't want the money! I didn't have anything to do with it!"

"But it's your story—the story of Charlie Campion! It's a great success, Charlie—very popular. Why look at what it's done for me!" He struck a pose, but was serious about it. "They've promoted me to senior correspondent. I feel better, I look better. I haven't had a drop of booze in three months." He came close to me, confidential. "What are you doing now?"

"Draying with my mules."

"How much money are you making?"

"None of your damned business."

He snickered. "Pretty tight, eh? Things pretty tight?"

"Oh, I manage to keep the mules fed and manage a roof over my head."

"How much money have you got in the bank?"

"Look here!" I said. "My bank account is a private matter. Now—"

"Nothing in the bank, eh? *Charlie Campion, Boy Pauper.* Now I don't want you to think I'm nosy, Charlie. There's a purpose in what I say. What about that girl?"

"What girl?"

"Why, Annie, of course! The one you talked so much about when you were at Fort Jackson. By the way, Alonzo Hacker is a major now. Anyway, when you talked about Annie your face lit up with a holy light! That's a fact. But how are you going back to New York State and marry her without money, eh? Answer me that!"

In fact, that had been worrying me too.

"It costs money to travel so far," George said.

"I'll sell the mules," I said, though the words made me choke. Dan and Beersheba—to sell such faithful friends!

"But you ought to have a little nest egg in the bank." He pressed the bills into my hand. "If I can help with anything else, Charlie, just write me at *Harper's.*" He stuck his head into the back room to thank Mrs. Duffy, and went out into

Manila Street so quickly I didn't know quite what was happening.

"Wait a minute!" I called, running out on the front stoop. "George! Just a minute!"

He was gone. I stood there gawking at the roll of bills. In spite of myself I grinned. George Keeler, that hardbitten and most unsentimental of men, had been greatly moved by the two hapless lovers, Annie and Charlie Campion, *The Boy Hero* or whatever he was.

"You old coon!" I whispered, and closed the door.

⸺⸺Chapter 21⸺⸺

I sold the mules, of course. There was no way to take them back with me, much as I would have liked to. A teamster I knew on the docks gave me a fair price for them and the wagon.

"Treat them kindly," I said to Burke. "They're good animals. They'll work their hearts out for you."

Gentle Beersheba nuzzled me, looking for sugar. Dan slyly tried to kick me, good black-hearted old Dan! "Joe Burke," I said, "if I ever hear of these mules being mistreated, I'll come back here and cut out your gizzard!"

He looked goggle-eyed at me.

"Do you hear me?" I shouted.

"What in hell is the matter with you? You know I treat my animals right!"

"Yes," I said. "Yes, that's right. I'm sorry. Well—"

When I went away he was still looking after me, astonished.

I was a long time getting back to Utica. Steamship—train across Panama—steamship—train—coach. All very dull, very tedious. They took a long time and a lot of money, more than I had thought. I was grateful for what George Keeler had given me; it was almost used up when I got near Utica.

I remembered that day so long ago when I had stolen a pair

of boots from a merchant in Fort Plain. On shank's mare, now, I trudged through the town. It had not changed much, though I had. Where was that long-ago boy, that cocky jigging precocious child, so sure of himself and his fortune? The blood of kings ran in his Irish veins, he was marked for destiny, he sang and laughed and dreamed dreams. Where was he? Where had he gone?

Fumbling in my pockets, I came up with less than two dollars in notes and coins. That was all I had. I went into the store where I had stolen the boots. Damned little thief! And yet I could not restrain a sad affection for him. Well, I would make what apologies I could.

A round little man in steel-rimmed spectacles looked warily at me as I entered. I was not particularly presentable. All my money had gone for my passage. Travel-worn and stained, I still wore my deerskin shirt; my hair was long and caught back with a strip of otter-fur; my boots had long since gone to pieces and I was in moccasins again. Smelling of dry goods and millinery, he hustled to meet me, hooking his spectacles firmly over his ears. "Yes—yes! What is it? What do you want?"

I will admit I didn't look a likely customer for Brussels lace or embroidery-hoops. Holding out the last of my funds I said, "Here—take it."

He drew back as if he'd been offered a hot stove.

"What's this, now? What's this?"

"A long time ago I stole a pair of boots off your rack. I was a child then and didn't know any better."

"What kind of a trick is this? Say, where are you from? I don't remember anyone that looked like you!"

"Nor do I," I said, "but that's beside the point. Here, take the money ."

"I don't remember any stolen boots. What are you trying to put over on me, young man?"

"Nothing," I said patiently. "Nothing at all. It's just as I told you, an old debt. Will you take the money?"

He backed away. "Where did you say you were from?"

"I didn't."

Barricading himself behind his counter, he became more belligerent. "You look a queer one to me! Now you get out of here! I don't want any trouble in my store!"

A lady came in, then another, and looked astonished and uneasy. A small boy came in too, who seemed captivated by my beaded shirt and not frightened at all.

"I'll call the constable! Jimmy, go see if you can find Mr. Buckley. Quick, now, I'll give you a penny!"

I knew when I was beat. Leaving, I gave a handful of pennies to the wide-eyed Jimmy. "Go buy some jawbreakers," I said, and ruffled his red hair, so much like mine.

When I got to Gillentine's farm I was footsore and weary. How the farm had run down! That was not like old Gillentine— he was a good enough farmer, I'd give him that. In gray winter the gate hung on one hinge. The house huddled unpainted in the dusk, and a wind rustled the shocks of corn like old bones rubbing together. As I started up the lane a cold drizzle started. It had been raining when I left.

Boards were missing from the veranda, and one post had collapsed, worm-eaten, so that the porch roof sagged. No lights in the house. Where was everybody? To come so far, and no one here? Annie, at least—where was Annie? I knocked on the door, and waited. No answer. I knocked again, harder. Annie, at least . . . Where was my dearest Annie?

"Is anybody in there?"

Behind the colored panes of glass that edged the door I saw a waxing radiance. Someone was coming with a lamp.

"It's me!" I shouted. "Charlie! Charlie Campion!"

The light seemed to halt, and tremble. Slowly, rustily, the knob turned. Impatient, I spread the growing crack with my hand. "Who's there? It's only me—Charlie!"

The door opened wide. In the lamplight I saw a small thin woman. The rays of the lamp cut her face with sharp planes and shadows.

"I—I'm Charlie Campion," I said. "I used to live here. Where—where is—"

Her eyes opened wide. "Charlie! Is it you?"

"Annie!" I cried. "Don't you know me?"

Throwing my arms round her, I hugged her hard, at the imminent risk of setting us both afire.

"Charlie! You've come back!" She was weeping, and I was weeping, both bewildered at the way we'd changed, but happy and choked with feeling.

"Yes," I said, "I've come back, Annie. A long way back." A small boy in night dress appeared in the lamplit hallway, his eyes round and frightened, and rushed forward to cling to Annie's skirt.

"Follett," she said. "Take the lamp, dear."

"Follett!" I said. "Is that Follett?"

She knelt, putting her arm round him. "Follett, do you remember Charlie?"

Fingers in his mouth, he looked gravely at me. "You were the king."

"He remembers," I said. "Lord, he remembers! Yes, Follett, I was the king."

We went into the kitchen where there was fire in a grate and tea in a pot. "But where is everybody?" I asked. "You pa and ma, and the rest of the children?"

In the brighter light I could see how she had got thin and worn, and Follett looked pinched and somehow consumptive, with an unhealthy bright flush to his cheeks. But she was still my Annie, with her violet-blue eyes and fragrant dark hair. Only now, she was a *woman,* though a woman who had had a hard time of it.

Her eyes glistened a little, but she went calmly on slicing bread for me and frying eggs in a pan. There was something lovely and graceful in the way her slender brown hands moved and her body bent over the iron stove.

"So much happened after you left, Charlie. Papa was furious at you, you know. He spent all his money hiring detectives, trying to find you. The farm ran down, but he didn't seem to care. All he wanted was to bring you to justice, he said."

"I know. I—I remember the detectives."

"One day he had apoplexy. The doctor came all the way from Utica, and put him to bed. We were all so scared. The next night he—he passed on, still calling out against you."

"I'm sorry, Annie. I wasn't worth that much hate, not really."

She put the meat and eggs on a plate, and sat across the table from me, Follett on her lap. I ate, trying to remember some table manners.

"After that, Mama just gave up. She got a man to run the farm on shares, but he wasn't very honest. Finally, she got sick, too. They took her and the children to the poor-farm. She's—she's—" Annie's voice broke in spite of her. "She's dead, now, and the children all scattered. . . ."

"Don't cry. Please don't cry, Annie. Look, do you remember that day in the hop-vines?" I was trying to make her laugh. "That day I stuck myself with the knife? Wasn't that crazy?"

"I remember."

"We were children then."

"Yes." She gave a piece of bread to Follett, who chewed at it, and continued to stare unblinking at me.

"But you and Follett. You're both still here, Annie."

"Yes." She didn't look at me, only stroked the boy's hair. "Follett was poorly. He was always poorly. I—I couldn't let them take him away, he'd die. He wasn't strong enough. So I stayed here. I told them I wouldn't leave. I'd stay here and work the place myself and tend to Follett." Slowly she raised her eyes to mine, lovely dark eyes with depths I'd never seen. "You said you'd be back. You said we loved each other best of all, and you'd be back. I—I wanted to be here when you came back. I wanted you to have a place to come back to, Charlie, when it was time."

"Annie," I said, overcome. "Oh, Annie!"

I leaned over and kissed her for a long time, Follett watching astonished.

"It's time, now," I said. "It's time. I've come back, Annie. I guess a man always has to go away and see how things are in the world, and a woman waits. It's hard, but that's the way things are." I put Follett on my knee. "But everything's all right now. Tomorrow I'll fix those boards in the porch, and prop up the roof. We'll fix things up, and get the farm going again. It was a good farm. It just needs a little work. And— and if you'll have me, Annie, we can go into Utica and get married." I was fumbling and awkward in the way I said it. "I mean—well, how would it look?—me living here and us not even married. . . ."

When we fell into each other's arms Follett slid off my lap and started to cry. I let him cry for a while. He might as well start in learning that life isn't all comfortable and easy and predictable. After a while I put him on my lap again, while Annie bustled round cleaning the table and washing dishes in a pan and sweeping the floor. Rain rattled against the windows, and a shutter banged somewhere, but inside it was cozy and warm.

"You know," I said, "it's funny."

"What's funny, Charlie?"

"Well, I looked all over the States for my father. I needed a father, I needed one desperately. I couldn't grow up without a father. But I never found him. And now I'm home. I grew up somehow—I don't know exactly when or how—without a father. In a way, I figure I was cheated. And in a way, it's too late now, because"—I watched Follett's finger touch the Indian beads on my shirt—"I guess I'm a kind of father myself now. I have to leave off being a son and become a father."

Chores finished, Annie sat beside me, holding my hand so tight it hurt. *"I* think it's very nice. Follett needs a father."

He raised big eyes toward me. "You used to tell me about kings."

"You remember?"

He nodded. "Tell me about kings."

"Well," I said, "I used to think I knew a lot about kings. But I don't. All I know about is Annie and me." I put a finger on his button nose. Lord what a finger! Long and brown and scarred! "So I'll just make up a story about kings. All right?"

"Fine," said Follett, and curled up in my arms, waiting.

Bestselling Books from ACE!

Bestselling Books from ACE!